SPIRIT STEALERS

Step in through the gateway
Let your imagination free.
Come oh magical child
Share an adventure with me!

KYM JADE

Published in 2009 by New Generation Publishing

British Library C.I.P.

A CIP catalogue record for this title is available from the British Library.

Email: kymjade@yahoo.com

Design and layout by Tricia Stubbings

The "Spirit Stealers" series is dedicated in loving memory of:

Jean and Fred Denman

We miss you Mum and Dad

Glossary of Terms

Bird-spiders	Large spiders
Bull-ants	Large ants
Darkening	Night-time
Funnel-web	Type of Spider
Leaf fall	Passing of time
Lightening	Daytime and passing of days
Rain-bringers	Clouds
Spirit	Life or living
Sustenance	Eating or food
Water drip	Passing of time
Wedge-tailed	Type of Eagle

PROLOGUE

Brother Sun's rays slid past the flowers of the wattle, teasing them open to greet the lightening of the woods. Still in the darkening's shadows, the King of the Kookaburras waddled out of his tree hollow, onto the gum tree's branch and stopped. Taking in a deep breath, he drew in his wings and called to his brethren to announce the coming leaf falls.

In response to his call the forest erupted with a morning chorus of laughing kookaburras and chanting cicadas. As the shadows of the Darkening withdrew, a new Lightening of the Woods was born.

Far below the branches of the mighty gums, Mon Mouse hopped with all his might through the undergrowth. Flipping himself over a dew-laden flower, spraying water everywhere, he called back to his friends, "Hurry up! The lightening of the woods is upon us and we have mouse lengths to travel." Pushing the lush grasses aside, he rushed on.

Crashing out into the small clearing, Wit of the Wombats complained, "Do I have to come, Brother Sun's rays hurt my eyes so? Can I please stay here, in the remaining shadows and wait? Hurrying is not something we wombats do well, anyway."

Squeezing past, Wit's large furry behind, Enla the echidna snapped, "Suit yourself, Wit. You do realise that some leaf falls, you can be such a cry-baby."

"Ouch, watch your spikes Enla. You jabbed me right in my rear," Wit moaned, as he rubbed the sore spot with his hind leg. "I shall lie here under the shade of sister banksia tree, and wait for your return." With that, Wit lay flat on his belly, his eyes squinting in the light.

"Cry-baby," Enla teased, running up the small track.

Wit did not even raise his head to answer; instead he took a deep breath and prepared to slumber. He did not see Mon come hopping back toward him.

"Come on Wit," Mon pleaded, tugging at the wombat's whiskers. "Tya is going to tell us about when the Large Pale Ones first came to our woods. Remember, I told you, it was the same lightenings the invaders came. She has promised stories of battles and to tell me more of my ancestors: The Family of the Great Silky Oak. So please join us." The little kangaroo mouse grabbed a set of whiskers in each front paw and pulled with all his might.

Wit opened an eye and looked at his friend's pleading expression. "Will there be wombats in the story?"

Releasing the whiskers, Mon hopped backward and put his front paws on his hips. "Of course, dear Wit; those of your kind were renowned for their wisdom and strategies. So will you come?"

The small wombat sighed as he pushed himself up. "Well," he said, moving forward, "what are we waiting for? Climb up on my back, Mon, and guide me to your friend."

Leaf falls later, Enla turned to the loud crashing noise coming up behind her. Her tiny eyes struggled to see the image that was bearing down on her small body. By the time she focused her vision, she barely managed to roll out of its path. Looking up from the grasses, she could not believe what she saw; there was Mon, sitting on Wit's shoulders, tugging at the wombat's ears to guide him. "Hey, watch it, you two! Do you realise you nearly ran me over?" Composing herself, Enla stood and followed.

"Who is a cry-baby now?" Wit retorted, charging straight through some fronds.

On the other side of the ferns, both Mon and Wit had their vision stolen from them by the bright rays of Brother Sun. No longer able to see where they were going, Mon drew back both of Wit's ears at the same time. "I feel it is important that we slow down and exercise caution, rather than be so impetuous."

Still rushing blindly ahead, Wit called to his friend, "Impetu... what? I am still trying to work out what tugging on both my ears is supposed to mean? Do not throw big words at me now."

Noticing the trunk of a familiar palm go by, Mon realised it was time to stop. "We must stop at this very leaf fall. Wit we are here!"

The small Wombat dug all his feet in at once and came to a complete halt.

The little mouse flew into the air and tumbled down to the ground. Standing and brushing his fur, Mon turned to his friend. "Way to go with the stopping, Wit. Do you know I had no idea you could move that fast?"

Puffing, Wit replied, "We wombats possess many hidden talents, dear friend."

Running up to Wit, Enla jammed her paw down on his. "There, that is for being so thoughtless." Spinning around the echidna surveyed the small clearing. All she could make out was a large tree with a boulder near its base. "Where is this friend of yours, Mon, I see nothing? If you have been telling us tales again, I will not protect you from the Elders' wrath."

Smiling, Mon walked over to a dark hole in the boulder

and called, "Tya, Tya, Tya..." his voice echoed over and over again.

As two large eyes moved toward the small kangaroo mouse, he hopped back seven jumps. When Tya of the Tortoises' head emerged from her large shell, Mon could not help laugh at his friends' expressions.

"How many times, Mon Mouse, have I told you not to yell in my shell? You have no idea how deafening such a thing is." Straining her eyes, she could see Enla and Wit staring at her in disbelief. "Oh do close your mouths, young ones; I would hate to think you may accidentally swallow a native bee or something."

"You are a ttttur..." Enla stuttered, moving forward.

"Turtle! Oh by Father Sky, no, they are my cousins. I am a tortoise, a very old giant tortoise may I add. You see, I was abducted from my beautiful homeland by the large pale ones, so many lightenings ago. One darkening a storm on Sister Sea pushed their enormous hollow log onto rocks. If it had not been for my cousins, the Sea Turtles, my spirit would have been lost. They bravely helped me reach your land and even taught me your common tongue. We share a common language, we of the tortoise and turtles, you see." Stretching her neck out she moved her head to each native in turn. "However that is another tale, I can share with you, perhaps another lightening." Tya gazed at the young ones' wide eyes, full of wonder, and smiled. "For if I am not mistaken, this leaf fall you have come to hear of the troubles that came to your woods, many, many lightenings ago."

The children, already enthralled by Tya's story and manner, simply nodded in reply.

"Fine then, move to either side of me and listen. Listen to my voice and allow your minds to soar to Father Sky. Close your eyes, young ones, and I promise you a wondrous journey to the lightenings when the invaders first came."

Complying, the young natives found themselves mesmerised by Tya's calm voice.

The old tortoise grinned as she watched the three friends motionless bodies sway back and forth to her words. "When you open your eyes, do not be afraid. For in my prayers I have asked the spirits of our past to guide us back through the pond of remembering to their lightenings. Lightenings, full of trouble and adventure for our friends. You may open your eyes."

The trio gasped when they saw a pond-like image surrounding them. An intense light laid in the depths of its centre that appeared to call to them.

"Say not a word my young students as we travel back, back to our past." Tya swayed her head from side to side as she spoke, "Concentrate on the bright light, submit to its call. Allow the story to unfold before your young eyes. Come with me as we fly on the breeze of time, leaving our troubles behind, to the old world where we will become privileged observers."

Like a soft thistle seed, floating with the breeze, the children allowed their minds to ride the currents in a wondrous whirlwind of adventure. One leaf fall they were gliding effortlessly along the ground, the next they shot to the sky, where they were left suspended to look down on a motionless world.

Tya's voice, so wise, guided them on. "Silently, we drift with the air currents past the world as we know it, to our new world for a leaf fall. Here, we are safe from harm and can share in the adventures of our soon to be friends. Look, young ones, in the middle of the great forest a gigantic silky oak tree, how noble it stands. Do not be fearful as the breeze stalls and we float down onto the ground.

"Ah, we are finally here! See over there walking along that root, it is Chief Antoni Ant of the Bull-ants. Listen carefully and try not to speak. Perfect! Now, let the adventure begin as we become nothing but shadows in the woods, undetected."

LIGHTENING OF THE WOODS

"Splosh and bother," Antoni grumbled, under his breath, walking along the enormous root. "Splosh and bother, I tell you. Ten lightenings of the woods, on foot, is just too much to ask of me. I know Mar is my oldest friend and together we have seen many adventures, but ten lightenings! All I can say is, it better be important! Though it was not Mar's fault, the rains came particularly early and turned my trip into a challenge; which at my age, I was not prepared to meet. I should have ridden Squorth that is what I should have done. Splosh and bother!"

Antoni dodged from side to side attempting to miss the raindrops, which were still teaming down after five lightenings of continuous rain. "Do the Great Grey Rain-bringers not realise what a drop of rain feels like to an ant? Every splosh is soaking me to my very spirit. I warn you, my patience is wearing thin," he declared, shaking his front leg at the clouds above.

As yet another drop hit Antoni, saturating him to his very soul, he screamed with rage. "For Queen's sake leave me alone," he yelled, placed his front leg into the centre cavity of the weapon strapped to his side and withdrew it.

His every move fuelled by frustration, he swung the spider's fang in the air. Rage's fire lighting his eyes, he used it as a sword and lashed out at the drops. "You want me, then you have me. I shall run no further. Come attack me once more you beasts of drops and I shall shatter you to a million droplets with my sword."

With that, Antoni swung it around the top of his head, until the sword started to roar. "Ah wet me will you. Take that," he screamed, jumping around, dancing a fine jig.

"Not far to go now the battle can still yet be mine." He reached the end of the root, leapt off with a back flip and landed in front of a large knothole at the base of a giant silky oak.

Safe, under the cover of an overhanging piece of bark, he turned, laughed at the rain and put his sword back in his belt. Picking up a pebble, from near by, he banged on the door several times before it finally opened.

"Boyor, Antoni," a tall kangaroo mouse greeted, in a soft, gentle, voice.

Antoni bowed his head and swept a front leg across his chest. "Metcha, Trix, of the Oak. After such a long and perilous journey, I am certainly glad to hear such a beautiful voice, speak my native tongue."

"I beg you please enter, old friend, let me find you some warm sap and a place by the last glowing embers." Trix opened the door wider and bid him enter. "I am sure the children will be interested to hear of your journey."

As Antoni passed through the door he turned, placed his first leg on his chest in tribute and said, "Chang mot ableeming don holer." Turning, he opened his mandibles and smiled. "Translated from my native tongue, it means: 'May there always be food and love in this hollow'."

Content to have finally reached his destination Chief Antoni admired the new leaf etchings adorning the hall's dirt and wood walls. "Did your young mice do these?" he asked, without stopping.

"Yes, there are two from each."

"They are really very good."

Proud of her offspring's' efforts Trix smiled and waved her front paw toward the hollow of rest.

The ant nodded and without warning let out a loud piercing squeak, "EEEEEEEE," which echoed through the oak's hollows.

Snuggled down by the embers, a young female mouse's ears twitched as they received Antoni's signal. She knew immediately her adopted uncle had arrived.

Standing, she rushed to the doorway and with a large smile said, "Boyor, dear, dear Uncle. Oh I am pleased to see you." Gently, she bent down and kissed Antoni on the forehead; right where his mark of warrior ant sat proudly on his scalp.

"Metcha, Hatty." He stood back, examined her every feature and continued, "You have certainly grown since we last met. What is it now?" Antoni said, placing one foreleg on his chin as the other rested on Hatty's shoulder, "Why I must have taken sustenance 450 times, since we last sat and talked."

Hatty was just about to answer when a rumbling started somewhere in the tree above them, growing louder and louder.

"By my Queen, are we under attack?" Antoni asked, reaching for his sword, which was no longer there.

Hatty smiled broadly, as her brothers, Dodd and Toemouse, entered the room.

"By the Great River Stones," Antoni exclaimed, "Dodd you near block the archway. Why, you must be bigger than your father now, Latchkey. And look at Toe with his fine blonde fur, by my Queen, son, you look every bit a prince if ever I saw one."

Rushing forward, Toe smiled and hugged Antoni.

Dodd waited for their greeting to end, puffed out his chest, strode up to Antoni and took one of his front appendages. "Boyor, Antoni," he said, in a deep voice.

"Metcha, Dodd. But may I ask who gave you leave to call me by my name, without uncle in front of it?"

"I did, Antoni! You see I have grown and am no longer an infant. So, by my way of thinking, I am your equal in every way now. Furthermore, I think it would be more appropriate if you treated me as such," Dodd announced, walking over to stand near the place of the glowing embers.

Surprised by Dodd's attitude, Antoni turned and looked at Trix, standing in the archway. "By your leave, dear Trix."

Knowing full well the bull-ant's intentions, Trix smiled and nodded. "Of course, Antoni, please make yourself at home."

With a wink of mischief, Antoni sprang off a small rock stool and landed on Dodd's back. In a flash, two of his legs pulled Dodd's ears inward as he dug two other feet into the mouse's ear holes. No matter how much Dodd danced and jumped, Antoni would not relinquish his grip.

"Go, Uncle Antoni," Toe yelled, with glee.

Hatty and Trix stood back thoughtfully and watched as Antoni brought Dodd's large frame to the ground.

"Who am I, Mouse?" Antoni demanded, placing his last two feet over Dodd's eyes.

Conceding defeat Dodd smiled as he said, "Sir, you are my Uncle Antoni, Chief Warrior Ant of Queen Zana and protector of all those who are good."

"So be it," Antoni said, dismounting, "You are a strong young fellow Dodd; I certainly could use somebody like you."

Dodd turned to his mother with a pleading expression.

Trix smiled gently shaking her head, "Not these lightenings, dear Dodd, you have not yet completed your studies."

"Blod," Dodd mumbled under his breath, without even realising everybody heard him.

"Dodd, Kangaroo Mouse, how dare you use such language in my hollow," Trix chastised, waving the tip of her claw at him.

Letting his head dip in shame, Dodd apologised, in earnest. "Sorry, Mother."

"Please, Trix, I beg your leave, do not be hard on the mouse. At this leaf fall, he is at a difficult age. Why, I remember the same time as if it was the lightening past. Ah, the things their father and I used to get up to with Gregor before he moved away."

"Please tell us, Uncle Antoni," Hatty said, handing him a small gumnut filled to the brim.

"Later perhaps, for now I must take rest and drink this lovely warm sap." After swigging down some brew, Antoni looked around and enquired, "And where is my old and dearest friend?"

Trix poured some more sap into the Chief's cup. "Only a matter of leaf falls ago, Mar was called to help dislodge some debris clogging the stream. Something needed to be done before it back filled and flooded the whole commune."

"Ah, thus explaining the water depth around the smaller plants and roots," Antoni interjected and took another sip of the warm brew.

"Yes, I expect it does. Mar and a few others have gone in this direction from the tree." Trix pointed. "I would say approximately 1000 mouse lengths away."

"So that is why I did not cross their path. You see, I came in from the opposite direction to the knothole of this grand old oak. If he does not return by the time I have dried off and rested awhile, I will seek him out. Perhaps Dodd could come?"

"We shall see. Dodd have you finished your studies of the edible roots in our area and beyond?" Trix asked, in a strict tone.

"Yes, Mother," Dodd replied, scraping his hind paw along the dirt floor.

"Fine then, after we have a nibble and dear Antoni is rested, you may go."

"What about me, Mother?" Hatty asked, standing to show her obvious size against her elder brother.

Dodd leered at her and mumbled under his breath.

"Not this time, Hatty, and before you ask, Toe, most definitely not. Now let us have a nibble of some nuts and roots while Antoni tells us of the goings-on in Queen Zana's court."

Trix went out for a moment and was soon back sitting, waiting for Antoni to begin.

Antoni took a long gulp of his warm sap, which gave him a comforting glow, looked around and began to tell them all about the attempted coup by the Queen's cousin, Princess Leta.

#   #   #

An ominous mist drifted across the forest floor, concealed the workers for a leaf fall before moving on.

A grey kangaroo mouse, standing atop the barrage, soaked to the skin, hopped to its centre. Kneeling, he examined the structure of the built up debris.

"No matter what we do, Chieftain, we can not shift the intertwined branches and twigs. At this rate it will only be a matter of leaf falls before the whole of the lower commune is under water," Aldo said, with deep concern in his voice. "I wish we had just one of Brother Wombat's kind with us as it would clear this in one shove. Sadly, they and the echidnas, all moved to higher ground lightenings ago."

"When you consider they can not climb, like we natives who stayed behind, it was a wise choice." Mar turned to a small chubby mouse, standing to his right paw and touched him on the shoulder. "Stump, go back and get all the lower dwellers to leave their homes and head for the Great Silky Oak, Trix will know what to do with them."

"Yes, Mar," Stump said, bowed and hopped away.

The Chieftain of the Oak watched his old friend disappear into the foliage and turned to the others. "We must break through this or all the lightenings of work preparing our lands with crops will be lost. Aldo, you and the other creatures stay here and try to weaken this section.

"Summer, you and ten of your best natives follow me. We must stay to the high ground," Mar announced, jumping up on a log. "While on our travels we must each find a large branch to use as a lever my friends. Follow me."

"Where are we going?" Summer yelled, above the teaming rain.

"Quickly, to the latest windfall, my friends. We must move a log into the strongest current and send it hurtling into the wall of debris."

"How will you make sure it stays in midstream?" Aldo asked, concerned.

Mar looked down, water dripping off his saturated fur. "I and a few others will ride the log keeping it in midstream with our branches. Then at the last moment we shall leap off."

Aldo jumped onto a small stump and raised his from paw in protest. "No! Surely, it is too dangerous! You will be lost in the rush of water when the wall breaks."

"It is a risk, which must be taken for the good of many." Surveying the scene Mar noticed some branches hanging low, near the dam of twigs. "Aldo, dangle as many vines as you can from those branches," he said, pointing. "We will jump for those." Mar walked a few paces and stopped. "Aldo, when you hear my warning cry, make sure none of our fellow creatures are on this haphazard structure. Now, my friends, we must leave."

#   #   #

Antoni Ant was just at the point where his spider's fang pierced the chest plate of Deago, the Princess's Ant of Arms, when he heard a loud cry came from outside the oak.

"Everybody to the Great Oak; Chieftain Mar commands it," Stump trumpeted, hopping in and out of the underbrush.

"By all that is holy," Trix said, immediately realising what it meant. "Quickly children up the tree and make sure all passageways are clear. It appears likely we will have unexpected visitors."

Antoni dashed to the front door and flung it open as Stump followed by the low dwellers started pouring up the large root.

"Boyor, Antoni, Boyor," he said, in his broad low dweller accent.

"Metcha, Stump. Tell me of Mar and the others."

Stump reached out and moved Antoni out of the way of the rush of low dwellers, swelling at the doorway and began to explain, "The debris has built a huge dam, I am afraid if this rain keeps up the only thing left will be the very tip of the Great Oak. I also fear other such dams breaking further upstream and washing all in their path away."

"Well, mouse, what are they doing about it?

"They are trying to displace it, Antoni, but it could all well be for naught. I am worried we shall lose many of our best natives this lightening. That is all we need with the latest threat, from the place where Brother Sun rises, heading our way."

While guiding some refugees toward the higher hollows of the oak, Trix could not help overhear the conversation. "I beg you, Antoni," she called over the top of a sugar-glider's head, "to find Mar and help him."

Keen to help Dodd left his task and rushed up to her.

Trix looked into her son's deep, brown, pleading eyes, sighed, reached out, touched him on the forehead and gave him her blessing. "Dodd, use your strength, my son, by all means. Please, my darling mouse, let wisdom and Antoni be your ultimate guides."

Shaking, she hopped over to the bull-ant. "Dear Antoni, once again I ask you, please bring my husband, and now my son, back to rest safely in the warmth of the oak."

"That I shall do." Antoni sprang back inside to put on his belt and sword. "Aga," he yelled, in bull-ant, as he rushed past and disappeared with Dodd into the crowd.

"Aga, Dodd, Stump and Antoni. May the warmth of Brother Sun's rays protect you." Her heart heavy with fear, Trix returned to directing the influx of animals; determined to show only strength in front of them.

#   #   #

Mar ducked under a small sapling's branch, hopped a few paces and stopped mid-stride. Certain, he could hear something above the pounding rain, he swung his head back. When he heard an eerie cry, reverberating through the woods from downstream, his ears twitched and he smiled.

"May Brother Sun be praised! I would know that cry even amongst the most powerful howls of a storm. It is Antoni." Lifting both paws to his mouth Mar let out an unnerving, "E E E E A Y A Y," in reply.

19

Relieved he slapped Summer on the back. "We will soon be joined by a great bull-ant warrior. Things may bode well for us yet, my friend."

Repeatedly answering the call, Mar, and his mice, made their way to the nearest windfall and started rocking it.

A leaf fall later Antoni, Stump and Dodd burst out from the underbrush.

To show he carried no weapons, Antoni bowed and swept four legs in front of him. "Greetings from Queen Zana, oh noble Mar Mouse."

"Greetings," Mar replied, with another push on the log.

Antoni and Dodd waded into the water and put their weight against the log. Locking into the rhythm of each push they gave it all they could until it started to roll toward the stream.

The leaf fall it splashed into the muddy water, Mar, Summer, Antoni, Stump and two others grabbed a stick each and leapt onto the log.

"I think you know the routine of logging, Antoni. Or has your memory gone in your old age?" Mar said, guiding the log into the current.

"Old age indeed," Antoni protested, water streaming over his small frame.

Mar dug his stick into the bottom of the stream and pushed. "When I give the signal, everybody is to follow my command. Jump for your lives and grab the vines Aldo will have in place for us."

As Dodd attempted to scramble onto the log his father turned, placed a paw on his shoulder. "Thank goodness you are a strong swimmer my son. I beg you though, do not press me to come on this perilous journey, I shall only have to refuse your request." As the log started to move faster, Mar turned his head toward the bank.

"Return to shore, Dodd. Please go home; our people need a leader which you must be for now."

"May a soft breeze, refreshing and kind, guide your efforts, Father," Dodd screamed, running along the bank.

With surprising speed the log hurtled down the stream and was soon only a matter of 600 mice lengths away from the now swollen wall.

"SQUEEEEEEEEEEEEK!" Mar shrilled, to the mice ahead still attempting to clear the debris.

Upon the signal, Aldo cleared his natives off the structure and scurried up one of the closest trees.

Unseen, Dodd had managed to keep up and sprang into a tree above the wall just before the log hurtled into the haphazard structure.

"Oya," Mar yelled, to tell the others to leap off.

Obeying his order the others leapt into the air and caught the vines. Safe, dangling above the rushing water, Antoni was shocked to see Mar still frantically attempting to keep the log on course.

"Jump, Mar, for the sake of the life giving spring rains, jump!" Antoni screamed and crawled up the vine.

Oblivious to his friend's plea, Mar focused on ensuring success, steered the log into the dam.

Horrified, Antoni watched his friend flung into the air by the force of the impact. Then as the structure began to break up, he went to move forward; only to realise how futile an attempt to help would be. Panic fuelling his every thought he caught a glimpse of a shadow moving along the trees on the other bank.

Suddenly, out of nowhere, Dodd swung down into the water and grabbed his father's paw. In an amazing feat of strength, he gripped the branch with his hind paws and lifted his father out of the water.

"I have you, Father," he cried, straining every muscle to hold his father up.

Mar looked into his son's eyes as he pulled him onto the branch. He said nothing as they sat and watched the breech grow larger and larger. Success theirs, he turned to him and held him close to his heart. "Nature blessed me, my son, the lightening you were born," he whispered, into Dodd's ear.

Dodd, shaking, held his father close to him. *I had not realised how important you are to me,* he thought, *until the threat of never hearing your voice again became a reality. I only acted on impulse, driven by my love for you. Who would have thought, all the years of play wrestling with Hatty, Toe and my friends would pay such a dividend?*

Leaf falls later, as they all waded across the now shallow stream, Antoni announced, "Bigomambo." Slapping Dodd on the back with four legs, he laughed.

Dodd turned puzzled and looked at his father. "Antoni paid you a very large compliment in bull-ant, son, it means, 'One with the heart of a warrior'."

"Babvaloon, Mar," Antoni said, to Mar embracing him.

"What does Uncle Antoni mean, Father?" Dodd enquired.

Giving Antoni a look of apprehension, Mar replied, "Never mind, Son."

Antoni smiled broadly and lifted his fore legs above his head, saying, "Well, Chieftain, it is true."

"That is not fair," Dodd protested. "What does it mean, Uncle Antoni?"

"I shall leave it up to your father, to explain," Antoni said, allowing diplomacy to take charge.

After all, Antoni thought, *it would not be fitting for Mar's son to find out it means, 'very large fool'.*

"Come friends," Mar beckoned, "honour me with your company, at the Great Oak, to toast my son; a young mouse who, this very leaf fall, has shown himself to be a hero. This darkening, may we enjoy each other's company and the sap run all the darkness. We must celebrate the good fortune the waking hours have brought us. We shall all rejoice until the next lightening of the woods."

"I bid you tell me of this trouble, Stump mentioned?" Antoni asked, looking around at the muddy creatures trudging along behind them. He was proud of the twenty or so creatures who, only leaf falls ago, toiled so nobly on nature's dam, in an attempt to bring it undone.

"Indeed, Antoni, it is bad news. I have been told invading rats are moving inland and are attacking other communes as we speak. They, old friend, show no mercy," Mar confided, shaking his head.

Tipping his head up, Antoni asked, "What of our allies the native rats, reptiles, marsupials, cockroaches, ants and birds? Are they not with us?"

Mar laid his paw on Antoni's head as they walked. "Yes they are still our allies, but many lightenings of peace has mellowed their will to fight. They, my friend, have lost their edge. I am afraid the allegiance of natives is a rusty blunt sword at best. Worst still, the invading rats have brought with them a large army of foreign mice and cockroaches as their allies. They outnumber us, so we are told, by thousands. Sadly, dear friend, more land with each lightening of the woods is being lost to them."

"You were right to send for me, Chieftain. While my army fared well against Leta's, we still lost many of our most valuable fighters. I am afraid, with those I must leave to defend the Queen, we will only be able to rely on a few hundred to join our cause. Nevertheless, I shall ensure they will be well trained." Antoni assured his noble comrade.

"By the Great Gumnuts, it is good to see you." Mar wobbled the bull-ant's antennas with his paw.

Antoni's face lightened. "Indeed, Mar, it has been a long time and too many lightenings of the woods since we took sustenance together."

"Oh yes. I have contacted the Highest Wedge-tails and she has promised her assistance and as many of her kind as she can muster. First, however, she has offered to take us toward the place where Brother Sun rises, in the next lightening, to take measure of the invaders' strength." Mar turned and saw Dodd catching up from behind, still struggling to get away from the hero's welcome he was receiving. "Enough talk of the future, Antoni, in the darkening we shall enjoy the celebration with some sap and I dare say a few of your tales."

Antoni realised Mar was attempting to shelter Dodd from the worries his title, 'Noble Oak Mouse', brought with it and fell silent.

"Father, can you ask your followers to stop hitting me on the back? It is really beginning to hurt." Dodd said, turning. "Look there, the brutes have flattened my fur and my skin is red and sore. I do not know if I can take being a hero. Well, being a hero is alright, it is the acclamation I am not very fond of. How do you stand it, Uncle Antoni?"

"I will tell you how Antoni takes it, son; he wisely disappears before the celebrations begin if he is the one considered the hero of the moment. Ants can do that you see," Mar said, patting Antoni on the head.

"Yes, Dodd, there are many advantages in being small, strong and fast. In fact, it is those very same things that have saved mine and others lives on numerous adventures." Looking up ahead, Antoni noticed the word spreading and the crowd of creatures swelling on either side of the Great Oak's roots. He simply smiled saying, "Brace yourself, mouse, because here comes the onslaught."

Dodd's fur went quite grey, as the crowd began to chant his and Mar's name, both in their own languages and in the common, chosen, tongue. He was, however, very pleased to walk along the slightly raised root above the crowd than in amongst it.

Antoni smiled, "Well, young mouse, are you fully grown yet?"

"Well not really, I suppose, dear Uncle," Dodd replied, waving and gazing around.

Without another word, Antoni slipped his leg out in front of Dodd and with a flick of his elbow flung Dodd into the adoring crowd. "You soon will be, mouse," he laughed.

As Mar and Antoni entered the doorway, they turned in time to see Dodd thrown up into the air and the crowd swarming fifteen deep around him.

Trix greeted Mar lovingly and then suddenly slapped him on the shoulder. "Mar Mouse, who do you think you are nearly getting yourself killed?"

"Nearly, is the word, my dearest, the Great River Stones shone for me this past leaf fall. That is why I am still here."

"Rubbish it was due to your son, from what Stump has told me, river stones indeed," Trix grumbled, and glared at him.

"Of course, it was them after all who sent Dodd to us so many lightenings ago, was it not?"

"Oh, yes, and we had nothing to do with it. Well, I never, and I suppose they took our Adin away from us as well?" Trix sensing her words piercing Mar's heart leant forward to kiss him. "I am sorry, my dearest mouse."

Having overheard their conversation, Antoni lowered his head in thought. *Even though many lightenings have past since their young Adin disappeared, I know they both still carry enormous guilt. None of us can be sure what happened to him.*

25

Antoni remembered too well, the tension which had resulted from the search for this young mouse. He shuddered, as he thought of how a long standing treaty between the predators and smaller creatures was nearly broken.

The Chief Ant knew life would have never been the same with the breaking of a treaty derived from ancient times. After all, it was agreed, the large meat eaters would only take the commune's dead from a sacred place, in celebration of sustenance. Those left behind did not mourn the others passing, instead they accepted it as a fact of their existence. Antoni shook his head trying to remove the visions, flooding his senses, of the carnage and havoc that would exist without such a treaty.

DARKENING OF THE WOODS

Mar looked around the gathering area, which lay in an enormous cavern beneath the Great Oak. Despite the labyrinth of roots shooting out of the moist walls in every direction, blocking his vision, he could sense the atmosphere of jubilation. *I am proud of Dodd,* he thought, *and it is only fitting they honour him so. I fear the coming lightenings will not allow such celebrations.* A paw gently touched his shoulder, making him jump.

"Is it not wonderful, my life mate, to see the meeting area so alive with happiness?" Sliding her paw down Mar's soft grey fur, she took his. "Come, walk with me. It is important they see the Chieftain of the Oak amongst them. So stop skulking in the shadows and let them see your handsome smiling face." With that Trix grabbed both his front paws and pulled him into the faint light.

Walking amongst their fellow natives, Trix and Mar nodded and greeted their friends with cheer. Entering an area devoid of roots, they both smiled when they noticed a crowd of the younger creatures gathered around Antoni.

Trix stopped and squeezed Mar's paw. "Please may we linger a leaf fall and hear Antoni's tale." Adoration

shining from her deep brown eyes, Trix looked up into
Mar's.

Antoni, aided by some warm saps, was in the midst of
reliving a magnificent battle. Glancing to his side, he
noticed Mar standing there and winked. Ah m*any an
adventure we had,* he thought, *before you took a mate
Mar.* The Chief Ant shook his head as he tried to focus
through the haze, brought on by the intoxicating affects
of the warm saps.

The creatures listened contentedly as Antoni told them
of their fight against a gathering of red back spiders.
"Where was I?" he mumbled to himself, "Oh that is right;
we were pinned in a corner tired and beaten."

The air was damp and darkness filled the cavern as
Antoni went on:-

"Suddenly, a flaming arrow hit the ground in front of
us, setting the grass alight and scattering the gathering.
Seizing the opportunity, we slashed our way out. Only to
turn and see many of the spiders perish in flame as their
webs burnt away.

"Still unknown to us, was our mysterious saviour.
Looking around in all the plants above the gathering
area, we could not see any sign of an archer.

"'Come out, I beg thee, so we may show our gratitude',
Mar had pleaded.

"But we heard no reply. As we sat there on a rock,
exhausted, we noticed a piece of the greenery move and
then yet another. For indeed the battle had worn me out
and so I thought, my eyes were playing tricks on me.
Until that is, I heard, 'Ha, Ha,' emanating from some
leaves.

"Then as our weary eyes focused, through the haze of
the redness, we spied two proud green figures. In a
water drip they moved forward, one still devouring a

spider's leg.

"'Allow us to introduce ourselves', the grasshopper had said, 'I am Gregor of the Grasshoppers and this is my long time companion, Preta of the Preying Mantises'."

Antoni leant back on the small rock and crossed two of his legs. "And that, my friends, is how we met two of our greatest allies and the noblest of warriors." With that, he finished the story.

"Tell us more, tell us more," the crowd pleaded.

Antoni, too tired to go on, excused himself. Crawling over the young creatures' legs, he went to seek out Mar and Trix. He found them talking to some of the commune's elders by a large pile of warm stones.

"Ah, Antoni, another successful tale I trust?" Mar said, offering his friend another cup of sap.

"Yes, Mar," he replied, "but please, I ask your forgiveness, for I have no wish to partake of anymore sap. This is not a sign of disrespect but a need I must not fulfil. I have told the tale of our struggles with the Red Back Spiders, as you know. Anymore sap, I fear, they shall haunt me in my dreams this darkening. Chieftain and Lady, I beg your leave to seek refuge in a place that does not spin before my eyes."

"Your leave is granted, dear friend, and may sleep bring you fond memories of riches and conquests," Mar Mouse said, laid a paw on Antoni's head and bowed.

"Again, thank you, dearest Antoni, for what you did for us this lightening of the woods and good rest my friend," Trix said, as he graciously kissed her paw.

Even the elders were impressed with Antoni's obvious respect as he bid all good darkening and retired.

KYM JADE

LIGHTENING OF THE WOODS TWO

Antoni woke to the noise of a happy home preparing for a new lightening. As he lay there, listening, he could not help thinking how very different Mar's life had become. Since being elected the Noble Oak Mouse of this small outlying commune, with his lovely mate, Trix, by his side, he had managed to turn a struggling outpost into a thriving community; a sanctuary for the smaller creatures in the forest.

Hatty wandered down a long hollow, following a rather loud snoring noise. "Good lightening, Uncle Antoni, father bids you join us for breakfast," she said, peeping into the tiny alcove Antoni chose to use as his room. "Indeed, Uncle, we have been searching everywhere for you since before lightening."

"I had no idea, child. Please accept my deepest apologies. You see, as I wandered tired last darkening, I happened across this area which I felt would be ideal for a creature of my stature. In truth, I was worried about being stepped upon by one of the larger creatures, such as a bandicoot perhaps. So I took this as a safe haven,

30

for indeed the only other creature who could fit in here would be another ant."

"Wise, as always," Hatty replied, walking off. "I shall see you in the eating area, Uncle."

Antoni stood up and placed his belt and sword together carefully in the corner. Out of a small opening in the oak, he could see the grey rain-bringers had broken up and the blue of Father Sky gracing the land with its presence.

"A fine lightening of the woods," he said, stretching and walking out into the long hollow. "Now all I have to do is figure out where it is exactly, I am in the Oak. Too much warm sap will do that to an ant. Although, I suspect on this lightening many other creatures will join me in the vagueness such an over indulgence brings."

Walking, down the long hollows of the Great Oak, Antoni could not remember when he had last seen so many creatures, of the commune, gathered and sleeping in the one abode. One particularly large bandicoot blocked the passage, he felt sure, would lead to the great eating hollow below. Ever so carefully he squeezed past, with his back against the wall, leaving the sleeping bandicoot snoring away.

Finally, Antoni walked into the large hollow, which lay near the food storage areas. Smiling, as best a bull-ant can, he made his way down the long table to where Mar and his family sat eating.

"Good lightening," Mar said, raising his head from the grass and root breakfast before him. "I bid you, dear friend, join us."

Trix stood, entered the preparation area and to Antoni's surprise returned in moments with a selection of sugars and small crumbs. "I hope this will be to your liking, Antoni. If I am to understand, what Mar has told me, you both will be soaring this lightening on the Highest of Wedge-tails. I should imagine you will need a lot of strength," she said, laying her paw on his shoulder.

"Indeed, I will," Antoni replied. "You may well realise what Father Sky's winds can do, at such great height, to a creature my size. Why, the slightest breeze could see me flung off, that is, if I let my mind wander."

"Excuse me Chieftain," Stump said, bowing as he drew nearer. "A finch has told me the Highest of Wedge-tails will wait for you upon the staggered rocks toward Brother Sun. She begs you not to dally long, she feels it in her talons the weather may turn against your search."

"Thank you, Stump. I hope you offered the finch some sustenance for its kindness?"

"That, I did, Chieftain. Good lightening, Antoni," Stump said, placing himself down next to him. Then with beckoning eyes, he looked up at Trix and continued, "I do hope I have not interrupted your sustenance?"

Entering the storage area Trix smiled, she knew exactly what Stump was after. Turning she asked, "You will do us the honour, dear Stump, of joining us?"

Stump smiled, accepted and glanced around. *I know what you all think; an appetite far outweighing my size has brought about my bulk. Being of rather short stature, for a kangaroo mouse, I realise you think me podgy but I know it is muscle.*

"I would have thought you would have eaten, Stump?" Dodd said, gathering his leaves.

"To tell the truth, young Dodd, I had. However, may I point out that was leaf falls ago, before the lightening of the woods. Someone had to stand guard," he announced, sticking out his chest.

"Yes, I see your point, friend," Dodd said, smiling mischievously as he patted Stump's rather large belly. Then before Dodd could reach the last empty leaf, Stump devoured it.

Not wishing to alarm the other creatures, Mar stood, rubbed noses with Trix, and ushered Stump to the side of the hollow, "Well, Stump, were there any unwelcome visitors in our midst last darkening?"

"No, Chieftain. Aldo and I searched around our commune, for many mouse lengths, and not a sign of strange rats did we see."

"What of our brother rats, have they heard anymore from the rising of the sun?" Mar asked, looking around the hollow.

"I did have reason to speak to a brother rat last darkening. While they have heard many things too, they can not be sure if the tales are of the sun struck or truth. As you know, Mar, the new menace do not use our common tongue nor do they speak brother rat's."

"Indeed, it was a dark lightening when those large pale creatures landed, their logs on our shores, bringing those rats, mice and cockroaches with them. The large pale ones tear apart our fellow natives' dwellings, creating massive lands of waste; while these other savage creatures spread and breed beyond imagining."

"Cockroaches?" Stump said, thoughtfully, "I could not be sure they were not about last darkening. Though, I have never gazed upon one, am I to understand they are dark themselves and would blend with the darkening? Is that right?"

"Sadly, Stump, it is. I leave you with the protection of the commune this lightening." Mar laid his paw on Stump's shoulder and leant toward him. "Keep well, my friend, and ever watchful."

"I will, Mar; I shall never fail you or the commune." Stump bowed as he left.

Mar caught Antoni's attention and signalled for him to join him in the shadows. As Antoni walked across the hollow, Mar's mind drifted for a moment. His heart skipped a beat with the sight of his beloved, Trix, standing in a ray of light adorning their hollow.

"Chieftain," Antoni said, stood on his back legs and swept a leg across his chest.

"I suggest we leave before two more leaf falls. We can call council as soon as our search is over. To be honest, my friend, I fear all does not bode well for our kind."

Antoni sensed darkness in Mar's voice. He had not felt so uneasy since the great battle with the funnel-web spiders.

"Why did the Large Pale Ones have to come to our beloved bush?" Mar asked Antoni.

"I really can not say. I have heard my cousins, in and about, where these strange creatures live have fast become lazy gatherers and find an abundance of food in their dwellings." In an attempt to lift Mar's spirits Antoni continued, "Fear not, I have sent word to my cousins, the wood eaters, to partake in some covert operation against this terrible creature. I am not sure how successful they will be, but indeed they will feast on their dwellings." Antoni laughed. "So once we are able to understand the creatures strange tongue we shall instantly have many spies in their midst to convey messages."

"You never cease to amaze me, Antoni! Your strategy of war is incredible, fancy sending in an advance party of white ants to feast on their dwellings. Why, the creatures will not even be aware of their presence until it is too late."

Antoni stepped closer to his friend, whispering, "It is good, at least they have stopped fleeing from the progress of the Large Pale Ones. I dare say a fight has begun that will still be going on thousands of leaf falls from this lightening.

"A change is coming across our homeland, Mar. I too fear it will alter our destinies to such an extent, even the tales of our ancestors will disappear. If we can not at least stop the advance of the rats and cockroaches, the way we live now, in our life giving bush, will change not for the better, my friend. Now, I must return to my lodgings and gather my things for the journey. Tell me, would brother bandicoot have moved by now?"

"I doubt that, Antoni, you know how they love to sleep in the leaf falls of the lightening. I bid you do not disturb him as he too aided Stump and Aldo in the protection of the commune last night."

"Fear not, Mar, not a piece of his fur shall I ruffle in passing," Antoni announced, as he gave a salute to his chest upon leaving.

Mar and Antoni met again outside the Great Silky Oak; where they found Aldo and Stump waiting to bid them a safe journey.

Aldo looked Mar in the eye. "We wish we were soaring with you, Chieftain."

"Perhaps next time, my friends." Mar placed a paw on each of their shoulders, turned and walked away.

Hiding in the shadows, Dodd and Toe watched on wishfully as their father and Antoni moved into the underbrush.

Before disappearing into the deep foliage, Mar yelled, "Farewell and good lightening. We shall see you again before Brother Sun sleeps."

Not far into the journey Mar looked down at Antoni, "Please do not think me disrespectful, my friend, but would you mind climbing on my shoulders, so we may make better time. I am eager to get this journey done and return to my family."

Without hesitation Antoni bounced off a pebble, spun in the air and landed on Mar's shoulders. The kangaroo mouse smiled and then hopped away at a great pace.

In only a few leaf falls they reached the edge of a small clearing at the base of the staggered rocks. There in the middle sat, "Sqweara" the Highest of Wedge-tails.

"I bid thee good lightening, Highest of Wedge-tails," Mar said, bouncing up on a rock before her.

"Ah, Chieftain Mar of the Great Oak, I return your greeting. However, for the rest of our journey I suggest you call me by my chosen name of, Sqweara," she replied, her head held high; ever watchful.

"Hail, Sqweara, greatest of all Wedge-tails," a small voice said.

"Why," she said, looking down at the rock Mar and Antoni stood upon, "I would know that voice anywhere. Hail to you, Antoni, Chief Warrior Bull-ant of the mighty Queen Zana. I hope all bodes well in your Queen's kingdom?"

"That, my lady, is a long story, which I shall gladly share with you on our journey."

"Well, we shall waste not another leaf fall. Mar I have had my ladies in waiting fasten a vine, around my neck, for you to hold on to. Antoni, so I can hear all the latest gossip, I should enjoy you placing yourself near my right ear; if that is convenient?" Sqweara asked, putting her head down next to the rock they were standing on.

The giant eagle waited for her passengers to make themselves comfortable, ran a few paces and flapped her enormous wings. Soon they were soaring high above the eucalyptus and rain-forests; Sqweara effortlessly riding the air currents to their advantage. Not many wing flaps later they were thousands of mouse lengths away from the Great Oak.

Mar had forgotten how bright Brother Sun's rays could be, free from the shelter of the forest and bush. He found the brilliant clear blue, and the accompanying brightness, blinding for a while until his eyes became accustomed to the surroundings.

Antoni was enjoying the journey immensely as he re-acquainted himself with Sqweara, who had also shared some of their early adventures. How he loved the bird's eye view of the land. *It humours me,* he thought, *to see that all creatures take on the look of my fellow ants from this position. It gives me an understanding, a oneness, with all creatures who wish only to exist in peace.*

With her incredible eyesight, Sqweara gave a continuous narrative of what she could see below. Leaf fall after leaf fall they travelled on. Until, even Mar and Antoni began to notice more movement down on Mother Earth's surface.

"Sqweara," Mar yelled, "Do you think we could land near that gathering of animals?"

Many of the ground dwelling creatures scattered as the cry went out warning of Sqweara's approach.

"How strange?" she commented, landing with a gust from her wings. "These creatures are afraid of me."

Mar soon dismounted and shot off into the partly

bushed area. "Hold, friend," he shouted, hopping at great pace. "I only seek information," but the other mouse had long gone.

"What are you doing riding on an eagle's back, small one?" came a voice from the scrub beside the clearing.

"Come forward, so that I might see you, oh one who speaks the common tongue." Mar politely beckoned.

"Sorry, I can not, the lightening hurts my eyes. I beg you come closer to me," the slow, soft, voice implored.

As Mar drew closer he could make out a distinctive outline. "Ah, Brother Wombat, I bid you slowcomb," he greeted, in wombat and bowed.

"Thank you, kind mouse, and metcha to you. Now what are you doing riding on the back of the winged one? Do you not realise how dangerous it is to associate with such a powerful creature?"

"We are long time friends, so do not fear, their kind and ours have a treaty."

"Treaty huh!" The wombat grumbled and laid down in the shade. "We used to have treaties, in our homelands too, until those vile creatures came. They have been removed from the bush for so long, they can not even speak the common tongue."

"Do you mean the Large Pale Ones, I have heard talk of?" Mar asked, eager to hear news.

"Yes, I most certainly do. They are stripping our forests and bush. Not only do they bring the breaker of treaties with them, they also have brought giant creatures. The strange things have very hard feet that do not suit our terrain and they also eat our grasslands."

Crouching down beside him Mar enquired, "Treaty breakers. Do you mean the rats, who have come from where Brother Sun rises?"

Just then Antoni walked up behind Mar and sat on a small rock beside him.

"Is the bull-ant with you?" Wombat asked. "I have never had a lot of time for bull-ants, always getting in my tunnels and biting me."

"Slowcomb," Antoni greeted. "Perhaps, if you watched where you were going, my kind would not have to bite to let you know where we are."

"Hm," the wombat said, turning his head away from the two friends.

Mar hopped a few paces forward. "Please, Brother Wombat; do tell me more of the treaty breakers? I promise my friend will do his best to let others know how you and your kind feel."

The wombat returned his gaze to Mar and huffed. "Huh, I somehow think such days are past in the forests and bush. Creatures caring for others with mutual respect; how I wish for those times again."

"Please go on," Mar implored.

Slowly, the wombat began to speak once more, "Yes, see those strange rats have been taking everything they can get their paws on, food, babies and even the great eagles' eggs. Not so, any creature would notice mind you. Always in the shadows lurking, waiting, they are. So now no creature trusts another and all treaties are off. And as we become displaced and move into other communes the anger travels with us; spreading. Where it will end, only Father Sky and Mother Earth know."

"How far do you feel the treaty breakers may be from this clearing, friend?" Antoni asked, sketching a rough map of the area.

"I do not know what, that is, you are scratching in the earth, Ant. All I know is I have walked four lightenings since the last time I saw one of those despicable creatures. Tell me, Brother Mouse, how far is it to this commune where treaties still hold?" Wombat asked, blinking at the light.

"To tell you the truth, Brother Wombat, I can not say. It is so difficult to judge when you have soared on an eagle's back." Mar held his paw to his chin and continued, "If you walk toward the ending of the lightening, perhaps, it may be as near as five lightenings away. Before you ask, my brother, I can guarantee you will indeed be welcome. Look for a great silky oak, standing on the outer edge of the rain-forest."

"That I will," the wombat said, standing, "May the River Stones protect you on your journey." Looking down at Antoni, he continued, "Both of you. Please remember Brother Ant to convey my message."

"I shall without delay, oh peaceful one," Antoni yelled as the wombat disappeared into the foliage.

Within the wink of an eye Antoni and Mar dashed back to Sqweara and relayed the news.

The wedge-tail waited for her comrades to finish, tilted her head on the side and said, "No treaty exists between the creatures of this place because of those rats, why wait until I can get my talons on them. Peace, which has existed since the pebbles were boulders, destroyed by deceit. Come, this is not a safe area for us anymore, we must return and have council with our allies."

"I beg you, Sqweara, grant me one more boon," Mar said, climbing into position. "Take us a bit further toward the rising of Brother Sun."

"Granted, Mar Mouse. I too, am more than interested to spy ahead, toward the great water we can not drink; where my cousins live and prosper."

Mar and Antoni held on tight as the great wedge-tail flapped her wings and took them into the hands of Father Sky.

For many leaf falls nothing appeared to change on the ground below while all around them the grey rain-bringers gathered. Then suddenly, as a grey rain-bringer moved from beneath them, their eyes gazed for the first time upon the devastation created by the Large Pale Ones.

Life giving Sister Trees lay on their sides while the pale creatures stripped off the protective branches and leaves. Amongst the now naked areas stood strange creatures; none had ever heard tell of before Brother Wombat mentioned them.

"The rain-bringers are angry, no doubt due to the stupidity of these creatures. We must return as they are starting to grumble," Sqweara announced, completing a large circle of the area.

Neither Mar nor Antoni were in a position to argue, they were both dumbfounded by what they had seen.

"By the Great River Stones, I had no idea they had come so far and created so much devastation," Mar yelled to them both above the wind currents. "We can not fight or defend ourselves against such enormous creatures. Not even my mighty cousins the kangaroos could withstand them."

"That may be true, Mar, nevertheless we can stand against the smaller creatures who are new to our land. I admit the battle will be long and hard but we must prevail," Antoni interjected.

"What of our large friends who blend with the darkening?" Sqweara squawked. "They have shared our life with us for so long."

"I really do not know," Mar said, turning around to gaze down on the scarred landscape, watching the smoke billow into the sky.

DARKENING TWO

"**A**ldo, I hope no ill fate has fallen upon Chieftain Mar or Antoni on their perilous journey. Mar did say they would return before darkening," Stump whispered, nervously patrolling the outer edge of the commune.

"Fear not, Stump, the Highest of Wedge-tails has carried Mar on many such journeys, she will not fail to return them safely to the protection of our commune," Aldo replied, poking around behind some branches.

Without warning the leaves in front of them rustled as both mice heard the strange laughter of a young creature.

"Halt, in the name of The Commune, identify yourself," Aldo commanded.

There was no reply.

Only mouse lengths on, the strange muffled laughter bounced off the leaves around them again.

"I command thee, in the name of Chieftain Mar of the Great Oak, to show yourself," Aldo screamed, now more than a bit annoyed.

Stump jumped as a small pebble, hurled from the bushes, knocked Aldo's leaf hat clean off his head. "How dare you?" he said, bending to pick up his hat. His temper then erupted as another pebble ricocheted off his posterior.

"We are under attack," Stump cried, running into the bush toward the noise.

"Ah, gumnuts!" Stump moaned.

Aldo circled around their position and crouched under a large gum leaf that was conveniently leaning against a small log. Moving forward, he gazed in all directions, expecting an attack at every turn.

"Aldo, please get me down," Stump pleaded, seeing him drew nearer.

There dangling in front of him, Stump was more than a bit embarrassed, a vine wrapped tightly around his hind paw.

It was obvious to Aldo; a child had set the primitive trap. "If I get my paws on whoever did this, when our commune is facing such a threat, I will strangle them!"

As Stump crashed to the ground both mice once again heard the impish laughter of a child. However, the more they pursued it the further away it seemed to go. Sometimes it appeared to be in the tree-tops. Other times it came from deep dark hollows where no commune creature would ever dare venture.

Nervous, Stump's whiskers twitched. "Do you think it was one of those rats?"

"No, it was one of our own. I could tell by how well it knew our habitat. The question is, who?" Aldo said, rubbing his rather sore tail area. "All our young ones know of the impending threat and stay in the secured areas."

While Stump and Aldo pondered the strange occurrences they continued on their rounds. Not a sign of the young creature did they see or hear. Their duty ending they returned to the gathering place in front of the Oak.

While sitting indulging themselves with some warm sap, to take the edge off an unnerving darkening, they heard the cry come down from the staggered rocks, "Mar, Sqweara and Antoni have finally returned."

"May the River Stones be praised," Stump said, his warm drink tightly clasped between his chubby paws.

#   #   #

"Farewell, Sqweara, I thank thee with all my heart. I will send word, upon mid lightening, of the place and time of High Council. May Father Sky keep you safe in his arms." Mar Mouse bowed, sweeping his paw in front of him.

"It was indeed a pleasure, Mar, to share in such an important journey with you and Antoni. Again, I only wish it had been better news we returned with and not some so bleak. I bid thee good darkening." Sqweara flapped her wings and was gone.

On the way back, to the gathering area, Antoni walked by Mar's side. Neither said very much but were glad of the company.

While Mar walked, he formulated a proposal as to how exactly the news should be broken to his fellow creatures.

"Hold, dear friend, give me but a moment before we enter the clearing," Mar asked, sitting down on a log.

"Of course," Antoni replied, but remained standing.

"You and I are survivors, of many crusades, yet even I must admit I was shaken to the core by what we saw this lightening. Brother Wombat's words still echo in my head."

"I know exactly how you feel, Mar! I, too, am at a loss for words to describe such a happening."

"So, friend, my point is: If it has affected you and I so severely, might it not send a wave of panic through our fellow creatures?"

"Ah, I see your point. Wise as always Mar! However, they must be told." Antoni argued, "Otherwise, how can we all prepare for such an onslaught?"

"You misunderstand me. I fully intend to tell them of

the darkness that invades the lightening. What I ponder is, in how much detail? Besides I fear they shall all know soon enough."

"You lead friend and I shall follow as always. Your wisdom has not led our deeds astray, thus far."

Mar shook his head, stood feeling old beyond his lightening and walked on.

Entering the clearing, near the beginning of one of the oak's surface roots, the comrades were greeted by a crowd of animals. "Hale, Chieftain Mar and Chief Antoni."

It did not take long for word to spread of their arrival. Within a leaf fall many natives had gathered to hear their news. Creature after creature jammed into the area until there was no standing room left. That is all except the echidnas, who stood quietly in the background to prevent jabbing a fellow creature with one of their quills.

The gathering hushed when Mar raised his paw. "First we must give thanks," he announced.

You could have heard a leaf falling through the air in the darkening as Mar lead them in thanks:

"Father Sky and Mother Earth we, your children, thank you for sustaining our humble lives. Sister Trees, who give us food and shelter, we pledge our protection. Grey Rain-Bringers, the children of Father Sky, we thank thee for the kindness of bringing us water. By the great River Stones may we always be thankful.

"We here acknowledge also, that as the lightenings pass, we may cease to exist and in our passing our bodies will sustain others. For this we give thanks."

"For this we give thanks," the crowd rumbled.

"Brothers and Sisters on this lightening, thanks to the Highest of Wedge-tails, Chief Antoni and I soared many mouse lengths away from our oak. On our journey we met a brother wombat who lived closer to the rising of Brother Sun. He told us of evil deeds, carried out by the invading rats, ending all treaties amongst our fellow creatures in his area. Therefore, we must be ever watchful of such deceit in our presence and believe in our long standing friendships.

"We soared further than we expected this lightening in search of answers. Sadly, we saw the devastation; the Pale Large Ones create through their very existence. They appear to have armies of creatures at their disposal. These animals are much larger than even Brother Red Kangaroo and Sister Dingo."

A cry came out of the gathering. "How far are they away from our commune?"

"Fortunately, we had favourable winds, as our gift from Father Sky on this lightening, and they are many lightenings away from us. Perhaps they may even stop their push forward and we may all yet live in peaceful coexistence. We must, however, prepare ourselves for the worst and move much of the commune deep into the rain-forest to start again."

"No, we shall not leave our homes," many voices yelled in unison.

Aldo and Stump moved forward and held up their paws. "Let Chieftain Mar speak," they yelled above the rumble of discontent.

Mar waved both his front paws. "This is only a precaution; firstly, it must be agreed too by the Elders and the High Council. We must also prepare ourselves for fellow displaced creatures, who will soon cross our boundaries, confused and homeless. We can not allow the anger they carry to spread amongst this commune. So I beg thee, talk the common tongue amongst yourselves. Cherish thy neighbour, let us stand as one, all creatures of Father Sky and Mother Earth."

The chants and cries of the gathering erupted in so many different native tongues, it was deafening.

Mar walked over and rubbed noses with Trix. Soon Dodd, Hatty and Toe were standing by their father's side hugging him lovingly.

Trix sensed immediately, something was terribly wrong as Mar's fur under his eyes looked darkened.

"Father, oh Father. What is it like to soar? When can I go, Father?" Toe screeched.

Laying his paw, quite heavily, on his little brother's head, Dodd threw out his chest and said, "I shall be first Toe, will I not, Father?"

"And I suppose you consider female mice not important enough to soar?" Hatty growled, at Dodd.

"Correct," Dodd replied, not even looking her in the eye.

Hatty punched him in the arm and with a, "Huh," stormed off into the Great Oak.

"Well, Father, will it be me?" Dodd asked again.

Mar holding up his paw growled, "Enough," and walked off to where Antoni was talking to Stump and Aldo.

"Ah, Chieftain Mar," Antoni said. "It appears we may already have some trickery in our midst.

Mar listened intently as they told him of the strange occurrences of the early leaf falls of the darkening.

"We shall double the guard and send some of our best creatures to create outposts, in a giant circle around our commune. Stump, enlist some of the faster creatures to act as runners for the passing of messages."

"Yes, Chieftain," Stump replied, before running into the dispersing gathering.

"Also, I need to know the precise number of creatures

willing to stand and fight for the commune. Along with those who will venture further to search for a new location and begin preparations. Nothing too elaborate though, I still hope a move will not be needed."

Aldo was gone in a flash to contact all the other commanders of the commune's defence forces.

"And what of I, Chieftain Mar?" Antoni humbly asked.

"You, dear friend, will remain by my side. We shall attempt to convince, the peace loving Elders and the Winged Council that we must form a War Council in all haste. It is imperative we prepare strategies for many lightenings to come."

"That, I shall proudly do. I think perhaps, with your permission, I may send one of my fellow ants to my Queen Zana's kingdom to inform her majesty and seek assistance. Also, Chieftain, I would like to send for Squorth."

"Squorth, by the rushing stream, is that devil still alive?" Mar asked, astounded.

"Yes, my Chieftain, and she still enjoys a good battle. Since the Funnel Web Wars, she has lived in solitude, shunned by her own kind. Even though the Funnel Webs are now, hopefully, our allies they have not forgiven her indiscretions. In regards, that is, to protecting me after I saved her life prior to the war."

Within an instant of his antenna moving, a fellow ant stood by Antoni's side only somewhat dwarfed by the great bull-ant's size. "Dark Ant, take this leaf etching to Queen Zana." The bull-ant dashed over to a large leaf, placed his scent on it and returned. "Also take this message to Royo, my commander; he will know what to do."

Honoured to be asked, the small black ant struggled with the two leaves and took off down the large root. The little ant mumbled a prayer to himself. "Please do not let a larger native step on me, especially when I am carrying such important leaf messages!"

Only a few leaf falls later Mar was sitting on his rock, in the great eating hollow, surrounded by the commune's elders. Those too big to enter, stood patiently outside looking in through a large hole; usually covered by an enormous stone the former entrance is only open for special meetings.

Briar the Elder Mouse walked over to his student, bent down and whispered, "Quite a speech, Chieftain Mar."

"Thank you, Elder Briar. To be quite truthful though, I did not disclose all we learnt this lightening," Mar confessed, turning his eyes from side to side.

"I thought not. The Pale Ones are much closer than you let on and these foreign rats and cockroaches precede them, do they not?" The old grey kangaroo mouse took his position directly in front of the chieftain.

Mar laid his paw on his mentor's shoulder. "Does nothing escape your ever watchful gaze, old one?"

"On the contrary, Chieftain, with each passing lightening more and more slips by me unnoticed. I fear too many lightenings, and perhaps too much warm sap, are finally seeking their revenge on my weary body."

"Never. You are as sprightly as when you trained me in combat techniques."

"Ah, to look at life through young eyes again and to believe everything is possible. What I would not give to have your youth again, Marcus."

#   #   #

Slowly the hollow filled and the meeting commenced. Many expressed grave concerns about the talk of possible confrontations with fellow creatures and proposed immediate negotiations commence. They put forward, a messenger be sent to the rats first, as they were the most immediate threat.

It was hoped, a meeting would be arranged so a treaty may be signed. This would ensure peace and successful assimilation of the new rats' kind into their beliefs and political system.

Tired of their banter, Mar stood in protest. "How would you talk to them? They do not speak the common tongue, native rat or any other language we know."

"You are certain of this?" Pitra the Possum asked, from her position hanging above the meeting.

"I have heard," Mar replied.

"So you can not be certain. I appreciate your view of the problem, Chieftain Mar, but a great majority of the creatures in the commune are peace loving creatures and have no taste for war. I move we send a messenger. Perhaps a native rat, if any creature should be able to find a way to communicate with them, should it not be a Brother Rat?"

"Aye, that makes sense," the room rumbled.

Mar held both front paws above his head. "Yes, yes I agree to such an action. I only asked we form a Council of War, as a precaution. We must also look for a new site for the commune, further into the rain-forest."

"Yes, your suggestions are wise," Wolla the Roo commented from outside. "Sadly, I doubt we shall find another area which will suit all of our brothers and sisters. This will mean the commune will be split, perhaps for all leaf falls."

Rina the native rat stood up, from his position in the back of the hollow, his distinctive bravery locket gleaming in the moonlight. *Even though I know, the new threat is not related to my kind, I feel somewhat responsible.*

The brave rat took in a gulp of air, swallowed it and called, "I shall venture out into the unknown and seek out these rats' council and put forward all which has been laid down this darkening."

With that Binja the bush cockroach, his loyal friend, made his way into the centre of the hall and stood on an eating stump. "And I shall do my best to find these new cockroaches and explain our wishes."

"No," Damp cried, from the back of the hollow, fearing for her lifelong mate's spirit.

"We salute you both! By this coming lightening we will have settled upon the messages to be conveyed," Mar Mouse announced. "Now I must implore you to allow a War Council to be formed."

"War is such a harsh word," Pitra sighed. "Could it not become a self fulfilling prophecy to have such a council?"

Brother Wella the wombat, positioned in a new extension to the oak's hollows, walked out of the shadows. "You speak wisely as usual, Lady Petra."

"Perhaps an Alternative Action Committee," Betra the bat screeched from high in the eating area's ceiling.

After a round of talks it was decided; Chieftain Mar, Chief Antoni and King Damon of the Dark Ant would head an Alternative Action Committee, consulted by Briar the Elder Mouse and Elder Bega of the Bandicoots.

Later, sitting to leaf etch the council edicts, Mar felt a familiar paw on his shoulder. "Mar, judge not badly the council's decisions."

"Please, Briar the Elder, do not think me in disagreement of a peaceful resolution. I beseech Mother Earth and Father Sky, to allow us such a solution. I too remember, have a family I long to protect from the horrors of war. Horrors, neither side ever really benefit from."

"Ah, they made a wise choice when they approached you to be, The Noble Oak Mouse. Indeed, you have once again made me a proud old teacher."

"Thank you, Elder Briar."

"Please, if I may address you quite bluntly, as my time is short. I ask you to allow for some of our fellow creatures lack of worldly knowledge, such as yours. For while they are the elders of our commune they are not always correct. Always remember, Mar, while the passing of leaf falls is inevitable the gathering of wisdom does not necessarily follow."

Before Mar could lift his head from the etching on the leaf, Briar was gone. Astounded, he stood and called out to him but received no answer. "For an Elder, that mouse can certainly still move swiftly," he mumbled, going back to work.

Illuminated by a single sliver of Sister Moon's light, Mar sat back down on the gumnut and continued his work until the lightening once again touched the woods.

LIGHTENING OF THE WOODS THREE

Rushing into the hollow, Stump found Mar slumped over his work. "I have some grave news," he announced, rocking him with his paw.

Bewildered, Mar leapt to his feet. "What, what is it mouse? Tell me, have the rats attacked?"

"Chieftain, it is Briar the Elder. His mate, Ma, reported his spirit left his body last darkening. It happened when he was partaking of a warm sap after the meeting. May Mother Earth and Father Sky bless him and his." Stump said, solemnly holding his paw to his chest.

"No, how can it be? Briar the Elder was here, with me, not leaf falls ago in the darkening. We spoke of the council," Mar declared, confused.

"Sorry, it could not have been so. His mate prepares his body for transport to the Stone Circle this very leaf fall. The word has gone throughout the commune and the procession is already forming. His body will lead this lightenings offerings to the way life must be," Stump announced. "Chieftain you look pale, may I get thee something?"

"No, go now, Stump! I will wake Trix and the children

and lead the procession myself." With his mind clouded by shock and disbelief Mar set off toward the hollows leading up the oak.

Standing at the entrance to his private hollow, Mar took a large breath. Leaning against the archway he stared at his children asleep in their notches. Slowly, he gathered himself and entered Trix's chamber, where she lay fast asleep.

"Trix, my darling," he whispered, softly stroking her forehead. "Please wake from this darkening's rest. I have something that I must tell you."

Lovingly, Trix reached her paws up, placed them around Mar's neck and rubbed noses. "Good lightening, my life mate. What a beautiful lightning it is," Trix said, gazing out of the knothole near their bed. "How did the meeting of the Elders finish?"

"Satisfactorily, my moonbeam. My news is not of such matters though. This lightening, we are to mourn the passing of a friend and celebrate the sustenance of life," Mar announced, pulling Trix closer.

"Who is it, Mar?"

"Briar the Elder passed last eve, after the meeting. My mind is perplexed as I am sure he came and spoke to me, not many leaf falls ago during the darkening." Mar looked pale and confused.

"Your bond together was great, Mar. Perhaps you sensed his passing coming and dreamt of him. You look so tired, my love."

"Perhaps, but it was all so very real; as real as you and I sitting together right at this leaf fall." Mar's brown eyes were deep and puzzled.

By the time the Oak's family emerged to lead the procession, the path leading to the Great Ring of Stones was adorned with colourful flower petals. The surrounding trees were alive with the brilliance of the commune's parrots lining the path in tribute. The whole gathering area was also a torrent of sounds, with an ancient song, in the common tongue, spreading around the forest.

> *"We live a life of happiness*
> *We pass to a land not seen*
> *We provide others' sustenance*
> *The way it has long since been."*

Even though it was an accepted part of their existence, Mar still felt sorrow at the passing of his teacher and friend.

Ten creatures were to be transported, the few hundred mouse lengths, to the stones where words would be offered and the crowd would disperse. The local bird life, who participated, with a number of reptiles, waited a distance in the bush as a sign of respect for the passed ones' families".

Mar marched proudly alongside the creatures carrying Briar's body as did Antoni, Dodd and Toe. Trix and Hatty joined Briar's mate Ma to show support. In his belt Mar carried a carved wooden sword known as 'Tongue the Bringer of Truth' which Briar had presented him with, after a twenty lightening quest toward the setting of Brother Sun.

As the commune's natives placed the bodies of the departed out in the circle, Mar watched on. Then as the kookaburra guard of honour began to give the traditional salute, in their native tongue, his mind drifted to leaf falls long since past:

"No, no, young Mar, you must learn to use your tail as another paw, an extension of your will so to speak. Allow

it to sense what may lie behind you," Briar said. "Never underestimate an opponent, my dear mouse, never."

"I shall try not to teacher," Mar exclaimed, turning to face Briar.

"Be ever on your guard, young one, and expect the unexpected," Briar said, bowing his head to the stick Mar had pointed at his heart.

Mar had no idea what hit him as Elder Bega the bandicoot's tail lashed out from the bushes like a whip and knocked his stick from his paw. Stunned, he looked up at his teacher in shock; Briar simply smiled as he waved his paw.

Within leaf falls the small clearing was filled with many of Briar's fellow trainers. "Tell me, mouse, did you really think we were alone?" Briar asked, lowering his brow.

"Yes, I did teacher. I had no idea," Mar answered, quite embarrassed.

"Ha," Briar laughed, lay his paw on his favourite pupil's shoulder and continued, "always be aware, Mar, that in our wondrous world, where Father Sky watches over us and Mother Earth supports us, we are never alone, never alone..."

Briar's words echoed in Mar's ears as Trix took his paw, held it to her mouth and licked it. "It is time for us to return to our homes, my dear mate. Most of the others have departed already. We shall all miss him dearly," Trix whispered in a voice so soft and understanding.

"I learnt many of life's messages through the wisdom of that mouse's teachings. He was of a breed, I feel is disappearing far too quickly for my liking. Trix, my darling mouse, I feel it is time for Dodd to enter into the Learning Circle. If it is alright with thee, I shall ask Bega to teach him in the ways of knowledge and defence?"

"Whatever you see fit, Mar. Now let us depart before our Servicers' of the Circle get restless and look to us for sustenance," Trix said, nervously grabbing Mar's paw and pulling him away.

After Mar and Trix made their way down the ceremonial path, the stone circle came alive. The highly honoured Brother Goanna entered first and gracefully carried that which gives sustenance away, then came Brother Snake, followed by Brothers Crow and Kookaburra. They in turn ventured back to their dwellings where they gave thanks to Mother Earth and Father Sky and took sustenance with their kind. And so it had been since the givers of life had deemed it so.

Upon reaching the Great Oak, Mar was greeted by Ma, Briar's mate, standing near the doorway.

Even though every creature recognised and celebrated the giving of sustenance it did not stop tears welling in her eyes as she spoke to him, "While my Briar would never have told you so, Chieftain Mar, he loved you dearly as if one of his own litter. Our young mice have long since grown and left our commune in search of adventure, and I know not where they are. May Mother Earth and Father Sky protect them in this time of great impending darkness."

Mar moved over, put his arm over Ma's shoulder and held her tight, "I am sure any child of yours and Briar's would be more than safe. Pon, Fila and Jun are great mice as their father was. I have little doubt, they would have completed their quests and settled somewhere in the bush or forests."

"Thank you, Chieftain Mar. Briar asked me to hand you this on his lightening of passing." There from behind her back Ma pulled a diamond encrusted scabbard, "This, Briar told me, belongs to Tongue Bringer of Truth, that which he drew from its sheath so many leaf falls ago, which now adorns your belt."

Humbled by the gift Mar accepted it with pride. He did not even realise, until that leaf fall, such a beautiful creation existed.

Bowing, before she excused herself, Ma said, "Chieftain, I believe it is known as 'The Mouth' from which 'Tongue the Bringer of Truth' comes." Then slowly, deep in sorrow, Ma walked away down the long oak root to her dwelling.

Mar held the scabbard up into one of the rays of light, filtering through the canopy. It is indeed dazzling, he thought, as he drew Tongue from his belt. Then as he inserted Tongue, the Bringer of Truth, into Mouth, the scabbard, a sudden chill which made his fur stand on end struck him.

Trix's eyes sparkled at the sword's brilliance. "It is indeed very beautiful, Mar! Look the handle of your sword now appears to radiate with the same beauty as its sheath. How can that be?"

"Perhaps the reflecting rays of light have shown something to us, we had not seen before. Or it is only when the two are joined the true beauty of their existence can be realised." Mar, reached out, drew Trix nearer and whispered, "As did our marriage make me realise about life."

Dodd, returning from the gathering at Stump's dwelling, immediately noticed the sheath. "Father, where did you gain such a thing?" he asked, staring at the beams of coloured light reflecting in the early lightenings sun.

"Briar the Elder bequeathed that I should have it." Mar handed them both to Dodd.

Holding them in front of him, Dodd shook his head. "And the sword, Father, where did it come from?" he asked amazed.

"It is the same sword, I carried on so many

adventures, my son," Mar said doing his best to summon a smile.

"How can it be, it appears so changed, Father?" Dodd said, holding it out in front of him at full arms length, "and what does the writing on the sheath mean? It is in another creature's tongue because I do not know it by sight."

"Writing!" Mar exclaimed. Walking over to Dodd, he studied the scabbard for a leaf fall. "It is of an ancient tongue, of long before the common tongue was used."

"Where did Elder Brain gain such a prize from, Father, do you know?"

"Well, Dodd, I really do not know."

"Ah, Tongue the Bringer of Truth has returned to its Mouth and so it should be," Bega the Bandicoot said, approaching from behind the oak. "It does my old eyes good to see such brilliance, such purity, again."

"Tell us, Bega the Elder, what does the inscription mean?" Mar asked, passing the set to him.

Bega squinted in the light trying to focus. "It has been so many years, since I read these ancient words, I am not sure if I can still translate the tongue."

"Please try," Dodd pleaded.

Trix, sensing one of Elder Bega's famous stories coming on, snuck into the Oak and summoned Toe and Hatty to listen. Just as she returned Bega adopted his position on the Great Root, signalling for the younger natives to gather round.

"Let me see," he began, "perhaps if I recall, Briar the Elder's and my quest then the words may return to me."

Eagerly, the children sat waiting as Bega's face searched for answers in the air around him:

"It was many leaf falls ago when Briar and I travelled many thousands of mouse lengths toward the falling of Brother Sun. We had crossed rivers and huge mountains in our adventure or quest, to find and document other communes. It was on this adventure we first met, Dena, Sister Dingo and her kind. I remember now as if it was only the lightening before this. Ah, for it to be so.

"We were both very pleased to have travelled so far and find the common tongue still spoken. Most of all it filled our hearts to find all the treaties still stood strong. For many lightenings we enjoyed the generosity of Sister Dingo and her commune. She was indeed a suitable noble of the Great Rock.

"It was she who took Briar and I deep into the dry ground that burnt under Brother Sun's rays. There she allowed us to watch the large ones, who blend into the darkening, paint pictures of fellow creatures on cave walls. You see those large ones believe, as we do, in Mother Earth and Father Sky, and the importance of the Celebration of Sustenance.

One lightening, by river's edge, one of Sister Dingo's pups wandered off. For many leaf falls we searched for what was its name? --- Crin, that is right," Bega said, scratching his head. "Briar, being the experienced tracker he was, eventually took us to the opening of a great tunnel from which we could hear a sad yapping sound. Sister Dingo was horrified as the hole was not big enough for her to enter. It was then she told us..."

"Told you what Bega?" the children shouted.

"Hush and I will tell you. She told us of an old snake named Pyra the Python, who had given up the Celebration of Sustenance ritual and refused to recognise any treaties.

"Suddenly the gravity of the situation hit Briar and I, like a limb off a tree. Briar quickly gathered some vines and we made our way down the long tunnel which, I must admit, was even difficult for me to manage. Quietly, upon reaching a flat area, we allowed our eyes to adjust to the darkness. Always remember, young ones, to allow time for your eyes to adjust, do not rush in, understand!"

"Yes Bega," the small natives answered.

"Finally, there before us stood a large hollow where at one end stood Crin and at the other, Pyra the Python."

"Ooh," some of the young audience cried.

"As Pyra moved forward, poking her tongue before her, it was obvious what was about to happen."

"What, Bega? What?"

"Hatty, you tell them," Bega said, nodding.

Hatty, wrapped up in the moment, said, "Well, I can not be sure, mind you, but I would say Pyra was about to," pausing, she turned to the little ones and jumped shouting, "EAT CRIN."

"Ah," the young ones screeched jumping in fright.

"Yes, that is right. Well, Briar would not stand for it and jumped in between them both.

"'Hold, I command thee, in the name of Mother Earth and Father Sky. I give thee warning to abide by the treaty between your kind and other creatures. A treaty which has been in place since the pebbles were boulders,' Briar commanded holding up his staff.

"'Ssurely you jest little one, I am Pyra and I believe in no ssuch treaty. Though I must thank you for adding to my meal, a nice entree you sshould make, I think. Breathe easy pup I sshall take but a leaf fall to dispose of this annoying little morsel'.

"By that time I had managed to sneak around behind the great snake by another tunnel. Thinking quickly I grabbed Pyra's tail and tied it around a root.

"'What is going on? Deceit treachery,' she hissed, trying to free herself.

"Fortunately for me she could not turn around, so I returned to watch Briar try to convince her to abide by the ancient laws. When Pyra once again refused, Briar turned quickly and told Crin to run to me. As soon as she did I started to help her up the steep portion of the tunnel. Then as I turned to tell Briar, we were clear, I saw Pyra lunge," Bega announced, jumping forward.

Many of the smaller creatures scattered and stood near their parents who also were now listening. "What happened next, Elder Bega?"

"Briar was gone; Pyra had swallowed him in one movement. My heart pounded, my soul laid heavy with guilt, as I had been sure I had tied her tail enough so as to make her advance impossible. Looking across the hollow I noticed the distinctive rocky outcrop, I had used as a point of judgement. To my surprise, in the excitement, Briar had actually moved forward so as to allow the evil one to devour him."

"But why?" Toe screamed.

"Well, all looked lost, when suddenly Pyra started to screech 'Sstop it. What are you doing, mouse? How dare you? Leave my tooth alone.'

"Briar was inside the snake's mouth with his staff knocking her teeth out, one by one. Then when he was finished, he simply pried her jaws open, using his staff on her gums, and hopped out.

"'You beastly little creature. Now what am I ssupposed to do for ssustenance?' she asked with a very pronounced lisp.

"'Why return to the ancient ways, Python, then you can find sustenance at the appropriate time,' Briar boldly said, placing a front paw on each hip.

"'Never, never, never,' Pyra screamed, her forked tongue flicking in and out.

"'Then you leave me little choice,' Briar announced, bashing the stones above his head. 'Farewell'. With that Briar, the Elder, jumped across the hollow and was soon by my side. We climbed, for all we were worth to escape, just as a cloud of dust bellowed from the hole below.

"Well after that Dena awarded Briar with the ancient sword, but even she was not sure of its origin. She mentioned it once belonged to a noble race of animals which lived deep in the tunnels, who were neither creature nor large one.

"Upon receiving it Briar, to the commune's amazement, unsheathed the sword. Amazement, because no one in their remembering had ever been able to. It was then one of their elders told us what they thought the inscription read.

"How did that go?" Bega said, leaning back. "'Only one pure at heart and with the best of intentions may draw the sword when it is needed most'. Nobody really knew what it meant until out of the darkness Pyra sprung at Briar. In one swift blow Briar drove the sword into the evil python's underbelly before she landed upon him. The sword found its mark piecing her heart and killing her instantly. Tongue the Bringer of Truth had slain one of the most evil creatures we had ever encountered. The gathering of the Elders was shocked and dismayed.

"The Elder explained further that if Briar was to sheath

the sword now, after taking blood, he would never again be able to draw it forth. That is why Briar kept them separate for all these lightenings."

Mar's face grew grim with the realisation that after all his adventures, he would never be able to draw the sword again either. It was then he vowed to lay the sword in the Great Eating Hollow, in remembrance of Briar the Elder, a true hero.

"Thank you, Elder Bega, for a fine story," Trix said, rubbing her nose against her old friend's. "Come now children we must get on with our chores."

As the crowd broke up Mar walked up to Bega. "I seek your advice, Elder, as to the appropriate consultant to replace Elder Briar on the committee."

Bega held a paw to the whiskers on his chin, tugged at them and answered, "Well, to tell you the truth, after such a long peaceful existence, I am not sure if any such native exists. You know Briar was well balanced between understanding and force. But may I sleep on it this darkening, Chieftain Mar. For now, I suggest we convene the War Council. Hum, hum, I mean committee before darkening. If you like I shall pass the word as I return to my humble dwelling."

The Chieftain of the Oak reached up to touch Bega's paw. "Thank you, Bega, that would be much appreciated. Also please join us for sustenance this darkening."

"Indeed, it would be my pleasure," Bega said, walking off. "Until then, may Father Sky smile on you and yours."

"The same to you, Brother Bega," Mar replied, waving a salute to a wise old creature.

Dodd hopped out of the shadows and up to Mar. "Father, when will I be able to venture out past the commune's outposts, in search of adventure?"

"Soon enough, Dodd. Firstly, I feel it is time you entered the Learning Circle. This darkening I shall ask Elder Bandicoot to take you on as his student, if you wish?"

"Really, Father. Oh yes," Dodd screamed, running off to tell his friends. "I shall see you then."

"Dodd, what about your chores? Dodd," Mar yelled.

"Let him go," Trix said, walked up and leant against her mate. "It is time, Mar, he is of age. I can no longer expect the same of him anymore,"

"Where have the leaf falls gone?" Mar sighed, tilted his head and lay it against hers. "He has grown so fast and soon will seek a mate. I only ask Mother Earth and Father Sky it is in peaceful times our offspring and their young live."

Pulling her life mate closer, Trix rubbed his back. "Come in now, Rina the Loyal and Binja the Proud wait for you in the meeting hollow."

"Thank you, I shall gather the leaf etchings and go to them. Trix, could you place the sword and sheath in our chamber. In tribute to Elder Briar, I intend to lay it out in the Great Eating Hollow; for all to see."

"Proudly, my mate, proudly." Trix graciously accepted the sword and sheath and walked into the oak.

"A grand yarn Elder Bandicoot," a voice called from above Bega as he walked down a narrow well worn path.

"Who is it, who compliments me without showing their face?" Bega asked, looking around the dense foliage where he chose to make his home.

"I am above you on the large leaf. It is I, Antoni Chief Warrior Bull-ant of Queen Zana."

Focusing his eyes, as best he could, the bandicoot could make out Antoni's outline. "Ah, I wondered where you got to, Great Chief."

"Believe me, Bega, when there is a large gathering you will always find us ants up high or under something."

"I see," Bega replied. "So, to what do I owe the pleasure of your company?"

"I have a few questions, I would like to find answers for, and I was hoping you would be able to assist me, wise one?" Antoni said, leapt down and landed in front of Bega.

"Please continue, I beg you."

The bull-ant grabbed some sap off a low branch and began to nibble at it. "Briar the Elder, would you not say he was an exceptionally fit mouse, for his advanced age?"

"Yes, Briar was." The bandicoot let out a loud sigh, flicked his long tail into the air and lowered his posterior onto a rock.

"And would you not say, he appeared the picture of health last darkening?" Antoni added, pacing back and forth.

"Why, yes I would," Bega answered, beginning to grasp what the ant was leading up to.

"Did, at any time, Briar mention to you feelings of tiredness or pain, perhaps? Do not such conditions give one warning of something being wrong and the possible loss of spirit? "

"No, not a word had he mentioned to me. Am I to understand, you suspect a fellow creature removed his spirit from his body; in an act of evil?" Unnerved by the revelation, Bega reached up and scratched his ear. "Why, who would think of such a thing in our commune?"

"That, I can not be sure of, but I would lay my life on it being linked to the invading cockroaches and rats. All I need is proof, then there will be no suggestion of a peaceful resolution with such deceitful invaders. You see, I fear for Rina and Binja's lives; for once sent upon their mission, I have a feeling they shall never grace us with their company again."

"How can we prove such a claim? In doing so, we must act quickly because the two unfortunate creatures are destined to leave this darkening. So whatever we do, is in all urgency." The large bandicoot pushed himself onto his hind legs and began a trek back to the oak.

DARKENING THREE

Not far from the clearing, where Mar had met Brother Wombat, two mice were working hard in the early darkening. The two brothers were gathering edible roots and bulbs for their communal store.

"Pon, most of the other creatures from the commune have fled. Should we not follow the same course of action?" Fila asked, filling the large leaf pallet next to him.

"Yes, yes, Fila we shall soon follow. I only wait to hear Jun's report." Pon scrapped up another bulb with his paws. "Here, Fila, help me with this one. If we can return it to our under-dwelling it should last us many lightenings to come."

Fila hopped to Pon's side and leant down to help. "Jun has been away for so many lightenings of the woods. I am fearful he may well have met with trouble."

"Ha. You mean any creature who has crossed Jun's path, in anger, has met with trouble," Pon laughed. "Now come help me, we shall return to our under-dwelling. The full darkening will soon be upon us."

"You know, Pon, I had the strangest dream state last slumber," Fila declared, returning to his leaf pallet.

"Really," Pon said, standing next to his younger

brother.

"Father came to me and asked that we return to our commune of origin with our families," he confided, in a distant tone.

Pon was amazed as his brother described his dreaming. It is nearly the same dream, he thought, I had during the darkening. So real I could have sworn, on the River Stones, father's paw touched my shoulder. I will not mention my dream yet.

"He warned me of a great darkness sweeping our land. Of something the rats, we have heard tell of, carry with them. Apparently, without warning and unseen, it may kill many of our fellow creatures. I admit the reality of it all chilled me to the very core," Fila said, with a worried look on his face.

"Unseen, what could it mean?" Pon asked, puzzled, thinking out loud.

"So you believe it is a foretelling of lightenings to come?"

"Fila, you know I do not believe in such things." Pon replied, attempting to remain confident and in control. "Now, we must definitely leave this place as your talking has taken up precious leaf falls."

"I miss Mother and Father," Fila announced, as they both dragged the laden leaves along the bush floor. "How we all used to laugh when you and Father tail wrestled. Do you remember, Pon?"

"Yes, Fila, I remember. I never did manage to beat him, did I?"

"No but, by the River Stones, you came close. Tell me, did it bother thee Mar was the only one who could better father?"

Pon was about to answer when they both felt the ground shake.

"By Mother Earth, what could be making her grumble

so?" Pon exclaimed, watching their supplies rolled off the leaves.

It did not take many leaf falls before they had their answer.

"Pon, look out, our fellow creatures are on the move and headed straight toward us."

Jumping in front of Willa the Wallaby, Pon screamed, "Stop! Please tell us what has you all so scared?"

Without even stopping, she yelled, "The redness has come with the heat of Brother Sun. It comes up the hill over there. Hop for your spirits, hop."

"The redness? It is not yet the season for the redness! Why Mother Earth and Father Sky always send us warning of such a happening. By my calculations it should not be due for a least another two hundred lightenings of the woods," Fila declared, standing near an old gum tree.

"For the sake of our families stop thinking, Fila, and move. Leave the food. We must hurry to our commune and lead our families to the safety of the dampness, in our under-dwelling." Pon sighed and quickly, hopped away.

By the leaf fall the mice reached their commune the fire was hitting the outer area of their gathering place. Dashing inside their hollow Fila found none of their families inside.

"No!" he screamed, as he dashed outside toward the fire, only to be tackled by Pon. "Pon, no, I must find Ji, Nell, Nila and Fena. I beg thee let me go."

LIGHTENING OF THE WOODS FOUR

High in Sister Trees, native bees' wings could be heard buzzing as they busied themselves collecting pollen from the eucalyptus flowers. Brother Sun's rays had barely started to penetrate the early lightening's mist when natives began to gather at the foot of the Great Oak. A sombre mood hung over the commune, with no joyful chorus of birds or cicadas to greet the coming leaf falls.

Not far from the Great Oaks' main root Mar sat, on a rock, reflecting upon recent events. *Elder Briar's passing of spirit,* he thought, *has affected me far more than I expected. My mind appears to be shrouded in a fog of uncertainty and self doubt. In these dark times, am I truly fit to lead my commune?* He lowered his head into both his front paws and rubbed his tired eyes.

Trix walked up to her mate and placed a paw between his ears. Her eyes widened when she felt the dampness of Mar's fur. "You are soaked to your skin. I came to you to ask why your straw had not been slept in, but I believe I have my answer."

Crouching down in front of him, Trix gently lifted his face to look at hers. "You have been out here sitting like this all darkening, have you not?" Tears welled in her eyes at the sight of her love's darkened and worried face. "I beg you, come in and take sustenance with us. The children are worried about you, as am I."

Reaching out, the Chieftain of the Oak brushed a tear from her deep brown eyes. "I shall be along in a few leaf falls. It is my duty to be here for those who are leaving this very lightening." Mar's voice was distant and pained. "You go along and I will follow soon."

Placing an up turned paw under her mate's chin, Trix read his thoughts. "It is not your fault; Binja and Rina are being sent on such a perilous journey. Remember, my dear mouse, it was the Council's edict not yours." Standing she moved to walk away. "If you have not come to Celebrate Sustenance in a few leaf falls, I shall send the children to fetch you. Your mind and body will not function without being fed."

Nodding a reply, Mar watched on as many brave creatures, of the commune, said farewell to their families. *Why could I not make the Council understand*, he thought, *that these invaders could well be dangerous? It is not right; they believe new creatures to our lands will have our same philosophies. Binja and Rina are two of my most faithful friends; I have no wish to see them harmed.* Tired beyond his lightenings, Mar forced himself to stand and began to walk toward his friends.

Watching, those assigned to the outposts disappear into the undergrowth; Mar felt so many misgivings in his heart. His shoulders heavy with responsibility, he hopped up to where Binja and Rina stood. Raising his head to look up at Rina the Rat's noble face, Mar's stomach churned; so confident and so trusting was his friend's expression, he found himself at a loss for words.

Breaking the tension, Rina stood on his hind legs, moved forward and embraced Mar. Picking the much smaller mouse up off the ground, he hugged him and said, "We will have many a warm sap upon my return, dear friend." Lowering him again, Rina ruffled the Chieftain of the Oak's fur on his head, smiled and walked off into the bush.

Moved by the occasion Binja the Bush Cockroach, scurried to Mar's side, leapt to his hind legs and hugged him also. Before Mar could reciprocate the cockroach released him and ran into the undergrowth after Rina.

"How I wish I was going and not you, my dear comrades," Mar mumbled out loud without realising.

"You males are so stupid," Damp, Binja's mate, snapped. Crawling up to Mar she spoke with venom in her voice. "They are the most loyal of your followers and both idolised you, how can you send them to their deaths?"

Caught unawares by Damp's comments, the Chieftain of the Oak looked down at her with a blank expression on his face.

"You, Mouse, are more trained in war and battle than any other. Why could you not make the Council listen to you?" Tears streaming from her eyes, Damp ran away to the side. Picking up a ball of mud she hurled it at Mar's face, screaming, "Coward."

Upon the impact of the missile, Mar's head twisted to the side. As if in a dream, he reached up and tried to wipe the mud away. Other than Bega and Antoni, not another native in the commune knew how he had approached the Council in protest after the meeting. *I had no choice,* he thought, *after Petra the possum and Betra the bat joined, with others, in opposition to any change in the plans. Should I have pushed harder, even if it meant the Alternative Action Committee would be disbanded?*

As the lightening progressed the Grey Rain Bringers grew dense, in Father Sky, high above the canopy of the forest. Lost in himself, Mar moved amongst the group of creatures chosen to seek another site for their commune. He could hear a voice talking to him, but it seemed mouse lengths away.

"Chieftain Mar, I beseech thee to squash the Council's edict and allow Stump and I to stay by your side?" Aldo asked, quite openly, as Mar walked past.

Brought back to the current leaf fall, Mar turned to him. "Aldo, you two are amongst the best defenders in the commune. Within these ranks are surveyors and gatherers who need your strength and wisdom. Please take your position with honour and lead them back to us safely," Mar asked, patting his commander on the back.

"Yes, Chieftain, I understand," he replied, lowering his head.

"Now remember, you have the echidnas from our Defence Force with you, so ensure the others stay within the designated areas when they are resting. The echidnas will protect them through the darkening."

"That I will, Chieftain," Aldo replied as the expedition commenced to shuffle to order. Raising his right paw in salute, he said nothing more.

His mind a whirl, with possible outcomes of the current actions, Mar called, "May Mother Earth and Father Sky protect you all." Holding his paw to his chest, he followed them with his eyes for a few mouse lengths, sighed and sat on a root.

Bravely, the expedition marched on into the deep leaf cover, toward the place where Brother Sun sleeps.

DARKENING FOUR

A slight shimmer of Sister Moon's light slid through a split, in the Oak's trunk, illuminating the meeting area. There, in a secluded hollow of the cavern, Mar sat in deep discussion with Antoni, Bega and Damon, King of the Black Ants.

"Forgive my intrusion, Chieftain Mar, but Slur the Queen of Snake seeks council with you immediately." Ro, the Bilby, informed them.

"Thank you, Ro. Please ask Queen Slur to meet me in the gathering area in five leaf falls," Mar said standing, "We will postpone our discussions, fellow creatures, and meet with Queen Slur."

Ro turned back as he was leaving. "Sorry, Chieftain, Queen Slur was very specific that she meets with you alone. Forgive me, I should have thought to mention it," Ro said, lowering his head in salute before scurrying away again.

Swinging around to face his friends, Mar raised his front paw. "All the better then, Bega, please continue in my absence, I am sure anything decided will be well justified."

Hopping across the damp floor, Mar made his way to

the outside gathering area at the base of the oak. "Hale, Queen Slur," he called in salute. "Whose kind services the Stone Circle."

"Ah, Chieftain Mar, I am afraid I have come on a matter of grave importance."

Mar could tell by the tone of Slur's hiss, she was disturbed and restless. "Then tell me, oh wise one, what is it my kind can do for yours?"

"Nothing I fear," Slur said, moving her head as she drew closer to Mar, "You ssee, three of my kinds' young lie without sspirit this darkening. Yet another two are in a way I have never sseen before. I fear they too will join the others. Chieftain Mar, I accept that is the way of our lives but ssomething is different this time." Drawing even closer to Mar, the Queen's forked tongue flicked in and out.

Pushing himself onto his hind legs, Mar pivoted on his strong tail. "I am deeply sorry, Slur, but we all accept that the passing of spirit can occur at any leaf fall. It is the way it must be so others may celebrate sustenance."

"Yes, as I ssaid, I accept the ways of Mother Earth and Father Ssky. This time I fear my kind's young sspirits did not leave their bodies, but were forced out by treachery," Slur hissed, agitation clearly evident.

"Treachery," Mar declared, hopping a few paces forward.

"Yes each ssnake, who lies without spirit or is ssick, partook in the Celebration of Ssustenance the lightening of the woods before last. And each I tell you, ssustained themselves on the body of Briar the Elder."

"What can this mean?" Mar asked, more than disturbed, "How can such a thing happen?"

"Know not I, Chieftain. It is obviously treachery on your kinds' part. To make matters worse one of my elders, just outside the gathering area, not long after the Celebration of Ssustenance; overheard that old fool Bega, bragging about the sslaying of Mother Pyra. We had heard tell of a great ssnake who was viciously murdered by a ssmall creature and now we know who. Sso your kind also keeps ssecrets too now, Chieftain Mar." Slur hissed even louder.

Reacting to the accusations, the Chieftain of the Oak's expression darkened. "I do not know what your Elder told you. Did they mention that Pyra had broken the treaties and returned to ways long since past? Nobody would allow her to unjustly devour other natives. Ask your Elder to tell you again. I will even come with you and look in his eyes as he speaks."

"Ssorry, that is not possible, oh Noble One. He, at this leaf fall, lies with his family around him while the sspirit leaves his body. I must warn you, Chieftain, my council are on the verge of removing our kind from any treaties and returning to the ancient ways. Now I must go and help prepare the bodies for the Celebration of Ssustenance in the coming lightening." Turning, Slur began to slither away.

"Slur, stop!" Mar leapt forward and in one bound blocked her way. "I beg thee do not commit the bodies, of those you have lost, for Celebration of Sustenance. Something is amiss, something I say none of our commune have ever experienced."

"Chieftain Mar, you know that we must follow the rituals of ssustenance. That is the way it must be," Slur said, finally slithering away into the shadows.

Standing, there in the darkness, the words of the strange wombat came back to Mar, 'Always in the shadows lurking and waiting, they are.' "The Treaty Breakers are here," he yelled, racing back to the Alternative Action Committee.

Bursting in through the archway, Mar announced, "They are here, the Treaty Breakers are amongst us. Antoni and Bega, I want every new arrival in the last five lightenings checked out. They have come to destroy our commune's trust and thereby weaken our defences. Go now, please, to every dwelling, find this remover of the spirit."

"Mar, what has happened?" Bega asked with urgency.

"Briar and three young snakes have passed before their given time and the snakes are accusing us of treachery."

"Snakes accusing us!" Bega lifted a paw and shook his head, dumbfounded.

"Their council, at this very leaf fall, is considering returning to the ancient ways. You see they too knew of the Pyra story, Bega, only differently."

"How so?" Bega asked, placing his gumnut of warm sap on the bark table in front of him.

"An Elder, whose spirit may leave him, heard your tale. Only in their version, a small evil creature slew Pyra. Thanks to your story they know it was Briar the Elder. Now in passing, his body appears to have slain at least three young snakes. So do you see?" Mar asked with both paws, on Bega's shoulders, looking him in the eyes.

"May Mother Earth protect us. I am nothing but an old fool. May the commune forgive me." Bega slumped back onto the rock.

"Antoni and Damon go and find this treacherous creature. Then it may be brought before a combined council of the commune and Servicers' of the Stone Circle. It is our only hope. Please make haste," Mar pleaded.

With a quick salute, both ants took off into the long hollow outside the arch.

Bega sat with his head in his paws moaning, "What have I done? Such a fool am I; such an old fool."

#   #   #

"There you are, Toe, come inside immediately! Mother has been looking for you all over the Oak. Where have you been?" Hatty chastised.

"Nowhere," Toe answered. His head held high, he walked passed her into the small opening at the back of the Oak.

Hatty looked into the darkness and shook her head. "What were you talking to out there in the dark, Toe?"

"I was not talking to anything," Toe replied, with a strange pitch in his voice.

Toe's sister hopped up, laid her paws on his shoulders and twisted him around to face her. "Now now, my dear young brother, you should know better than trying to tell me untruths. I distinctly heard you talking to somebody over near the dark valley. You know we are not supposed to talk to strangers, especially near that scary place."

"Alright, I was talking to my friend. Well actually, he does not really say much, so you could say I was just talking," he said, pushing her away and scurrying up the hollow toward their chambers.

"Oh," Hatty said, pursuing him. "You mean you were talking to your imaginary friend again."

"He is not imaginary! How many times do I have to tell you that!" he called back, quite annoyed.

"Really. If he is not imaginary then describe him to me, this instant."

"I can not."

"And why not?"

"Well you see, I have never actually seen him. He always hangs around in the shadows. When he wants me, he throws a pebble at me, you see."

"What an imagination you have, dear brother. Tell me then what tongue does your shadow creature speak?"

"He only speaks a few words of mouse and about the same amount of the common tongue. I taught him you see." Toe stopped outside their sleeping alcove, placed both paws on his hips and faced Hatty.

"Well good for you, little one. Now you better get ready, for the long rest, before Mother and Father find out. You know you are forbidden to be outside at such a dangerous leaf fall, let alone talking to a shadow," she said, ruffling his fur and tapping him on the tail.

"Good Darkening, Hatty," Toemouse said, climbing into his notch and pulling a fresh soft green leaf over himself.

"Good slumber," Hatty smiled and rubbed noses with him. "And Toe, I think it is time you invited your friend in. I would like to meet him."

"He will not come, Hatty. Though perhaps he will and then you can see he is not imaginary," he said, with a large yawn.

Hatty wandered down the long hollow toward the gathering, warmed by the love she felt for her family. When she entered the gathering area it was all a buzz with an unofficial meeting of the council.

Walking over to her daughter, Trix asked, "Hatty, did you find Toe?"

"Yes, Mother. What is wrong, you look terrible?"

Nervously, Trix looked around at all her friends' faces. "Three of the snakes' kind have lost their spirits. Oh it is so terrible, they were only babies."

"Yes but, Mother, that is the way things must be. It is the way it has been since the beginning of time, is it not?"

"Dear Hatty, it appears, it was not of the natural way of things. Some creature has come amongst us with treachery in its heart; a stealer of spirits!"

The young mouse's eyes widened and her fur stood on end. "How is it so?"

"Elder Briar, may his spirit soar with the eagles, was murdered by ways not of our understanding. Bega believes it may well have been a concoction of plants, we all know not to eat, which stole Briar's spirit. Then in turn, through the Celebration of Sustenance, the young snakes have had their spirits taken."

Even Hatty could sense the tension in the air. "Oh! I think I understand," she said, watching the area fill with even more natives.

Grabbing Hatty's paw, Trix took her to a small doorway. "My child, it is worse still. One of the Elder snakes overheard Bega's story and now he too waits for his spirit to leave him. So you see the snakes are pushing Queen Slur to end all treaties with the whole commune."

Hatty went quite pale and sat on a small piece of wood. She had always lived in peace, yet had heard tell of the ancient times where creature ate creature. Noticing Dodd, standing by Mar and Bega, she commented, "Why does Dodd not help us prepare for our guests, Mother?"

"That is his place now, Hatty. As of this darkening he has entered the Circle of Learning and Bega is now his teacher. Sadly, it is the way it must be," Trix said, with a wistful tone in her voice.

"Fine. Why, that means that in a few lightenings of the woods, I too shall enter the Learning Circle. Who do you think will be my mentor?" Hatty asked, standing beside her mother, both paws on her hips.

"Female mice do not enter the learning circle of the males. We have our own, you know that mouse."

"No! I shall enter the Circle of Knowledge and Defence. I have no wish to enter the Circle of Management and Negotiation, until such time as I have completed training with Father or Bega."

"Sorry, child, it is not to be," Trix said, rubbing noses, she walked away to the meeting to find Mar.

"We shall see about that," Hatty muttered, threw her nose in the air, huffed and went to help prepare food for their guests.

Trix's eyes sparkled when she caught sight of Mar in a glimmer of light. She nodded politely as she weaved in and out of other natives, walked over to his side, bent down, hugged him and sat. "How goes it, life mate?"

"We wait only for Slur and her elders. I fear we should have held more of such meetings, lightenings ago."

"You know that, since memory, such meetings have only come when Sister Moon shines fully upon us. Mar, many of the creatures in the commune still fear the snakes' kind and the other creatures who feast on bodies. Simply because it is the way it was meant to be does not mean it is right. When Mother Earth, Father Sky and Sister Trees provide us with such an abundance they do not understand the need to eat a fellow native's body. To those that eat grasses, one creature sustaining another through sacrifice is creepy."

Ro the Bilby dashed up to Mar and bowed. "Queen Slur is here, Chieftain Mar, she, at this leaf fall, is talking to Elder Bega through the large opening behind you."

Standing, Mar smiled at Trix and bowed his head. "Thank you kind, Ro," he said softly as he walked over to where Bega and Slur were in heated debate.

"Why tell ssuch stories, old one? Our kind and yours have lived in peace for many lightenings of the wood. Ssurely, Bega, you could have told one of your other tales. If I am to understand correctly, you and Elder Briar had many ssuch adventures," Slur stated while moving around attempting to get comfortable.

The large, greying, bandicoot knelt before her, placing a paw to his chest. "Please, Queen Slur, forgive an old fool. The story I told was the truth, I swear by the Great River Stones it was so. Indeed, I only told the story so that those of the commune could understand about Tongue the Bringer of Truth and its sheath called Mouth. Truly, I meant no disrespect to your kind."

Slur's old eyes gazed past Bega, for a leaf fall, to the legendary sword. "Sseeing it glow, in Ssister Moon's beam of light, I have no doubt you told the truth from your perspective. However, I understand you failed to mention Pyra's children, who were left behind motherless. Indeed it is ssaid, amongst our kind, upon that lightening the babies watched on as their mother was sslain. Sso sshocked were they, many of their descendants refuse to learn the common tongue and only sspeak in a sstuttered native hiss in protest."

Turning to follow the queen snake's line of sight, Bega noticed Mar standing behind him. "Forgive me, Slur, I had no idea. I am nothing more than an old stupid bandicoot." He lowered his head in respect.

Stepping forward, Mar placed his paw on Bega's

shoulder in passing. "Surra and good darkening again, Queen Slur, I thank thee for gracing us with your presence," he said, looking around behind her and continuing, "Will your elders be along or are they elsewhere around the Oak?"

"Ssorry, Chieftain Mar, my elders refuse to leave Elder Ssimon's nest. Ssadly, they are not only on the verge of breaking the treaty, there is ssome talk of war against your kind for ssuch deceit. It is against their wishes I am here conversing with you now."

"I am deeply sorry to hear such news, oh Noble One," Mar said solemnly. "I should have told you, about the evil that threatens to destroy our peace, straight away. We, at this very leaf fall, are faced by an invasion of foreign rats and cockroaches. They travel before the giant pale ones who devour our lands and destroy our homes. Thousands of fellow creatures are headed toward the setting of Brother Sun. I have no doubt they will reach us with anger in their hearts."

Slur could sense the truth in his words. "Please continue, Chieftain Mar. I have heard rumours of ssuch happenings."

"These rats, I was told by a brother wombat, break treaties between creatures through deceit and treachery. Then their kind move in, after the others have returned to the ancient ways, and feast on the remains."

"Very interesting, Chieftain Mar. Indeed, I understand why you tell me this now. I think in future perhaps our kinds sshould meet more often. Perhaps ambassadors of each kind could relay messages to the others' councils. Tell me and what was your councils' edict on ssuch a threat?"

"We have sent Rina the rat and Binja the cockroach ahead, to try and contact the newcomers, in hope of peace. We have also placed creatures in outposts with runners to tell us of impending attacks. Furthermore, we have sent many of the surveyors and gatherers to try and find a new site for the commune, deep in the forest?"

"And were my kind to be included in ssuch a move?" Slur asked intrigued.

"Of course, how could the Celebration of Sustenance continue otherwise?" Mar answered, confidence and truth clearly evident in his voice.

"Ah, the Celebration of Ssustenance; while I remember, I did manage to convince my kind that if we were to offer the bodies of the sstricken ones, we may well bring the wrath of the winged ones upon us. Ssomething our kind can ill afford. Sso this lightening we will remove them to an abandoned old hole."

"Thank the River Stones for that," Bega blurted out.

"I am very pleased that your wisdom prevailed on such a matter," Mar said bowing. "We have also formed an Alternative Action Committee consisting of Elder Bega, Antoni Ant, King Damon and myself."

"Hm, with ssuch creatures, sso well trained in the Circle of Knowledge and Defence, I would have thought a War Council would be more fitting a title. Tell me, Chieftain Mar, if these creatures do attack, would your councils allow us to assist by devouring and crushing a few."

For the first time that darkening, Mar felt a glimmer of hope for a peaceful resolution. "This I can give my word on, Queen Slur."

"Very well. With ssuch news I am ssure that my kind will reconsider their current course. Once I inform them, of the threat and the tactics the evil ones partake of, I am ssure much of the tension will ease. Chieftain Mar, I ask I too be allowed to join your committee, though I do prefer the title of 'War Council'."

Mar, more than pleased smiled with relief. "I could not think of any creature more suitable, oh Great One. I shall look forward to our next council." Moving closer he whispered, "I too prefer the title of 'War Council'; indeed it was Betra the Bat who put forward the other name."

"May the River Sstones ssave us from politicians," Slur said, smiling for the first time.

"Now, I must commence the meeting. If you will excuse me, Queen," Mar said, sweeping a front paw across his chest in tribute.

"Before you do, Chieftain Mar, I will return to my elders and pass on the news. I feel urgency may well be our best tool this darkening," she said, starting to uncoil herself.

"Chieftain Mar," Antoni announced with a swift bow as Slur turned to leave. "I have found the scent of something strange in Elder Briar's supply of sap. Outside his dwelling I found the scent of a creature, I can not identify, leading away into the bush. Tell me, Chieftain, do you wish me to pursue it?"

"I sshall leave now, Chieftain Mar, and convey the news to my kind." Slur turned and slid off without saying another word.

"Antoni, return and take Ro with you. Do not allow any other creatures near the area, I shall be with you in but a few leaf falls." Mar knelt down and looked into Antoni's eyes. "By the way, old friend, your timing to convey such news could not have been better."

"I merely do what is asked of me. It would be best, Mar, if I return before the scent becomes too weak. I dare say it will disappear if the Grey Rain-Bringers bless us this darkening." With that Antoni spun around and was gone.

Weaving through the gathering of natives Mar made his way to the centre of the hollow. Standing on a root, he held up his paws signalling for silence. Within leaf falls the crowd hushed.

"I hope you will forgive me if I dispense with the opening prayer. My friends, this darkening, I have urgent news to convey. At this very leaf fall, Noble Slur returns to her kind to relay the information we have received. Antoni Ant, Chief warrior Ant of Queen Zana, has found a scent of an unknown kind in Elder Briar's sap supply. Also, there is another scent of a creature, moving away from his dwelling.

"It is with the utmost urgency we must immediately pursue such a discovery. I, Bega, Antoni and Dodd, my son, shall follow this new scent this very darkening. Fellow creatures I feel that it is as we feared, the foreign rats and cockroaches are attempting to destroy our peaceful existence. They use deceit and treachery, so be ever aware." Hopping down off the root, Mar left in search of Trix.

Dodd was beside himself with excitement when his father walked over and laid his paw on his shoulder. "It is time, my son, for your learning to begin in the ways of tracking. I can not think of a better teacher than Antoni. Is that right, Elder Bega?"

Bega hobbled up to Dodd's side and ruffled his hair. "I could not agree more strongly. Now, my student, leave us and gather your things for perhaps a three lightening journey."

"Yes, teacher," Dodd said, bowing his head before running off. In the thrill of the moment he nearly knocked Hatty over in passing. Hatty did not respond, instead she sighed with envy.

Noticing Trix serving some of the commune's Elders, Mar excused himself and made his way to her. "We leave without delay, Trix, my moonbeam. I shall have King Damon get his kind to increase their patrols around the commune. Those guards who are left behind will be ordered to double their effort. Trix, if we can capture this Spirit Stealer and somehow gain knowledge, of these creatures, then our task will be all the easier. For how can you plan, strategies of war, if you do not know the enemy," he said, drawing his mate close to him. "If there is any sign of trouble send a messenger to Lady Sqweara. Her council has agreed to protect the commune against any invaders. Oh yes and Queen Slur."

"Yes, Chieftain," Trix said, gracefully lowering her head. "Mar, vow to me, on your father's spirit, that you shall return." And with that she knelt before her mate and let her feelings flow in a soft low love song, loud enough for only Mar to hear...

When she had finished, Trix looked up into her mate's eyes and whispered, "Please come home to me once more."

Gently, Mar reached down, deeply moved and lifted her from her knees. "That I vow. Fear not, my love, for I feel the main forces of these creatures are far to the rising of Brother Sun. The current evil in our midst is only to cause trouble amongst the communes." Rubbing noses, Mar embraced his mate and held her for a leaf fall.

Trix's heart sank as she released him and watched on helplessly as he rushed out of the meeting.

Mar was soon standing, with his staff in paw, watching Antoni hunt around Elder Briar's living area and out into the forest beyond.

Zigzagging across the debris on the forest floor, Antoni called, "The scent is strongest in Briar's storage area. The strange thing is though, when it enters that deep valley over there, it crosses another scent."

"Another?" Mar asked intrigued, "Could it be a foreign rat?"

Antoni stood erect, his antennas' flicking around in the air. "I think not, Mar. It seems familiar, like that of a mouse but yet it is not. For now, however, I suggest we follow the unknown scent. I suspect that with the absence of tracks it may well be a foreign cockroach we find."

#   #   #

The bush came alive with the rattle of the smaller winged ones returning to their nests as Bega strode ahead of his young companions. Not far from Elder Briar's dwelling Bega stopped and waited for Dodd and Rit to catch up.

"Come over here you two and stand under that tree, near those pebbles."

Wishing only to please his new mentor, Dodd complied.

"Good, now listen," Bega said, in an authoritative tone. "To be my student you must promise to concentrate and soak up everything I teach you like a sponge. Rit, it will soon be your turn to join the Circle of Knowledge and Defence too; so heed my words.

"One mistake in a dangerous situation can see the loss of either your spirit or a comrade's. I know some say I am overweight and my best lightenings are past but the mere fact I am standing here, after so many battles, is testament to my abilities. So I promise if you give me your all, no matter how many battles you face, you will live many lightenings."

Bega went to a clump of bushes and cut a staff for Dodd. "Now, come young mouse, the others are waiting." After throwing it to him, he walked off without another word.

Dodd held out the staff with one paw, reached out, hugged Rit farewell and followed.

Mar and Antoni turned to a loud rustling, emanating from the bushes, back in the direction of the Great Oak.

Within a water drip, Dodd and Bega joined them. Dodd, with a smile on his face nearly as big as the green staff he now possessed.

"A fine staff, son," Mar commented, looking him up and down.

"Yes, Father, Elder Bega cut it for me with his sharpened stone axe," he announced, throwing the rather large staff to his father.

"So I heard, Dodd," Mar replied, giving Bega a strange look.

"Oh the noise; I am sorry Chieftain, I thought no harm in it so close to the Oak. Besides, I gained the staff from the very same plant that yielded yours and Elder Briar's all those lightenings ago."

"Really," Dodd said, sticking out his chest so far it appeared close to bursting. Watching on, his mind raced with excitement. "Fancy that, the same plant as Father's."

"A fine weapon, Son." Mar walked over, returned the staff to him, placed a paw on his shoulder and turned to address the others. "We must be aware that at this very leaf fall, a Spirit Stealer may be observing us." The Chieftain felt uncomfortable as he stood looking into the dense undergrowth ahead. "Please do not take me for a fool, but I most definitely sense eyes upon us."

"I too," Antoni added.

"So let us be gone with all urgency and quietly," Mar said, looking directly at the bandicoot and hopped away.

Unfazed, Bega simply shrugged his shoulders and followed.

LIGHTENING OF THE WOODS FIVE

A slight mist hung low over the woods, caressing the green grasses and flowers, promising a beautiful lightening would follow. Above Father Sky smiled in all his brilliance upon Mother Earth, who in reply appeared to be blooming in all her beauty. The birds of the forest called their early lightening greetings to each other and sang their songs of praise in thanks.

Yet, intent on following the faint trail, Antoni was oblivious to it all. Many mouse lengths into their journey, he was having ever increasing trouble tracking the scent. *No other creature could have followed the smell into such small confines and so far, he thought. I am afraid it only confirms my suspicions that it may well be a foreign cockroach.*

Creature after creature they crossed paths with, in the outskirts of the commune, had not seen nor heard anything. Indeed, two of their outposts, with well trained creatures in them, had also not detected any movement. As darkening once again came to the woods the searchers decided to rest by a crystal clear stream.

 DARKENING FIVE

Sitting under a large leaf, going over the lightenings' events, Mar heard a splash in the stream. Standing, with his staff in his right paw, he moved stealthily to the edge of the water. The feeling of being observed, for so many mouse lengths, had left him disturbed and nervous.

As he stood there, straining to see out over the stream, a spray of water hit his face, with such force, he fell backward. "Who dares, to do such a thing?" he yelled, leaping onto his hind legs.

Saturated, he stood prepared for another assault. However, even this did not stop him from falling backward, when hit with another powerful blast.

"Coward!" Mar bellowed, pushing himself up. "Show yourself, so that you may feel my staff's sting."

"I be no coward, oh sodden mouse," a young voice replied, from the middle of the stream.

"Then who are you, Sprayer of Water?" Mar questioned, straining to see the unidentified creature.

"I be, Platy, daughter of Pint of the Platypi. Who might thee be, drippy one?" Platy asked, in an impish tone.

"Well, child, some people call me 'Mar', while others choose names I can not repeat."

Moving up onto the bank, she enquired, "Tell me Mar,

of the Mice, where do you hail from this darkening?"

Hopping down the muddy bank, Mar could see Platy's distinctive outline. "We hail from the very centre of the commune. The Great Oak, in fact."

"Hm, I have heard tell of such a place, I believe my father has travelled there on occasion. It is too far away from my beautiful stream for me. To tell the truth, I do not like busy places and could not even be bothered visiting one," Platy announced, now lying on the bank.

"Chieftain Mar, are you there?" Bega enquired, from under their camp's fern canopy.

"Yes, Elder Bega, I am talking to a new, young, friend by the water. Her name is Platy and she is the daughter of our old friend, Pint of the Platypus."

"Well, may the River Stones be praised," Bega replied. "Give me but a leaf fall and I shall bring Dodd and Antoni."

"Did he say 'Chieftain'?" the young platypus asked, quite embarrassed.

"Yes, Platy, I am 'Chieftain Mar of the Great Silky Oak'. But please call me 'Mar', as all my friends do."

"Oh, forgive me, Chieftain. My father has spoken of you at many a sustenance. He will punish me severely for such stupidity."

"What stupidity is that, young one?" he said smiling, holding out his dripping arms in the dim light.

"Why, the stupidity of spraying you, Chieftain. Oh please forgive me."

"Spraying me. Why I am sure I fell in the water and you kindly helped me out," Mar said, gently touching Platy's bill.

Platy's eyes sparkled as she shook her head. "Chieftain, you know that is not what happened. Nevertheless, if that is the way you want to convey it to my father, I shall be grateful."

"There is no need for your father to know at all."

"He will know, once I summon him to speak to you. You see, he would punish me even more if he knew I let a friend pass without informing him. He will wish to offer you the safety of our dwelling," Platy said, sliding back into the water.

"Please do not child, we are in a hurry. I have no wish to offend your kind by not participating in the platypi ritual greeting." Mar's pleading was too late, Platy was gone.

At that very leaf fall Bega came crashing through the bushes. "Where is she?"

Mar looked at Bega, a grim expression on his face. "She is summoning Pint and you know what that means?"

"What, father?" Dodd asked, hopping down to stand by his father's side.

"We will be expected to ride on the platypus' back," Mar's eyes widened as he continued, "underwater, into their den to celebrate the ritual greeting."

"Wow," Dodd replied very excited, until he realised what underwater meant. "You mean we have to hold our breath and go under the great quencher of thirst?"

Antoni moved forward. "Does the child know I am here? For if she does not, I will make camp on the bank and wait for you; I do not want the taste of warm sap to put me off the scent."

"As you wish, Antoni. I shall explain you are out checking for tracks and can not be found. Though, I too hope to avoid the ritual if possible." The Chieftain of the Oak plodded back up the bank.

"I doubt that you will, without offending Pint and his kind. Be it, they are normally solitary creatures, when they do have visitors they are animals of heavy celebration," Bega said, sitting on a rather large river pebble. "As for me, I am too old and fat to be carried into water on a platypi's back. I fear we would both drown!"

"Ah." Bega heard from the moonlit water. "So Brother Bega, you consider I have become weak with my advancing lightenings." Pint, the platypus, slid gracefully onto the bank. "Metcha, Chieftain Mar, Ona Bega," Pint said, quite formally and continued, "and who is this young mouse with you? I do not believe we have met."

"Patti, Noble Pint," Mar replied, "this is my eldest, Dodd of the Great Oak,"

"Metcha, oh large one." Pint opened his bill in a smile. "You certainly must feed your family well, Chieftain Mar, why the young mouse has easily outstripped you in height."

Dodd bowed. "Patti, oh Noble Pint of the Clear Running Waters, I am indeed honoured by this meeting."

Bursting with pride, Mar looked across at his son.

"You have taught him well, Chieftain Mar. Why, Dodd you were smaller than a gum nut the last meeting we had. How, the lightenings of the woods have slipped away. Now onto my den, where we may celebrate your coming." Pint began to dig his webbed feet into the mud, so he could turn.

Hopping forward, Mar held up his paw. "Please, old friend, do not be offended if we decline your gracious offer. We are on the trail of a creature who is suspected of taking Elder Briar's spirit."

Pint's expression changed and his tone darkened. "Elder Briar's spirit has elapsed, this is indeed solemn news. Surely, in the darkening there is little point in pursuing. Can not Antoni find the scent in the morning?"

"How did you know Antoni was here?" Dodd asked amazed.

"Young one, I can smell that rebel many platypus' lengths away. We have been through too much for me to forget. Now where was I? Oh yes, Chieftain Mar, I am afraid your search could well end here. For at this leaf fall there are many creatures, within this province of the commune, who do not belong. What type of creature is it, you seek?"

"We believe it to be, a dark cockroach, one who does not speak the common tongue."

"Hm. I am sorry to give you such news but in amongst the bush on the other bank are many such creatures in camps. They have come but this lightening. I know this, as I have seen them with my own eyes. I have also, on occasion, tasted their flesh. Quite crunchy and tangy it is." Pint turned with a wink and a smile.

Pint sensed Dodd's horror immediately. "Worry not, young one, I attempted to communicate the common tongue greeting, and the native cockroach's, before consuming them. Now, they fly across the water to avoid my kind, we will not stand for their underhanded ways. Why, they are always stealing things from dwellings. I must also mention, in my defence, no treaty exists with such savages."

"We do not judge you, Pint." Mar scratched his left ear, deep in thought. "We must capture this creature and bring it to trial. This Spirit Stealer nearly caused a treaty between Brother Snake's kind to be broken."

"How so, Chieftain?"

"You see the servicers consumed Briar's poisoned body, as a result three young snakes died."

"Yes, I can understand how such an event could destroy trust. I do hope no other creatures have consumed the young ones' bodies. By the River Stones, if they did, the results could well be catastrophic," Pint said, splashing the water with his large flat tail.

Mar moved forward in an attempt to quell Pint's increasing anger.

"Oh, I am sorry, Chieftain Mar, did I wet you with my splash?" Pint asked, noticing Mar's wet fur.

Shaking his head, Mar replied, "No, old friend. I did it

99

not leaf falls ago. I fear, I am getting old and clumsy,"

"Sorry, father, it was I who wet Chieftain Mar," Platy announced, swimming up behind him. "I thought at first he may have been one of those strange mice, who do not hop nor speak the common tongue. That was of course, until I heard him speak."

Pint swung his head around to look his daughter in the eyes. "Why, child, fancy soaking the Noble Oak Mouse himself. You are certainly foolish! Besides I have told you to stay away from those creatures. Platy, listen, if you annoy them, they could well jump on you. Now, if that happened while you laid on the bank you could be overpowered. Only Father Sky knows what they would do with their great numbers."

"Other mice?" Mar interjected.

"Sadly, yes. Toward the rising of Brother Sun, on the bend of the river, there are hundreds of the creatures. So now, rats, cockroaches and mice, are invading us. Also, I have heard tell of a sickness which spreads with their coming," Pint sighed, returning to the water. "Why, if I get my spurs into any of them, they soon will be without spirit. I have seen them; they respect nothing of our ways and take everything."

"You have seen them?" Bega asked. "What do the rats look like, Pint?"

"They are darker than our brothers and somehow their ears are different. Their leaders wear the skulls of native creatures between their ears. Evil they are, pure evil. Now please, at least, join my kind for a sap. I promise we have a brew that will suit you, free of any traces of water creatures remains."

Mar slid down to the water's edge. "Please do not think me rude, my friend, if I still decline. You see, I am now even more fearful for the commune. When we soared on eagle's back, not long ago, Antoni and I saw nothing to the scale you have mentioned."

The old platypus lowered his bill into the water and withdrew it. "That does not surprise me, as they all keep to the shadows. Every single one of the invaders' kind does. Oh do come, please, for your safety's sake."

"Antoni is still out searching, we can not go and leave him," Mar said, looking off into the bushes.

"Oh he is, is he? That is interesting." Crawling up the bank, a length, Pint sniffed the damp air and said, "You may come out now, Chief Warrior Ant of Queen Zana, I know you are there. You should be ashamed of yourself, hiding away, listening to others' discussions. I promise I will not eat you again."

"Again!" Dodd gasped, raising his paw to his mouth.

"Yes, Dodd," Pint replied, levity evident in his voice. "It was entirely my fault. Many lightenings ago, I happened to swallow Antoni while he was crossing my stream. Immediately, when I realised my mistake, I did spit him out and apologise. Not before Antoni bit my tongue though. Why to this lightening, I feel ill to the stomach when ants are left, as tributes in the still pond. To tell you the truth, I allow others of my kind to partake in their sustenance. No disrespect meant, Antoni."

Antoni who had waited, hoping he would not have to reveal himself, walked from the bushes upright with two of his legs in the air. "No disrespect taken, friend. Mar I am sorry, I can not find any trace of a scent, it appears the creature may have taken flight."

"Flying cockroaches, what next?" Bega exclaimed, throwing his front paws into the air.

"Boyor, Antoni." Pint pushed his daughter onto the bank with his tail. "Please allow me to introduce my off-spring, Platy."

"Patti, Noble Platy of the Clear Waters," Antoni said, sweeping down in an exaggerated bow.

Platy giggled and slid back into the water without

saying another word.

"Now, please will you all join me. I shall send word to brother Hena, of the heron, to carry you back upon the lightening of the woods."

Determined to have his way, Antoni folded two legs across his chest. "Forgive me, Pint, I will stay here, I have no desire to be wet by riding on your back and absolutely no hunger to ride in the so called safety of your mouth. Noble Pint, I have had that experience once and that was enough."

"That will not be necessary. Since, we crossed paths; I have employed Mourie Mole's assistance in creating another entrance to our dwelling. Well hidden from prying eyes it is. So now you have no excuses at all." Pint insisted.

"I agree, Pint," Mar said.

"Now, Bega and Mar climb on my back. Dodd if you do not mind, you can ride on Platy's with Antoni," Pint suggested.

"I shall walk, Pint, I really have not got the temperament for riding on platypi's backs. No offence Platy," Antoni said, bowing again.

"Very well, I shall leave Mourie at the doorway so that you can find the entrance. You do remember where our abode is, Antoni?" Pint asked cheekily.

"Yes, Noble Pint, I do," Antoni said, setting off.

Pint, with his cargo on board, continued teasing the bull-ant, "Then, Antoni, I suggest you turn around and head in the other direction."

Bending down, Antoni replied, "Oh you are a funny one, Pint. I was only gathering my belt and sword from the bushes,"

LIGHTENING OF THE WOODS SIX

Toe lay in his notch with both front paws behind his head staring at the wood above him. *Soaring high over everything*, he thought, *how wonderful it must be*. His mind drifted a little longer and then the spark of an idea began to grow. *I have it!* Bounding out of bed, he snuck out of the sleeping chamber. *The last thing I want to do is wake Hatty or Mother as they will stop me and spoil all my fun.*

Slowly, Toe climbed up all the hollows, of the Great Silky Oak, until he could go no further. Then, just as the lightening of the woods began, he squeezed through a knothole, not much larger than himself.

Sitting motionless, he watched on in pure wonderment as Father Sky allowed Brother Sun to lighten the woods. There, slightly above the canopy of the eucalyptus forest, he marvelled at the glory of his home. For the first time, he imagined what it might be like to soar on eagles back.

As Brother Sun began to warm him, Toe could hear the Royal Cicadas begin their chorus. The birds followed with a greeting to the lightening, sung in their native tongues.

Not far into the choral overture, the cicadas' chorus

grew to such a deafening pitch it drowned out the birds. Despite having never heard the warning in his lifetime, Toe realised the commune's alarm was being sounded. Jumping up, he scrambled back through the knothole into the hollows.

#   #   #

"Toe, oh Toe; where are you? The invaders are here in the commune, we must seal the Oak!" Hatty yelled, as she frantically looked for her brother.

The next thing Toe heard was the muffled cry of his mother calling, "Hatty, take Toe and flee to the staggered rocks. Sqweara and her kind will be waiting there for word to attack."

"Mother, it is too late to seal the Oak and I can not find Toe anywhere. Mother, are you there?"

Hearing no reply, she ran down through the tree, to the meeting hollow, only to have her progress halted by a dark cloud of cockroaches; swarming along the dirt floor. Thinking on her feet, she climbed out of a viewing hole and scurried into the bushes. She discovered the gathering area, outside the Oak, full of dark rats squeaking a strange tongue. She did her best to listen but not a word could she understand.

Hoping to avoid capture, or worse, she hopped further into the bushes. Hatty was totally stunned to find foreign mice, riffling through the underbrush, searching for the commune's creatures. Using all the skill she could muster, she dodged and ducked across the path to the staggered rocks.

#   #   #

Toe watched in horror as the Great Oak filled with the invaders. Finally, when he felt it was safe enough to move, he stepped out of the darkness and into a long passage. As he walked along, in the semidarkness, he could hear areas of the Oak being torn apart.

After passing his family's chambers he began to cry. *My family has been taken,* he thought. Suddenly, from out of nowhere, he felt a paw go around his mouth and he was dragged helpless into the darkness. Shaking, kicking and biting Toe tried in vain to fight his captor.

Finally, to his surprise, Toe heard a familiar voice murmur, "Quiet, Toemouse. Safety, seek we must." It urged in an unusual native tongue.

Becoming quieter, Toe turned to look up into the face of his mysterious friend from the shadows, for the first time. Somehow, the wild creature's features looked hauntingly familiar, even in the poor light.

The large gentle creature led him across the room to an old knot marking in the wall, where Toe had often imagined he could see faces late in the darkening. With one push his friend swung the knot half open. He dragged a speechless Toe inside a narrow cavity and closed the knot door behind them.

"We must find my Mother and Hatty. Where are you taking me? We must stay and fight them," Toe commanded.

"Mid darkening noise, Toemouse be making, no sound. Game now, we must play," his friend whispered, clasping his paw across Toe's mouth again.

Through the occasional cracks, in the secret passageway's walls, Toe could make out they were somehow working their way down inside the Oak. Eventually, they came to a position where, through a small spy hole, he looked out into the meeting chamber. There, in one small glimpse, he caught sight of hundreds of black cockroaches and mice fighting over the Great Oak's store of food. Tears welled in his eyes as he was pulled on into the ever darkening passage.

Hatty broke out of the undergrowth pale and breathless.

"They are here. Are they not, child?" Sqweara declared, spreading her gigantic wings.

"Yes, the Highest of Wedge-tails, they came upon the lightening," she replied, gasping for air.

"Why was my kind not called immediately? We could have been waiting in the trees." Sqweara screeched, turned her head and nodded to twenty pairs of eagles behind her and a further thirty hawks gathered behind them.

Watching them take flight Hatty screamed, "My mother, they have my mother."

"Listen, child, we will do our best. I have already sent winged ones ahead, who should have reached the Oak by now. Have the reptiles been called? And again why were we not summoned?" In her annoyance, Sqweara's neck feathers stood on end.

Hatty hopped forward holding both paws in front of her. "We did not suspect an attack despite warnings. My father and the others are away tracking a Spirit Stealer, this very leaf fall."

"There are no leaf falls left for explanation, child! We must act swiftly. Climb on my shoulders. Brother Highra Hawk," she called to her lieutenant. "Take flight and summon all the Servicers' of the Stone Circle. This lightening, we battle for our commune's continued existence." Sqweara squawked and took flight.

"How will you tell who are friends, Lady Sqweara?" Hatty asked, hanging on tightly as they arrived at the gathering area.

Like arrows, they fell from Father Sky, the winged ones' talons pierced the invaders. In a flurry of feathers, they engaged the enemy, ripping at them with their beaks. The gathering area began to run with the blood of those who dared invade the sanctity of the commune.

Soon after, Queen Slur and her kind arrived. Their assignment was to seek out the Spirit Stealers in the hollows and to crush them. While Gewa of the Goanna's kind took on the rats and mice head on without hesitating.

"What a feast," Gewa yelled, to his kind, as he snapped the neck of a rat wearing a skull.

Hatty felt sick to the stomach as corpse after corpse appeared piled on the ground below. Then suddenly, scared half out of her wits, she noticed a circle of echidnas. Always noble, they had formed a ring to protect some young natives of the commune. Only one leaf fall past before the rats turned on the fortified enclosure.

She gasped as the invaders piled dead bodies around the echidnas, to avoid their spikes, and over ran them. "Sqweara! The babies are being attacked! Toe oh Toe!" Hatty howled above the noise of the wings.

Sqweara heard not a word, as she tore with her talons and flung another dead rat over her shoulder with her beak.

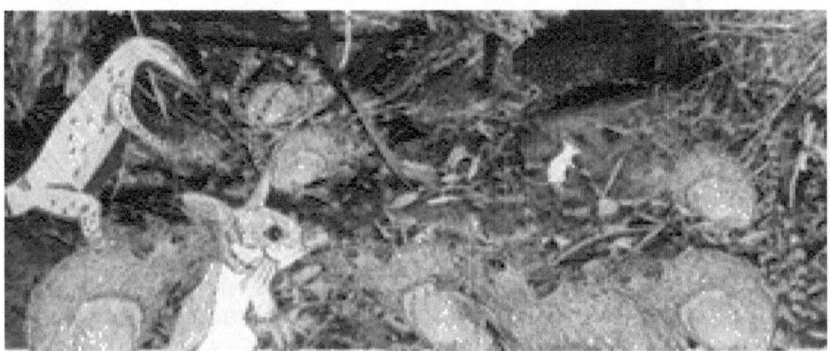

Breathing in deeply, Hatty leapt off the eagle's back and dashed across the gathering area. Jumping, over a black rat's body, she ran toward the young creatures only to be stopped by another rat, its bloody teeth glaring. Hatty saw her short life flash before her when the creature leapt at her.

Out of nowhere Ro the Bilby sprang, a rock tightly clasped in his paws, and hit the aggressor across the snout. "Run to the bushes, Noble, Hatty," he yelled, as twenty rats took him down. Ro fought on valiantly, only to be bitten and torn again and again until his spirit left him.

Seizing one of the sharpened sticks from the ground, in front of her, Hatty did a short jump onto a rat's back and flipped herself into the circle of echidnas. There she stood bravely, stabbing at the invaders as they attempted to penetrate deeper into the protective circle.

"You shall not hurt our young natives!" With her eyes turned red, from tears and rage, she shook from head to tail.

Unaccustomed to battle, the small commune's creatures soon tired. Helpless, they watched on as the echidnas found themselves overrun. Hatty standing proudly, ready to let her spirit go fighting, held a baby possum in one arm and a stick in the other. Unexpectedly, when she felt her death was imminent, the rats stopped attacking the circle and a dark mouse walked through them as they bowed.

#   #   #

"Father," Dodd yelled. "Is this like soaring on an eagle's back?"

"Eagle's back, indeed," Hena, the Heron, protested. "I will have you know, mouse, I have flown thousands of wing strokes to places your precious eagles have only ever heard tales about."

"Sorry, Noble Hena of the Long Legs, I meant no harm."

Hena turned his long neck around to Dodd in mid-flight. "No harm taken, young one; why when I think about it, I should imagine it would be like a ride on cousin eagle's back. In fact, I now feel quite flattered."

On the other hand, Mar, Bega and Antoni's heads were spinning from an over indulgence of sap. Through hazy eyes they gazed lazily down on the blurred ground before them.

"Never, shall I drink a platypi's so called sap, again!" Antoni declared to Mar.

Many leaf falls later Hena and his two brothers landed in a stream down from the commune. As they stood there saying farewell, Hena looked down at the water and noticed it ran red. The bird arched his long neck over the water and looked upstream. "What can this mean?" he said, pointing with his beak.

After so many battles in his life, Mar knew exactly what such a sign meant. Without a word the Chieftain of the Oak leapt off his ride and ran toward the commune.

"Father, where are you going in such a hurry?" Dodd yelled, climbing down off his bird's back.

Antoni bounded onto Dodd's back and said, "Dodd, follow your father with all haste. And, mouse, ready yourself."

"Ready myself for what?" Dodd asked, seizing his staff off the ground and moving to follow.

Bega rolled down from the Heron, stumbled to his feet and ran forward. While he did his best to keep up he soon fell behind, gasping for air.

Nothing could have prepared Mar for what he found that lightening. Not far outside the gathering area there was body after body of the invaders. Then as he drew closer to the oak, more and more of the commune's creatures, their friends, laid slain. *We were tricked*, he thought, moving with great caution toward the gathering area.

As the clearing opened up before him, Dodd gasped in horror at the sight of hundreds of bodies covering the area. Overwhelmed, he swung around and became violently ill.

Antoni, a battle hardened veteran, sprang off Dodd's back and drew fang from his belt. "By the Great River Stones I have never seen anything like this in all my lightenings," he declared, running off.

The Chief Bull-ant soon found some ants, busy carrying some of the smaller creatures toward the Stone Circle, and began to converse.

Desperate, Mar dashed from creature to creature, frantically, checking for signs of life. To his dismay, the noble Oak Mouse found not one with spirit. Broken hearted, he lifted himself up from yet another body and as he did noticed Sqweara not far ahead.

"Hale, Sqweara," Mar called, running up to her. Standing there, encircled by the bodies of at least twenty rats, she stared down at him in a trance. "Sqweara, when did they come?"

"They came, upon the lightening of the woods. Like a dark shadow, across Mother Earth, they crept. Not a sign of warning, did we get, until it was too late. If it had not been for Hatty's bravery, in seeking us, many more would have lost their spirit"

"Hatty," Mar declared. "Where is she, Sqweara, and what of Toe and Trix?"

Buckled over, Dodd took deep breaths and tried to regain his composure, after being so ill. Suddenly, a rat sprang out from the bushes and poised itself to pounce. Scared, the young mouse froze, only to hear two cracks whip through the air.

One crack had been from the tail of Bega to disarm it. The second, from the bandicoot's staff, snapping the rat's neck.

Know thy enemy, Bega thought as he moved over to examine the body. Noticing Rina's bravery amulet glistening through the black rats' fur, he fell to all fours. Tears building in his eyes, he rolled the rat over only to find it wearing a bush cockroach's shell chest plate. Even his old eyes could see it was Binja's shell.

Looking to the heavens the Elder screamed, "May Father Sky and Mother Earth protect their spirits." With that, he ripped the amulet from the rat's neck.

In shock and bewildered, Mar wandered around the gathering area, until he found Ro's body amongst several rats. "Faithful, Ro," he sighed kneeling. "So far from your native home, how I failed you and the others." Standing, raging with anger, he hopped into the Great Oak calling for his family. Not one reply did he receive.

Entering the eating area he came upon Slur, slowly interrogating one of the rats. "Sspeak you foul creature. Why do your kind join with the mice and roaches to wreak ssuch devastation on a peaceful land?"

Mar watched on as Slur constricted the rat's last breath of air out of its lungs.

"What yet another, who fails to inform me?" She let the crushed body fall. "I sshall sseek every last one of you out and crush you until one of you sspeak to me. Mind you, it must be in the common tongue. Answers I sseek," she hissed, moving her head to the side.

Stepping out of the darkened arch, Mar walked across the crushed bodies to where Slur mumbled to herself. Before he knew what hit him, her tail had come around behind and had him in a vice like grip. When she turned to face him, he could see her eyes red with anger.

"Sso yet another dares to approach me."

"Hold, Queen Slur! It is I, Mar Mouse of the Noble Oak."

"Chieftain Mar," Slur said, leaning toward her tail.

It was then, Mar noticed her eyes were swollen from the ferociousness of the battle.

"Yes, it is you," Slur said, flicking her tongue at him. "Please forgive me, Noble One, we ssnakes sshould never have doubted your kind. I am just sso deeply ssorry." Her tongue flicked to within a whisker of Mar's face.

"Forgiven. Now please may you release me from your mighty grip," Mar pleaded, pushing with his paws. "Have you seen Trix, Toe or Hatty, Queen?"

"Not I, perhaps one of these vile creatures may tell you." Slur looked around.

Looking down at the carnage, Mar shook his head. "Slur, their spirits have long since gone."

"Sspirit? A creature which sseeks out another to make war for no reason, has no sspirit.

Mar noticed movement out of the corner of his eye, but before he could act, Slur struck with her fangs.

"How can you be sure, Slur, you do not take one of our own? Why you can hardly see at all due to your injuries."

"I ssmell them, Mar, they carry the sstench of darkness on their fur. None of our commune carry ssuch a distinct evil odour," Slur said, sliding the rat into her coils. "Now rat, why did you come? What, sstill no answer? Then evil one's sspirit be gone." Then with one twist, yet another rat breathed its last.

"Forgive Sslur, forgive me," she cried, as noticed Mar move away to search for his loved ones.

Soon Dodd joined his father and together they checked every crack and hollow of the Great Oak. In their chamber they found signs of a great struggle and the bodies of many cockroaches. Hope waned as they found no real sign their family may still have their spirits.

By the leaf fall they reached the eating hollow again, Slur had moved on. For the first time, since the lightening after Briar's murder, the wondrous gleam of Tongue, the Truth Bringer and Mouth did not illuminate the small stump on which it had laid. As with Mar's family it too had disappeared without a trace.

Leaf fall after leaf fall the father and son hunted around the commune but could find no trace of family. The only glimmer of hope being the fact their bodies were not amongst the others. Therefore, a ray of hope lingered in their hearts that perhaps they had escaped.

DARKENING SIX

A sombre shroud of death hung over the Commune of the Great Oak.

With the massive task of clearing the bodies from the commune complete, the survivors tried to come to grips with the disaster. They reckoned out of the two hundred natives, who had lived in the commune at the moment of the attack, only fifty ground dwellers had survived.

In regards to the Servicers' of the Circle, there appeared to be twenty winged ones missing. One of whom was Noble Highra the Hawk, who had last been seen in pursuit of a band of foreign creatures. These Spirits Stealers had broken away in the heat of battle and headed in the direction of Brother Sun's rising.

Toward mid darkening the most fearful revelation hit the survivors, when they realised there was not one child found, dead or alive.

"You were right, Chieftain Mar," Petra said, in a solemn tone, from her tree on the side of the ceremonial path. "There was no dealing with such creatures; in fact, our peaceful creatures had little hope. That was until the winged ones and the Servicers' of the Circles arrived. We are just not creatures of violence and as such all we ask is to live peaceably in our beloved bush. Why did they come?" Tears rolled down her cheeks and shattered on the pebbles below.

"I feel Queen Slur was right when she said the Spirit Stealers are without spirit, Petra. Now our challenge is to track them down and bring back our children. For without our children we have no future, be it peaceful or otherwise," Mar said, formulating a plan in his mind.

LIGHTENING OF THE WOODS SEVEN

Sound asleep under a large leaf, Toe dreamt of better leaf falls as his mysterious saviour hovered around in the tree tops above him; watching and listening.

Looking down at Toe he smiled. "Toemouse safe, hide him, I will," the strange creature said, holding up a large stick with bumps on the end.

#   #   #

"Chieftain Mar," Antoni said, rushing into the meeting of the Elders, "we have four rats and a mouse that were caught in traps on the edge of the commune. And they live, my Chieftain."

"Well done, Antoni," Mar declared, "I shall question them on my way."

"Where to, Chieftain?" Antoni queried, reached up and scratched behind one of his antenna.

"I leave this very leaf fall to follow those who left the battle. The council has ordained it."

Hesitantly, Petra, Betra and Bega nodded.

"And Antoni it is no longer 'Chieftain Mar'. I, of this leaf fall, have resigned as the Noble Oak Mouse," Mar said, standing and moving to the arch.

"No, Chieftain," Antoni protested, rushing forward.

Mar lowered his head."I must leave as I feel a heavy spirit in my heart. In a way it was through my actions that the commune lost so many. After all, if it had not been for my suggestion, Stump, Aldo and many of the defence force would have been here to defend our loved ones."

"Yes, Chieftain, and they too would have been slain," Antoni argued, stepping in front of him. "The evil invaders are well learned in the strategy of deceit. It was not you who split the commune but they. By depleting our numbers, sending us every which way, they destroyed our strength of unity. Not you, Chieftain Mar."

"Forever a friend," Mar said, affectionately touching Antoni's shoulder. "Petra is now the duly elected Noble of the Oak. She will need your knowledge, Antoni, while you are here."

"Petra has my loyalty, Chieftain Mar, but soon Royo, my commander, will arrive with one thousand of our best Bull-ants. He is more than capable of helping protect the perimeter of the commune. So I beg thee, Chieftain, let me come with you," Antoni said, lifting Mar's paw off his shoulder.

"Sorry, Chief, I shall go alone. I fear even a small force will soon be detected. Antoni dear friend, I am hoping they have my family with them. I am afraid any mistakes could instantly cost them their spirits."

"Father," Dodd protested, "I shall not allow you to travel such a perilous road without me by your side."

Looking Dodd deep in his eyes Mar whispered, "You, my son, are all I may have left; I would not risk your spirit for all of the river stones, swords, jewels or creatures on Mother Earth. Besides you are not yet trained in the Circle of Knowledge and Defence."

Bega stood to protest but upon seeing the resolve in

their former leader's face held his tongue. Helpless, the bandicoot watched as his friend walked nobly out of the Oak.

Mar did not look back as he hopped down the Oak's root and disappeared into the undergrowth.

"We can not allow him to go by himself," Dodd said, picking up his staff.

"I agree, young Dodd," Petra said softly. "Antoni, how long before your forces arrive?"

"From what one of King Damon's ants told me, Noble Petra, they will not be any longer than one lightening of the woods away."

"Fine and messengers have been sent to inform the expedition what has occurred?"

"Yes, Lady Petra," Bega answered. "Chieftain Mar sent word within leaf falls of seeing the devastation."

"Also the Servicers' of the woods have moved in closer to protect those that remain, have they not?" Petra said, her eyes squinting from the brightness of the light she was still unaccustomed too.

"Yes, Petra," Antoni replied.

"Well, I see more urgency in you and Dodd assisting the Noble Mouse's search. Antoni, could you not train Dodd, in the ways of the Circle of Knowledge and Defences, as you go?"

"Our ways are far removed from yours," Antoni said, scratching his chin, "but yes I am sure I could teach the mouse enough to survive."

"Fine, that is settled. I Petra, duly elected Noble of the Oak, command you to help Mar in his quest. Even he will not disobey my edict," she said, letting out a sly grin. "I shall ask Prince Crier of the Cicadas to pick some of his best creatures to accompany you in the trees, they will surely go unnoticed. Betra of the Bats, could not some of your kind be ever watchful in the darkening and even scout ahead?"

"Yes, my Lady," Betra squeaked, from the darkness behind Petra.

"I must say I am impressed with your thinking," Bega said, bowing humbly to Petra, "oh, Noble Oak Possum."

"Thank you, Bega, but the title is one, I shall only bear until Mar returns. Then I shall return it to the shoulders that deserve it more than I."

"Chief Antoni, you are needed in the gathering area immediately," Belor the Blue Tongue Lizard, hissed loudly from the entrance to the gathering area.

"Very well, Belor. Please excuse me, Petra, Bega and Betra."

Before the others could say a word in reply Antoni was gone, across the floor, up the vertical wall and out through a small crack in the side of the Oak. Belor, clearly agitated, stood at the entrance pointing his tongue wildly towards a small bush near the edge of the clearing.

"What is it, Belor? Calm down and speak the common tongue. All I can hear now is hissing."

Blue tongue is such a difficult language to grasp, Antoni thought.

"Funn fun fff funnel-web ssspider," Belor finally hissed clearly, nervously flicking his tongue about.

Belor was surprised when Antoni casually walked down the Oak's root and began conversing with the dreaded spider.

Lizards of Belor's size had no need to be afraid of such a creature, as these spiders only take sustenance from much smaller lizards, frogs and the occasional small bird. Still Belor feared it, because while there had been talk of the funnel-webs' joining the alliance, it had not yet happened. Also as a veteran of the funnel-web wars Belor took no chances. In the end, he need not have worried.

Antoni brought Squorth forward and introduced her, "Belor, may I present, Princess Squorth, a companion of mine on many an adventure."

"Sya, oh sky tongued one," Squorth said, in a deep rumbling voice.

"Ento, oh Great Eight Legged One. I have heard many a tale of your might in battle." Belor bowed his head in respect.

Squorth turned and looked at Antoni. "Knowing my friend, Antoni, I would probably say exaggeration could well be afoot."

"Why, Squorth, you know I am not one to exaggerate a battle." Antoni protested, standing on his hind legs with his centre pair on his hips.

"Belor, could you summon Noble Dodd from the eating and gathering area? We must leave immediately." Antoni turned away and stroked Squorth gently above her eyes.

"Yes, Chief Antoni," Belor said, leaving as quickly as he could.

"You sound anxious, Chief Antoni, what has happened?" Squorth asked, enjoying the attention.

"The lightening of the wood past saw an attack on this commune that took 150 spirits. Not to Celebrate Sustenance, but in an act of aggression never seen in our lands before.

"Upon the early lightening they came, black cockroaches, strange mice and many black rats. They stole everything they could; including it appears the young ones of the commune. If it had not been for the Servicers' of the Circle, I fear all would have been lost. Only leaf falls ago Chieftain Mar left us to follow the creature's tracks."

"Alone!" Squorth grumbled, wriggling her legs.

"Yes. That is why we must start immediately. Our only

hope is to catch him before he leaves the area where some unknown hunter has trapped some invading rats. So we are taking Dodd, Prince Crier and some of his best along with us. We will also have many of the bats kind as support in Father Sky during darkening." Antoni turned to walk away.

"Why did you not go with him, Chief Antoni? Did he not summon you here for help?" Squorth asked puzzled.

"They have Trix, Hatty and Toe, Mar fears they will take their spirits if they sense a force following. He also forbade me from going," Antoni announced, shaking his head.

"Then if I know Chieftain Mar your interference will not be well received. Perhaps his actions are for the good of all, though I can not see what one kangaroo mouse could do against such overwhelming odds," Squorth said, crouching down onto her belly.

A wicked grin formed on Antoni's face and a gleam came to his eye. "Ah yes, but Mar resigned his title and now Petra the possum is the Noble Oak Presider. She has ordered us to pursue and help Mar."

"Hm," Squorth grumbled, "Antoni, whether Mar be Noble Mouse or not, you still realise he carries a mighty temper when agitated."

"Yes I do, but by the River Stones, I am not going to let him fight a battle without us guarding his back and that is all there is to it," Antoni declared, stomping his forelegs against the Oak's root.

#   #   #

"Where are we, strange one?" Toe asked, clambering up the tree.

"Home, me be. Toemouse safe. See with eyes further traps me made work, yes?" The wild native smiled and pointed.

Toe gazed toward the movement many mouse lengths

away. "I see very little of anything except bushes. Um what will I call you or do you have a name already?" Toemouse scratched the fur behind his ear deep in thought.

"Name not have, my home be where me stand." The strange creature did a flip and stood in front of Toe.

Unexpectedly, the ruffled wild mouse leapt forward and took Toe's paw, shaking it furiously.

> "Metcha Mouse I be me
> A creature of the bush that be me
> I speak native wasp and even bee
> While others work hard, I be free
>
> "Not staying clean and sitting still
> Not a creature would I kill
> I swim through the water like Sister Fish
> Eat wild herbs and roots, that my dish
>
> "Every plant and creature be my friend
> On me to protect them, they depend
> In the shadows I do hide
> Watching and learning from inside
>
> "I be, air, tree, water and earth
> I make grasses laugh with my mirth
> With my friends I do fly
> Then with laughter I do cry
>
> "I be me, I be me
> Creature of the bush that be me
> While others work hard, I be free
> My home is here in Sister Tree."

"You mean you live here in Sister Trees, all of the time?" Toe said, sitting on the branch.

"Do me," the creature answered, still watching the

movement in the distance.

"I think you mean, 'I do'. Anyway, I must call you something, let me see. Hm as you live high in the trees and it is your home, while we live largely on the ground, I think I will call you 'Attic Mouse'. Signifying one who lives above others; what do you think, Attic?"

"High me live. Ever watchful see," Attic said, pointing toward movement in the distance.

Toe's heart leapt when he saw his father hopping through the undergrowth below the tree. However when he went to call, Attic covered his mouth and muffled his cry. Toe's heart sank as he watched his father disappear.

Attic smiled knowing full well Mar was heading to the traps where he had successfully snared some invaders.

"Safe not cry out," Attic whispered into Toe's ear. "Many dark ones hide outside area. If found we lose game." Attic crouched down, his eyes sparkling in his knotted fur.

"But, Attic, that was my father. We must find him, he will know what to do," Toe pleaded, pushing Attic's paw off his mouth.

"Live here, ever watchful must be. Father, what is father?" Attic asked, still staring at the activity on the ground.

"He is the one that loves you, cares for you and teaches you," Toe explained, tears dripping down his cheeks. "You must let me go. Father will know what to do. He will know if Mother and Hatty are alright. Please."

"Toe point ears to my noise. See leaves on this tree there, never touch, sting they do," Attic said, reaching out his long forearm.

"Yes fine I will never touch. Now can we go?"

"Me care for you, Toemouse, love, me do, now me teach. Does this not make me father?" Attic asked smiling.

"No, it most certainly does not," Toe protested. "And

how is it that you now speak so much common tongue?"
Toe folded his arms and began to pout.

"All existence me watch, listen, gather words. This is
how," Attic announced tumbling backward.

"Then why did you struggle with speech when I was
teaching you?"

"Toemouse say, 'Toemouse'. me say 'Toemouse',
same way." Attic lifted gumnuts and stored them on the
branch.

"Oh my goodness, you were not learning from me, you
were mimicking me. I taught you nothing you already
knew." Toemouse huffed and slammed his hind paw
down.

"Mimic, what does mean?" Attic asked, rolling one
gumnut at the others he had placed further down the
branch.

In an attempt to explain, Toe did his best
impersonation of Brother Green Tree Frog croaking,
"Whoop."

"See, me now," Attic replied and then went on to
mimic all the birds of the area perfectly.

"Unbelievable," Toe gasped, leaning back against the
tree. "Please can we go now?"

"Safe not. Dark shadow move about in bushes outside
area," Attic said, pointing to the undergrowth Mar had
just passed through.

#   #   #

"Halt, go no further. Who dares approach without
warning?" Lea of the Frill-necked Lizards questioned,
puffing his fan-like neck out.

"It is I, Mar. I have come to seek answers from those
who have been captured," he announced, standing quite
still in the undergrowth.

"Come forward so I might identify you," Lea

commanded, signalling for four of his lizards to circle around behind.

Cautiously walking out to greet Lea, Mar came across the primitive trap. For the first time he gazed into the dark eyes of a black rat, suspended by a vine in front of him.

"Sorry, Chieftain," Lea said, lowered his frill and walked up to greet him.

"Sya, Lea. I would expect no less from one learned in the Circle of Knowledge and Defence. Now have you managed to gain any information from the creature?" Mar stood mesmerised by the creature's evil eyes.

"No, Chieftain, I have tried several dialects but none seem to penetrate the evil ones' thick skull." Lea's tongue flicked about in frustration.

"Very well, I shall also attempt to gain knowledge," Mar said, as he spun the creature around with his staff.

After using many native languages Mar also failed to communicate with the creature. Leaf falls later Mar turned, frustrated beyond belief, and told Lea he personally was going to leave and follow the other creatures' tracks.

"Alone, Chieftain, I will not allow it!" Lea protested, signalling for his guards to come in. "Allow us to assist these vile creatures' spirits out of their bodies. Then I, and two of my best lizards, will accompany you."

Just as Lea finished speaking, a loud crack came out of the bushes and then yet another. Instantly, within a wave of Lea's tail, the loyal lizards formed a circle around Mar with their necks flared ferociously, creating a daunting sight.

Out of the undergrowth several rats sprang at Mar and the others, giving them no time to formulate a plan.

#   #   #

"Toemouse stay. Shadow's creatures make more play," Attic announced, as he went hopping off from tree to tree.

Toe could not have followed even if he wanted to. There many mouse lengths from the forest floor, Toe watched the rats swarm across the ground below.

#   #   #

The frill-necks hissed and ripped at the rats as they attacked and poured over them. Mar cracked his staff across several of the demons' necks and lashed at their dark eyes with his tail. Sadly, all looked lost, as the attackers released the captive rats.

"Lie on ground you will," a cry came over the noise of the battle. "Lizards close circle".

Seeing little choice but to listen, Mar dropped to the ground in front of the trap. Suddenly, from the trees, three large logs hurtled across the air smashing into three of the rats. Then yet another rat seemed to disappear up a tree with a vine around its neck, instantly killing it.

Mar and the lizards stood as one, once again, renewed by the mysterious assistance and fought on.

Although intrigued by the help from above, Mar had no time to seek out their saviour as the onslaught continued.

Then with a roar, from above, Prince Crier and his Royal Guard swooped down at the rats scratching at their eyes. Father Sky went dark as Betra and the bats' kind, dropped from the tree tops blocking out Brother Sun's rays.

The rats, shocked by the attack, fled into the bushes.

Exhausted, Mar lifted his staff. Bracing himself for another impending attack, he stood defiantly. Then when the rats attacked again his heart sank into despair.

With a gigantic thud, as if out of nowhere, Dodd, Antoni and Squorth leapt into the circle of lizards. There they formed an inner circle around Mar for his protection.

Antoni thrust his sword in all directions, while nipping at the rats with his powerful jaws.

Squorth moved backward and forward, thrusting and biting with her fangs.

Dodd using his staff, with amazing agility, knocked some of the rats on the head. While his blows were not hard enough to kill, it did send some running.

After many leaf falls the battle was over, the creatures of the native commune victorious.

Mar and Dodd crouched exhausted, one leaning against the other's back.

"May Mother Earth and Father Sky be praised that we are still with spirit," Mar declared, breathing heavily.

"Ah, that was a good battle indeed." Leaning back Squorth stretched her front legs. "Why I think I enjoy these invading rats company after all." Looking around at the dead she added in a dark tone, "Yes, I do, exactly as they are right now, without spirit."

Raising his staff in thanks, Mar signalled to Prince Crier and the bats, who had taken to the trees. "Thank you all for saving a foolish mouse's spirit this lightening."

He lowered his head in tribute.

As Mar thanked Lea and his Lizards, the trees erupted with the sound of cicadas chanting a rhythmic melody in celebration of a great battle.

"Antoni, thank the River Stones you followed," Mar said, as he summoned enough strength to stand, "You my son and Squorth, I thank with all my heart."

"Well to tell the truth, Mar, it was Petra who commanded us to follow and protect you," Antoni said, placing fang back in his belt. "They are quite cowardly these rats when faced with resistance, are they not?"

"It appears so." Mar's brow furrowed as he leant against his staff. "Antoni, do you expect me to believe you did not push to be allowed to follow?"

I knew full well, Antoni would do exactly what he did. Despite our friendship, I did not have the right to ask him to risk his spirit on such a quest.

"It was indeed masterful, of you, Marcus, to have laid such traps in the trees," Squorth said, looking at the large logs suspended around them.

"It was not I," Mar said quietly. "At first I thought it must have been you, Squorth, as the voice that called to us sounded oddly familiar. But as I did not have time to set such traps, that appears unlikely."

"Odd indeed," Antoni said, circling the area on all six legs, sniffing. "Mar, do you not recognise many of the traps sprung here? They resemble primitive versions of those taught in your Circle of Knowledge and Defence."

Astounded, by the ingenuity used in creating the traps, Mar hopped around studying the site.

"Indeed, Antoni, I believe you are right. Why this hunter must be one of the chosen." Holding his front paws to his mouth Mar called, "Come out so we may thank you, oh Great Trapper."

#   #   #

Amazed by the cicadas and bats' attack Attic scurried back to the base of the Stringybark and made his way back to Toe. He smiled when he saw his young friend still sitting on the branch.

"Are they alright, Attic? Is father alright?" Toe asked, leaping to his feet.

"Fine they be. Father and tall mouse make mighty fight. Others help too. Loud wing ones come, you must see them come." Attic shook his head and waved his arms about mimicking the winged natives.

"Yes, I did. It sure was a sight to see Brother Sun blacked out as they passed." Toe answered, while trying to push past his scruffy saviour.

Attic placed both his front paws on Toes' shoulders and bowed his head. "Me sad, Toemouse." Tears formed in his eyes and started to roll down his cheeks.

Toe pushed even harder fearing the worse. "But why, Attic, if they are alright?"

"In some way, yes me pleased. Sad because, area me make to play in, gone. Took long to build such place. When lightness come again, me was to take you there to play. Now gone. Why must old creatures play so hard, Toemouse?" Attic asked, released Toe and extended his front paws.

"I am sorry, Attic, but I am afraid none of it was play," Toe replied, staring up into his wild brown eyes.

"In area of play me build, must be play. Me rule, me thought all must obey." Confused, Attic shook his head.

"No, it was as real as Brother Sun is above our heads." Toe reached out and touched him on the shoulder.

"Me not understand. First they come play, as me see others play, so me think we hide. Then me see some in play area, swinging around as other creatures speak to them. So me think all is good when creatures play together. Now you tell me, not so." Upset Attic seized

Toe's wrist.

"Poor, Attic, you have not ever been taught the tales of great wars before the treaties, have you?" Toe said, touching Attic's face with his free paw.

"Toemouse, tell me, when breath stop coming out of mouth, what does that mean? Me have watched the creatures take others from the sacred place. The ones they take are without breath, are they not?" Attic asked, leaning his head into Toemouse's paw.

"Yes, it means their spirit has left them and the Servicers' of the Circle may take sustenance from their bodies."

"Breath come back ever, Toemouse?"

"No, I am afraid it does not." Toe's face went ashen.

"Oh, me think me did bad this lightness," Attic said, moving away from Toe and putting his head in his own paws.

"Even at my age, I know the problems that now exist in our land can not be fixed by adults deciding to play together. Oh innocent Attic," Toe held out his arms and pulled the much larger mouse to his shoulder.

As Attic sobbed with grief, at the thought of taking a spirit from the rat, Toe held him like a mother would a child.

Mar mouse sat on the ground twirling the end of his staff in the dirt. "Antoni, please do not think me of shaky spirit. Now I have had time to think, the voice sounded like Elder Briar's," he confided. "Yet somehow different, perhaps much younger."

"That is indeed odd, Mar. Are you sure you are not mistaken?" Antoni replied, chewing on a piece of grass.

"After all the hours of training, I endured from Elder Briar; I would recognise his commands anywhere. Especially, when he or it yelled, 'Close circle'."

"Indeed, that is one of Briar's commands. Well, that

has settled it then, somewhere in the bushes we have a fellow defender."

"Yes, that must explain it." Mar murmured, as he and Antoni stood to rejoin the others.

Lea the lizard sent three of his brothers back to the commune, but insisted he and two of his best lizards joined the crusade.

As they gathered their things, Antoni spoke to Prince Crier who had received word of the invading rats' pack ahead.

Antoni let out a screech of joy. "Eeya, Eeya."

"Antoni, what is it?" Mar called, from under a sapling.

"Prince Crier's scouts are sure they have seen Trix, Hatty and the others, not more than one lightenings walk from here." The ant informed them doing a strange little dance.

"Why indeed, the River Stones and Mother Earth have blessed us," Mar exclaimed, running up to Antoni and slapping him hard enough to knock him over. "We must leave within the leaf fall. Antoni, could you ask Crier if they saw Toe as well?"

Antoni turned and spoke to Crier in the common tongue of insects.

Mar could tell, by the look on his old friend's face, what the answer was immediately.

"Mar, fear not, they say many of the commune's children are within their ranks. Sadly, for some reason, their numbers decrease with every stop the marching creatures take." Antoni informed Mar and walked away into the shadows.

#   #   #

Attic raised his head suddenly. "Toemouse, wrong! Long time past me watch creatures in circle fight and fall but always they stand again."

"Circle," Toe mumbled, thinking aloud. "Oh you must

have been watching the Circle of Knowledge and Defence." Toe rolled a gum nut back and forth between his paws.

"Yes. Much me learn from the large one," Attic said, standing and rolling his paws in front of his stomach, "whose belly nearly blocks out Brother Sun. Lightenings me watch him, teach and show. Many things he did, me can do now me grow."

"Sorry, Attic, it is not the same." Toe flicked the gum nut into the air.

"How so?" Attic asked, catching it.

"They were pretending to fight as part of their personal development, to make them better creatures in themselves. I too, as my father was, am destined to enter. Nobody is supposed to know where the ancient circle is. So Attic you better not tell anybody, not even me. After all, I shall know soon enough anyway. So now please, will you take me to my father?" Toe pleaded standing and moving toward the trunk.

"No not me. Look they leave the area of play. Now me learnt from you, it be too dangerous for you to join them," Attic said defiantly, with his arms crossed, blocking Toe's progress.

Toe began to sob and sob.

"Stop water now, Toemouse! Shadows likely to attack father again and again. Not safe for little friend, me tell you. Commune not either."

Toe just cried louder.

"Stop noise from mouth, Toemouse, now. Me take you to follow from safety of trees. Behind we be alright." Attic embraced the smaller mouse.

Toe stopped crying and lifted his head to look straight into the hauntingly familiar face.

Attic just smiled broadly and ruffled Toe's fur between his ears with his paw.

DARKENING SEVEN

In a distant part of the forest, in a hollow at the base of the great spotted gum, Elder Briar's sons Pon and Fila sat mystified.

"I have searched as far as my legs can carry me. While I found many charred remains there was no sign of any of our family," Fila said despondently, sitting in their dwelling etching in the dirt with his toe.

"I can not understand why they were not here in safety. Neither Nila or Fena said they were going anywhere that lightening, did they, Fila?" Pon asked, going over the events of the past lightenings of the woods repeatedly in his mind.

"Every creature I have asked has said they saw nothing," Fila replied, without lifting his head.

"Impossible! I realise the Large Pale Ones are nearly upon us, but some creature must know what happened. We must seek them out wherever they may be." Pon stood determined to find answers and left the damp hollow. Venturing out into the darkening he beckoned, "They must have fled from the redness. Come Fila; etch a message at our entrance, for me, before we leave."

"But, Pon, where will we go?" Fila reluctantly stood and moved up the small passageway.

"We shall search every hollow, tree and valley until we find Fena, Nila, Nel and Ji. I know I shall not rest until I do." Pon grabbed his small bow as he left the opening and walked out into the darkening's smoky air.

"The redness has turned everything dark for many mouse lengths around our humble home. There are no tracks to follow, Pon. Why, there is barely a blade of grass or tree left unscathed. Even brother Keira the Koala has lost many of his kind. I fear all our efforts will be for naught," Fila said, as he finished etching on the tree trunk.

"You think too much, Fila. Now come, we shall walk in straight lines from our dwelling, each in opposite directions. No matter how far we travel, upon mid lightening we will return here. If we find something or not we must always return. After resting we will leave messages for each other and set out again." Pon placed his paw on his brother's shoulder. "Understand."

"Yes, Pon, I shall do my best." Fila picked up his small sword, made from the rib of a bandicoot, and set off.

LIGHTEING OF THE WOODS EIGHT

Belor entered the Oak's gathering hollow looked up and announced, "Noble Petra, the Highest of Wedge-tails seeks an audience with you on the uppermost branch of the Oak,".

"Indeed and did she say what it was about, Belor?" Petra asked, from her dark corner.

"No, my Lady, but I fear it is grim news she brings upon this new lightening of the woods." Belor's tongue glowed with a brilliant blue as he spoke.

"I do hope it is not bad news! I really do not think I could take much more. Is it not enough that Mar was nearly killed and that Trix, Hatty and the surviving children are captives of those distasteful creatures?" She sighed and moved toward the Oak's entrance.

The brightness of the early lightening stunned Petra's eyes. For a nocturnal creature, in the habit of sleeping most of the lightening and into the darkening, the climb would not be an easy one. Sleep deprived, the possum was already feeling the pressure of her new position in the commune.

By the leaf fall she had scrambled up to the highest branch, where Sqweara sat waiting, her eyes had partially adjusted to the light.

"Eeark, Sqweara, Highest of Wedge-tails, " Petra said, puffing as she curled herself up in some shade.

"Raa, oh Noble Petra of the Oak. I am afraid I am the bearer of bad tidings. Upon this lightening, many of the creatures that assisted us in the defence of the commune are ill in their nests; winged ones and no legs alike," Sqweara said, her head turning ever watchful.

"Oh this is indeed grave news. Have you any idea what it could be?" Petra lifted her head up in an attempt to see Sqweara's face.

"Every ill creature is one who, against my advice, partook of the invaders' flesh. They are as warm as Brother Sun's rays, sickly to the stomach and have a strange redness on their chests. Noble Petra, I have never seen such a thing in all my lightenings." Sqweara shook her head and sighed deeply concerned.

"Forgive the interruption, Noble ones," Grey the Gecko said quietly, popping his head out of a crack in the tree. "Belor has asked me to relay a message to you both. Many of the land dwelling creatures who drank some of the running water, down from the Oak, are sick with pain and hotness of the flesh." With that Grey was gone.

Even with the treaties, still intact, the little lizard thought hurrying away. *I do not feel safe around Sqweara.*

"What evil have these detestable creatures brought to our peaceful commune?" Petra growled, her head held down in thought.

"It seems we have yet another enemy amongst us. Only this one we can not see to sink our talons into," Sqweara said, digging her right leg's talon deep into the tree in frustration.

"Sqweara, what if the unseen evil spreads? Oh, great Mother Earth, where will it end?" Petra prayed quite openly, tears soaking the fur on her cheeks.

Unaware of the attack on the commune, or the sickness that now ravaged their friends, Aldo and Stump continued to look for a new site.

"Well what do you think, Aldo? Does this area not suit as a possible site for the commune? Look there is a beautiful rain-forest, and not much further a clearing leading to another forest of the great gum," Stump said, pushing his way through the dense undergrowth.

"We must wait until the surveyors and gatherers look over the area, before making a decision. Stump, there may well be an existing commune within this area. Though, I must admit it seems strange that we have barely seen a sign of any other creatures." Aldo scrambled to the top of a small sapling to spy ahead.

"I would say that could well be because of my kind," a voice echoed from above.

Stump and Aldo jumped, at the sound of the high pitched voice, and drew their swords from their belts.

"Fear not, little ground dwellers. My kind recognises all the treaties set down since ancient lightenings." The voice assured them.

Looking around, neither mouse could find the creature from which the grating voice had emerged. Yet they could sense movement in the branches above.

Hit by the realisation of what was to occur; both mice hit the ground as a large dropping fell between them.

Forewarned, Aldo jumped to his feet and sprinted to a small sapling in an attempt to stay out of the line of fire.

"Please forgive me, but my kind do that sort of thing all the leaf falls. We also enjoy loud raucous debates about the goings on in the woods," the voice screeched. "But we never gossip, mind you."

"Really and what kind of creature are you then, oh dropping dropper?" Stump grumbled, while holding his nose.

"I really do not know if I feel like talking to you, oh fat one, after such a remark. After all I was hanging here long before you came upon this spot. Surely, you can see the evidence of it around you, or are you without sight, oh short and fat one."

Aldo sensed the discussion deteriorating. As things sometimes have a tendency to do, when one side refuses to see the world through the other creature's eyes.

"Please forgive my friend. Allow me to introduce myself. I am 'Aldo', second in command of the Great Oak's Defence and this is my Noble Lieutenant, Stump," Aldo said, bowing while looking up at all the droppings on the leaves above their heads.

"Ah now that is more like it. Yes, I know of the Great Oak, my kind has had occasion to fly past it in search of sustenance. I am Free of the Flying Foxes, and you Oak Mice are on the outer edge of our camp. Tell me, what is it you seek here?" he asked, hanging with one wing closed while the other fanned cool air around himself.

"We are looking for a possible new site for our commune. You see, to the rising of Brother Sun, large pale ones have savaged the land. Though at this leaf fall that is not our main concern," Aldo stated.

"Yes, I have indeed seen these pale creatures. They throw things at our kind, to stop us from taking what has always been ours to share. The sweetness of the gifts Sister Trees give us is to be shared and now they dare try stop us. Bother to them, I say. Just do as my kind and many feathered wing kind do and place a well placed dropping on them. Ha that makes them dance and wave about." Free laughed, flapping his wings.

Aldo lowered himself into a sitting position and said, "I wish it was so simple. Sadly, they have brought new rats, mice and cockroaches to our land. They are our greatest threat. You see, we have been told they deceitfully destroy treaties and create wars. Then they move in and take everything in their path themselves."

"Hm, they do sound distasteful creatures. Well, my new found friends, if you can stand some noise every now and then, usually when we return from feeding, you and your commune are most welcome. I, as an Elder, can assure you that much. I also guarantee some sky support for your fellow creatures," Free announced swinging on the branch.

"Thank you, oh Noble Free of the Flying Foxes. We shall take that into consideration when making our choice. Would you mind telling us approximately how many of your kind live here and about?" Aldo enquired, his neck becoming stiff from looking up.

"Our camp is a modest 200,000 but all are friendly and agreeable creatures," Free said in a friendly tone. "I must admit it would be nice to have other creatures close by to converse with. How many would you say are in your commune?"

"Well including the outposts, runners and this expedition it would be around 500 altogether," Stump said, re-entering the conversation, astounded by the size of Free's camp.

"Really, oh one of roundness, I am impressed 500,000 creatures. Why it might be a squeeze, but I am sure we can all fit in the area. While there are other communes about none have really staked claim to this spot. Mind you, I can not really understand why when it is so scenic."

"Sorry, Free, you misunderstood, our commune is only 500 creatures strong. Oh yes and then there is a similar number of the Servicers' of the Circle," Stump replied, rolling about trying to stand.

"Ah yes the Servicers. Tell me do they all follow the treaties strongly?" Free yawned and crossed his bat-like wings.

"Oh yes," Stump replied, rolled forward and finally stood.

"Well fine, we shall welcome them too," Free said with a screech. "Are you sure that is all your commune exists of? Please do not think me rude, but is it not rather small?"

"Aldo, Aldo," a cry came from the undergrowth, "A runner has come from the commune."

"Send the creature in," Aldo commanded, brushing his fur clean.

Leaf falls later a red meat-ant entered the clearing and ran up to Aldo. With a salute, he handed Aldo a leaf etched message.

As Aldo read the grim news his expression changed and he fell to his knees.

Stump hopped to his side. "What is it, Aldo?"

Speechless, Aldo handed Stump the message instead.

"You know I can not read such things," Stump whispered embarrassed. "What does it say?"

"The lightening of the woods after we left, the rats came just as Brother Sun rose." Aldo's voice was distant and mournful.

"Yes, go on," Stump pleaded.

"They attacked our kind and killed more than 150 of those we left behind. If it had not been for the Servicers' of the Circle all would have been lost. Noble Mar wants you and me to return immediately. We are to leave Breaker, the Bandicoot, in charge." Aldo stood again and attempted to compose himself.

Free, hearing the bad news swooped down from the tree, impressing both Stump and Aldo by his obvious size and strength. "Please do not think me rude but I could not help but overhear. While one does not wish to interfere, may I suggest I return you both to the Great Oak with haste? I shall ask my kind to watch over those you leave here. Indeed, I will also gather a few thousand of our guards to accompany us in this dark hour."

Aldo shocked but elated by Free's generous offer did not hesitate to accept.

Leaf falls later; Aldo looked down at Mother Earth from Free's back in wonder. "Stump this is a journey we will remember many lightenings. It is amazing how Free's kind glide so effortlessly from sister tree to sister tree." The kangaroo mouse glanced back and gasped. "Look at the size of the guard column following, Stump. Why there must be at least ten thousand flying foxes amongst it."

Wind buffeting his face Stump turned to his friend. "Forgive me, Aldo, if I fail to look. I am afraid my stomach churns so much that if I were to turn I would empty its contents."

 DARKENING EIGHT

Mouse lengths from the base of a giant Stringybark tree, the captives sat tied together. Fear raced through their minds as they huddled together and tried to rest.

Trix sat upright, when she felt the vine attached to her and the children loosen. *What is happening*, she thought.

Unbeknown to her mother, Hatty slipped away into the darkening. "That demon rat can not be allowed to harm another native," she mumbled to herself, crawling through the grass.

Quietly, she snuck to where the mouse who had stolen her father's sword slept. There from the shadows she reached out her shaking paw and grasped the hilt of the weapon.

Her heart stopped when the invader rolled to face her. *Steady yourself mouse*, she thought, *he is still asleep*. Gathering her courage again she slowly dragged the sword back into the darkness.

"Now to do what father would, for the sake of all natives." Hatty moved swiftly to the rat commander's temporary nest.

Hatty ducked under a large fern frond and stopped. The dark rat, deep in slumber, let out a loud snort as she approached. She paused and watched as the rat's chest raised and lowered. Certain it was asleep she moved out of the darkness to its side.

Her heart pounding she stood examining the large rat's ugly features. Then as a vision of her lost friends flashed, before her eyes, she drew the sword and drove it into the demon creature's chest.

The rat's body contorted and then the vile creature's heart beat its last.

Tongue the bringer of truth hissed as she withdrew it, only to let out a moaning noise as she placed it back into mouth the scabbard. *What have I done?* she thought, *surely now they will punish us even more.*

The echo of a stick cracking, not far from her position, captured her attention. In panic she darted away and returned the sword to the mouse's side.

They could well lay the blame for the murder on him and leave us natives alone, she thought dashing back to the captives.

Trix wriggled uneasily as the vine moved again. "What on Mother Earth is going on?" she whispered to herself.

Leaning forward she looked down the line of children toward Hatty.

Sensing her mother's unease, Hatty raised her arm to show her mother all was well.

Even in the darkness Trix could see what appeared to be a liquid dripping off her offspring's paw.

"Oh, Hatty what have you been up to?" Trix sighed, well aware of her daughter's independent streak.

LIGHTENING OF THE WOODS NINE

Meric, the Prince of the black mice, woke as the sun's rays filtered through his makeshift dwelling's leaves. Standing, he stretched and moved to the entrance.

Leaning against a sapling, Meric gazed out at his captives. *What is my part in all this? How could I be a party to such savagery?*

The grasses before him parted, an invading mouse appeared and bowed. "Prince Meric, upon this morn, a guard went to wake Captain Rol of the Rats and found him slain," Lenthric said, nervously looking around the long grass.

Meric ran back inside and picked up the sword. Feeling a sticky substance on his paw he held it up to a slither of sunshine and found it covered with blood. Dumbfounded, he attempted to draw the sword from its sheath, only to throw it to the ground in frustration when it would not release.

"Prince, do you think the creatures of this land may have tracked us down? They may well lay in wait to kill us, one by one." Lenthric's whiskers twitched, as he backed away staring at the bloodied sheathe.

"Fear not friend. It is more than likely one of his kind killed him. After all he was not well liked. I too would have run him through on numerous occasions given the opportunity. In fact, go back to where he slept, cover him with leaves and say nothing of it to the others. Let them think him a deserter."

"My Prince, there is more."

"Go on."

Lenthric moved close enough to whisper, "A small creature's bones were found near his camp."

Meric's eyes went dark with anger as he crawled out from under the large leaves, his worse fears confirmed.

"Lenthric, have our captives brought into the shade of these trees. Who ordered them placed in the open?"

"Rol did, my Prince." Lenthric moved to carry out his orders.

"Hold, friend, I shall walk with you. Do you know why he did it?" Meric asked, waving his paw toward the captives.

"To use them as bait to draw the birds away from us."

"Idiot! They will not attack them. It is obvious some kind of agreement exists between the animals of this land. Have you not noticed the winged ones watching us? Come Lenthric, you must have wondered why they had not attacked."

"Of course I had."

"It is obvious they have been sent to observe not to confront us. They fear for the safety of these natives and as such will not attack while they are in our possession. That is another reason why Rol was an idiot," Meric declared, kicking a pebble.

The Prince drew closer to Hatty, stopped and did something unusual for him; he examined Hatty's vine shackles. Noticing some blood, rubbed on the grass near her, the Prince smiled broadly, raised an eyebrow and walked on.

Trix cringed as the dark mouse came toward her, bowed politely and walked past to summon the other invaders from their sleep.

#   #   #

Deep within the confines of the Great Silky Oak, Petra of the Possum, sat dismayed. Upon returning from surveying the sickness in the commune, she had asked Belor to summon Bega.

"I am sorry, Noble Petra, but Elder Bega can not be found, and his dwelling has not been used." Nervous, Belor's tail swung back and forth.

"Send word to Prince Crier's and Betra's kind, that a sickness has come upon the commune. Beseech them to pass that news on to Chieftain Mar and the others."

"Immediately, Noble Petra." the blue tongue lizard rushed out to find Grey.

Grey of the Gecko scurried up the noble Oak to pass on the grim new to the cicadas.

#   #   #

"Antoni, tell me do you feel that we are still being observed?" Mar asked, pacing around a small stinging tree.

Antoni climbed a small trunk to retrieve some sap and leapt down. "I do, Chieftain, but I would have thought it only to be expected with our sky support. The bats and cicadas do watch over us and constantly survey ahead."

"Hm, I suppose that could be so. However, I feel something more; it is as if somebody or something is watching over us. Do you still believe in spirits, without bodies, Antoni?" In mock battle, Mar swung his staff against a dead branch.

"After all the things I have seen in my lightenings, I can not honestly say, I do not believe in spirits." Antoni drew his sword and thrust it into the sap.

Sensing movement approaching, the friends raised their heads.

"Forgive me, Chieftain, Prince Crier's kind have received a message from Betra Bat's guards. The invaders are breaking camp, what are your orders?" Lea respectfully asked, bowed and revealed his wrinkled frill neck.

"Antoni, how many mouse lengths to you think we have gained on them?"

His mouth full of sticky sap, the bull-ant found it impossible to answer and shrugged instead.

Mar shook his head in disbelief, hopped toward Brother Sun and spun around, "Lea, wake the others, we must depart this leaf fall."

#   #   #

"Toemouse, wake now," Attic said, undoing the vines that had held Toe in the gum tree during the darkening. "Father and others leave, we follow, yes?"

"Attic, is there any sign of the vile creatures that are trailing behind father?" Toe asked, rolling the vine up and tucking it over his shoulder.

"Last darkening, me look back where we came from. Yes, still some shadows follow. This lightening, though not as many as last," Attic said, flicking his vine out like a whip to catch the branch of the next tree.

Toe walked along the narrow branch."Attic, did you take the breath from them?"

"No, not me. Large one from commune behind. He takes breath, not me. Now come," Attic said, grabbed Toe under his arm and sung to the next tree with the aid of the vine.

147

"Attic, could we at least change these large leaves, we wear to help us blend into the trees? They make me itch so."

"No. Leaves good until sun sleeps, then we change. By then, different trees we must blend with." With that, Attic repeated the process and swung to another tree.

"I see," Toe replied, as they scurried down its trunk.

They lay on the forest floor, scrambled across a small clearing and up another tree.

Gripping the bark with all four paws Toe reflected, *With every leaf fall I learn so much from you, Attic. So much, in fact, your knowledge of the bush astounds me.*

#   #   #

The Chieftain of the Oak gazed at the dense underbrush ahead, turned and noticed one of his comrades missing. "Where is the Princess, this lightening?"

Antoni lifted his head to look at his friend. "Squorth begs your pardon, Mar. She left last darkening to scout ahead, as only she can in her way," he replied, a strange look on his face.

"Yes, I remember her scouting expeditions in the Red Back Wars. How many was it, we calculated, she left without spirit?" Mar hopped along quietly through the dense leaf cover.

While Antoni took the high ground, along a log, in an attempt to keep up with his friend. "I am not sure, Mar, but it did exceed Gregor of the Grasshoppers, Peter of the Preying Mantises, yours and mine, combined. That I do remember."

"I had hoped that to be my last taste of battle, Antoni. To tell the truth, I grew weary of adventure many lightenings of the woods ago. That was why I took the position of Noble Oak Mouse. Now here this leaf fall, I pursue yet another enemy, only this time, they have all that I hold precious," Mar said, lowering his head.

"War is something I think any knowledgeable creature dreads. Made worse, when it is against others of ones own kind, so to speak. When it is with such creatures, who were your long time neighbours and friends, it becomes too difficult. I have no wish to slay any creature, let alone a friend. It upset me to such an extent that I very rarely take sustenance on any bodies left in our Stone Circle. In truth I have taken to eating more vegetation," Antoni spoke honestly, as he scurried along at Mar's shoulder height.

Without warning, one of Prince Crier's kind landed on a tree in front of Mar and Antoni.

Antoni rushed ahead and spoke to the messenger. Mar could tell from a distance, by the speed of the insect's tongue, the news was not good.

"Tell me, Antoni; is it news of Trix, Toe and Hatty?" Mar called, thrusting at a sapling with his staff in anger.

"Sorry, Mar, it is news of the commune I have received." Antoni's tone was deep and solemn.

"Go on," Mar implored, still practising.

Antoni walked back and placed his front leg on Mar's shoulder.

"Many creatures are sick by an unseen enemy. Some of the Servicers' of the Circle, who took some of the dark creatures' flesh, are dying. While others who drank the water down from the commune, are ill. Petra is fearful that many spirits will be stolen this very lightening."

Mar held up his paw, stopped the march and informed the others of the commune's plight. Sadly, he, and his friends, knew they could do nothing other than pray to Father Sky and Mother Earth for the commune's survival.

There beneath the leaves of the banksias, with the

scent of wattle flowers in the air, they knelt in prayer.

#   #   #

Forced to push their way through thick grasses the captive natives struggled along the bush floor. Trix tried her best to keep the younger ones from thinking of what was yet to come. Both she and Hatty sang songs, in the common tongue, of their much beloved home.

Prince Meric enjoyed the soft melodies echoing through the trees around them. Somehow, it reminded him of the songs his mother used to sing to him long ago. *How I long to leave this land, where it was always hot, and journey back to my country of origin.*

Homesick, he allowed the prisoners to pass and fell back to Lenthric's position at the very rear of the column.

"Ah, to smell the great pines again and to drink from the cool sweet water of the lakes, aye, Lenthric," Meric said to his old friend.

"I too dream of such things, my Prince," Lenthric replied, as he walked behind the last of the captives.

"You know, even though the rats are our cousins, I still have no great love of their kind. Most of all I hate their savage ways. Why on this earth my father let Yahn, the King of the Brown Rats, talk him into such a journey mystifies me?"

The prince leant in closer to his friend. "I believe he deliberately deceived my father and the others into boarding the giant wooden crafts. Now, many months away from home, they wage war on creatures for whom I have not got one feeling of hatred.

"I and others feel the same, Prince."

"The rats are fools! If it had not been for them over populating, the food supplies would not have run so desperately low. It was that alone that made them turn away from the ports and head inland for survival. Now, the rats have discovered how easy it is to take what they want from peaceful creatures.

"Nothing but greed drove the powers that be to send our forces out to sweep the land and make it theirs. They disgust me! Now the fat leaders, yes even my father, sit in their nests having food brought to them. To make matters worse, to ensure continued supplies, they have taken to abducting these natives and now force them to do their work. What was found near Rol, also confirmed my greatest fears." Meric's head hung heavily on his shoulders with sorrow.

"What is it, Meric, that troubles you so?" Lenthric asked, reverting to how he addressed his friend when they were young.

"I fear the detestable rats have actually taken to devouring native creatures. Worse still, they have actually acquired a taste for their flesh." Throwing caution to the wind Meric screamed, "I hate this land and what I am being forced to do!"

Then as the tail end of the column broke out of the undergrowth into a field of wild flowers; his heavy heart lifted for a moment.

#   #   #

At the head of the column, Chieftain Mar began to formulate a plan as they grew closer to the kidnappers.

While at the rear, Dodd practised manoeuvres with his weapon. As the staff returned to his left paw, the young mouse sensed something behind him. Falling back, he heard a loud crack come from the bushes.

"I will hide under the shadow of the next tree," he mumbled to himself, and disappeared around the trunk to wait.

Within leaf falls an odd looking mouse stumbled through the undergrowth.

His foresight rewarded, Dodd jumped out from behind the tree and yelled, "Hold,"

For but a leaf fall, their eyes met before the strange mouse leapt at Dodd, a sharpened stick in its front paw.

Stunned by the ferocity of the attack, Dodd dropped his staff and was soon in a wrestling match with his opponent. Rolling over and over on the moist ground they tumbled amongst the leaves.

"Stop! Stop!" he yelled, fending off the attack. "I have no wish to hurt you. I wish only to ask some questions."

The other mouse, screaming in a foreign tongue, took little notice of his pleas. It nipped and ripped at Dodd's arms while attempting to drive the stick into his heart.

Finally, after leaf falls of holding the mouse off, Dodd tucked his powerful legs under his opponent's body and pushed with all his might. He would remember the mouse's face, forever, as it flew across the small clearing. Hitting the ground with a thud the mouse did not move.

Dodd pushed himself upright and waited for another onslaught. When it did not come he held his staff out in front of him and carefully moved forward to investigate.

"By Mother Earth, what have I done?" he gasped, realising the mouse was without spirit.

Upon closer inspection he noticed what appeared to be a large wound in the mouse's side. *Could I have done that,* he thought, *or was it the struggle that reopened it?*

Remorseful, he stood looking down at the mouse. "You appear not to be too much older than me."

With tears in his eyes, he knelt and wept for the departed spirit.

Ever cautious, Mar turned and checked the numbers in his squad. Unable to see Dodd he jumped up onto a log and checked again. "Lea," he shouted, panic struck, "where is Dodd?"

Lea sprang round, flared his neck, pushed some grass aside and was amazed to find Dodd gone.

"Chieftain, he was here but a leaf fall ago," Lea replied, raising himself onto his hind legs to look over the undergrowth.

Chief Antoni, immediately took off in one direction as Mar, Lea and the lizards went straight back down their path.

Antoni called to the cicadas, in their tongue "Have you seen Dodd?"

"No," Crysalid answered, taking flight to search.

Not too far away, Mar was relieved to see Dodd up ahead in a small clearing.

"EEE," Mar squeaked in a high whistle, recognisable only to his son.

The Chieftain watched in horror as a dark shadow plummeted from the sky above Dodd's head. "Look out, Dodd," Mar screamed, pointing up to the sky.

Still in shock from his fight, Dodd staggered toward his father unaware of what was coming up behind him.

"No, stop," Mar screeched, in hawk, waving his staff above his head.

In the end he could do nothing but helplessly watch the mighty Hawk scoop Dodd up in its talons.

Antoni, who had come around behind Mar, also shrieked with anger as he watched the hawk disappear into the distance.

The searchers did not have long to ponder Dodd's fate as out of the bush, on the other side of the clearing, a band of five large invading rats crashed out into the sunlight.

Ducking down into the leaf cover, Mar and Antoni watched on as the rats looked over the mouse and checked the clearing.

"It won't be long before they find our scent; I hope Lea

and his lizards get here soon."

"Perhaps we should return to the others, Chieftain." Antoni whispered, in ant. "There are too many for you and me to face alone."

The leaf fall he finished speaking, Lea and his lizards, necks fully flared and ready for battle, rushed into the clearing. Leaving them little choice but to confront the creatures, Mar and Antoni moved forward. Soon four ferocious bearded dragons appeared from nowhere and entered the foray.

#   #   #

I must escape, Dodd thought as he struggled with all his might to free himself from the hawk's talons. Despite the fact he knew he would more than likely fall to his death, he continued to squirm.

"Stop struggling, young one," the hawk commanded.

"No. I shall struggle until you drop me. I would prefer my spirit to leave me as I hit the ground then lose it as you tear at me with your beak."

Dodd felt Father Sky's wind rush past him as the hawk stopped in mid-air and began to dive again. All his short life flashed before his eyes as he hurtled toward the ground while in the hawk's grasp.

"Stop wriggling. This is difficult enough with you held in my talons," the hawk protested.

Dodd took no notice and struggled even harder while poking the hawk's underbelly with his staff.

"Stop it now, mouse, or I will drop you. By the River Stones, you are like your father, stubborn!"

"You know my father?" Dodd asked relieved.

"Of course I do. I am Highra the Hawk, Servicer of the Circle of the Great Oak. Did you not recognise me, mouse?"

"Well," Dodd yelled, above the sound of rushing air.

"Forgive me, Noble Highra, but thankfully I have never seen thee from this position before this leaf fall. Why is it, you took me in such an odd way?"

"Look ahead on the ground to where we came from. I saw those rats coming upon you and could see little choice but to take such an action.

"I have been following them since the lightening of their attack, on the great Oak, along with my brother hawks," Highra squealed, put his wings out to slow their descent and let Dodd fall to the side of the clearing onto some soft leaves.

In one swift movement the hawk had swept low across the grasses and was in full battle with the rats.

Dodd, quite dizzy from his rapid descent, could do little more than watch on as the mighty fight came to a successful conclusion for the commune's creatures.

Mar ran to his son and embraced him with all the strength he could muster, "Praise Father Sky for delivering you back to us safely. And of course you, Noble Highra of the Hawks, eeek to you."

"Metcha, Chieftain Mar, tell me was your mouse a terrible wriggler as a young mouse?" Highra asked, winking at Dodd.

"What else was I to do? I thought you were going to make a snack out of me." Dodd pushed his father away to search for his staff in the bushes.

"Never, young mouse, you are indeed already too tough for me," Highra exclaimed, turning to Mar with another wink. "Do not fear the winged ones of this area or ahead. My brothers have already told the tale of the evil creatures attack on our peaceful commune. They only find sustenance on the foreign mice now and are aware of the commune's captives in the lightenings ahead."

"How can you tell from such a great distance oh Noble Highra, who is who?" Dodd innocently asked.

"Oh we can see, my dear child. I must warn you though not to let any of your followers, Chieftain Mar, sustain themselves on the brown or black rats' meat. One of my brothers took but a taste and was ill to such an extent, we left him behind in a cousin's nest." Highra held his head high turning to survey the area.

"Sadly, we have worked out such news for ourselves. You see Highra our commune is stricken with the sickness. Petra has sent word to us, it may strip the spirits of many of our fellow creatures," Mar informed the hawk, while gazing with pride at his son.

Highra went silent, deep in thought for the family he had left alone on that fateful lightening. He could only hope they had kept to the Celebration of Sustenance after the battle and never partaken of the invaders' flesh.

"Now, Chieftain, I await your command and I shall summon my brothers to attack the kidnappers of children and consumers of eggs ahead," Highra said, holding his head proudly in a salute to Mar.

"Thank you, Highra, for your wisdom. I only wish I knew when we could attack the creatures so as to ensure our families' safety.

"As of yet the reports we have received have told us that our loved ones are bound and continuously guarded. What I fear most though, is that with any sign of trouble the dark ones will slay them.

"So helplessly we still wait and watch." Mar said, his mind now back with the rest of his family.

#   #   #

From high above the canopy of the forest Free, of the Flying Foxes, caught a glimpse of the Noble Oak. Her branches appeared to be beckoning him to her embrace.

"Shall I land in the Great Oak, Commander Aldo?" Free asked, approaching the commune.

"Yes, that would be excellent. Free, could you ask your kinds' guard to land before the commune? I am afraid my friends have hardly ever seen such a force, en mass, and it may well make them fearful," Aldo called, the current ruffling the fur around his eyes.

"I understand." Free turned his head and squawked to Screecher, his wing commander, "Flying foxes land immediately and wait for further orders."

Without a sound, Free glided into the Oak about halfway up the trunk and landed on a main branch.

Leaf falls later Grey the Gecko popped his head out of a small opening. "Oh it is you Aldo and Stump, may the River Stones be praised," he said coughing loudly. "Now go away!" Without another word Grey turned and disappeared into the darkness.

"What an unusual greeting," Free said, peering into the hole. Even though they are a large bat, flying foxes still have quite remarkable sight.

It was not long before Grey popped out again only this time with a leaf-etching. The little gecko gave Free a peculiar look, handed the leaf etching to Aldo, and disappeared with, "Now go away, without delay, or risk falling sick."

As Aldo read the message out loud the tone of his voice changed dramatically:

> "The commune has an unseen enemy which is stealing many creatures' spirits. Please seek out Mar, directly toward Brother Sun's rising. The invaders have taken some of our young and he will need your help.
>
> "It is not safe for any of our creatures to leave this area for fear we may take the Spirit Stealer to attack other harmless natives. We must wait and pray that Mother Earth and Father Sky will

deliver us from these dark lightenings.

"It is signed with Petra's paw."

Fearful, Free looked around at the ground below. He could just make out small piles of creatures' bodies lying out in the open. Unbeknown to the flying fox, before him were the bodies of one of every species of creature in the commune.

Aldo rolled up the leaf etching and held it in his shaking paw. "Free, we must leave. Could you ask your guard to return to the rain-forest and tell Breaker not to let any creatures return here? Stump and I must go on to the rising of Brother Sun in search of our Noble Mar," Aldo said, as he too looked down at the once bustling gathering area; now a field of death.

The flying fox draped his wings across his chest. "I shall do as you wish. However, I shall send but a few back to warn our camp and your creatures of expedition. With your permission I, and others, will accompany you on your quest. I feel it imperative we stop these invaders. In the meantime my kind will aid those winged ones, who are able, in the defence of your commune here."

"Indeed, you have amazed me with your kinds' generosity." Aldo bowed.

"One never knows, what another creature is like, if they do not take time to talk. Now do they?" Free nodded and laid his wing down for them to climb up. "Now, I am to take it your Noble Mouse is many lightenings away from here. So even on wing it is best we leave without delay."

The large bat jumped off the branch and was soon aloft again heading for the spotted gum tree where his wing commander.

Screecher, hung with his wings draped around him looking at the ground below in horror.

Up in the trees not far from Mar's position, Attic and Toe remained undetected. Attic walked back and forth nervously, neither of them aware of the attack on Mar's rescue party.

"What is wrong, Attic, you look puzzled?"

Attic sat on the branch of the stringybark still searching for signs. "Me not sure where go, many smells in area confuse nose." He rubbed his nose with his paw as if trying to clear it.

"You mean we are lost?" Toe asked, very concerned.

"Lost, what be lost?" Attic turned, his deep dark eyes looking for answers.

Toe thought for a moment and answered, "Lost is when you can not find your way home or what you are looking for." Toe tried to sound as wise as possible under the circumstances.

"Hm." Attic lifted his paw and scratched his scruffy chin. "Then we not lost, can never be lost. Me home in trees and this where we be," he said, stroking the rough bark beneath him like an old friend.

"Oh, you do not understand," Toe said, groaning in frustration.

"Ah, now me know where go," Attic said, springing up to his feet and sprinting along the branch.

"How so? Have you seen father?" Toe asked, pushing himself up.

"No! Look there, in long grass, is large one from commune. He goes where we go, so me and Toemouse follow large one." The wild mouse pointed toward the bandicoot and leapt onto the trunk.

Looking in the direction Attic had pointed, Toe noticed the large form of Bega crash out of the long grass with his staff lashing from side to side.

Before Attic could do anything Toe had let out a large scream that echoed throughout the trees for some distance. "ELDER BEGA UP HERE! HERE! HERE!

HERE."

Attic scurried back up the trunk and shoved his paw across Toe's mouth and whispered, "Not safe, Toemouse, not now. No noise you make, understand!"

"By the River Stones!" Bega exclaimed, looking around, "That sounded like Toe."

From the darkness of the foliage three invading rats swamped Bega, instantly pinning him to the ground. The bandicoot could do nothing as they ripped and tore at his flesh.

Attic looked at Toe with disappointment in his eyes as he said, "Stay, Toemouse, or me tie to tree trunk and come back when mother and father found safe."

Within an instant Attic was whisking across the tree-tops leaping from branch to branch. By the time he reached Elder Bega, the bandicoot had regained his stance and was taking on the three rats with his staff.

Even though Bega had quite an advantage in size, he did not, however, have the vitality his youth once gave him in a fight and began to tire. With one rat attacking his back and two lunging at him from the front Bega knew he had little hope.

Using the advantage the height of the trees gave him, Attic hurled himself at the rat on Bega's flank and landed square on its back. Digging his legs into the rat's neck and squeezing, he grabbed the rat's ears and lead it full gallop into one of the other rats, successfully knocking both of them out for an instant.

Realising the fight was lost the third invader fled, like the cowards their kind are, leaving the other two to fend for themselves.

Bega turned and looked at Attic for the first time. Somehow he was transported back many lightenings to when he and Mar Mouse had fought side by side. Blood dripping from his brow, he let out a sigh, "Mar," before he collapsed in front of Attic on the ground.

Attic disappeared into the bushes and returned with some herbs and vines. With the vines he hog tied the two shadow creatures up to a tree, in an open area for all eyes to see. Then he proceeded to mix the herbs with mud and smear them on Bega's wounds.

"Many cuts large one," he said, gently touching Bega's forehead. "Soon you be better. Me watch over you, as me see you do for others so many times."

"Look out," Toe cried, now hiding behind a wattle sapling near by.

Jumping up Attic saw the face of the other rat racing towards him. Standing still, and straight, as a young sapling he waited without a flinch until the rat was practically upon him. Then he reached up with one leg while pivoting on the other and in one swift precise blow kicked the rat in the windpipe.

Shocked, it fell to the ground gasping for air at Attic's feet.

"Quickly, Toemouse, more vines," Attic yelled, leaping onto its back.

Toe rushed into the undergrowth and grabbed some more vines.

Within leaf falls of receiving the vines Attic also had it hog tied.

"Toemouse told stay," Attic said, without a missed placed puff of air after dragging and tying the three rats together.

"I know, Attic, but I thought I could help when I saw the rat circle around and return," Toe replied, pointing with his paw to where the shadow creature had emerged.

"Hm. I think Toemouse perhaps did good." Attic lifted Toe off the ground and whirled him around as Dodd had done so many times.

Once again, Toe was struck by the uncanny

resemblance between Attic and his brother Dodd.

"Now we hide and protect large one," Attic declared, lowering his friend. "Toemouse, help drag large one into bushes over there, yes."

Slowly, the two struggled to move Bega's large body into the shadows of the ferns where he would be safe.

The talented wild mouse soon used some vines to sew together some ferns into a humble dwelling. "Stay," he said to Toe, and within a leaf fall was gone.

Attic returned just before darkening, checked the three rats' vines and made his way back to Toe and Bega.

"Where did you learn how to care for others?" Toe asked, as Attic pounded some roots with a stone.

"Watch, Toemouse, me always watch. Now give this to large one, then he will rest all darkening. In lightening, he will be somewhat better." Attic's large brown eyes glistened as a reassuring smile crossed his face.

DARKENING NINE

Bega lay moaning while Attic carefully wiped his face with a damp piece of moss.

"Mar, where are you?" Bega called, with a ghostly cry, in his native tongue of bandicoot.

Attic turned to a worried Toe. "Toemouse take moss to stream and lay in water. Bring back with haste."

"Attic, I have no idea where the stream is. Can we not get enough moisture off the leaves, as we have been doing?" Toe reached up and pulled a leaf down only to find no water at all.

"Not right leaf fall," Attic replied, without lifting his head from the task at hand.

Sniffing the air, he turned and pointed past the grey gum that stood high above the ferns. "Water there, no more than forty of my lengths away. Now go, and be quiet."

Pulling up some moss, Toe began to creep out of the small dwelling into the grasses.

"I make noise of large one, with giant eyes, so you can find your way back," Attic whispered as Toe left.

As quietly as he could Toe hopped the short distance to the stream. Just as his hind paws splashed in the water he heard a subtle, "Mopoke," from where he had come. Wasting no time he lowered the moss into the water, damped it and turned.

"Plop," was the noise Toe heard from the other bank of the small stream. Crouching, he watched on as two small mice, speaking quietly in neither native mouse nor the common tongue, came to the water to drink. Waiting and watching, as they sat on the bank, Toe wondered what they were doing there at all.

"Mopoke," Toe heard again breaking the silence of the darkening.

It seemed like an eternity to Toe as he waited for the invading mice to leave. Silently, he popped out from the bushes and gently immersed the moss in the water again.

"Mopoke," the call came from behind him for the third time at a regular interval.

Rushing back through the unfamiliar undergrowth Toe lost his bearings. Out of nowhere he heard a second, different, "Mopoke" sound cut through the air.

Stopping for a leaf fall he tried to see any familiar plants that would possibly identify the direction he was to travel. Sadly, as he rushed away, he had failed to take note of any landmarks. Staring up from this position he thought, *all the trees look the same to me*.

"Mopoke," came from one area. Then, nearly straight afterwards, Toe heard another "Mopoke," from the opposite direction.

Confused, the poor little mouse made a decision and hopped toward the closest call. Gazing around the area he found no shelter but instinctively sensed some large eyes fixed on his every movement.

"No!" Toe blurted out thinking quickly. Within a breath of wind, a large boobook owl stood before him on the ground. Looking up into the creature's eyes, he shook with unbridled terror.

"Metcha, little native. May I ask, what on Mother Earth

are you doing wandering the woods this darkening when the evil creatures lurk about?" Perched on an old fallen tree the owl turned her head from side to side.

"Mo, mo....," Toe stuttered, staring at the bird's large talons.

"Oh fear not, child, my kind still follow all treaties with our fellow natives. Allow me to introduce myself, my title is Breath of the Boobook Kind," she said, bowing with grace, "and you are, child?"

"I am Toe of the Great Oak, son of Chieftain Mar the Noble Oak Mouse," he said, proudly but nervously, returning the bow; reluctant to take his eyes off the owl.

"Ah, now that is more like it." Hearing a distinct "Mopoke", Breath turned. "What is that creature doing using our call for meeting?" she questioned.

"It is my friend, Attic. He uses the call to guide me back from the stream. You see, it was my job to wet the moss for Elder Bega. Our Elder, has been badly injured by some foreign rats." Toe looked down at the moss in his paw and was relieved to see it still moist.

"Injured," Breath exclaimed, obviously concerned.

"Yes, he was attacked by three large rats this past lightening. Attic is aiding his spirit to stay in his body by looking after him." Toe held out the moss in his paws. "This damp moss is meant to help him."

"How very interesting. Come, I shall take you to your friend. The winged ones of this area have been told, by Brother Highra, that your father and others are amongst us. Climb on my neck child and we will be there in but a leaf fall." Breath lowered her head to the ground.

Toe quickly climbed up and held on tightly to her feathers. Finally, I will soar, the little mouse thought. His heart lifted as the owl took off into the darkness. Watching on he smiled as the large Sister Gum Trees whizzed past. Within what only seemed the wink of an eye, they had landed near the ferns where Breath had tracked the quiet "Mopoke" call.

Attic knew long before Breath landed a winged one of the night was drawing closer. When he heard the ferns bend, as Breath landed, he dashed out from the dwelling with a leaf in each paw.

To Toe's amusement the wild, larger, mouse began a strange comical dance.

Breath did nothing as she stood proudly and watched on.

Toe, not realising what was happening, went to dismount only to hear the owl whisper.

"Stay child, he is not finished! We do not wish to offend, do we?"

Without giving a verbal greeting Attic spun in a circle, as he danced with the leaves held out like wings, then knelt before Breath.

"Bravo, young native, bravo. You have indeed honoured me this darkening. How delightful," Breath exclaimed. "Well indeed, I have not been greeted in my kinds' traditional dance by another creature, why it must be in hundreds of lightenings of the woods. Thank you, young mouse and metcha," Breath said, deeply flattered by Attic's greeting.

"Me heart feel light, at your sight, oh Large Eyed One." Attic laid the two leaves in front of him signalling the end of the greeting.

"Oh you speak ever so nicely." Turning to Toe, concealed in her feathers, she said, "You may hop off now, child."

As soon as Toe hit the ground, Attic leapt to his side and hugged him. Holding him out at arms length, he said, "Where you go, Toemouse? I hope you not annoy oh Great Seer of the Dark. Now take the moss, you must put on large one's head. Go."

Toe rushed into the bushes, where Bega lay still unconscious and gently duplicated Attic's caring ways.

"Your brother was no trouble at all, native. Indeed, I am glad he found me, as I am still tingling from your wonderful greeting." Breath lowered her head in gratitude.

"Me know not the meaning of brother. Toemouse be friend," Attic said, scratching his left ear.

"Oh, how odd, I just assumed when you looked so alike that you must be from the same litter, never mind. Tell me, oh Dancer in the Dark, can I help you in any way? Or perhaps, I can call some of my kind and we can relieve you of your prisoners." Leaning further down she continued, "You see, in all honesty, our kind have found we can sustain ourselves on the dark ones as long as we do not touch the inners."

"Me guest you be," Attic said, pointing to where the rats looked on wide eyed.

"Farewell." Breath flapped her wings, seized the rats' restraints and with a gigantic push lifted them off the ground. "May Father Sky watch over you," she hooted disappearing into the darkness.

"Attic," Toe quietly called, "Bega is stirring."

Happy, the scruffy kangaroo mouse hopped into the rough shelter, pulled Bega's eyelids up and looked into his pupils.

"Good, he soon be of one spirit and body." Looking up into the trees Attic grabbed Toe's arm and stood. "Soon lightening comes, now we must leave for trees before large one wakens."

"No," Toe said, wrenching his paw back and stepping to Bega's side. "I will not leave." The small mouse plonked himself down with defiance, on the damp grass.

"Alright, Toe, but me leave. Sad me be," Attic said, turned and hopped away.

"If your sad, then why not stay," Toe pleaded, standing again to administer more herbs to his patient.

"Not sad because go, as me never alone. Sad because this lightening, me was going to teach Toemouse Stinger's tongue, so you be friends,"

Attic reached up and pulled the vines from around the ferns. Instantly the shelter was gone as if it had never been there at all.

"Are you sure he will be alright?" Toe asked, looking down at the large Bandicoot, he cared for like a grandfather.

"Me sure, as Brother Sun rises. So come now?" Attic did a little jig of joy.

Toe leant down and gently hugged Bega.

Attic walked over and put his front leg over Toe's shoulder. "We watch and protect him from high."

As Toe and Attic left, Brother Sun began to filter through the canopy. Silently, they donned their camouflage and sat in a tree above Bega to wait until he wakened.

LIGHTENING OF THE WOODS TEN

Each carrying a baby creature Hatty and Trix stumbled along the forest floor. The invading rats marched up and down checking their captives as they went.

Prince Meric, of the foreign mice, came across an area where the bush began thinning out and pushed some saplings aside; before them lay great strips of land void of trees.

"Hold," Meric commanded. Turning, he looked for Lenthric to consult. "Do not move the prisoners another inch, Borton. I am going to find Lenthric."

Walking back down the line of prisoners, to find his second in command, Meric noticed a rat glaring at the native captives.

"Do you not think their hearts are not full of fear enough, rat, without you glaring at them so? Go to the front of the column and report to Borton." Meric walked the few paces to his friend.

Lenthric moved forward to greet Meric so their conversation would not be overheard. Sweeping his paw in front of his chest, he greeted, "Good morning, my Prince." Bowing his head, he continued, "I see a pleasant night did not improve your feelings toward the rats. I must warn you, to be careful in your dealings with them, Prince. I have heard grumblings in their ranks; they could easily slay us and claim it was done by the creatures of this land." Lenthric's head and eyes moved nervously from side to side.

Placing a paw on his friend's shoulder Meric smiled, "Let them try. I am starting to think I would prefer an early death than to carry out the orders of the king rat."

"You may have a death wish, my Prince, but I have a family that I wish to return to."

"Alright, I promise not to start anything. Now, Lenthric, we must wait here again until nightfall. It is here I have arranged to meet the other advance party. So be a good mouse and guide all the creatures into the shadows and wait. I shall dash across the field and wait for Reon near that great tree, as arranged."

"Meric, some of the other mice have asked if we should leave these creatures bound here and make for our home with haste. With each day that passes they have become certain we are being followed. After all, our captives are only dumb savage creatures far removed from ourselves. Why they can't even speak our tongue," Lenthric said, in a matter of fact kind of way.

"Lenthric, I am surprised at you. Have you never thought it is we who could well be the savages? It is after all us who are new to this land. No one in command even thought to try to learn their tongue, before attacking them so savagely," Meric said, angrily turning to head for the tree, about three hundred mouse lengths away.

"I do hope you have not gone soft, Prince Meric," a voice called from the shadows. "You know what my king does to mice who turn away from his chosen ways," the despicable rat Velor said, crawling out from under some banksia leaves and squinting his eyes at the rising sun.

Running to the head of the column Meric completely ignored the rat's comments. Velor, not far behind sneered as Meric stopped near Trix.

Softly, Meric put his paw down on the baby pigmy possum's head, Trix carried, and smiled. "I am so deeply sorry for my part in your capture," the Prince whispered. "You, dear mouse, with your kind ways, remind me of my mother." With that Meric straightened and moved on.

Further toward the front of the column, Hatty kicked at the prince as he passed. "You shall not eat that baby, you barbarian, I vow that with my life." She continued to kick and lash out even after Meric had passed.

"Hatty," Trix cried, "do not annoy the leader. I feel he may be our only hope, amongst all these creatures. I see kindness in his eyes."

"Not likely!" Hatty protested, glaring at Velor as he passed. "I think he was testing the tenderness of young Pe and soon will devour him."

Leaf falls later; the guards came and pushed their captives back into the dark undergrowth.

Trix grimaced as Hatty kicked and scratched at them too. She became fearful, more than ever before, that her daughter's strong will would see her without spirit in the leaf falls to come.

Despair, a dark companion for anybody, filled her heart once more. Trix mumbled to herself as if in prayer, "Father Sky and Mother Earth let me know Mar, Dodd and Toe are safe. Please let there be survivors in our beloved commune."

Tears filled her eyes as she realised all hope of rescue may well be in vain. All these thoughts went through her mind as she huddled under the ground plants with the children snuggled close to her.

Suddenly, Trix felt the ground move beneath her feet and she jumped as a hairy leg gently rubbed against hers. She was not afraid as she looked down under the slightly lifted leaves, into the dark eyes of Princess Squorth of the Funnel-web Spiders.

"Come," Squorth whispered, as she snipped the vines with her powerful fangs.

Trix started passing some of the small babies down under the leaf but stopped as one of the rats came and sat nearby staring straight at her.

"Trix, I shall return for you and the others do not worry. It is only that we dare not take too many, at once, for fear of being detected." With that the leaf was down and Squorth and three of the children were gone.

Brother Sun was high in Father Sky before Meric arrived back.

Within leaf falls of his return, Trix noticed more rats and mice than before. The rats had other captives gathering at the edge of the clearing. Reaching down, she wisely tied the vines up securely, to hide all trace of the missing creatures.

Brutally, the rats herded the new arrivals up, poking them with sticks and nipping at them with their dirty long teeth.

Trix was stunned as prisoners from another commune joined their group.

Upon being tied together, Trix and Hatty's eyes met, for the first time, with Fena, Nila, Nel and Ji; Pon's and Fila's families.

"Metcha," Fena whispered to Trix as they were herded together, "I be Fena of the Ghost Gum, wife of Noble Pon."

Could it be, Trix thought as she reached out and gently touched Fena with her paw.
"I am Trix of the Great Oak, wife of Chieftain Mar. Tell me, did your mate talk of coming from the Oak?"

Fena simply nodded as the rats closed ranks around them, halting all conversations. There they sat, jammed closer than grains of sand, with more foreign rats and mice scattered amongst them, than ever before.

Hope of Squorth helping anymore to safety was lost.

\#   \#   \#

Tired from their forced march, Mar and Antoni took to the shadows to rest.

"Antoni, how far back do you think Lea and the bearded ones must go to ensure our safety? If we are to save my family, it is imperative that they succeed; we can not afford to face anymore surprise attacks. For if the invaders catch us unawares, exhausted as we are, they will defeat us," Mar said, resting in the shade of a tree.

Antoni took another bite out of a root and passed it to his friend. "Lea is good at his chosen field, he has already proven himself many times since we left."

Further back down the path Dodd sat quietly, with some of the frill-necked lizards, rubbing a long hard piece of stone he had picked up. Using a hard rock as a bench he pushed it back and forth polishing it.

"Ah," Dodd said, picking it up and looking down its length, "perfect."

Searching around him, he found a sliver of rock harder than his polished stone. Rubbing it between his paws fast enough to create friction, he managed to drill a hole for a vine to be tied on the end. Standing, Dodd moved to a tree and started scratching around in the grass.

"This vine should do the trick," the young mouse said, attaching it to the end of his long stone.

With a smile on his face, Dodd walked into a small clearing and began to swing his creation above his head. Waving to attract his father's attention, he never expected the stone would start to roar.

"What is it Dodd is waving above his head so wildly?" Mar asked standing and moving to get a clearer view.

"No, it could not be!" Antoni jumped to his feet and screamed, "Stop."

The warning was in vain, as the stone let out a huge humming roar.

Shocked, Dodd let the vine go and watched helplessly as it flew into the bushes.

Mar rushed to his son's side. "Where on Mother Earth did you learn to make such a thing? It is a tool of the large ones, who blend with the darkness, used to send messages."

"Bega!" Antoni declared, running up beside them.

"Very clever, son, such a thing may come in handy. Please, I beg you, do not use it again until you are ordered to do so. We dare not bring anymore attention upon ourselves. Now off you go and find it." Mar reached up and ruffled the fur on his son's forehead.

Still shocked, Dodd rushed off in the general direction the stone had travelled. Soon he was down on his paws and knees looking for his creation in the grass. Finally, he found it near a large furry sapling, in a small grove of similar saplings.

As he grabbed his stone and stood he banged his head on what he thought was a low branch. To avoid doing it again, he put his paw straight up and grabbed it. Hit by the realisation it was something he had never felt before, Dodd had the sudden urge to flea.

Turning to run, he found his passage blocked by a massive spider. *By the stars,* Dodd thought, *it is at least seven times larger than Squorth.* Speechless, he just stood and stared at the giant creature's massive fangs.

"Metcha, Mouse," Bur of the Bird-spiders said, in a rumbling voice.

Looking around Dodd found that the grove of saplings were actually the legs of twenty bird-spiders. Feeling the blood rushing to his head he began to pass out without answering.

"Perhaps you did not hear me properly, metcha mouse," Bur repeated, to no reply. "Looks like we have another invader, brothers. Web HIM.

Instantly, web flew from all directions, entombing Dodd from his hind legs up.

"If you do not mind me interrupting, Bur, but do you not think the mouse is too good looking to be an invader?" Brior asked, concerned.

Just as the web reached his mouth Dodd managed to mumble, "Ento," the spider greeting.

"I told you so," Brior snickered, and the brother spiders joined in.

Bur stopped and looked down at the mouse wrapped like a mummy, "Did you say 'Ento', little one?"

"Mm......," Dodd replied, nodding his head as best he could.

When Bur's fangs touched his fur, the poor mouse started to shake uncontrollably, his heart skipping beats.

"Your elders should teach you to speak up faster, young one! Why you were nearly a meal for sustenance later this lightening," Bur rumbled, as he gently snipped away the webbing.

His mouth free, Dodd moved his head from side to side. "I do apologise, oh Giant Spider. It is only that I have never seen a spider as large as you in all my lightenings, let alone twenty," Dodd announced, stammering.

"Why, thank you," Bur said, standing on his hind legs in salute.

It was then that Mar and Antoni saw the giant spider's head emerge from the undergrowth. Neither waited for the other as they dashed toward where they knew Dodd went to search.

"Quite a noise we heard before. Was that you little one?" Bur asked, returning to all eight legs.

Before Dodd had a chance to answer, Antoni had leapt onto Bur's back and Mar was in front of the spider poking him with his staff.

"Stop it, Ant. I beseech thee for Mother Earth's sake. Why are you tickling me? Metcha, Chieftain Mar of the Oak." Bur bowed onto his front legs nearly tipping Antoni off.

Slowly, all of the spiders joined in the greeting and stood before Mar with their heads down.

Deeply moved, Mar welcomed them all, "Ento large ones." Mar waved his staff signalling for them to stand. "What brings you to our humble presence, oh Giant Spiders?"

"A distant cousin of mine, Princess Squorth, has told me of your troubles. We have come to offer our might against these breakers of the treaties." Bur turned to his brothers and growled until the other spiders joined in. Soon the undergrowth rumbled to the noise of the mighty spiders.

"Tickle indeed," Antoni protested, leaping off Bur's back.

"Ah, a bull-ant, you must be Chief Antoni. Squorth has told me many wondrous things about you, little one, Boyor," Bur said, rising on to his back legs again only this time all of his companions did so as well. "There is one thing she did not tell me though."

"Yes, pray tell me, oh Hairy Legged One?" Antoni asked, moving around all the spiders showing no fear.

"She failed to mention you gave such invigorating massages, little one," Bur added, before the air rumbled with the trill of the spiders' laughter.

"Hm," Antoni said, as he turned and scurried away.

"Come back little one, we have travelled a long way to join you."

Antoni stopped and turned back to face them.

"Great Chief Warrior Ant, grant me a boon," Bur requested, in a formal tone.

"Thank you for remembering my rank, Eight Leg. What is the boon you ask?" Antoni stood his ground with two of his front legs on his hips.

"Do you think you could give my brothers one of your special massages as well? I am sure they would be grateful," Bur said, before rumbling with laughter again.

Even Mar grinned at the enormous creature's sense of humour. However, when he saw the look on Antoni's face, he soon changed the topic. "Noble Bur, did Squorth return to you when she finished scouting?"

"Squorth has gone even further ahead." Sensing Mar's fear, he continued, "Do not worry, Chieftain Mar, she will do nothing to risk harm coming to any of your commune's creatures. She has a plan to burrow underneath and retrieve them at every stop.

"Also as she proceeds, many invading mice and rats lie in her wake, bound of web, without the other vile creatures even noticing. She intends to drop the children off to the side, where she has arranged for some of the echidnas' kind to guard them. We shall come across them soon enough."

"Thank you," Mar replied, hoping that Squorth was sure of the path she had chosen to follow.

Stepping past Mar toward the place where Brother Sun rises, Bur grumbled, "Now, Chieftain Mar, I suggest we move on. I shall carry the little mouse who can roar, in return you can tell me of your home."

Bur crouched on his haunches in front of Dodd.

He looked at Mar for approval and was pleased when his father nodded.

Leaf falls later; all the creatures mounted on the

platoon of great spiders, scurried along the forest floor.

#   #   #

Bega rolled onto his back and looked at the rays of light dancing off the large ferns above his head. Slowly, his clouded thinking cleared and he realised where he was. Reaching up and touching his head, he found the poultice Attic had left secured with a strong piece of grass.

"By the Great Burning Ground," the bandicoot moaned, sitting up.

"Toemouse, see large one wakens. Now we must go on," Attic whispered, to his little companion in the trees above.

Elder Bega stood, staring around the area, searching for a sign of his mysterious saviour.

Toe watched on, longing to call Bega's name to let him know he was not alone.

Bending over carefully, Bega picked up his staff, turned toward the beautiful bush ahead and step by step went on his way.

Lumbering along the forest floor he, for the life of him, could not work out what had happened. He wandered in a mental fog, the invading rats' blows having stripped him of his recent memory.

Bega found himself haunted by the vision of a young Mar mouse helping him. "Get a grip on yourself, you old bandicoot, it could not have been Mar."

Ever so quietly the two, young, angels of mercy jumped from tree to tree or crawled along the forest's floor, following Bega's every step. Toe, after a while, found the pursuit quite enjoyable because they stayed close.

Attic, while wishing to stay concealed, wanted to stay nearby in case the large one needed help.

The Grey Rain-Bringers formed, over Father Sky, as Bega popped in and out of the undergrowth. Shadows began to grow longer and a stillness fell over the bush.

Many bandicoot lengths into his search, Bega stopped when he sensed something ahead.

"I am in no condition to fight," he mumbled, rolled up into a ball and quickly disappeared into a clump of undergrowth.

Silently, he listened as the steps grew closer to his position. However, when he saw Lea and the bearded dragons slip past him, he sighed with relief.

Standing, still unsteady on his feet, Bega stepped out onto the small track behind the lizards. "Hold, Lea of the Frill-necked. Have you time, to speak to a fellow creature of the commune?"

Spinning around, in a flash, Lea and the bearded dragons were amazed to see Bega standing there.

"Ona, Elder Bega," Lea said, putting his foot to his chest. "Where in the name of darkness, did you spring from?"

"Sya, Lea. Sya, also to you, brave bearded dragons. Why, Lea, I thought I had taught you better than to walk past a large creature like myself," Bega said, with the look of a scornful teacher.

"Sorry, Teacher, but I did not expect a creature of your size. You appeared nothing more than a large stone, there in the shadows. We seek foreign mice and rats. I praise the River Stones, to this leaf fall, we have not found one of your stature," Lea said, looking up into Bega's dark eyes.

"Flattery will not make any difference. Always expect the unexpected," Bega warned, walking over to get better acquainted with the bearded dragons.

"Yes, I remember Elder Briar's words. How I wish, he was with us upon this journey." Lea solemnly lowered his head.

Laying his paw softly on the frill neck's head Bega replied, "So do I, little Lea, so do I."

The lizard raised his head. "Tell me, Elder Bega, how are things at the commune?"

"Fine, when I left. Why do you ask?"

"Then you do not know of the unseen spirit stealer that is amongst our friends and families?" Lea's voice was sad and distant as he spoke.

Bega leant against a tree. "I know nothing of it. I beg you inform me."

"While on the trail of the kidnappers we have faced attacks from the foreign rats and mice. Also during this time, our commune has been struck by a sickness brought by the invaders. I will tell you more details when we have finished our patrol and have reported to Mar."

Saddened by the news, Bega felt guilty for being so impulsive and following Mar's trail. *Perhaps*, he thought, *I may have done more good by staying and helping Petra face the unseen enemy.*

"The darkening will soon be upon us, I feel we have backtracked far enough, now we shall return to our companions," Lea said, turning his back on Brother Sun and striding off.

Bega was pleased for the company as they made their way along the path, Lea had marked. None of the group, however, detected the two young mice that followed.

"Tell me, Teacher, how did you come to be so ruffled and beaten?" Lea whispered.

"I must have been in a fight, Lea," Bega answered, raising his paw to his brow.

"Teacher, you will never change. Your modesty is only challenged by your size and strength. To this leaf fall, I have never seen a creature better you. When you feel so inclined, I would dearly love to hear the details of such a fight,"

"So would I," Bega grumbled, under his breath.

"What was that, Teacher?"

"Nothing, Lea. How many leaf falls or lightenings are we away from the others?" Bega asked, already tiring.

"It is hard to say, Elder, for I do not know the terrain ahead of Chieftain Mar."

DARKENING TEN

As Brother Sun's rays slipped away, Meric's guards stirred their prisoners. Savagely biting, kicking and prodding the children, their captors forced them into action and so began the trek across the clearing.

"Stop it, you beasts," Hatty protested, pushing one of the guards away from a young native.

She felt a blow to the back of her head and fell stunned to the ground.

Abruptly, out of the darkness, a black shadow appeared and dragged the guard responsible back into the bushes.

Fena helped Hatty to her feet, with the aid of Fila's son. "Careful, child, these creatures care nothing about who they hurt. They are evil vile creatures, who will not hesitate to steal your spirit and leave your body to rot under Brother Sun's heat," Fena warned. "Those who you see around you, from our commune, are only half of what set out.

Fena's words rang in Hatty's ears, as Ji put her paw over his shoulder and helped her along.

"Female, must not stop to rest," Ji whispered, "they have no pity."

Unable to reach her beloved daughter, who was at

least thirty creatures ahead of her, Trix helplessly watched on.

The small dust storm, kicked up by the hundred or so creatures, quickly became stifling and many of the commune's creatures began to cough violently.

A few of the guards, from the other expedition, raced into the captives' ranks and dragged the offenders down into a small gully. Leaf falls later, only the guards returned.

Trix looked up to see two large birdlike shadows cross the sky. With a gush of wind, the returning guards disappeared into the darkness.

"Mopoke, Mopoke, Mo." Trix heard and smiled.

The natives of the night had begun the retaliation.

Reon shuddered as he heard yet another rat squeal.

"What, the great Reon, fearful of creatures of the night," Meric said, with a laugh as they met under the old gum.

"Not I, Prince," Reon the rat replied, looking around nervously. "Meric, do you think it possible that the creatures of this land, despite varied species, can converse as we do?"

"Of course they can. I would even go so far to say, from my observations, they live in peace together," Meric remarked with contempt evident in his voice. "Something, may I add, that was never achieved in our homeland."

"Prince," Reon said, "I am sure I have heard cries from my group of captives, answered from the trees."

"Interesting," Meric murmured intrigued. "Well there you have your answer."

#   #   #

After watching Bega and Lea make camp for the darkening, Attic grabbed Toe's paw and took him to the side.

"Now be good for Toe meet friends," Attic whispered, grinning from ear to ear. "You become skilful in surroundings, with every leaf fall. Young mouse now move long ground, like bush cockroach."

Toe raised an eyebrow and smiled.

Not far from the trail, Attic found what he had been looking for. "Toemouse stay here. I see if small friends home."

Toe looked on in amazement as Attic walked over to a tree stump, covered in a papery substance, and gave out a low pitched buzzing noise. Astounded, he watched a group of native wasps emerge and begin to converse with Attic.

"Hmm, buzzzzz," Attic greeted, as he performed another ritual dance of welcome.

Leaf falls later, Attic signalled for Toe to come forward but he hesitated. As a very young mouse he had been, accidentally stung by a stinger and had no wish to go further. He would never forget the pain or swelling up to near twice his size. Finally, trusting Attic's wisdom, he cautiously moved forward.

"Toemouse, this King Stab of Stingers. He is a cousin of King Jab of your commune's nest." Attic proudly introduced his friend.

"Mmm," Toe said, and bowed.

"To fulfil cousin's promise, King Stab agree to help protect you. This be despite his kind have no fight with shadow creatures." Attic searched around in the bushes for a leaf fall, and returned. "Here Toemouse, when you need help blow in stick. King Stab say no matter where you be his kind help. OK."

"But why should stinger kind help me?" Toe asked, putting the strange looking stick to his lips.

"All me lightenings, stingers and me friends, me talk

and play with them. So now try Toemouse." Attic jumped around with excitement.

Blowing gently into the stick, Toe heard nothing until a rumble started to come out of the nest. He stood perfectly still and watched on nervously as the air filled with the stingers' best guards.

From where Attic stood, it appeared they had landed en-mass upon Toe's body. Only from Toe's position they were a good paw's length away. The mighty wasps had formed an impenetrable suit of protection around Attic's young friend.

Doing a back flip, Attic did another dance, only this time of gratitude. "Me promise to always be the King's friend," he squealed with happiness.

"Attic," Toe yelled, above the hum of the wings, "how do I get out?"

"Blow again, Toemouse, blow again," Attic told him with his paws on his knees, smiling with delight.

Within a leaf fall, of the whistle blow, the wasps moved into a cloud above Toe's head.

"Again, Toemouse, this many times," Attic said, putting up two fingers, "and point at sapling."

Toe was totally dumbfounded as the wasps left him and seemingly attacked the small sapling.

"I do not hear anything, when I blow the stick. What is happening?" He asked, mystified.

"I hear, stingers hear, very high whistle. Maybe you hear too soon," Attic said, reaching into his fur and pulling out his special stick. A kind of flute he had carried since he was a baby mouse who could barely crawl.

"How can you talk to them, Attic? I have only ever seen my Uncle Antoni, of the bull-ants, have dialect with them."

"Me grow in bush, listen and copy. Me talk to stingers, they talk to me. Long time they look after me and me look after them. Toemouse not know stingers lonely, and would like to talk to other creatures, but scared."

"Oh," Toe replied, moving over to Attic's side.

"Indeed, young mouse, you are lucky to have such a friend," King Stab said, in the common tongue. "You see we teach the common tongue in our learning places. May I ask did you ever learn wasp?"

"Sorry, oh Noble King, I did not. Well, no more than the simple greeting," Toe replied, quite embarrassed.

"Well there you have it. Nobody seems to have the occasion anymore to get to know other creatures. Why, the wondrous things they could learn if they just talked. Now you must excuse me, my kind are holding council over the happenings in our lands and I must return. Just one more thing, child, we of the Paper-wasp carry a painful sting so use your protection wisely." Then, like a flash of light, King Stab was gone.

"Attic, will you teach me the native tongue of wasp?" Toe asked, as he walked over to examine Attic's flute.

"Yes, me do that. Toemouse think stingers fun like me do?" Putting out his arm, Attic gave a small whistle and giggled as hundreds of wasps landed on it. "See, Toemouse, now me like tree that stings," Attic declared, with a gigantic smile on his face.

#   #   #

Silently a dark figure landed in the branch above Lea's head and hung with its wings spread.

"Pardon, Noble Lea," a voice called from the shadows, "I bring word from Chieftain Mar."

"Enter our circle, oh one of the night," Lea replied.

"Sya, Lea. Mar's band of searchers have joined with twenty bird-spiders and at this very leaf fall are making up lost ground. They hope they will reach the area of devastation before Brother Sun rises. He asks, for your group to continue and seek out the echidnas. Princess

Squorth has them guarding the young ones she has liberated. They rest off the path near a great wattle bush, which is in celebration of its life with colour."

"Good for Squorth," Bega said, stepping out from behind the large gum.

"I beg your forgiveness, Elder Bega, I did not know you had joined Lea's band," the bat said, flapping its wings across its chest in salute.

"Tell me, Night Flyer, have you heard word of the commune?" Bega asked.

"Early darkening one of my kind relayed word that the sickness seems to have subsided." The bat changed its grip on the small branch supporting it.

"Great news indeed," Bega said, slapping Lea on the back hard enough to knock him off his feet.

"Sorry, Elder, but many creatures lost their spirits. Your commune of ground dwellers now stands at but a pawful. Tree dwellers have also prospered badly. The greatest loss has been many of your Servicers' of the Circle."

Bega turned away heavy with guilt and groaned.

"However, there is some good tidings. I have word that my large cousins, the Flying Foxes, are coming this way under the guidance of my kind. They bring Free the Mighty, Commander Aldo, Lieutenant Stump, and twenty thousand flying foxes, to aid Chieftain Mar's quest." Night Flyer proudly announced.

"By the River Stones," Bega exclaimed, flicking his staff around in front of him.

Lea clambered to his feet. "Highra and his brothers have also joined us,"

"Why, what a mighty force, flying foxes, cicadas, bats, bird-spiders, hawks and the Mighty Lizards," Bega said, smiling at Lea.

Lea moved out of Bega's reach. "Most importantly, there is Chieftain Mar, Chief Antoni, Princess Squorth and yourself who lead us. Surely, with such a wealth of experience we can not fail in our quest."

For the first time since leaving the commune, Bega felt his heart begin to fill with the glimmer of hope.

LIGHTENING OF THE
WOODS ELEVEN

Relentless in their quest to find their families Pon and Fila searched for any possible sign of them still being with spirit.

As Fila examined a small wattle sapling a knowing smile grew on his face. "See I told you we were following the right tracks. Here is another leaf bent, like only Nila can," Fila declared gripping the leaf in his paw and pulling it out.

"I never doubted you, Fila. I only hope we can reach them soon," Pon said, quietly moving up to examine the leaf.

Pon, also an excellent tracker, was more worried how many of their family they would find. They had lost nearly two lightenings of the woods, before he had found Fila waiting impatiently for him at their dwelling.

Even then it had been very difficult for them to find the trail again. Yet despite all the damage to the forest, by the all consuming redness, Fila had been successful. Secretly, what concerned them both the most, were the strange mouse and rat prints surrounding their families' tracks.

Puffing, Lenthric ran up to the commander of the

invading mice and bowed. "Prince Meric, a new column of rats and mice have arrived from the temporary nest. I am sorry to report they have with them the flame, Commander Reon asked for."

"Flame! I did not order the flame!" Meric replied, his rage clearly evident. "Summon Reon to me at once."

Meric stood looking at the tufts of grass, which remained around the tree they had chosen to shelter under during the day.

To move, he thought, *during the hours of the sun will mean certain death to either some of our captives or my own kind. The large creatures, with whom we travelled to this land, have cleared great areas of trees and torn the ground into long dangerous ditches that are exhausting to cross. So to venture beyond this shelter, I am certain, will mean an attack from either the large creatures or the native birds.*

"Prince, you summoned me," Reon said, half bowing in contempt.

Meric turned and looked into the rat's dark, evil eyes. "Reon, who gave you leave to summon the fire back from our main camp again? We have all the captives we can handle, surely that will please the two Kings."

"Oh, Prince, please do not tell me you failed in your duty. I should not need to remind you, Meric, we were told to leave the land behind ravaged by flame. This was so ordered by our kings! Have you forgotten your training in war, which always taught us to avoid being followed? You know I will be obligated to report any such violation," Reon said, disrespect oozing from his words and demeanour.

"How dare you address me in such a tone, Reon? I did everything necessary to ensure a successful completion of our mission. So tell me, rat, what do you plan to do with the flame now?" Meric stood leaning against a blade of grass his paw on the hilt of the strange sword.

"I have already sent the chosen carriers of the flame that were with my mission, to scorch the earth beyond where we were yesterday. This, in my opinion, should stop any pursuit that may have occurred thanks to the Prince's lack of foresight," Reon said, with deep disdain evident in his voice. "These flame carriers are merely here to ensure every possible hiding place for any savages are destroyed."

"You have done all this without consulting me?" Prince Meric looked across the path, they had trodden the night before, at the smoke and flames rising from the bush.

"Oh yes, Prince, and more! I have also placed strategic groupings, of our most seasoned fighters, to capture or kill any creatures driven out into their path. So, Meric, if you do not mind I shall return to my destiny." Without the customary bow, Reon turned and dashed out into the furrows toward the flames.

#   #   #

"Tell me, Chieftain Bur, do you not feel that the air is becoming scarce from heat?" Dodd asked, leaning down to make himself heard.

"Not that I have noticed, oh Mouse who Roars," Bur replied, charging across the floor of the forest with Dodd on his back.

"Antoni," Mar yelled from atop his mount, "do you sense, as I, that the air is becoming thick, dark and heavy?"

"I do, Mar. I fear that we may well find misfortune if we keep pursuing at such a pace. This area is strange; the signs that present themselves contradict each other. I can not make it out, it is hot and yet my smaller ant cousins ready their nests for rain. Look around us, they are raising the entrances at every nest." Chief Warrior

Ant Antoni said, bouncing up and down on his spider's back.

Leaf falls later; as they rose to the top of a crest they received their answer. The spiders and their riders froze as they looked on. Stirred by the wind the redness leapt in all directions, devouring the small valley in front of them.

"Strange," Mar said, as he dismounted, "not a creature have I seen pass us. Where could they be?"

Before Mar could fathom the answer, the wind changed and sent the redness hurtling up the ridge toward them.

"For all that is sacred we must flee," Antoni screamed as the flames roared up the small hill like an ancient creature determined to devour them.

Mar mounted quickly and his spider began to run. Sadly, as he turned to see how close the evil was, he saw two of the noble spiders, a bearded dragon and one of Lea's brothers perish into the flames. His heart sank, but he had no time for grief, as he and his fellow searchers leapt through the bushes only just in front of the advancing redness of death.

As if protected by spirits sent by Father Sky, the ground dwellers found themselves plucked from the burning earth and lifted aloft. Only leaf falls later the part of Mother Earth beneath them erupted in the red spirit stealer.

"Metcha, Noble Mouse of the Great Oak. Ento, oh great one with eight legs," Highra the Hawk said, without a misplaced puff as he hurtled into the sky, attempting to avoid the thick smoke haze and life draining heat.

"By the River Stones, Noble Highra, you and your followers could not have chosen a more opportune leaf fall than this one to pass. Once again, I find myself in your debt," Mar said, as he gazed on at the massive devastation below. "In all my lightenings of travels, I had only ever seen the demon redness but once and indeed I have no wish to see it again."

"Nor I," Highra screeched above the wind. "How a fellow creature could do such a thing is beyond my understanding."

"Fellow creature!" Mar exclaimed.

"Yes, as we scouted ahead I saw a foreign rat setting the redness loose. It was then I felt the need to return and warn you. I am afraid many of our fellow natives have perished, including some of Betra and Crier's scouts. Not to forget many of our Sister Trees, who have been darkened beyond recognition." Highra's voice was solemn as he continued to climb.

"What about those we seek?" Mar squeaked holding onto the hawk's feathers with all his might.

"Sorry, Chieftain, of this I can not be sure. I am afraid with my limited knowledge; I may only give you half truths if I were to enter an opinion. I pray to Mother Earth they are alright. I see little reason for the invaders to bring them so far, just to take their spirits with the redness. No, I think they must have other plans for them," Highra said, as he glanced around and started to descend toward a cool stream.

#   #   #

Sensing something coming Pon grabbed Fila and dragged him into the dense undergrowth. "Quiet, Fila, there is something moving about ahead of us. Can you hear it crushing the dried leaves?"

Hiding beneath some leaves they both watched silently as the foreign rats past.

"Did you see that, Pon? One of those strange rats was carrying the redness on a flat rock while the other fed it with sticks." Fila crawled forward to get a better look.

"So that is what those creatures, I have heard tell of, look like. Indeed, they are an ugly creature; totally unlike our handsome native rats. Still we should at least make contact." Pon stood and stepped out onto the path, "Re, oh Brown Ones, I am Pon of the Grey Gum."

Before Fila could even crawl out the rats had turned and were rapidly approaching Pon. Unexpectedly, they both stopped and with an evil glare set the redness free.

Bewildered Pon and Fila watched on as each rat chanted in their strange tongue, laid a paw on their chest and rolled in the redness. Mesmerised, the two native mice stood frozen as the two rats with their fur well alight rushed toward them.

"They are using their bodies to spread the redness. Their cries are haunting." As if hypnotised, Fila did not move a mouse length.

"Get out of the way you fools." The dark shadow flashed across in front of the rats and knocked the mice to the ground. "Escape to the running water we must. Follow me." With that the strange figure darted back into the shadows.

Finally regaining their senses Pon and Fila followed the dark stranger as it disappeared into the thicker brush. After many mouse lengths of running, they sat puffing in the water as the bush around them disappeared into redness.

"Ento." Without looking up Pon realised a spider had saved them.

"Metcha, Pon, son of Elder Briar," the spider calmly replied cooling itself in the water.

Both Pon and Fila looked up at their guide to salvation through the haze and finally recognised the face of Princess Squorth.

Squorth smiled. "Fancy, you forgetting me, Pon and Fila. Why I used to take you for rides when you were only babies."

"Forgive us, Princess, as indeed we did not expect to see you in our lands." Pon did his best to stand and bow only to have a spider's leg hold him down.

"Please, dear friend, stay in the water. As for being in this land, I did not expect to be. You see, I am on a quest with Chieftain Mar to safely return his family to the commune." Squorth spun around in a circle and watched the redness consume all in its path.

"Return?" Pon questioned, ducking his head under the water to wet his fur. "Where have they been?"

"The invading rats, two of which you just met, attacked the commune of the Oak and took Trix, Hatty and other younger creatures captive. Now they return to where, I fear, many such an evil one exists. It is our quest to free them,"

It was not the redness, which drove our family away, Pon thought. *In all likelihood they have found a similar fate.*

"Tell me, Squorth, did they free the redness that devours, on the commune of the Oak as they did ours?" Pon asked, looking Fila in the eyes wondering if his brother had come to the same realisation.

"No, for some reason they did not; though it may have been because the Servicers' of the Circle attacked and prevented such action. I really can not be sure." Squorth huddled between them with a leg draped over their shoulders. "Tell me, how is that elder brother of yours, Jun the Tormentor?"

Fila moved even further under Squorth's embrace. "He has been missing now, for many lightenings of the woods. The last we saw of him, he set out toward the rise of Brother Sun, seeking answers to the rumours of the Large Pale Ones."

"I see." Squorth's brow furrowed. "I have no doubt he will have found many a creature to torment by now. By the Stone Circle, he was certainly good at that and fast with it."

"Tell us, Squorth, what of our father; is he on the quest with Chieftain Mar as well?" Pon could not believe the power the redness was demonstrating. Never in his time with spirit had he seen it from such a close proximity.

Looking around as the bush darkened with smoke, Squorth took a deep breath and replied, "I am sorry to tell you this, in such a place, but your father is without spirit. Antoni told me, it appears he was given a strange concoction of plants in his warm sap, which took his spirit prematurely."

"Father gone," Fila groaned, slumping back into the water.

"What creature would do that to another?" Pon asked, clasping his bow tightly in his paws.

Squorth turned to face both of them. "They believe it was one of the dark winged cockroaches that band with the mice, brown and black rats from other lands."

"By the River Stones, I shall gut the creature when I find it," Pon declared, his eyes as red as the flames around them.

Not even the steady rain that began to fall from Father Sky would extinguish the anger that now burnt in his heart.

#   #   #

Perched up in a tree near Bega and Lea's party Toe watched the strange black clouds as they rose. "Attic, what is the darkness that bellows up toward the rising of Brother Sun?"

Attic thought for a moment as he stared across the land toward the giant cloud. "Me hear tell of such darkness in the lightening, when me listen to Bega speak to others who listen and learn."

Toe stood carefully and moved forward along the branch. "Really, then what is it?"

"Bega call it 'redness'. This creature devours everything in its path. It knows but one enemy which comes from Father Sky," Attic said, concentrating to remember the lesson.

"Devours all before it; should we not warn Bega and Lea, so they can protect themselves?" Toe said, watching the strange plumes of smoke twisting into Father Sky.

"No need worry Bega. Redness not reach us, its enemy soon take its spirit," Attic said, as a smile crossed his face.

"What enemy? Oh why can you not speak like the rest of us?" Toe said, tiring of their difficulty in communicating.

"All signs say, soon enemy of redness comes." Attic pointed to the ant nests on the ground as a drop landed on his forehead. "See enemy already here, redness not reach us now. We wait and it soon be gone." Attic grabbed Toe's paws and began a little jig. "Dance to welcome wetness from grey rain-bringers, Toemouse."

"Rain," Toe announced as it began to team down.

"Yes, yes, yes, Toe. It is the redness enemy." Attic squealed and did a back flip.

Protected under their camouflage leaf clothing, Attic and Toe watched on from high in the tree as Mother Earth started to quench her thirst.

#   #   #

Bur scrambled up to Highra and bowed. "Eeek, Noble Hawk, I Bur of the Bird-spiders thank you for our salvation this lightening."

"Ento, Noble Eight Leg. I am sorry we did not come sooner and save the passing of spirits that did occur. Please accept my condolences for your kinds passing."

Highra stood nobly watching over the survivors as he spoke.

"Accepted," Bur said, turned and scurried toward the gathering on the riverbank.

The hawk hopped, flapped its wings and landed near Mar. "Chieftain, I have great difficulty in explaining what I have seen but I must try. Before the redness came I saw rats, of a foreign kind, carrying and fuelling it," Highra squawked to the gathering, turning his head from side to side.

"So you are saying they carry the flame with them to use against us," Mar said, finding it more and more difficult to breathe in the dense smoke.

Highra looked off into the distance before answering, "Yes, it is hard to believe, but what my eyes saw will haunt me always."

Antoni walked up to stand near the bird's talons. "What is it, Highra? Please go on."

The great hawk lowered his head between Antoni and Mar. "They laid the redness down on the ground and fed it to make it grow. Then, they themselves rolled in it and ran through the bush chanting in their foreign tongue. By the highest tree, I will remember those chants until my spirit leaves me and more than likely beyond that," Highra whispered, so as not to alarm the others.

"What insanity is it we face when a creature would give its spirit in such a way?" Mar asked, totally stunned.

"Insanity it may well be, Chieftain, but they use the redness to divide and conquer our fellow natives. Indeed, not a lightenings flight from here I have seen armies of rats waiting to capture or kill natives that resist their ways." While Highra did not express his fears, he was beginning to wonder if they could win any battle against such numbers.

"Why do they take so much and kill so many?" Mar

mumbled, thinking out loud, as he sat on a submerged river pebble in the stream.

"I know not why, Chieftain." Highra fanned out his wings around his friends creating a sound barrier. "But I do know their numbers far outstrip any numbers we can muster in both ground dwellers and winged kind. Even with our power we could make but a dent in their legions. I fear these creatures must mate without thought of consequences, thus their numbers have increased to such an extent they need more of everything."

Mate without consequences, Mar thought. *They are breeding themselves into a massive plague that may sweep across all our land if not stopped.*

 # *DARKENING ELEVEN*

Bega's large nose swung from side to side, his nostrils' flaring. Despite the rain he knew there was still great danger ahead from the redness.

"Lea, my senses are heavy with the darkened air around us. While the wetness falls, praise be to Father Sky, we must still follow the waters flow on Mother Earth to ensure our safety. We shall come back to the trail as soon as we can. Now, Lea, we make haste."

The old bandicoot knew exactly what they would find ahead, if they were to continue on their present course.

How is it possible, Bega thought, *for our beloved bush and forests to be alight with the redness? As a young bandicoot I saw the large ones, who blend with the darkness, use the redness to burn undergrowth and capture creatures for Celebration of Sustenance. Since, I have not seen anybody else use it in such a way. That was except for the occasional lightening finger of Father Sky, when it hit Mother Earth, during a Rain-bringers battle.*

Still deep in thought Bega crashed through some ferns, spraying water everywhere. Stopping, he turned to ensure Lea and his companions were near. Placing a paw on a moss covered stone to balance himself, he felt it slip instead. In the wink of an eye he tumbled down a bank and into a fast flowing steam.

Sometimes my own stupidity amazes me, the old bandicoot thought while being swept away.

No matter how hard Bega tried, he could not free himself from the stream's grasp. All he could do was use his staff to keep away from sharp rocks, as he found himself continuously immersed in a substance he had no fondness for at all.

Lea rushed along the bank calling out, "Elder Bega, Elder Bega, where are you?"

Bega, however, could not answer as he bobbed up and down like a furry cork.

His large ears stood upright when he heard a new roaring sound ahead. "By Mother Earth, please do not let that be what I think it is."

Bega spat water out of his mouth as he lifted his head to watch the water disappear from in front of his eyes. Wisely, he held his breath as he flew into the air. Then, within leaf falls, he found himself hurtling back into the water and falling down, down, down into a large lagoon. He sighed with relief before the current once again took hold of his body.

Totally exhausted, he laid on his back as the water took his large body down some more rapids. Slowly, his old eyes closed, he could no longer even hear the rushing water past his ears. He felt his spirit slipping from him and then there was nothing.

Finally, I shall know what lies beyond our bodily existence, he thought as he heard Elder Briar's voice calling him. Then as he saw a light coming closer, it disappeared.

Unexpectedly Bega found the sensation of pain return, as his body went into spasms due to a very large thumping on his chest.

"Harder, Dodd, bounce harder!" Antoni commanded, nervously running around the bandicoot.

Terrified of hurting his teacher, Dodd gave yet another gigantic bounce on Bega's chest.

"Pla, pla, pla...," Bega coughed with a gigantic splutter of water. Rolling over the bandicoot opened his eyes to see Antoni and Mar staring anxiously into this face. "By the River Stones, what were you hitting my chest with?" he spluttered.

"Dodd," Antoni answered, now quite calm. "Ona, Elder Bega. May I say you have not lost your talent for making discreet entrances?" Antoni leant over caringly and did what he could to help Mar and Dodd right Bega's gigantic frame.

"Boyor, Antoni. Metcha, Chieftain Mar and Dodd. I must say, I am pleased to see you." Bega's hind legs shook as he tried to stand.

Then as if being struck by lightening, Bega remembered what had happened when the rats attacked him. Staring at Dodd and Mar in front of him, he said, "You were there Mar, you saved me when the rats attacked. I heard Toe's voice warning me and then you came. Only it was not you, or was it?" Bega was confused. "Tell me, how could you have been so much younger?" The bandicoot's voice became extremely agitated and he fell back into the water with a loud splash.

Mar waded into the stream. "I do not know what you may have seen, my old friend. Since leaving the commune I have not ventured back, other than being forced back by the redness last lightening."

As they helped him to the pebbly bank, Bega mumbled confused, "Dodd, then it must have been you. You cared for me. Tell me where did you find young Toe?"

Without a word, Dodd sadly turned and walked away.

Abandoning his old friend, Mar walked over and gently lay his paw on is son's back. "We shall find them, do not worry my gentle giant."

"Have I said something wrong?" Bega enquired concerned.

Antoni leant down and whispered into Bega's ear, "They have not had word of Toe, since we returned to the commune,"

"What on Mother Earth is going on? Somebody saved me and treated me in the ways of the Circle of Knowledge and Defence. Who could it possibly be?" The bandicoot rested his front paw under his chin deep in thought.

Antoni sat on a large pebble trying to make sense of what he had heard. "Lightenings of the woods ago, we saw signs of a creature with such knowledge. It aided Mar in a battle with the invaders, not personally but with traps it had created. Only back then, Mar was sure he heard Elder Briar's voice warn him. The unknown creature also called commands to Lea and his kind."

"Hm," Bega said, shaking himself dry and saturating the bull-ant in the process.

"Splosh and bother," Antoni protested. "As if I am not wet enough, you old bandicoot. You have to saturate me to my very inners."

As the rain became heavier and heavier Lea and his companions finally caught up, to the now motionless team of searchers.

Together they sat quietly in the warmth of a hollow log, passing ideas back and forth as they planned their next move. With the darkening upon them and the rain pouring down, there was little point in venturing further.

#   #   #

Toe sat in a knot hole of a gum, crying and angry. "Why did you stop me from helping Bega when he fell into the water?"

Uncertain as to what to do Attic crawled over and held him close.

"Oh, Attic, Father and Dodd's gone, Mother and Hatty too and now Bega. Will we ever find them again?" Toe sobbed into Attic's damp shoulder.

"We find them, Toe, not worry anymore. This we will, me promise," Attic said, looking around the tiny area.

"How can you be sure? We are now so very far from the commune. Have you ever been here before, at all?" Toe asked, crying even louder.

"No not me but all creatures are friends in bush. me know they will help, Toemouse. You see blow stick." Attic rubbed his little friend's shoulder trying to comfort him.

Toe pulled out his hollow stick and blew it. Within leaf falls, his wasp guards were buzzing around the entrance. He listened as Attic talked to them in their native tongue.

"Friend wasp pass word to search for large one and Toe's father."

Standing Toe walked over, did a small dance of gratitude and said, "Buzzom Grando."

Impressed with Toe's attempt at their native tongue, the wasps were inspired, returned the thank you and left.

"Now, Toemouse, rest," Attic said, laying some damp grass on the floor. "Me speak peace to you as you rest.

To Toe's surprise, Attic began a soft melody of the creatures' of the forest calls; soft reassuring calls from the cicadas to the lyre-birds.

The young mouse's eyes became heavy, as Attic impersonated the sound of the breeze and the running brooks in a haunting tune.

Just before his eyes closed, Toe said to Attic, "I shall return your kindness, Attic, as is the way of our bush, and sing you a song my mother has sung to me all my lightenings.

"Rest my darling child dream of wondrous things
While your mother cuddles you and lovingly sings
Upon the darkening Brother Sun sleeps behind Father Sky
Now Sister Moon illuminates us and owls and bats do fly
Silently your eyelids close and you enter rest once more
May Mother Earth and Father Sky protect you for ever more."

The words he was hearing overwhelmed Attic. Something deep inside him stirred, as he began to whisper the song before Toe even finished it.

As if deep in a trance Attic sat and listened, warmed and yet mystified by the hauntingly familiar words as Toe continued,

"Softly does the raindrops fall upon the gum leaves broad
Softly does my baby sleep as I rock you back and forward
Rest now my darling mouse in your mother's arms"

But before Toe finished the young mouse fell asleep snuggled next to Attic.

Gently, with a tear in his eye, Attic reached down and touched his young charge and said, "Sleep well my child, here in Sister Tree, away from any harm," and finished the song.

#   #   #

Dodd sat honing the edges of his stone watching Bur, of the Bird-spiders, in amazement.

"Here, young mouse, I have finished weaving one of the strongest webs possible. I think it will make your long stone, even easier to spin above your head," Bur said, moving over to where he was working.

"Thank you, Noble Bur." Dodd reached out and received the gift. "Why, it is indeed much lighter than the vine." Holding it in one paw, he pulled with another. "Yes and strong."

"Now mouse, attach it and show me how it roars in the rain. If any of those detestable creatures are around, it should surely strike a note of fear in their hearts." Bur leant down closer to Dodd and whispered, "As it did to me, to be quite honest, on the lightening we met."

The large mouse attached the web rope to his stone and made his way out to a small clearing. There in the pouring rain, he started to spin the stone furiously above his head. The bush began to roar with a loud moaning noise, such as one would expect from a large creature warning others away from its territory.

Brrr, Brrrr, Brrrr the sound echoed across the hills and along the stream's bank.

Bur watched on hypnotised by the sound, smiling as best a bird-spider can.

#   #   #

"What is that noise, Attic?" The young kangaroo mouse sat up abruptly, scared beyond belief. "Is it

Bega's spirit come back to scare us?"

Attic sat and listened. "Not spirit of bush. Me know not what it is." The wild mouse stood, went to the small opening and gazed out into the rain.

The Brr Brrr appeared to be bouncing off the trees, making it hard to determine its direction.

#   #   #

"Dodd, enough," Mar commanded as he walked out from the hollow log.

"Forgive me, Chieftain Mar, it is I who requested Dodd demonstrate his roar," Bur said, coming to his friend's defence. "Please do not chastise him for something that was of my doing."

"There is nothing to forgive, Noble Bur. Perhaps Highra and his kind brought us far enough away from the creatures that they would not have heard such a sound." Mar turned to his son. " Dodd, I still do not want you to use that web on stone again until I give you permission, understood?"

"Yes, father," Dodd replied, his head lowered in shame. However, his mood lasted only seconds when Bega walked up behind him.

"By the great ferns of the rain-forests, you made this, mouse? You made a tjuringa which works so well, by yourself," Bega said, as he reached down and held up the stone to examine it. "Fine work, young one, the balance is perfect; fine work indeed. You are going to make a great student when we return to the commune. For now though, I suggest you listen to your father. Now come and I shall tell you this darkening more of our ways."

"Yes, Elder Bega." Following his mentor toward the hollow log Dodd turned and yelled, "Thank you, Bur."

"A fine mouse," Bur said to Mar, as they walked up the bank of the swelling stream. "Tell me, Chieftain, do we venture further this darkening?"

Mar looked to the grey rain-bringers in the sky. "Despite a great need, we must be satisfied with waiting for the rains to subside. The very bush around us is becoming awash and I fear at any moment we shall have to seek higher ground."

"I see, Chieftain. My kind and I await your command. We have made camp under those ferns." The spider lifted his front leg and pointed. "Please do not hesitate to call us if the need arises. For now aya."

Bur walked slowly over to his camp where his kind were to hold vigil for the spirits they had lost.

Mar, soaked to his very core, looked out into the darkness. "Please forgive me my darling Trix. May Mother Earth protect you, Hatty and Toe until we meet again."

#   #   #

Prince Meric walked up onto the crest of a furrow; his right paw clenched on the stolen sword's hilt.

"Why do you bother with that thing, Prince? It is useless if it can not be drawn to kill."

"Lenthric, do you not think it is beautiful? In truth one of the most beautiful things we have seen, since coming to this forsaken land." Meric said, holding the sheathed sword up into the air. "There is a mystery to this weapon and I swear by the fjords of our homeland, I shall learn it."

Lenthric noticed a messenger moving toward them and fell back for a few moments. After they spoke he returned to Meric's side.

"Prince, there has been word of Reon and his army," he reported.

"Really," Meric said, with obvious distaste. "I hate those detestable rats! In my opinion, it would be a good thing if they were all washed away."

"They have captured many of the small creatures, who were forced from the forest by flame. Prince, they have also slain many. Apparently, they feast on them at this very moment." Lenthric's eyes closed for an instant. "No creature deserves such a fate."

"Vile devils," Meric mumbled, as a sod of ground slipped into the running water below the crest. "Tell me Lenthric, what of those insane rats that carry the flame?"

"Apparently those who did not give their lives to the flame have had their precious cargo extinguished," Lenthric replied with a gleam in his eye.

"Wondrous news. Why that means they can not lay waste to anymore countryside, until they regain the flame from the nest. Lenthric, please ensure none of the rats that are members of the Order of Flame come near me. I am not in the mood for their endless ramblings about their worship of the flame and how it is the only answer."

"Yes, Prince." Lenthric moved close enough to whisper and continued, "May I beg you, not to talk so openly of your distaste for the order and brother rats? You realise to them, giving your body to flame is a higher honour than to die in battle. Prince, I am fearful for your life, if word of such talk gets back to Reon." Lenthric kept checking around the area as he spoke.

Trix, Hatty and the others straggled along behind Meric, their paws sinking deeper and deeper into the mud.

"I am so totally exhausted," Trix mumbled to herself. "Even if an opportunity came, I would not be able to escape."

With each large native carrying a smaller one, they trudged along in the darkness. They dared not speak to each other for fear of retribution, so they suffered in silence.

I must have hope, Trix thought, *in my heart*. She was

sure somehow the guards around her were decreasing in numbers. When she heard the cry of a mopoke she smiled.

Further back down the line Hatty, with a baby mouse in her arms, became unbalanced and slipped down into the mud. Gently, she felt Ji's strong arm reach down and lift her once again. Even as the guards whipped the young mouse with their tails, he simply smiled into Hatty's eyes to reassure her.

#   #   #

Frantic, Kea, a commander in the rat army ran up to his leader. "Reon, Reon, some of the rats have broken ranks and are fleeing toward the city."

"Cowards! Send the Order of the Flame to hunt them down. Tell me, Kea, what has disturbed the rats so? They know desertion means certain death," Reon said, gnawing at some meat.

Kea moved closer and seized a piece of meat. "The word is that as the flames were extinguished, they heard a roaring noise coming from deep in the forest. Some fool shouted it was the spirit of a great cat coming to devour them for laying waste to the land. Well, soon panic spread as quickly as the flame and just before the roar ended many took flight."

Spitting out a bit of gristle Reon grunted, "May our gods protect us, Kea, from the weak minded. Go forth and ensure no mercy is shown to them when they are caught."

"I shall, Reon," Kea replied, bowed and headed into the darkness.

Moments before Kea reached the camp of the Flame Carriers, he found himself scooped up in the talons of one of Breath's of the Boobooks kind. His message destined never to be delivered.

Close by one of Betra the bat's scouts hung high in the branches waiting for messages to relay back to Chieftain Mar. *The ground below begins to flood,* the bat thought, *and as the water rises, so does my concern for the captives.*

LIGHTENING OF THE WOODS TWELVE

The rain had been relentless all through the darkening. It was as if Father Sky had sent the Grey Rain-bringers to cleanse Mother Earth of the evil spread by the invaders.

After spending a restless darkening, Mar felt water lapping at his feet. Realising what was happening, he attempted to stand, but was knocked backward by a massive jolt. "By the River Stones," Mar yelled, trying to balance himself. "The stream has swollen to such an extent that we are afloat."

Lea and the others leapt to their feet as the log began to move, rolling and swaying.

"Quickly to the top of the log," Mar screamed, hopping toward Lea.

Antoni, Dodd and Mar ran straight up Lea's tail, over his back, and scrambled through a hole in the log above their heads.

Lea and his brothers soon followed, leaving Bega behind. Half asleep, the bandicoot lumbered outside and the instant he did, a rush of water knocked him on his back. As the log tossed in the violent current, Bega reached up with his front paws and dug them into the bark.

Immediately Dodd and Lea ran to the opposite end in an attempt to keep the log balanced. Antoni and Mar rushed to aid their old friend. Summoning all the strength they could muster, the two friends pulled with all their heart.

"His fur is too saturated," Antoni whispered. "He is too heavy. We will never lift him."

Still exhausted from the past lightening's events; Bega sensed his actions were putting his comrades at risk. Looking deep into their eyes, he said, "May Mother Earth and Father Sky be with you, my dear friends, always." Then he flung himself into the water.

Watching him give his life so that they may live, Mar screamed, "BEGA, NO!"

Antoni tackled Mar before he could dive in. "Bega did it to save our spirits, Marcus. If you jump in after him, more than likely two spirits will be lost this lightening."

The sky grew darker as a dark shadow descended upon their position.

"Chieftain Mar, leap for your life," a small voice yelled as the dark spectre drew closer.

Unexpectedly, the searchers found themselves flung into the air as the log went over a waterfall. Mar, Lea, Dodd, Antoni and the others, were plucked from certain death as Free and other flying foxes descended and caught them.

By Mother Earth, Mar thought dangling in the air, *there are so many of them, they have blocked the rain from falling."*

The flying fox ducked under a branch, swooped over another and dropped Mar on a large bough. Gliding in a full circle Free returned and landed next to the chieftain. "Metcha," he said, draping out a wing.

213

Mar bowed. "Screech and thank you," he said, and watched in amazement as Stump and Aldo slid down the giant bat's wing.

The friends jumped when Antoni fell onto the branch beside them. Standing on his back legs the bull-ant shrugged and pointed to his saviour landing in another tree.

Relieved to see the others, Mar nodded at Antoni in passing, walked up and laid his paw on Aldo's shoulder "Your timing is excellent, as usual, Commander."

There from high in the tall ghost gum, they could see the extent of the flooding for the first time.

Aldo bowed his head. "I am deeply sorry we could do nothing for Elder Bega. There were too many overhanging branches for Free's kind to save him. Perhaps, he made it to safety on his own accord."

"We can only hope," Antoni mumbled as he examined Stump from head to tail. "Why, Lieutenant, you look like you have lost some fat, since we last met."

Pleased somebody had noticed, the chubby mouse sucked in his stomach and pushed out his chest. "I must admit the fur around my waist does seem loose." Stump smiled and turned toward Free. "Chief, please allow me to introduce, Free, the leader of the flying foxes."

The bull-ant found Free's size amazing. "Screech, oh one of the Skin Wings," he said, bowing. "We owe you our spirits this lightening." Antoni turned in a circle and did his best to estimate how many of Free's kind were hanging in the trees. "It is quite a force you have here, Commander."

"Please call me 'Free', Chief Antoni," he requested, sweeping his wing down in salute.

"You know of me then?"

"Aldo and Stump have been telling me of your adventures. Very interesting indeed," Free said, peering down at Antoni.

Doing their best to keep up with Bega, Bur and his fellow bird-spiders sprinted along the stream's bank. However, when Bega went under the water yet again he decided to split his forces.

"You ten follow Mar, while I and the others help the Elder," Bur ordered, already heading to a gum not far ahead of Bega's tumbling body.

I hope we can get to the overhanging branches in time, he thought.

Climbing the tree the bird-spiders leapt from branch to branch spinning webs. Using those webs, they then swung to other trees until they were closer to the bandicoot.

Bur and two others leapt onto some passing debris, trailing webs behind them. Then as they past Bega, each spider reached out and gently grabbed him with their strong legs.

"Eeor," Bur yelled in bird-spider, with that his kind took up the slack and started to pull. Slowly, Bur, Bega and the others reached the safety of a tree.

Within leaf falls, Bega's lifeless body lay stomach down on a branch, cocooned in webbing. Bur moving forward, checked for any signs of life and was relieved to find a faint heartbeat.

"You are a tough old bandicoot," Bur grumbled gently piercing Bega with his fang, allowing some venom to enter his bloodstream.

When there was still no sign consciousness, Bur began to push up and down on his back.

Slowly, Bega opened his eyes. "By Mother Earth, I did lose my spirit," he said, looking down at the rushing water, as if floating in thin air.

Realising the bandicoot's confusion, Bur climbed underneath the branch to speak and reassure him. "You are safe, Elder Bega."

When Bega saw Bur's blurred face appear underneath him, it all became too much and he fell unconsciousness.

#   #   #

Not far ahead of the searchers, Meric of the black mice and his army were still driving the prisoners on.

"Prince Meric, do you really think it wise to keep going in the daytime?" Lenthric asked, as they struggled up a hillside devoid of any vegetation.

"Look behind us, Lenthric, the valley that we crossed is underwater. If these rains do not cease soon, this whole area will be consumed. We must risk attack or drown for certain. Which do you choose?" Meric stood nobly as rain streamed down his face.

Lenthric slipped in the mud. "I bow to your wisdom, Prince Meric, but what of Reon and his army back at the edge of the clearing?"

"They can swim, can they not?" Meric answered with a smile.

"Yes, Prince."

Meric's eyes narrowed. "Then they can journey back into the forest to safety, or work some of the fat from their brains by swimming. Truthfully, I care not. Besides, we are helpless to do anything to help such large creatures.

"Perhaps you could get some of our prisoners to talk to the birds, as Reon thought they could do. I am sure the native birds could be persuaded to carry them out of the water. No, better yet, ask the prisoners to get the birds to dine on the rats." Meric laughed as he reached the top of the hill, and gazed down at the large pale creatures' dwellings below.

"Trix," Fena whispered. "Have you noticed the guards' strength is much depleted?"

Noticing a rat guard moving closer, Trix held a paw to

her lips and nodded.

Silently, Ji slipped Hatty one of the two sharpened sticks he had made. Hatty discreetly slipped it into her pouch and said nothing.

#   #   #

High above the forest floor, Squorth scurried along the spotted gum's branch to Pon's position. "We could certainly use some of Jun's special mischief," she said. "Do you remember how he used to pluck hairs out of my legs in an attempt to make me drop you and Fila?" Squorth sat on the damp branch watching below.

"No, Princess, I can not say I do. But, I do remember how he used to tie your legs with your own web while you slept down in your chambers." Pon did his best to keep watch through the heavy rain.

"To this leaf fall, I can not work out how he achieved such a trick. He should have been caught up in my webs, long before he could reach me. I also recollect having to try and stop one of my cousins, a trapdoor spider, from giving him a sound thrashing. Fancy a young mouse, rolling such a large rock over another creature's dwelling entrance," Squorth said, smiling as she wriggled her legs trying to get comfortable.

"Princess! Pon! Look over there to the edge of that clearing," Fila called from the ground. "Behind that large clump of burnt grass is a camp of rats. They are eating our fellow natives and making their captives watch."

Climbing down onto the blackened, sodden, Mother Earth, Pon and Squorth followed Fila.

"If this falling water does not stop, we will all be washed away. Look beyond their camp, the Large Pale Ones have stripped Mother Earth clear of Sister Trees and life giving grasses. The ground there is now awash. That is why the rats camp here," Pon whispered, crawling along on his belly.

"How many would you say are in the camp, Fila?" Squorth asked, diving under some burnt leaves.

Fila followed. "I circled its perimeter, Princess, and I counted but three paws full."

"Fine. If you are with me, we will make this their last meal," Princess Squorth said, moving virtually invisible along the blackened ground.

Pon drew his bow and strung it. "Aye, Princess, we are with you"

Leaf falls later. A guard fell to the ground, a small arrow piercing his heart. Yet, another guard disappeared behind a log. There, it felt the wrath of Squorth's mighty fangs. Leaping from a blackened bush, Fila quickly dispensed of yet another rat, with a sharp stab of his bandicoot rib.

In the pouring rain, the three natives barely made a noise as they went about their deadly business. To avoid arousing suspicion, each left their victim propped where they had lost their spirit.

Finally, but one rat was left. The creature's doom appeared sealed as the three assassins approached from different directions.

Unexpectedly, out of the sky, Highra appeared and swooped the despicable creature up. Taking it to a great height, the mighty hawk twisted it in his talons and dropped it.

Within the wink of an eye, Highra landed near the bound captives. "Metcha and Ento," he said, "fear not ground dwellers, I believe in all treaties," and with that, he bent down and cut their bonds with his beak. "Now run with all haste toward the place where Brother Sun goes to rest."

Understandably the native creatures fled as instructed.

"Eek, oh Great and Noble Hawk, I am Princess

Squorth of the Funnel-web," she announced, introducing herself. "You have a distinctive manner in which you dispose of the invaders."

"I thank thee, Princess. I am Highra, of the Hawks, part of the Servicers' of the Circle of the commune of the Great Oak. I was informed that you were to be found ahead of Chieftain Mar's searchers, and indeed here you are. Now, who are these two mice that aid our cause so valiantly?" Highra lowered his head to peer inquisitively at the blackened waterlogged mice.

"Noble Highra, this is Pon and Fila of the Grey Gum. They are two of the sons of Briar the Elder," Squorth replied and pushed Pon forward.

"Ah, I should have known. Both appear of his character. Please accept my sadness at the passing of your father's spirit, Noble Mice," Highra said, draping his wing to the ground.

"Thank you, oh Noble Winged One. Tell us of Mar's quest, have they found the captives? We hope our family will be amongst them," Pon asked, turning back scanning the bodies of the native creatures around them.

"Pon, they are not here," Fila cried with relief as he finished searching.

"I am sorry to say, I have not seen Chieftain Mar since last lightening. At that leaf fall, my kind were forced to carry the searchers backward, to prevent them being devoured by the redness. Sadly, one of Lea's kind, a bearded dragon and two of the bird-spiders, expired before we came to their aid."

Squorth lowered her head in tribute to her cousins. "Highra, can you take us to the searchers?"

"Yes, Princess, but I am afraid it will be a slow journey as I am saturated and must only fly at short intervals. If only the Grey Rain-bringers would leave! Then my brother and sister winged ones could pursue with much haste. We dare not cross such a baron land with so few trees in pouring water, for fear we go down. We as you know, are not of the swimming kind."

"I understand perfectly. No matter how many stops or hops we take, be they small or large, we will still be heading in the right direction," Squorth wisely said, as the three climbed on Highra's back.

#   #   #

Attic did a tumble into the small notch in the gum where he and Toemouse had taken shelter.

Grabbing his friend's front paws, the wild mouse smiled broadly. "Toemouse, wasp friends say Bega alright. He is perched high in tree away from water. Downstream, they see father with many, many flying foxes. So you see, Toemouse, everything is good, yes?" Attic said, pulling Toe's paws and leading him out into the rain. "You and me leave, soon catch up."

"But how, Attic? They must be hundreds of mouse lengths away by now and it is dangerous for us to climb with this much water falling. I am just not good enough," Toe said, looking around at the water streaming off the leaves.

"We soon catch up, Toemouse," Attic said, as he walked over and chose a large leaf and gnawed at its stem.

It was not until the leaf fell to the ground and Attic turned it over that Toe realised what his strange friend was about to suggest.

"Do you really think we can ride the leaf down such a strong rush of water, Attic?" Toe asked, moving over to help him.

"Fun, lots of fun. Me do it many times, water me love. Toemouse help float leaf to main stream, yes? Any trouble wasps carry us to safety, OK?"

Attic pushed with all his strength, and with Toe's help,

soon had the leaf ready at the edge of the stream. "Toemouse get in. Then me."

With the help of the wasps, to steady the craft, Attic picked up a large stick with a flat end and lashed it to one end of the leaf.

"Toemouse sit. Now we have fun," Attic yelled as he launched the leaf into the stream and hopped in the stern of their craft.

Toe's heart thumped as the small craft picked up more and more speed. Attic just stood at the stern smiling and letting out the occasional scream of joy as the makeshift craft hit yet another obstacle.

#   #   #

Antoni rushed up to where Mar was conversing with Free. "Excuse me, Chieftain, but I have news from Prince Crier's kind,"

"I beg you go on," Mar replied, reached out with is paw and touched Antoni on the forehead.

"The Prince of Cicadas and his scouts are but half a lightening ahead, where some foreign rats have been forced to make camp. The rushing waters have blocked the rats' progress. Chieftain, they have prisoners." Nervous Antoni sensed a battle ahead.

Free lowered his head and politely said, "Forgive me for interrupting, if you would allow the flying foxes to escort you, we would be there in but a matter of leaf falls. You see, we fly in layers so that none of our kind have to remain wet for too long. Therefore, we can fly when the feathered winged ones can not."

Mar placed a paw on his chin and thought for a moment. "An interesting strategy, Free. Yes, I believe they would not expect any creature to dare travel in such a downpour. Antoni, what word is there of Bur and the spiders?"

"They are upstream from us, Chieftain. That is if any

survived that flash flood." Antoni had already begun his pre-battle exercises.

"I am afraid our ground dwelling forces are low, in fact, but a pawful remains. Free, could you send some of your kind back to bring our allies to us? We shall wait in the largest trees, toward where Brother Sun rests, this side of the rats' camp. There, we shall muster our forces and formulate a plan of attack."

"Yes of course, Chieftain Mar." Free turned and screeched.

Soon hundreds of his kind flew back upstream in groups; taking turns to block the rain from those underneath.

Antoni walked over to a cicada, conversed, and returned with a message. "Chieftain Mar, Prince Crier and his kind are donning their battle armour at this very leaf fall. They await your command to start the chorus of war cries."

"Excellent, then let us leave. Hopefully, by the end of this lightening, we will be reunited with our friends and families."

Free draped out his wing gracefully and allowed Antoni and Mar to climb onto his back.

Aldo, Stump, Dodd, Lea and the others, climbed onto Free's wing commanders as they landed.

Once again, the sky went dark above the searchers' heads as thousands of flying foxes took flight.

#   #   #

"Bega, you must wake. Some flying foxes have come to carry us to Chieftain Mar," Bur said, poking Bega with one of his hairy legs.

Still very drowsy, Bega replied, "Chieftain Mar, yes of course. Let us move then." However, when he went to move, he found himself still confined by Bur's web.

"Please, if you do not mind, Bur, could you release me and accept my gratitude."

"No need for gratitude. Are you sure, you will be steady enough on your feet? You have had two serious dunkings in the last two lightenings." Bur bent down and began to snip the web with his fangs.

"Yes, I am sure."

"Hm," a flying fox said, "Chieftain Free, did not mention we were to carry a bandicoot."

"If there is a problem, I shall gladly walk," Bega proudly announced, stood, wobbled and nearly fell off the very wet branch.

"No, large one." The flying fox turned and screeched toward a group of his followers, "EEE..."

Within leaf falls a larger flying fox, nearly twice as big as the others, landed on the branch.

"Small One, carry this bandicoot," the high ranking flying fox commanded.

"Yes, Commander Fla," she replied, draping out a wing.

"I am in your debt, Small One," Bega said, climbing aboard. "Screech to you."

"Ona, Old One," she replied, taking flight close behind the others.

Within wing strokes Small One was flying beneath the shroud of its brethren to keep Bega dry.

#   #   #

"Look up, Toemouse, now! See up in sky, is Bega. Every creature is having fun this leaf fall." Attic grinned, deliberately steering their small craft into another obstacle.

Toe looked up just in time to see the large flying foxes disappearing into the distance.

"Listen, Toemouse, to the loud roar up ahead. Soon we have more fun." Attic released the rudder, allowing the craft to spin.

As the roaring became louder and louder, Toe realised what was coming up ahead. *Father took me to see the great falls of the boulders during a time of wet, but this noise is even louder than them,* he thought.

"Toemouse, stand and look out of leaf. You must see, with eyes," Attic screamed with a sound of glee in his voice.

As Toe looked through the vale of rain ahead, all he could make out was a large mist that seemed to rise from the stream.

Searching around his fur, Attic said, "Keep looking with eyes, Toemouse."

"Attic, you have to do something; we are going to go over a waterfall." Poor Toe did not know what to do.

Unfazed, Attic kept searching. Finally, he pulled out his whistle and blew into it.

As the leaf hit the edge of the waterfall, Toe crouched down and screamed, "ATTIC."

Unexpectedly, a loud humming noise drowned out the

roar of the waterfall.

"What is happening, Attic?" Toe pleaded, only to receive no reply.

Standing up, he saw Attic flapping his arms and conversing with a few hundred wasps. To his surprise, the wasps were now carrying the leaf through the air.

"What fun, Toemouse! Do you want do again?" Attic asked, pointing back to the enormous waterfall just behind them.

Toe took a deep breath of air and shook his head as he looked down at the rocks below. "No th... th... thank you," the young mouse stammered.

Attic, simply lay back with his paws behind his head and began to sing another song of the bush. Only this time it was in a wasp hum, within leaf falls the wasps were all humming along in time with him.

"In future, Attic, could you tell me exactly what you plan," Toe said, in a stern tone.

"Plan, what is plan? Me know, not what me do. So me, can not tell Toemouse. Also, it would spoil fun."

"What if there had been no wasps around, Attic?"

Confidently, Attic declared, "Then, me call hornets or bees. Always friends close in bush." Attic stretched, quite relaxed, and threw his forelegs into the air.

Toe stepped toward his friend and looked down at him, "Does it not worry you, we may have lost our spirits?"

"Toemouse, he can be without breath? You may lose spirit?"

"Yes," Toe said, relieved to be finally getting his message across.

"Attic, know not what worry be? Perhaps you could teach me this worry later. Now tell me, Toemouse, did your heart not pump, screaming, 'Me with spirit, me with spirit'? Now, that how me tell when having fun." A huge smile erupted across the wild mouse's face.

Toe shook his head, looked over the side of the leaf at the steady rain, and asked, "How shall we follow them?"

"Toemouse, not know flying foxes. Wasps and I know what their nature be. Plenty leaf falls to go back and do falling water again. Toemouse say, 'Yes' and me get wasps turn round."

#   #   #

Turning his head, Highra, of the Hawks, announced, "We are nearing a camp of many creatures."

"What is that dark cloud, moving across under the Rain-bringers?" Fila asked.

"That, mouse, is the flying foxes from the rain-forest. If my eyes do not deceive me, they have passengers," Highra said, flapping his wings furiously to gain some height.

Soon, they landed in the branches of a large stringybark. Upon identifying themselves, the coverage of foxes allowed them to enter through, into the war council area. There in the darkness, all the searchers came together for the first time.

"Bega, you old bandicoot, how do you keep doing it? When we return, I shall ask Petra to bestow the Gum Nut of Valour on you once more," Mar said, hugging his large friend.

"Still hugging creatures, I see," a voice said, from the darkness.

Without even turning, Mar replied, "I know that voice, Pon, where are you?"

Pon moved closer and embraced Mar like a brother. "I am not alone, come forth Fila."

"By the River Stones, Fila too! What on Mother Earth, are you doing here?" Mar threw his forelegs out to greet Elder Briar's, third son.

"Our Grey Gum commune was set to redness. We think these invaders have our families," Fila said, with deep sadness in his voice.

"That is indeed grim news," Bega mumbled, beneath his breath.

Fila held Mar at forelegs lengths. "Princess Squorth saved us from certain doom. Then, when we attacked a small camp of rats, Chieftain Highra assisted us. We were seeking you out, when we saw the sky darken."

Mar glanced at Squorth. "Ento, Princess Squorth, and thank you." The Chieftain then turned his attention back to Pon and Fila. "Now tell me of Jun, is he with you?"

"Sorry, Mar, we know not where he is," Pon announced and lowered his head.

"Eeek, Noble Highra and thank you," Mar said, and waved a paw to summon his son from the trunk of the tree, "Pon, Fila this is my eldest, Dodd."

"Metcha, young mouse," Pon and Fila replied, moving forward and looking up into Dodd's big brown eyes.

"Perhaps, we should say, 'large mouse'," Pon added, with a smile.

Dodd nodded politely and squeezed past to find his teacher, Bega.

"Chieftain Mar, we have received word from Betra's kind that a swarm of native wasps is coming this way," a call came from outside the sanctum.

"Fine news. Antoni, do you still speak their tongue?" Mar asked the Chief Warrior Ant, who had been sitting quietly against the tree's trunk.

"It has been many leaf falls, but yes I should be able to. Chieftain, while it is not well known, they do speak the common tongue. They simply refuse to use it, in protest. They think it unfair that wasp is not taught in our places of learning," Antoni said, walking along the branch to the small opening the bats had left.

"Elder Briar's spirit be praised, you survived once more, Elder Bega," Antoni whispered, without stopping for a reply.

Antoni walked out to the very tip of the small branch. "Well, where are these wasps?" he asked the cicadas, straining to see past the rain.

"Sorry, Chief, they have landed not far away. There, to the crest of the hill, near the banksias," replied, a cicada in full battle shell.

#   #   #

Landing at the base of the banksias, Attic and Toe hummed a thank you to their wasp friends. In the whisk of a breeze, the two young mice watched them fly away again.

Unexpectedly, a wasp from another nest flew in and landed on Attic's paw.

Toe waited patiently as the two conversed.

With a loud hum, the conversation ended and the wasp flew onto a leaf.

"Toemouse, friend wasp tell me many creatures of the shadows ahead. Also they have native creatures tied together. Best me think, you stay here and hide." Attic placed both paws on his young friend's shoulders. "Too dangerous for you, me think."

Toe defiantly brushed Attic's paws aside. "No, Attic! I am coming with you. My mother and Hatty could be amongst them."

"Very brave you be, Toemouse. Alright, me send friend wasp to gather other friends. Hornets and bees, they be. Then together we help."

At that leaf fall a cloud of mist drifted away and revealed a giant tree covered in flying foxes.

"What on Mother Earth is that?" Toe pointed in disbelief at the phenomenal sight.

Having seen something similar before, Attic simply shrugged and said, "Me say many gather to talk best way of freeing fellow creatures. We wait back here under ferns until they move, then we follow and perhaps help, yes?"

"You mean I will be able to see father and Dodd?" Toe's face lit up with excitement.

"We see. For now, Toemouse, we make shelter from rain."

With that Attic crawled deep into the ferns and shook the rain from the fronds. Constantly learning from the strange bush creature, Toe helped him fashion a secure shelter by crossing the ferns in layers.

#   #   #

"Chieftain Mar, Bur has found some fellow natives hiding in the bushes. At this very leaf fall, the leader of the Bird-spiders is bringing them to the council."

"Fine Stump," Mar replied, turning to his comrades. He raised his voice so all those perched on the branches above him could hear. "It is agreed, just before the end of darkening that Princess Squorth, Bur and the other spiders shall enter the camp. Then with the assistance of Pon, Fila and Aldo they will minimise any risk of harm to the captives and create a perimeter.

"Upon the coming of the lightening, those mounted on Highra's and Free's kinds will come at them from Brother Sun. Hopefully; they will catch the rats by surprise. Bega, Lea and the others will quietly move in and assist in freeing the prisoners. Prince Crier and his army shall create an intense deafening war cry while swooping in an attempt to distract the foreign rats."

"Chieftain Mar, this is Ni, of the Great Fallen Logs commune," Stump announced, leading the native rat forward.

"Re, Ni, tell us of your commune?" Mar asked, looking

up into the large rat's eyes.

The rat bowed his head solemnly. "Metcha, Chieftain. My commune has all but been destroyed. What you see down in the camp below is all that is left, other than a few echidnas, some possums and lizards. We all wish to join you in battle, to free our commune's creatures."

Mar reached his paw out to touch the rat. "Good, Ni, we will be proud to fight by your side. Please call me, 'Mar'. Did you see any other creatures strange to these parts?"

"No. I am sure they have only our commune's survivors. There was, however, a small army that left, before the pouring of water, they held many prisoners. That army appeared to be led by your kind."

"My kind, do you mean a native mouse?"

"No, Mar, not a native."

"Then it was most definitely, not of my kind," Mar said, disturbed by being associated with the foreign invaders. "Those you see around us are my kind, the natives, Ni!"

"Forgive me, Mar, I did not mean any disrespect." Ni bowed his head again.

"Mar, Chief Antoni, come quickly you must see this," Aldo screamed, from outside the meeting area and immediately scrambled down the tree's trunk.

Making their way down the tree in pursuit of Aldo, Mar and Antoni smiled broadly as they looked out around the great stringybark's trunk. There before them was Royo leading the column of ten thousand bull-ants and another four thousand white-ants; on either side, stood thirty frill-necked and forty bearded dragons. Magnificent, Mar thought, with a lifted heart, when ten goannas crashed through the charred undergrowth and into the small clearing.

Royo ran straight up to Antoni, stood on his hind legs and threw a foreleg to his chest in salute. "We have marched since the lightening you left, Chief Antoni, and in our travels have gathered these proud allies."

"Boyor, Royo, and by Father Sky you could not have come at a better time," Antoni said, unceremoniously slapping his commander across the back.

"Boyor, brave Bull-ants," Mar yelled, holding up his arms. "Sya, noble lizards and great ones of the bush. Nena, oh white destroyers. I thank you all. On the coming lightening, we shall let these vile invaders feel the anger they have created.

"For now we must keep ourselves undetected. So when Chief Antoni gives the command, please break away quickly and hide as best you can. You see, not a rat, mouse or cockroach of the invader kind, must escape the attack. We can not risk word getting to those ahead."

Moving forward, Gre the head Goanna exclaimed, "Ahead! You mean you do not know of the great camp of rats and cockroaches that is on this side of the water? Why it is only half a lightening away, to this paw, of Brother Sun," he said, raising his large leg and pointing.

Stunned, Mar turned toward the tree trunk to gather his thoughts. "No, we did not. The last we heard it was on the other bank."

"How many rats and mice would you say are in the camp, you wish to attack?" Gre asked, walking up closer to the mouse so not all would hear.

Turning again Mar gazed into the lizards face. "Our scouts say that more gather every leaf fall. Last report, there were approximately ten thousand rats and but a few mice."

A groan rumbled from Gre's deep belly before he answered. "Well, I would say that there were at least twenty thousand rats in the other camp. On top of that, there are ten thousand mice and a plague of cockroaches."

"This is indeed grave news," Mar said, walking around in a circle with his paw on his chin.

Antoni stepped out from behind a sapling and interjected, "May I suggest, we leave half our forces here, Mar, and send the rest toward the other camp, under Noble Gre's command? In doing so, we should block any who escape from this camp summoning help. I suggest strongly though, they do not engage the other army until we dispense of this one and join them."

"Even then it may be best that we only watch the large army until enough natives are gathered to ensure a successful battle. I fear if any creature should escape, they may make their way to wherever the kidnappers are taking the captives." Mar lowered his head. "That would mean their certain death."

"You are aiding us, Chieftain Mar, in ridding our homes of these creatures. Fear not, we shall do nothing that may risk the spirits of your commune's creatures," Gre said, turning and heading in the direction he had indicated.

Antoni raised his leg, ordering his ant army to split. Then the Chief Warrior Ant scurried over to Lea and explained. Within, a fraction, of a leaf fall Lea had given the command and split his force of lizards. As the chain of command progressed the great gathering of natives separated. Those left behind disappeared into the charred undergrowth and remaining patches of green.

The Chief bull-ant marched over and stood at Mar's side. "Now we must wait until the darkening comes and goes. In the darkening, Betra's kind will keep a watchful eye on the camp for us, while brothers Boobook and Barn owls will diminish some more of the enemies' kind."

 # DARKENING TWELVE

The curtain created by the flying foxes' wings parted as Night Flyer, the bat, made its way to Bega.

Reaching the old bandicoot, Night Flyer whispered, "Elder Bega, I have word of the commune. The Highest of Wedge-tails has left with half of the winged servicers and will arrive upon the lightening. In her travels she hopes to gather more winged ones from as far a field as possible."

"Ee, Night Flyer," Bega said, looking around in the darkness for Mar and his commanders.

Journeying further along the branch, to where Mar sat talking to Lea and Antoni, Bega told them the news.

Sensing the preparations to free the captives were overwhelming his pupil Bega ushered Dodd to one side. "Stay with me tomorrow, Mouse, I shall ensure your safety. Have you sharpened the edges of your roarer, like I asked?"

"Yes, teacher, I have." Dodd stood shaking by his mentor's side.

"Good! On the lightening, when I give you the word, drop your staff and roar it with all your heart." Bega commanded, placing his paw on young Dodd's shoulder.

#   #   #

Prince Meric and his captives made their way up the narrow treacherous path to the nest's entrance. Despite the darkness the Prince had given orders the prisoners' safety was to be paramount, much to the disdain of the rats.

Entering the opening of the cave, which overlooked the Large Pale Creatures' dwellings, Lenthric smiled and said, "Ah, finally we have returned to the safety of our city."

"City," Meric grunted in disgust. "You mean a dirty filthy hole in the ground; we share with ever increasing rats and cockroaches. No, if I had a choice I would stay outside. The stench down there was overpowering when we left, I can not imagine what it shall be like now."

As the tail end of the army entered the hole, the owls' talons seized two more of the rear guard.

Without warning, a small figure dashed out to Fena and Trix. In the wink of an eye, it cut their vines and whisked them away into the surrounding rocks. Trix, however, struggled and soon returned to the captors' ranks, tying herself back into the line.

"What an odd thing to do?" the rescuer whispered, dumbfounded.

Fena recognised the voice immediately. "You were never one for foresight, brother of my life mate. Trix returned so that my escape is less likely to be detected. You see her daughter is still captive, as is Ji, Nila and Nel," Fena said, staring up into the scruffy fur where Jun's large eyes rested.

Jun looked down hard into Fena's eyes, "Brother of my life mate?" Suddenly in the starlight, he recognised Fena's distinctive grin. "Fena, by the Great Gum's Leaves, I had no idea. Tell me, what of Fila and Pon?"

Fena put both paws on Jun's broad shoulders as she told him of the fate of their commune. "I have no idea if Pon or Fila survived the redness." She also went on to tell him of the other communes, including the Great Oak's, which had been attacked and pillaged.

As they zigzagged up the side of the hill Fena asked, "Why did you not return, Jun, or at least send word?"

"When I travelled here, laid my eyes upon the devastation and the plight of our fellow native creatures, I could not. A number of the creatures I aided in escape, promised to spread the word of my actions. I had hoped you may have heard from one of them. Now come, it is not safe so close to their main entrance. I will take you to the others who fight for the freedom of our kind." Jun seized her paw and picked up his pace.

Leaf falls later; Fena and Jun were high above the invaders' entrance. Jun gave three raps on a small boulder with the gem glued on the end of his staff.

This is amazing, Fena thought, watching on as a large rock opened toward them.

Inside she found hundreds of natives quietly huddled

together in a large cave. Turning she asked, "How could this be possible?"

Sensing her wonderment Jun placed his paw to his mouth and whispered, "We are right above the invaders' main lairs. They have not yet thought we would dare such a tactic."

#   #   #

"Send the captives to the holding area, Lenthric, I shall be with my father," Meric requested, breaking away at the junction of two passage ways. The Prince, of the Invading Mice, turned as he past Hatty and smiled.

In reply, she reached down, filled her paw with mud and hurled it at his face.

Unexpectedly the guards stopped the prisoners on the edge of a large pit and moved back. Out of the shadows dirty black rats charged and with a sinister squeal knocked the captives into the darkness. The helpless natives, still bound by their legs, tumbled over and over until they hit the bottom; the bodies of other captives, the only thing to break their fall.

For the first time since their capture Hatty and Trix could talk freely and plan an escape. "The entrance is guarded too heavily and these walls are too slippery." Trix said to her daughter as she summed their situation.

Defiantly, they stared around at the wasting faces of the other creatures. "Oh Mother, they are so thin. These devils must not have fed them for many leaf falls."

#   #   #

Entering his father's area of the caverns, Meric announced, "Father, I have returned."

The Prince was, however, left in puzzlement. Despite

236

the incredible increases in population over the weeks of his quest, Meric found no sign of his family. In fact, he found very few mice at all. Those that had crossed his path ran from his sight in fear.

"Prince," a voice whispered from the shadows. "Come into the crevice."

"Beyan, what is going on, where is my father, the King?"

"I have terrible news, my Prince. The King of Mice and your family have been slain by King Yahn's first guards," Beyan whispered. "When supplies of food became scarce your father protested to the King Rat. He put forward that our fellow mice were not getting a share sufficient to ensure survival."

His blood boiling with rage, Meric demanded answers, "How so? When we left supplies were ample!"

"Many of King Yahn's latest brood have since been born and take priority over all our kind. The large creatures have also started attacking our food gatherers. Prince, they have even befriended some of the natives who now help protect their dwellings from our food raids."

"But what of my family?" Meric asked, watching the passing rats in the corridor.

"The rats turned to eating the captives, Prince, and your father protested, again with his most loyal mice."

Meric's eyes opened wide. "You mean he took up arms against the Rat King?"

"Yes, Prince, in this very lair. I and a few others, still loyal to you, are the only survivors." Beyan peered nervously out of the shadows.

"I would never have thought it possible," Meric said, amazed at his father's courage. Courage, he thought, long since perished in this land.

"They were all killed, Prince, and devoured, your whole family. Those loyal to your father are now forced into servitude. With each passing day our numbers become less, while many mice still loyal to the Rat King flourish. Tell me what to do, Prince, as I have been ordered to bring you before the King." Beyan lowered his head into his paws.

Meric grabbed Beyan by his shoulders and shook him. "What fool does he think I am? Come Beyan, we must find those still loyal to the ways of the homeland. Do you think some of our cousins, the brown rats, would join us in a revolt?"

"No, Prince, they are all of Yahn's mind."

"Then we must flee this city, Beyan. Somehow we must seek refuge in this country of harshness. Perhaps we may ally ourselves with the natives and return to destroy this evil place."

Fearful of detection the two mice stayed in the shadows as they began their journey out of the nest.

#   #   #

For a number of leaf falls, Hatty sat silently staring at the wooden gates across the cell. *How shall we escape this wretched place?* she thought.

"What is beyond that gate?" she asked, an old possum next to her.

"I can not be sure, young one, anybody who has gone through them has never returned. I did gather enough courage to push forward, when I was first captured, and look into the cavern. All I saw were thousands of young rats, newborns they were." The old possum's voice sounded tired and wheezy.

Hatty wiggled even closer to the possum. "What about our fellow natives, where do they keep taking them? Have you any idea why not one returns?"

The possum tilted her head toward Hatty and whispered, "Before my capture, I used to see the rats herding natives toward the large pale ones' homes. After some leaf falls the natives would then return with food."

"How could they make them do such a thing? Why, they should have refused!" Hatty exclaimed in anger.

"Judge them not harshly, child. For every native forced into service, the rats somehow know they have a friend or relative left behind in this damp, cold, place. Look around you, kangaroo mouse, those here are but a few of the many family members and friends of those dragged away to do the rats' work. It is fear for their family's lives, not their own, which forces them into servitude." The old possum sighed deeply and closed her eyes.

"So that is why they attack a commune at a time and keep us bound separately. Those vile creatures are using our love and loyalty against us. Yet, here in this pit, we are allowed to interact. I am afraid I just do not understand their logic?" Hatty's eyes remained locked on the gateway.

"Given leaf falls you will, young mouse. Look upon my ear," the possum said, pushing her ear forward with her paw. "See the notch cut out of it, that is how they tell which commune I was taken from. Once a lightening, well that is what I calculate it to be, the rats come in and force us into our marking groups. It is then; they will select the ones to leave. Usually two groups are chosen, one consisting of the fatter creatures and the other of the more agile natives."

"I have no such marking," Hatty announced, feeling around her ears.

Opening her eyes, the possum sat up, and examined Hatty's ears. "No, it appears you do not. Perhaps that is the way they will identify your commune then."

"Ji, Nel," Hatty called, "come over here."

"Yes, Hatty of the Great Oak." Ji nodded his head, leapt onto his hind legs and helped Nel to stand.

Standing, Hatty rushed to meet them. "Have you been

marked in any way by the invading rats?"

When the two young mice bent forward and revealed the marks on the very tips of their left ears, she frowned. "Why then, were we not marked in such a way?"

"One can not be sure. Perhaps, the leader who took your fellow natives did not believe in such a form of identification or it was simply, planned that way. Only that creature could tell you." The possum groaned, stood trembling and stumbled off into the darkness.

Hatty scratched around in the damp soil with her hind paws as she tried to make sense of it all. "Ji, all the other natives in this cell have said the redness was used to destroy their communes. Why is it that the same tactic was not used against ours? What was so different, about the foreign mouse who led the raiders against us?"

"Hatty, I doubt all these creatures are as evil as the invading rats." Ji's skin crawled as yet another patrol of black cockroaches circled the walls. "How I would enjoy taking my sharpened stick and piercing it through one of their dark backs." His eyes narrowed as he grit his teeth.

#   #   #

After keeping to the shadows throughout the night, Meric and Beyan finally reached the main entrance of the underground cavern. Undetected, they stood in a crevice of the tunnel's wall and watched.

Meric waited until the guards were furthest apart and touched his friend's shoulder. "We must move now, Beyan, before sunrise. Are you ready?"

Reaching down to the water, seeping through the cavern's wall, Meric grabbed some mud in his paw and covered his loyal friend's face and then his own. Their disguise complete, they moved into the flow of other animals leaving the city.

Meric breathed a sigh of relief as they began to pass the last guard. We have made it, he thought.

Until the rat noticed Tongue, the Truth Bringer, strapped to Meric's side as he past. "Hold, mouse."

Fully aware of the possible cost, Meric ignored the rat's command and walked on. "Go on, Beyan, I shall meet you behind the great boulder the one which points to the sun's rising."

"I shall not leave you. There is but two of the rats, surely we can take them." Beyan stood loyally by his prince.

"You forget this sword is but an ornament which hangs by my side. It is not your fault, they detected us. Leave! I have brought this upon myself through stupid vanity and greed. I should have left this where I found it. Now go, I command you."

Suddenly, the two rat guards pushed forward, through the other animals, and seized Beyan.

Defiant, Meric walked up, crossed his front legs over his chest and stood before them. "Release him."

"I do not take orders from mice." The rat sneered as he looked the prince up and down. "What is a mouse doing with such a prize?" The guard held out its huge front claw. "Give it to me or face my wraith."

Struck by the realisation of who stood before him, the second rat's whiskers twitched. "It is Prince Meric, Yon! We have been ordered to arrest him and take him to King Yahn, immediately."

"Ah, that is why you have such a thing of beauty. Well, mouse, you are Prince of nothing now. So give me the sword," Yon ordered, poking him with his claw.

Left little option, Meric undid his belt and held the sword out for the rat to take. Unexpectedly, out of the corner of his eye, he noticed the handle move slightly in its sheath. Weighing up the consequences of his actions he grabbed the sword's hilt.

Unlike the other times he had tried, the sword came free, its blade gleaming in the moonlight. "What magic is this?" he gasped, and within a breath lunged forward.

With a hiss of air, the sword entered the rat's rib cage and mortally pierced its' heart. Turning quickly Meric sprang over the dead rat's body and lashed out wildly at the other rat.

Stunned by the ferocity of the attack, the other rat relinquished its grip on Beyan and fled back into the cavern yelling, "Prince Meric is here."

Without a second thought Meric cleaned the blade on the dead rat's fur and calmly slid it back into its sheath.

Moments later, they both recognised the distinctive, reverberating, rumble of guards climbing the passage.

"Beyan, run," he ordered, seized at the weapon's hilt and prepared himself to fight.

Determined to avenge his family's murder Meric moved to draw the weapon, only to find it unable to leave the sheath. Dumbfounded, he dropped the sword next to the body and joined the ranks of gatherers.

Free of any form of identification both mice slipped past the other guard posts before word of their escape spread.

By the time the sun's rays began filtering across the valley they were safe; high on the hill above the cavern.

LIGHTENING OF THE WOODS THIRTEEN

Brother Sun's rays broke through the canopy and illuminated Mar as he climbed up onto a rock to address the natives.

"It is time," he announced. "May Father Sky and Mother Earth, guide and protect all of us upon this lightening. All gathered here know the risks we take in engaging the invaders. Remember, the captives are our first priority; all that we do this lightening must revolve around their safety. Squorth and Bur have been digging since before darkening, so by now they will be close to securing the captives' safety perimeter."

Mar turned to the giant flying fox next to him. "Free, can you send your brothers into Father Sky."

In reply, the commander let out an ear piercing screech and took flight.

Within leaf falls, the large gum trees of the area became bare as the remaining ten thousand flying foxes followed Free. At first they flew in the direction of Brother Sun's rising and then turned back toward the rats' camp.

At the same time the Bull-ants, led by Chief Antoni, came out from under their leaf camouflage and began their march.

The dampness of the topsoil worked to the searchers' advantage as the ground above them silently slid away. Undetected, Squorth, Bur, Pon, Fila and Aldo, backed by the remaining bird-spiders, appeared from their tunnels behind the invading rats' lines. As silently as a feather blown through the air, the advance party went about taking the spirits of the closest guards and began releasing the captives.

As the first rays of light hit the dark camp-site the last of the small captives slipped down the escape holes.

Turning to the remaining natives, Bur grumbled, "Wait for the sign before we attack."

The rescuers and the larger liberated creatures stood side by side waiting.

#   #   #

Reon, the Rat Commander, walked amidst his army unaware of the impending attack. He smiled as he observed the remains of natives lying amongst his sleeping soldiers. *A fine feast had by all last eve*, he thought. *Why should we not benefit the most? After all, we were the ones brave enough to attack these pathetic native communities.*

"Commander Reon, look to the sun," a lookout called.

Reon then joined with hundreds of the other rats, who already stood staring at the cloud of flying foxes heading straight toward them.

"Never in my days, have I seen such a thing," Reon declared. "There are so many that they block the sun's rays." Turning to his army the rat donned his skull helmet, drew his sword and pointed to the sky. "Prepare for battle."

#   #   #

"Now," Highra of the Hawks called, from above the

cloud of bats.

On command, the flying foxes spread apart allowing the full force of the lightenings rays through. Down on the ground below, the manoeuvre temporarily blinded hundreds of the enemy.

As soon as the camp lit up, Bega and Dodd ran out from their hiding place. "Dodd, roar your bull-roarer like you have never roared it before," the old bandicoot commanded. "I pray that the sound will not only serve as the signal to advance, but that it will also confuse the enemy."

Dodd dropped his staff and started to swing his creation with all his strength. "Brrr, Brrr, Brrr," the roarer hummed, getting louder with every swing.

In answer to Bega's prayers, the enemy began to panic.

"A giant creature has come to devour us," was the cry that met Reon's ears. The commander could do little as the army of rats fell apart, scared out of their wits. Totally out of control the invaders began running into each other trying to flee, only increasing the chaos.

Standing on his hind legs, Antoni drew his spider fang from its scabbard and held it into the air. "Attack!" he called to his ant army.

Simultaneously, other creatures sprang out of hiding. Prince Crier's Cicadas, in their thousands started to chant a war cry as they too, donned in armour, flew directly at the rats. Squorth and the others then started their attack from within.

Highra, Pi, of the Peregrine Falcons, and the Brown Falcons swooped into the clear airspace. Soon Galahs, Black Cockatoos, Kookaburras and even Bower-birds joined in the attack.

When the flying foxes began to land, what little discipline left in the rats' camp disintegrated and they began to desert in droves.

Time after time the winged ones landed, seized an invader and flew off again. Soaring to a great height they twisted the rats' necks and dropped their lifeless bodies into the rushing flood waters below.

Dodd, as ordered, stayed by Bega's side swinging his stone. *I can not believe my old mentor can fight so well,* he thought. *It is astounding how quickly he moves for such a large creature. He whips at the rats' eyes with his tail and then strikes them cleanly across the neck with his staff. Thanks to his example, I no longer fear these rats.*

Eventually, the rats realised where the noise was coming from and turned part of their defence into an attack.

Dodd's eyes widened as at least thirty rats started coming toward him. Fangs dripping with blood and their fur stained by the burnt earth, the rats' appearance terrified the young kangaroo mouse.

Nevertheless, instead of retreating, Dodd stood his ground swinging his sharpened roarer above his head.

Rat after rat, found themselves slashed and cut by its razor sharp edge.

"Be warned rats that despite your onslaught and my fatigue, I will not allow you to hurt my mentor," Dodd screamed, the adrenaline pumping through his small heart.

When a rat leapt onto Bega's back, to puncture the bandicoot's neck with its fangs, Dodd let the roarer fly. Hissing through the air the stone found its mark, cutting into the rat's spine, crippling it instantly.

"Thank the stars for your talent, young mouse," Bega shouted, whipping another attacker with his tail.

While the battle went well in all the other sectors, Dodd and Bega found themselves constantly overrun. Despite the most valiant efforts of the few bull-ants that remained by their sides, the fight in this quarter was being lost. The barren scorched earth, so recently burnt by the redness, left nowhere for the brave natives to hide or retreat to. Consequently, the small band found themselves surrounded.

Just as Dodd's heart began to sink, out of nowhere his younger brother appeared camouflaged in burnt leaves. "Look out, Dodd," Toe yelled as he blew his whistle stick and pointed.

Like a giant arrow, thousands of wasps appeared from the sky and stung the rat that was about to attack Dodd.

"Toe," Dodd yelled, "How, what?" But when he turned, all he could see was a giant swarm of wasps.

"I am here in behind the wasps' protection. Do not worry about me," Toe replied, above the loud hum of the wasps.

Even with Toe's help, Dodd and Bega were still

beaten. Dodd, staff in paw, watched on helplessly as another two rats rushed toward him. *May Mother Earth and Father Sky deliver my spirit to the Great Circle*, he thought resigning himself to his loss of spirit.

Out of nowhere Attic sprang onto one of the devil creature's backs, dug his feet into its ears and steered it head-on into another. With great agility the wild mouse leapt off and landed directly in front of Dodd.

For the first time their eyes met. *How similar we are in size and appearance*, Dodd thought speechless.

Momentarily dazed, he stood as Attic lifted his leg, jumped toward him, knocked him down and kicked yet another rat in the windpipe.

From then on, Attic felt a strong bond with the large mouse and stayed guarding his back.

Attic smiled, reached into his fur, pulled out his stick and did a jig as he blew into it. Soon the air around them filled with native bees and hornets.

The small sting-less bees flew up the rats' noses forcing them to open their mouths to breath. This in turn signalled the hornets to fly in and sting the invaders' throats. Within a water drip, the rats' throats began to swell depriving them of air.

Bega stepped backward when a swarm of wasps came directly at him. "Hold wasps, surely I do not look like these demons?"

Humming a little, Toe made a small opening so Bega could see his face. "It is I, Toe, Elder Bega," he said, with a grin.

"By the River Stones, I have never seen such a defence," Bega said, as he whacked yet another rat across the neck with his staff.

As if trained together all their lives, Dodd and Attic fought, using each other as vaults to kick the enemy.

Attic shrieked with joy when his partner lifted a rat

above his head and threw it at the others. "Strong you be," he screamed with delight.

"Who are you?" Dodd asked, gasping for air.

"Me be air, water, trees, insects and creatures of bush. Me be all things, but Toemouse calls me, 'Attic'," he said, flipping himself over Dodd's back as he bent gasping for a breath of air.

The natives' surprise advantage soon disappeared when the rats gathered themselves together under Reon's command. Forming a large square they started to rush in the direction of the other camp.

If I can kill that commander, Mar thought, *the rats will be little more than a rabble.*

The leader of the commune of the Great Oak, rushed forward, leapt up onto a branch and waited. When the rats passed beneath him, he jumped boldly onto the top of the square and started running across the rats toward their leader.

After many years of battles together, Antoni knew what his friend was attempting to do. "Go under them my ants, bite their legs and sting their underbellies," he commanded, as he leapt under the group of invaders approaching him.

The rats screamed from the agonising bites received from the one and a half inch long bull-ant warriors. The square began to break, the goannas and echidnas moved in to ensure the rats stayed separated.

A piercing cry came from the sky as Sqweara, the Highest of Wedge-tails, and at least one hundred of her kind, gathered in her travels, dove into the foray.

The battle appeared to grow quiet in Mar's ears as he faced Reon. Concentrating on his opponent's eyes he balanced his staff in his right paw and waited.

Squorth and Bur silently crept up behind Reon ready to overpower him. To their dismay, Mar shook his head and held up his paw as a signal to stop. All around them lay hundreds of creatures, both native and foreign, without spirit and it sickened Mar to the stomach. "Now is the time for recompense, creature. I shall return you to hell personally, Devourer of Natives."

Reon stood on his hind legs. "Am I to take this as a challenge, you backward native? You can babble all you like in your primitive tongue but I shall never understand it. You see I am from a civilised world," the rat commander snarled with conceit.

For what seemed like an eternity they gazed into each other's eyes, then Reon laughed and sprang at Mar.

Whipping with his tail, Mar blinded Reon's right eye with a stinging flick. As if in one movement he rapped the staff across the rat's front teeth and smashed them.

Reon fell to the ground and lay still even as Mar approached him.

Doing his best to force his way to his father's side, Toe broke through the other fighting just as Reon fell. "Father," he yelled, without thinking.

Surprised, Mar turned to the sound of his lost son's voice.

Seizing the opportunity Reon leapt up, sank the remains of his jagged teeth into Mar's back and flung him across the ground.

Despite his wounds bleeding badly, Mar pushed himself up, stood and started to spin his staff above his head. Like the rush of a breeze the Chieftain of the Oak, let the staff fly at Reon. With the accuracy of a dart it hit the rat's windpipe depriving him of air.

His years of training with Elder Briar played back as he moved forward to take the advantage. With each pace, his wound took its toll, the world began to spin and his legs went weak. Exhausted, he fell to the ground; his fur saturated with his own blood.

"I give you this mouse, you can fight," Reon gasped, rising to his hind legs once more. "I shall take extra pleasure in devouring you when this battle is over." The rat pounced.

With surprising speed and agility, Toe, Dodd, and Attic appeared in front of Mar before Reon even landed. While to the side in a flurry of activity the hornets stung the last of the rats until they fell.

In an incredible demonstration of strength and determination, Dodd caught the large rat as he pounced on his father. "Now Toe and Attic," he screamed, holding it back.

Upon his brother's command, Toe sent in his wasps to sting Reon in the throat while Attic jumped on his back. Together, in an attempt to restrain Reon, Dodd strained to push forward as Attic pulled the neck backward.

"Hurry, Toe, take father away. I can not hold the weight much longer," Dodd pleaded, the fur on his brow saturated with sweat and his legs shaking.

"Your strength can not last out, mouse," Reon snarled, "I shall eat you first, you native sw..." The rat heard a loud crack and found himself robbed of his voice as his paralysed body fell to the ground.

How can this be possible? Reon thought as everything went black.

Natives and invaders alike watched on in amazement as the rat commander's eyes bulged, he shook and took his last breath.

A rumble quickly grew amongst the invaders' ranks telling of the commander's death. Within leaf falls the remaining rats broke ranks and fled.

The battle was over and the natives were victorious, the flying foxes hanging from the charred trees screeched loudly as the cicadas chirped in rhythm.

Dodd staggered exhausted only to fall to his knees beside Mar's motionless body.

Sending his wasps to pursue the retreating rats, Toe walked free of their protective armour to Mar's side. "Father, I am here," Toe cried, lowering his head onto his beloved father's chest. "Please do not lose your spirit. Attic, do something!" Toe looked to his friend for help but he was gone.

"Antoni, Bega," Dodd called, checking for signs of life. "Father is hardly breathing. What can we do?"

With a leap and a twirl, Attic landed safely beside Toe. Smiling, he held out a few small herbs, grasses, moss and plants. Crouching down, he crushed them between two small rocks and rolled them in mud. Nodding reassuringly, he applied the poultice to Mar's wounds.

"Here, Toemouse, give father this root. Little at a time, understand?" Attic lifted Toe's chin up, gazed into his eyes and grinned. "With family you be, Toemouse."

Without another word the wild mouse dashed across the battlefield, blew his whistle and disappeared into the sky carried by a swarm of hornets.

Dodd watched in awe as the mouse, he knew had saved his life, flew away. "Who was that, Toe? And where have you been?" Dodd questioned, crouched over their father.

Toe knelt rubbing more herbal medicine into Mar's minor wounds. "That, my brother, is my friend from the commune. The one, by the way, that you did not think existed. He saved me the lightening they attacked and I have been with him, not far behind you, all the time."

"Why did you not tell us? Father has been so worried. We all thought you were with mother and Hatty, captives of the invaders."

"Attic would not let me! He felt it was too dangerous for me to be with you," Toe said, raising his paws, "and as can be seen around us today, I would say he was right."

"So would I," Bega said, making his way up to them and wiping Dodd's roarer on a leaf before returning it. "I hope we shall meet your friend again, Toe, I have many questions to ask him. He seems very familiar to me in a strange way." Bega stood and looked into the blue of Father Sky.

"Attic does not answer many questions. He is very special," Toe said, stroking his father's forehead. "I have you, Father. I am sorry if I worried you."

"You will have to tell me of your journey, Toe. In particular, how did you acquire the wasp friends that hover above you in a cloud?" Bega asked, looking in wonder at the swarm that remained to protect the young mouse.

"It was Attic and I who helped you, Elder, after the rats attacked lightenings of the woods ago. I hope you are fully recovered now?" Toe said, helping Dodd lift their father onto a leafy bed which Antoni had prepared.

"What now, Chief Antoni, Princess Squorth and Elder Bega?" Dodd asked.

Squorth moved forward to help. "Sadly, I have word none of your commune's creatures were amongst the captives freed this lightening." The large spider began to spin leaves together above Mar to create a shelter.

Bega laid his staff down and sat on a rock. "Well, that means we must gather all the creatures we can, cross the floods and attack the invaders on their soil,"

"No, we must not!" Mar exclaimed. "We must try free our families before anymore attacks. The cost would just be too great." He whimpered and fell unconscious once again.

Bega summed the situation for a water drip as he looked around at the carnage. "Either way, we must cross the water." The old bandicoot looked up at the hawk sitting on a branch. "Highra, can you seek out Brother Duck's kind, Sister Water Rats and Pint of the platypus, to help us? We shall stay and make rafts for the larger creatures who can not be carried by wing."

"Yes, Elder Bega, I shall seek them out. May I also suggest we enlist brothers Egret, Cormorant and Pelican to assist?" Highra squawked flapping his wings and cracking his neck.

"Fine. The more we can muster knowledgeable of water, the more chances of success." Bega gazed down at Mar on the make shift bed.

It is the strange wild mouse that I am interested in the most, the old bandicoot thought. *He has much to teach us. Where has he come from? Why does he look so much like you my friend?*

#   #   #

Jun squeezed his way down the sanctuary's tunnel and nodded to fellow natives, huddled against the walls, as he past. Turning to his left, he lowered his head and entered a small alcove. He stood for a moment staring down at his brother's life mate asleep on the damp floor.

Gently pushing Fena's shoulder to wake her, Jun said, "Come with me, there is a very special native I want you to meet."

Trembling, she sat up, pushed him away and screamed, "Ji, Nel, Nila, where are you?"

"Hush, Fena, you are with me now. I shall protect you," Jun said, cradling her in his arms. "When you are ready we shall go and seek out the old one."

Leaf falls past as Fena slowly gathered her wits. She was still distraught from her capture and the ordeal of the forced march. She stood slowly, grabbed Jun's paw and waited beside his long agile body.

Taking her paw gently in his, Jun led her out into the tunnel. *By the Great River Stones*, she thought *these creatures are so thin.* Then as they passed row after row of natives, jammed together, taking sustenance on roots, nuts and grasses, she realised the enormity of the problem.

Tears rolled from her eyes and soaked the fur on her cheeks. "How do they survive?"

Jun turned her to face him. "Sadly, many lose their spirit with every lightening and then sustain those that must eat flesh. Even in such an environment we all still follow and respect the Celebration of Sustenance. It is best we do have natives that sustain themselves in the passing of those less fortunate, simply because we would not be able to dispose of the bodies in any other way. Every darkening those creatures well enough, leave and gather as much food as they can carry."

"How, do they achieve such a thing? There are so many of the vile invaders about. Surely it must be too dangerous." Fena looked up into Jun's large brown eyes, so deep and so feeling.

"We leave through an entrance to the setting of Brother Sun. We also use the same entrance to help others escape back into our beloved bush. Sadly, due to the Rain-bringers overabundance of water, we have not been able to send any creatures to safety for some time."

Jun spun her round and they continued their short journey.

"Could you really say it is safety anymore, Jun? There are just so many invaders, they are everywhere." Fena strained her eyes to see in the increasing darkness.

"I would say Mother Earth must still have places for her children and such places must be better than this. Well, I pray to her and Father Sky that it is so."

Jun took a sharp turn to the left and climbed down a damp slope to where light filtered through some overhead rocks. "Ah, we are here. Seanne of the Sulphur Crested Cockatoos, I, Jun of the Grey Gum, seek an audience with you, Wise One."

Fena took a step backward in fright as the old bird moved out of the shadows. *In all my lightenings, I have not seen a creature in such a poor state of health*, she thought.

Rocking gently back and forth as she walked, Seanne towered over the two kangaroo mice. Blind in one eye, she was practically without feathers, her pink skin exposed in places.

"Ah, Jun, Metcha, my friend." Seanne's head bobbed back and forth as she spoke in a squealed whisper.

"Ark, wise Seanne. This lightening I have brought my brother's life mate to meet you," Jun announced, pulling Fena forward so Seanne could see her.

Seanne lowered her head in respect. "Metcha, young mouse; it is indeed a pleasure to meet one of my saviour's family."

"Ark, wise Seanne. Tell me, why do you refer to Jun as your saviour?"

"Yes, I should have known as much, Jun has not told you how he saved me. As you can see young one, I am very old. Old enough, in fact, to have lived many, many lightenings before the large pale ones ever stepped a foot on our shores. Not long after they landed, a falling Sister Tree injured me and a young pale creature took me as a pet. Thankfully, he fed me things to sustain my life."

"Really," Fena said, surprised.

"There is good in all creatures, child! Never judge every creature of a type by the actions of a few. Unfortunately, the young boy grew and others came and took him. After that they hardly cared for me. There I sat in a prison barely fed, hardly alive.

"Over my time, with the large ones, I learnt some of their language. I came to understand that many of them did not even want to live in our land. You see the majority have been forced to come here by their keepers. The keepers are dressed in suits like penguins, rather silly really.

"Then one lightening, as I felt my spirit leaving my body, I heard a small voice call to me as he unlocked my prison. That was of course my saviour, Jun. He helped me through the shadows to this place, where I have been

257

ever since."

"What of your eye, Seanne? How did that happen, if you do not mind me asking?" Fena enquired.

"As I said, you can not judge all by the actions of a few. Once my young keeper left, another creature decided to poke a stick into my eye that was alive with redness. He wished to see if I would scream, which I did not," Seanne said, holding her head up high.

"I am sorry," Fena said, sitting down on a small rock.

"Now, child, Jun told me your commune was many lightenings from here. Pray tell me, how is it you are here?" Seanne tilted her head to the side and looked into Fena's eyes.

"Our commune was attacked. Those that were not killed, or devoured by the redness, were dragged to this place." Fena strained her eyes as she looked around the unusual chamber.

Moving her head to the other side, Seanne replied, "I am saddened by such news. It can only mean that their evil spreads."

Jun moved forward, to stand in a fine stream of light, so Seanne could see him better. "Tell us, wise Seanne, what news have you had from below?"

"Treachery, there has been." Seanne bobbed up and down. "The King of Rats had the King of Mice slain and now hunts his son. Sad it is, because the King of Mice showed promise and raised my hopes of a successful treaty between them and natives. Now the mice have reverted to breeding uncontrollably, as the rats do, and grow to massive plague proportions. That Fena is why they venture further and further for food. The King Mouse, for all his shortcomings, did edict self restraint when it came to breeding, now no such edict exists," she shrilled.

"You speak their tongue!" Fena exclaimed, joining Jun

in the light. "Tell me, have you heard of the rats' new prisoners?"

"Only that, they are this leaf fall in the pit and are soon to be separated."

Far down the tunnel, which snaked away from Seanne's chambers, a rumble of cries echoed through the refuge.

"What on Mother Earth?" Jun said, before he sprinted away.

Only water drips later, Jun ran head-on into some of his guards. The two blue tongue lizards, and five frill-necked, were escorting two of the foreign invading mice.

"Kill them," some of the natives had started crying. "Kill them now, before others come."

Sensing the danger increasing Jun led the two bound mice, flanked by the guards, straight to Seanne.

"Where did you find them?" Jun asked.

"Near the back entrance. We would not have risked being seen except they were so close." The head blue tongue grumbled, his tongue flicking in and out.

"Meric, they are talking to each other," Beyan whispered.

"Yes, it appears they are," Meric replied, as they were led forward into Seanne's chamber.

"So who be you, and why are you here?" Seanne asked, from the darkness where she stood once more.

Meric fidgeted nervously in the new surroundings, "How do you speak our tongue? Be you mouse or rat? Either way you must be a traitor if you live with these primitives."

"Neither, mouse," she said, moving out of the shadows into the beam of light, "I am Seanne, of the Sulphur Crested Cockatoos. Believe me; we of the natives are not primitive. We are knowledgeable in ways, your small minds possibly will not be able to grasp."

Speechless, Meric and Beyan stood staring at the awesome figure before them. How can it be speaking the tongue of the brown rat? Meric wondered.

Seanne leant forward, her beak nearly touching their noses. "Now, explain your presence. For indeed, there are many here amongst us, in this place, who would break our laws to see your hides used as mats."

"I am Prince Meric and this is my lieutenant, Beyan. We have fled the city for fear of our lives. I had hoped to muster an army of my faithful and return to defeat King Yahn, who slew my father."

"Jun," Fena whispered. "He is the leader of the army that attacked the Great Oak's commune."

Jun moved forward to Fena's side. "Seanne, this is the mouse that led an attack against the commune of the Great Oak. My community of origin was one of the natives' best."

"Are you the mouse who led an attack on a commune of natives, far from here near a great tree?" Seanne asked, with a judgemental tone.

"Yes I am. Yet you must believe me when I tell you, the rats use methods not of my liking, such as the flame. If I had not led that attack, a rat would have and many more of your natives would have perished." Meric turned to look at Beyan who had not murmured a sound.

"Hm," Seanne said, as she turned and translated to those present. "What do you want done with them, Jun?"

Jun stood staring at the mice. "Take them to the holding area, feed them and secure them to rocks. A gathering must decide their fate."

"Feed them, Jun? There is little enough as there is," a blue tongue grumbled.

"Do as I ask, friend." Jun turned deep in thought and left the chamber.

DARKENING THIRTEEN

When the wooden gates opened and the rat guards flooded into the pit, Trix waved her paw to summon Hatty to her.

Squeezing past some other natives Hatty made her way to Trix. "Mother, they have come to separate us all into groups."

Pushed against the wall furthest from the gate, they stood and watched as the rats chose four groups of twenty natives and left.

"Fear not, they will not come again until the next lightening. All must bode well for our kind, otherwise they would have taken more," the old possum whispered, from the shadows.

Nila's head bobbed up and down above the crowd as she pushed her way to the back of the cave. "Trix they have taken Ji and Nel."

Trix laid her paw on Nila's shoulder. "I am sorry, Nila. Do not give up hope though; they are both strong young mice."

"I do not understand. They pushed Ji into one group and Nel into another," she wept.

Hatty who knew full well what it meant, said nothing; she simply comforted Nila by stroking her head.

"We must formulate a plan. Tell me, possum, would they expect us to resist or even attack them?" Trix asked, sketching in the dirt with her paw.

"No, they would not, as the fight left many of us long ago. Surely, it would mean many would lose their spirit as beyond that gate are thousands of their kind. Perhaps, you mice and native rats could blend in with all the confusion, but we bigger creatures would have no hope."

"I see your point, wise one. I still think it best we plan something," Trix said, holding a baby feather-tailed-glider close to her chest.

You are about the same age my Adin when he disappeared, she thought studying its tiny features.

#   #   #

Chief Antoni walked amongst his army as they cleared away the native dead into piles. Standing on his hind legs, the bull-ant held his other four legs clasped behind his back thinking. *Never in my lifetime would I have thought that I could possibly see so many dead.*

By the time Antoni returned to Bega his heart was heavy and his senses were full of the stench of death. "How is Mar, Bega?" Antoni asked, scrambling under a large charred leaf.

"Those herbs and mosses, our mysterious ally placed on Mar's wound, are indeed incredible! All my existence I have learnt of such things but believe me, Antoni, I have never in my lightenings seen anything like it. We simply must find him again, we have so many questions to ask and so much we can learn."

"When do you think Mar will be ready for travel?" Antoni inquired as he swung under the branch of a sapling which immediately caught Bega in the stomach.

Pushing the branch aside, with a stern look, Bega replied, "He is already walking around with Toe and Dodd's help."

"Ah yes, Toe, what are we to do with him? In my mind, we should send him back to the Oak. He could go as a guide for the other natives who now are refugees," Antoni suggested, clearly speaking his mind.

Bega stopped and stretched with a yawn. "I partially agree. However, unless you can communicate with his mighty wasp allies I suggest he stays. Perhaps, Toe may be of some help in our quest."

Antoni scurried up a branch to look the bandicoot in the eye. "Bega, he is but a young mouse. He should be back in the safety of the commune learning about the environment."

"Antoni, my old comrade, I would say he has learnt more about the environment in the past few lightenings than he could ever learn in the circle of knowledge." Bega gently laid his paw on Antoni's head.

#   #   #

"Toe, tell me where has your friend Attic been? Why with all our patrols did we not ever come across him?" Mar asked, walking around propped over Dodd's shoulder.

Toe smiled and shrugged his shoulders. "Attic just says he has always been. In the trees, water, breeze and sky that is where Attic be."

Mar's eyes shifted from side to side surveying the scene. "Interesting; you say you met him when you first began to talk?"

"Yes." Toe placed himself under his father's free arm.

Mar turned to eldest offspring. "And you had never seen him before this battle?"

Dodd put his front leg around his father's waist. "Never, I swear, Father. Yet he seemed oddly familiar. The way he predicted my every move was like he had known me all my life."

"Perhaps he has! If it is as Toe says, his friend has

always been watching."

"Yuck, that makes my fur stand on end," Dodd declared, with a chill running down his spine.

"A Guardian he is," Mar whispered. "I have heard tales of such creatures, living in complete harmony with all that is around them. I must meet him, if only to thank him by looking in his eyes."

"His eyes, Father, are like a stream that shines your reflection back at you. They haunt me even now," Dodd murmured, his mind drifting back to his first meeting with Attic.

"Chieftain Mar," Antoni greeted, as he and Bega met them head-on in the undergrowth.

Mar straightened himself to let Toe free. "How are the waters, Antoni?"

The bull-ant leapt onto a small rock and grabbed some sap from a twig. "They are still swelling, Mar. There must be more water from the Grey Rain-bringers high in the mountains, adding to our problems."

"Yes, that must be it," Mar murmured, sitting on a small charred log. "Sons, I am proud of you both for your bravery. Could you please seek out Prince Crier, the Highest of Wedge-tails, Nightflyer, Highra and the other leaders? Please ask them to honour us with their presence at a meeting."

"Yes, Father," both replied, and disappeared into the darkness.

"Antoni, with the council's approval I hope you will be able to split the army. The larger natives to join the other army while the smaller creatures, including your bull-ants, cross the flood waters on ducks and platypi. I do not want to risk detection or the loss of anymore of our winged friends."

"Sqweara and Highra will not have it, Mar. They argue they can carry many creatures, drop them on the ground quickly and soon be gone." Antoni took a bite of his sap.

Mar placed a paw under his chin. "We must move only in the darkening from now on. How can they fly without the assistance of Brother Sun's light?"

Pulling some sap away from his mandibles, Antoni answered, "In that case then, Breath of the Boobooks' kind has offered to take some of our army."

"Antoni, I can not soar on winged one's back. Nevertheless, I must go on."

"Chieftain, I have been meaning to suggest you stay here. Perhaps, even return to the Oak with the next group that leaves."

"How dare you, Antoni!" Mar screamed, struggling to his feet. "I shall not run. I must find the rest of my family or lose my spirit trying."

Bega moved forward and placed his paw on Mar's back for support. "Dear friend, you can not blame us for trying. Then again, knowing you as we do, we have already sent for Pint of the Platypi to carry you."

"Also as many winged ones, who could be mustered, accustomed to journeying over water. Will you bow to the wishes of the council?" Antoni twirled the sap onto a smaller stick.

"Yes of course. You realise as well as I do that if the enemy gets any idea an army approaches, they will use our natives as shields or worse kill them outright." Mar's eyes were heavy with worry.

#   #   #

Not far from where Mar and Antoni were in deep discussion, Pon and Fila sat quietly making weapons out of sticks.

"Do you think they are still alive?" Fila asked, handing Pon a small arrow.

"Fila, they live; I can imagine it no other way. My Fena is a part of me that beats with every beat of my heart.

She is the very breath I breathe. Yes, Fila, they live."

Fila bent a twig and wrapped a piece of vine to both ends. Stacking it with the other bows, he confessed, "I can not rest for worry. Nila, Nel and Ji have never even left the boundaries of our commune before. I am not sure if they are tough enough to endure."

"There is one you should not give up on and that is Ji. He will protect the others." Pon rubbed a stick back and forth on a stone sharpening its edge.

"Ji is only a young mouse who plays with the other children."

Pon stopped and lifted his brother's chin with the weapon he had created. "You see him through a father's eyes; while I see him through a teacher's. He is quite knowledgeable in the ways of the Circle of Knowledge and Defence."

"How so, I only gave him to you but a few lightenings ago to teach?" Fila asked, quite intrigued.

A smile appeared on Pon's face. "My Brother, I have been teaching Ji for at least 900 meals. Surely you had noticed a change in his step and a gleam in his eye."

"Pon, I did not... Perhaps I was too busy to stand back and have a look at him from a different view. While I am pleased he is further advanced in his physical training than I thought, it is his lack of wisdom which concerns me."

"Fear not, Fila, as he is indeed like our father in so many ways."

Toe stepped out from behind a small sapling. "Excuse me, Noble Pon and Fila, Father asks that you join the Council."

"Yes, of course, Toe," Pon said, walked over, picked up the young mouse and placed him on his shoulders. "Come Fila, Chieftain Toe has summoned us. I shall act as his noble steed while you shall be his guard of honour."

Fila stood reluctantly but upon seeing the gleam of delight in Toe's eye found himself renewed. "Yes a hero like Toe needs a fine escort," he announced, as he pulled out his sword and began to make a noise like hitting a hollow log.

Sitting high on Pon's shoulders, Toe looked around at the partly burnt surroundings. *How different it is from earlier in the lightening; now Cara the Crows kind have removed the bodies.*

Dodd helped his father up on to a flat rock in the small clearing. Raising his front paws to Sister Moon, Chieftain Mar signalled for silence.

"Thank you for coming, my fellow natives. Before we start the Council's business, I would like to make an announcement; upon the coming of the lightening, there is to be a Celebration of Sustenance in the stone circle outside of Ni's commune, all are invited." Mar sat down on a gum nut and continued. "Now, Elder Bega, would you honour us with the words of thanks."

Leaning on his staff Bega hobbled forward into a slight shimmer of moonlight. Raising his head he looked around at the gathered creatures and nodded. The other natives, ground dwellers, winged ones and Servicers' of the Circle alike bowed their heads in respect.

"Let us say the words," the old bandicoot said, with reverence.

"Mother Earth and Father Sky help us,
A darkness has fallen upon our land.
This darkening many natives sit united.
We cherish our simple way of existence.
We share; we care and respect each other.

Since ancient times we have bowed
to the way things have always been.

We share you Mother Earth and Father Sky
with every creature, plant and Sister Trees.
Now our way of existence is being threatened.
Great ones we ask your blessing and guidance.

Father Sky and Mother Earth your children
thank you for sustaining our humble lives.
Sister Trees who give us food and shelter,
to you we pledge our love and protection.
Children of the sky, the Grey Rain-bringers,
we thank thee for thy bountiful gift of water.
By the Great River Stones we are thankful.

We acknowledge with the passing lightenings
we will age and eventually cease to exist.
Also that in the passing of our spirits our
bodies will be offered to sustain others.
For this we give thanks. So it must be!

"So it must be," the other natives said in unison as Bega ended the prayer.

The hush that followed was soon broken as Mar aided by Dodd and Toe stood to address the large gathering.

"Fellow natives, this past lightening we all fought a great battle against the invaders. I would be telling untruths, if I did not say I wished with all my spirit it had not been necessary.

"To engage the enemy further we must cross an angry Sister River. I fear if we cross the raging waters en-mass, they will detect our advance. If that occurs those members of our families we seek to rescue would suffer.

"I beg you to allow a small force to cross the waters by wing and on the water natives' backs. At this leaf fall, we have little idea of where to go, so an advance party is necessary. I have been told, by Noble Breath, that her kind will guide us on the other side by darkness, while Prince Crier's scouts will by light." Weary beyond words

Mar sighed and sat once more.

"What of the rest of us, Chieftain Mar?" Sqweara asked, from high in the wattle.

"I suggest you join Gre's army; then en masse, extinguish the evil light of the other army of invaders, before Sister River's waters drop.

"Chief Antoni, Bur and Squorth, I humbly ask you join Pon, Fila, Bega and myself, along with those of your kind, in forming a rescue party. Such a party will hopefully have less chance of being detected.

"Sqweara and Highra, I suggest you return to the commune after the next attack and if she is so inclined, bring Queen Slur to assist us. A force of no-legs should be of great help driving the invaders out into the open from their nest."

Antoni scurried on to a large banksias flower and called, "A fine plan, Chieftain Mar, but I feel you best return to the Oak with Highra immediately. It is important you are given time to convalesce and recover from your wounds. We shall journey ahead without you."

"Yes, Chieftain Mar, I think Chief Antoni speaks what is best," Sqweara agreed moving forward, her massive body towering over Mar. "We do not want to lose you, dear friend."

"What does the council say then?" Antoni yelled, before Mar could answer.

Highra turned and consulted the others. "We say send Chieftain Mar home with his sons, to safety."

Mar's eyes narrowed as he frowned. "Very well. I shall abide with the wishes of the council."

Dodd and Toe held their defeated father tightly as he made his way from the gathering toward his grass bed.

As he lay down with a groan, Mar whispered, "Go now, my mice, I must rest if I am to soar this coming lightening."

#   #   #

Trix sat with her back against the wall cradling the orphaned glider. Hatty, resting quietly, leant against her mother as two large rats entered their prison. "What are they doing here?"

The rats, standing on their hind legs, appeared to be looking for a particular creature. Unexpectedly they pushed their way straight through the other natives, who lay on the damp ground, and seized both Hatty and Trix.

"Let go of my mother!" Hatty bit and clawed at the guards as they dragged them away.

In the light of the flame, which hung on the wall near the gate, a rat noticed Trix was still holding a baby and flung it to the ground. His violence toward a defenceless child infuriated Trix.

"How can you be so heartless, you devil?" Trix twisted and jumped trying to free herself to help.

She felt relieved when Nila shot forward, picked up the baby and quickly disappearing back into the darkness.

Dragged through a maze of tunnels, they finally arrived in a great cavern adorned with many flames on its walls. There, on a broken stalagmite sat King Yahn with Tongue the Bringer of Truth leaning by his side. The floor of the massive cavern laid littered with blood and bones.

The King grumbled at the guards, "See if you can get these primitives to clean up this mess. It smells and is giving me indigestion." Yahn waved a paw as the other lay across his fat stomach.

After being shown what was expected, Trix and Hatty had little choice but to mimic the behaviour as the rats lashed at them with their tails.

"Mother," Hatty grimaced, "these are the bones of natives." The young mouse gritted her teeth as both rats lashed her.

Because during their time as captives they had

demonstrated a caring nature for young creatures, they were chosen to serve the King and his offspring. Therefore, the King had logically thought them passive and suitable to serve.

Working her way along the cavern's wall furthest from the King, Hatty noticed another large wooden gate. As she drew closer she saw Nel sitting with other natives feasting on an abundance of foods. *What is going on?* she thought as she picked up yet another bone and walked across to place it on the pile, now twice her height.

Hit by the realisation of what was occurring; Hatty looked down at the bone in her paw. Rushing to the gate she yelled, "Nel do not eat the food or eat very little." However, before she had a chance to finish speaking the guards seized her.

Nel watched on helplessly as two guards held Hatty's paws and yet another two whipped her until blood became visible through her fur. She became physically ill as the head guard moved forward and licked the blood with its long tongue and turned to the others laughing.

#   #   #

Poked and prodded through the darkness, Ji asked, "Where are they taking us?"

"We are to seek out food for their young ones," an old native rat answered, "You are here to replace the ones who lost their spirit last darkening, so be alert."

Ji had other ideas. As soon as the group was free of any light from Sister Moon, he leapt off to the side. Before anybody even noticed, he was blending into the surroundings, hidden behind a rock.

Making his way back towards the rats' city he came across yet another group of natives forced to gather. *How many groups of gatherers must they have,* he thought.

Thinking quickly, he lay down on the ground, covered himself with a few leaves and watched as the guard rats marched within half a mouse length of his position. Thankfully, with all the other captives so close, Ji's scent went undetected. Once the threat past, he quickly hopped away toward the foot of the mountain.

"Hold, young mouse," a deep voice whispered from a hollow log.

"Who speaks the common tongue to me?" Ji demanded, spinning around.

"I, Pena of the Possums."

"Raa, Pena," Ji said, clambering to the log.

"No time for formalities, young one. What are you doing out of the refuge, when you know it is not safe? By breaking Jun's and the Council's rules, you jeopardise all of our lives."

"Jun! My uncle, is alive and here. Forgive me, possum, but I am not of your refuge, this darkening I escaped the rats."

"Well done. Are you sure you have not been followed, young one?"

"Yes."

"Well, I think you had better follow me and quickly. No, I have a better idea, climb on my back and I shall carry you."

LIGHTENING OF THE WOODS FOURTEEN

Mar slipped away from the encampment as Brother Sun's rays began to filter through Sister Trees. His body beset with pain, he made his way to the river as fast as he could.

Standing there by the swollen water, he pondered his next move. Deep in thought he jumped when the bushes behind him swung open and out plodded Pint of the Platypi.

"Sorry, Chieftain, it has taken me so long to answer your call. I am not used to walking so many lengths to get anywhere. You see the water rushes so hard in Sister River; I can barely swim and navigate."

"Pint, my friend, you could not have come at a better time. I was just leaving, by order of the council, to scout across the water. By the Mighty Boulders, I can not think of a better companion," Mar said, as he stumbled up the muddy incline.

"Chieftain, are you alright? Your fur is stained with blood and your nose looks pale?"

"Worry not, Pint. I am only tired from the battle of last lightening."

"Ah yes, I have heard from others. I am sorry to hear of your family and pledge all my help and life to you Chieftain."

"Patti, Pint. Tell me, are you ready to cross?"

Pint looked out at the rushing water, filled with constant debris and took a deep breath before answering, "While it is against my better judgement, yes. May I suggest though that we move further upstream so as to use the swift water to our advantage?"

I did it, Mar thought, as he climbed up onto Pint's back. *Before anybody even notices I am gone, I will have already crossed Sister River to find my family.*

#   #   #

"Toemouse, wake," Attic whispered, nudging his friend while placing his paw over his mouth.

Toe, scared half out of his spirit, opened his eyes and stared into Attic's.

"Father gone, alone he is, we must follow."

The wild native mouse jumped as Dodd rolled over next to him. "Father is gone! We must help him. Tell me strange one, can you find him for us?"

"Us, what is us? Only Toemouse and I go, big one."

"Not this time," Dodd said, standing up a good head and a half higher than Attic. "I am coming with you."

"No! You too large, not be able to keep up. We must move swiftly through trees and on ground. Me have friend waiting to help us cross water. His name be Tree of the Turtle. Tell me large one, have you ever ridden on turtle back? Very slippery, it can be!" Attic rubbed one paw over the top of the other and smiled.

"No, I have not, but I insist on coming and that is the end of it," Dodd declared, reached down and grabbed his staff.

Silently, the three brave young mice crept into the underbrush and followed Attic's wasp scout.

Antoni felt a gush of wind move the fern leaf he had slept on during the darkening. Lifting his head, he saw Highra on a branch of a gum tree above him.

"Chief, Mar has gone and so have the children."

"Gone!" Antoni jumped up onto his hind legs.

"Yes, Bega and I have searched everywhere. I can not believe Mar would disobey the wishes of the council. However, to know he also took the young mice is unthinkable."

Antoni sprang off the leaf and rushed to where Mar had been resting. Hurrying in and out of the surrounding area he used his senses to assess the situation. Within a water drip, he returned to where Bega and Highra stood.

"Mar left before the young ones, as I suspected. The guardian mouse has joined Dodd and Toe. It is the wild mouse's scent, I now recognise from when we searched near Elder Briar's dwelling."

"You mean he may be the taker of spirits?" Highra said, amazed by the revelation.

Bega waved his large paw in front of him and shook his head. "No, not that one; I would say, it was no more than a coincidence. Now, we must summon the advance party."

Highra flapped his wings and turned his head from side to side. "What of the plans laid down last darkening?"

"Fear not, Noble One, we shall follow them. If we hurry, we may well catch up before trouble strikes." Antoni called, scurrying off into the charred undergrowth.

#   #   #

Standing, watching the strange activity in the refuge, Fena's curiosity overcame her. Turning to Jun, his back hunched over in the small tunnel, she whispered, "What are the moles doing, Jun?"

"They are digging access holes over the King's main cavern, in preparation for Seanne." Jun touched one of the moles on its head, brought his face close to its and smiled in greeting.

"Ah, so that is how the old one listens." Fena found the workings of the refuge amazing.

"Yes, it is surprising how well the sound travels in such a place. That is why we dare not make too much noise."

"Jun," Rilo the Native Rat said, "there is somebody here you should meet."

Ji's eyes lit up as he saw his uncle and aunt crawl out of the tunnels.

"Where did you come from, young mouse?" Jun asked, glaring into the stranger's eyes.

Fena, gently reached up to Jun's shoulder, pulled his ear close and whispered, "He is Ji, your nephew, Jun. Can you not see your family in him?"

Jun's fur stood on end as he gazed upon Ji, whom he had not seen since he was a baby. "By the Great Grey Gum, look at you, mouse," he sighed, and embraced him.

Fena moved forward and rubbed noses with him. "How did you come to get here, Ji?"

"I escaped when they took us out to gather for them."

"What of Nel, Nila, Trix, Hatty and the others of our commune?"

"Nel was taken in another group, I know not where, while mother remains in the pit."

"Oh," Jun sighed.

Ji's brown eyes widened. "Have I done wrong, Uncle?"

"No, young mouse, we shall work something out. Tell me, was Nel on the plump side?"

"Yes, Uncle, this she has always been."

"Then we must act swiftly, before they feed her up even more."

The female mouse could see Jun's expression

change. "What is it, Jun, you look terrified?"

Jun leant down and whispered in Fena's ear and she went faint at his words.

"What is it?" Ji called, sensing something very wrong.

Rilo had little choice but to move forward and cover the young mouse's mouth.

#   #   #

When the guards burst in through the gates the old possum stammered, "Ssomething is wrong, these are the guards who take spirits to set an example. They are looking for somebody?"

Nila shivered as one of the guards laid his paw on her shoulder and checked her ear. Noticing the baby in her arms, he waited while the other rat found another of her commune. Inexplicably, he then moved away from her to where the second rat held a small pigmy possum.

The captives of the pit cried in agony as the guard grabbed the young possum and quickly snapped its neck. They sobbed as the rats dragged the body out of the gates.

As she had known the young one all its lightenings, Nila was beside herself with grief. "Why? Pep had done nothing?"

"A creature from your commune must have escaped, Nila. That is the only time they send those two larger rats amongst us. They are the ones that kill our kind, for varying from their ways."

"Ji," Nila cried, "what have you done?"

#   #   #

Navigating the stream Pint groaned as another log hit his side, bruising him. "I am sorry, Marcus, but I am finding it incredibly difficult swimming on top of the water.

I am not used to swimming amongst so much debris."

"Pint, my friend, if it is too dangerous perhaps we should return."

"Either way, Chieftain; we are bound for more blows. We may as well proceed. It would be so much easier if I could but swim under the water. Perhaps if you were to climb into my bill, I could hold you safely in my food pouches."

"Do you think I shall fit?"

"Yes, Marcus, I am sure you will fit."

Slowly Mar climbed along over Pint's head and between his eyes. Then as he was about to enter Pint's soft bill, they were struck by another log and Mar was flung into the water. Pint searched frantically for his old friend, but could see nothing in the gloom.

Dodd near died of shock as Attic let go of Tree the Turtle and threw himself into the rushing river. "Toe, Attic is gone. Why would he do such a thing?"

Toe, tapped his brother on the shoulder and pointed to Pint searching frantically in the water ahead of them. Between them, they could just make out a small figure moving along under the water not far behind the platypus.

Mar, his back still badly injured from his battle with Reon, could do little more than try to stay afloat. Then as he felt himself sinking, his life long mate, Trix's face greeted him. Giving in, to his inevitable fate, the Chieftain of the Great Silky Oak smiled and stopped fighting.

With a sudden jolt, Mar felt his body lifted from the dark depths as Attic pushed him toward Pint. It was then that Dodd and Toe noticed, Attic did not raise his head from the water but swam like a fish, using his hollow stick to breathe through.

Gently, Attic pushed Mar into Pint's bill and climbed in as well. All went dark as the bill closed gently over them.

The wild mouse did his best, in the tight quarters to turn Mar on his back. Pressing on his chest, Attic blew air down his mouth with the hollow stick.

With a gush of water from his lungs, Mar's eyes slowly opened. Exhausted he lay there, completely unaware of his rescuer's identity.

Pint surfaced for a leaf fall, to take a breath of air and get his bearings. He was surprised to find Tree, of the Turtles, swimming beside him with Toe and Dodd on its back. Despite all the debris, they managed to see the other riverbank in the distance.

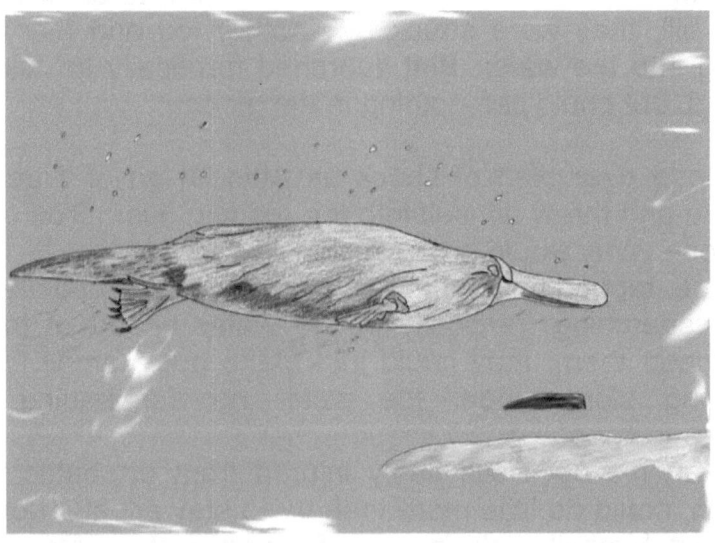

Against Pint's, of the Platypi's, better judgement he tried to stay on the surface as much as possible. Their crossing was hazardous in the dirty waters that swirled away toward the sea. With every water drip that passed, the current seemed to bring even more obstacles to cause a change in direction.

Toe turned his head to watch a large log whiz past behind them. "Did you see how close that was Dod...?"

Even before he could finish his sentence, a pile of leaves and branches ripped across the turtle's back and swept him away. Hanging on for his life, he could only watch as the branch sped downstream, away from Dodd and Tree.

Dodd reacted immediately, by leaping off Tree's shell onto a log. Carefully timing his actions, he then jumped onto another and another. Exhausted, he reached some debris near the large branch.

"Come on, Dodd, you can do it," he mumbled to himself. Sucking in as much air as possible, he waited for the right opportunity, sprang onto its widest part and held on with all his strength. Despite his efforts, he was still many mouse lengths from Toe.

"Dodd, help me! I am losing my grip," Toe pleaded and then disappeared under the water only to re-emerge.

Barely able to hear his brother's plea above the rushing water, Dodd dragged himself along the tree's trunk. In what seemed an eternity, to both the young mice, he reached Toe still caught up in the small branches.

Dodd stretched out his strong arm. "Grab my paw," he screamed.

With a gigantic thrust, he pushed himself forward to seize Toe as he once again slipped into the dark waters. Summoning all his strength, he hauled Toe back onto the log. Throwing himself over the top of his little brother to protect him, he could do little more than hold on and wait for help.

The large, brave, young mouse was relieved when leaf falls later, Tree's long neck popped out of the water. "We are indeed fortunate, young ones, as Sister River has washed you closer to her bank. I shall come in closer and you can climb back onto my shell."

With great caution, Dodd and Toe crawled back on, gripping every section of Tree's shell as hard as they could in their paws. "Hang on, here we go." Tree stroked all of her webbed feet at once to clear the tangled mess that surrounded them.

Not very far ahead, they could see Pint sliding up the bank. With a sigh of relief, they landed not far behind.

Unsure of his surroundings, Mar lay quietly beside Attic, in Pint's mouth. While he sensed the Platypus's movement, he had no idea what was happening.

Pushing and sliding, Pint finally found a grassed area safe enough to release his passengers.

Opening his bill he beckoned, "Pleased I am we have had a successful crossing." Politely Pint waited for the two mice to leave his mouth before he continued. "I was certain I had lost you, Chieftain Mar, before this brave young mouse came to your rescue."

Bewildered, Mar held a front paw above his eyes to block out the light. He had no idea it was the guardian who was helping him to stand. Instead, he thought it to be his son Dodd.

Attic swept his front legs under Mar and carried him further up the sodden shore. With the utmost respect, the wild mouse laid the Chieftain of the Oak down on some soft moss and moved away.

Dodd and Toe were soon by their father's side.

Rushing over to Attic, Dodd picked him up off the ground and swung him around in gratitude. "My wild friend, you saved our father. How can I ever thank you?" In their elation, the two fell to the muddy ground.

Still dazed, Mar watched on, barely able to tell the two apart.

Toe ran up to them both jumping up and down. "You are amazing, Attic. The way you jumped off Tree's back and swam like a fish, wow." Toe plopped his bottom down into the mud with, "You will have to teach me that."

Shaking, and terribly weak, Mar pushed himself up and began to walk toward them. Soon, his walk turned into a frantic, stumbling run. Like a mouse possessed, he knocked Dodd out of the way and headed straight to Attic. In one movement, he threw himself on top of Attic's soaking wet body and seized his shoulders.

While keeping pressure on the guardian's body, Mar moved his paws up the shoulders to his neck.

"No father," Toe yelled, jumping up only to slip in the mud and fall on his face.

Scrambling to his feet, Dodd grabbed his father and tried to restrain him. "Stop, Father, he is our friend. Please stop, he saved your life."

The young mouse was shocked that despite his father's weakened state, Mar still managed to find his mark.

Holding Attic by the nose, Mar reached down and gently parted the fur above the mouse's mouth. "By the Mighty Mountain Ranges," he screamed, when he saw the birthmark just above his lip.

Shocked, Attic looked up into the older mouse's eyes. "Me be friend, Noble One." His deep dark brown eyes, bewildered.

The expression on Mar's face changed when he realised he was scaring his saviour. Reaching down, sobbing, he embraced Attic.

KYM JADE

For a water drip, the guardian's mind wandered as he found a vague familiarity in the embrace. This not be possible, he thought.

Toe and Dodd were amazed as they watched their father, stand, lift the young mouse and place both paws on Attic's shoulders.

With tears streaming down his cheeks, Mar stared deep into Attic's eyes. "Adin, my darling mouse; how I have missed you." Weeping, he then pulled the guardian into his muddied chest and held him.

"Father," Dodd said, moving forward, "it can not be Adin. He was lost to us long ago. I have been to the place where you marked his loss of spirit, so many times. Come, Father, you must rest." Dodd gently released his father's grip from Attic and led him to a tuft of grass under a gum.

"It is him. Father Sky and Mother Earth have brought him back to us," Mar declared, placing his paws over his face shaking.

Crouching down, with his heart full of love, Dodd placed a paw on his shoulder. "If it is Father, then what stands before us is a ghost; if Adin had lived, why would he not have returned to us?"

"Adin! Who is Adin?" Toe demanded, stomping his paw on the ground.

"He is your elder brother. Years ago, he wandered away from the play area. By the time this was discovered, it was too late. We think a predator, who did not abide fully by the treaties, may have taken him," Dodd said, standing to rest his paw on Toe's head.

Slapping his brother's paw away, Toe walked off, "Why did you not tell me I had another brother?"

"Forgive me, Toe. We did not wish you to share the pain we all felt," Mar gasped, before he lost consciousness.

Walking up to his friend, Toe looked up into his wild features. "Attic, are you my brother?" he asked, reaching out.

Disturbed the sudden attention, Attic just replied, "I be me." Confused beyond belief, he ran off yelling, "I be me."

"Do not go, Attic! I would love you to be my brother," Toe sighed, watching his friend disappear into the distance. Soon, some of his wasp and hornet friends were following him.

A shadow moved across Mar and his sons, as the Grey Rain-bringers blocked Brother Sun's rays. Toe sat in the mud, held his father's head on his lap and stroked it.

Dodd walked a short distance away and stood staring in the direction Attic disappeared. *Is it possible, he is our lost brother?*

Within leaf falls, Highra, hawks and ducks landed, let Antoni and the others off quickly and departed. Finally, Sqweara came hurtling in, left Bega on the riverbank and flew away again. Like well trained soldiers, those left behind dispersed and took shelter.

Antoni scurried up the muddy slope to where Mar lay unconscious. "Dodd, your father broke the law of the council. It is my solemn duty to arrest him," he announced, standing on his hind legs.

Turning to look at his father, Dodd replied, "Arrest, father? How? Why?"

"Your father was told to return to the commune with you two and said he would. He broke the law and as the Noble Oak Mouse, he must be punished. Once the landing of the advance party is finished, he will be escorted back to the commune under guard. Believe me; it is for his own good." Antoni looked up into Dodd's eyes.

"Father goes nowhere, bull-ant!" Dodd screamed,

defiantly, impeding Antoni's progress. "You call yourself friend. Why, I should squash you." Dodd grimaced at the ant, a quarter of his size, and pointed. "Take your law, Chief and leave."

Antoni held his two front legs out in front of him. "Mar is my friend beyond spirit, mouse. I only wish to protect him."

Leaning forward Dodd growled, "Friend he may have been, but he is my father. You forget he gave up his title, of Noble Oak Mouse, to set forth on this quest alone. So, are you not the one who should return, if any? If you were to return my father in his current state, he more than likely would lose his spirit. He is such a caring creature, he would die from a combination of his wounds and worry in a very few leaf falls. By the River Stones, it is my mother and sister, he wishes to save."

Antoni stood his ground. "He will only be a burden,

young mouse."

"A burden, I shall carry proudly!" Dodd exclaimed, walked over, reached down, picked up his father and placed him over his shoulder.

Running across, Antoni moved to block Dodd's advance.

"Out of my way, ant, for we go on." Walking on, with a gleam in his eye, Dodd pushed Antoni out of the way.

"Stop! Dodd," Chief Antoni commanded.

Toe, tense from the past leaf falls' experiences, pulled out his stick and summoned his wasps into a cloud above him. Just, as he was about to order them to Dodd's and his Father's protection, Antoni spoke.

"By the River Stones, you are like your father. Mouse, you shall have your way. All I ask is; that you wait until the darkening, so we are less likely to be detected." The bull-ant turned, to look at the swarm of wasps above Toe's head and frowned.

Relieved, Dodd gently laid his father down on a tuft of grass and rested his head on some moss.

Toe walked past Antoni with a scowl on his face to join them.

"Would you have set your wasps on me, Mouse?" Antoni asked, in passing.

"Yes," Toe replied in a matter-of-fact kind of way.

Walking over to Bega, who now stood between Mar's sons and Antoni's Warrior Ants, Antoni commented, "How they have changed in so few lightenings. They have the courage equal to the heat of Brother Sun, Bega."

"Yes, Antoni, they have. I can not help but feel pride in my heart. Dodd, my pupil, did make a valid point, which would hold in the Circle of Knowledge and Defence. His father did relinquish his title and leave the Oak alone, forbidding anyone to follow. It is not his fault that we chose to do so." Bega, unceremoniously, plonked his bandicoot behind down in the mud and crossed his front legs.

"Alright Bega. It is only that I had no desire to see my friend, nay my brother; lose his spirit in such a way. I had hoped these days were long behind us."

"So did I," Bega sighed, letting out a large breath of air. The old bandicoot was pleased the tension had eased.

Looking at the two mice caring for their father, Antoni said, in a distant tone, "I shall send some bull-ant scouts ahead. Squorth and the bird-spiders, as planned, have already gone. For which I am glad, for if they had not they would have seen what has just occurred."

Toe busied himself collecting leaves and shaking off the moisture, to create a shelter for his father. Looking up at the Grey Rain-bringers, so angry in Father Sky, he knew more rain was coming.

DARKENING FOURTEEN

Water dripped down the muddied walls of Seanne's chamber where Jun paced up and down. The wise cockatoo sat silently on a root, pondering Jun's problem.

"She is my niece; I can not leave her to be devoured by the rats." Jun looked down and kicked a rock across the damp floor.

"Yes, I see your problem, Jun. If you were to set about rescuing your niece, it could well bring about the loss of many spirits. One of which, is your brother Fila's mate. Is that not correct?"

The leader of the sanctuary threw his paws in the air in frustration, "Why now, Seanne? All our plans to rescue the prisoners will be for naught, if we are discovered. Not only will the prisoners' spirits, be put in jeopardy but perhaps all the natives in this refuge as well.

"If the rats get wind of any attempt, they will swarm over this mountain in their thousands and surely find us. Our fellow natives here are not warriors but peaceful creatures. All any of us ask, is for our lives to go back the way they were."

Seanne turned her head to the side. "So you have decided to leave the young mouse to her fate?"

"No! I can not abandon my brother's child or mate. Whatever I do I must do it quickly, it will not be many leaf falls until King Yahn invites the faithful to feast. The idea of us attempting anything, with those insane rats that carry redness around, chills me to the bone. I have never in all my travels, seen creatures who search for death, like we search for food. They of all the creatures, new to our lands, are the ones I fear the most. How can one fight a creature that hungers to lose its spirit?" Jun sat on a small rock and placed his head in his front paws.

"May I suggest stealth, Jun? Perhaps, Mina the mole and his kind could open a small hole above the child's holding pen; Then you could shimmy down on spider's web and remove her without being noticed," Seanne suggested, once again adopting a lying position to enable her to listen in on the movements in the King's chambers.

"Yes, Seanne I have thought of something along those lines. However, the roof above the cell is nearly pure rock; any interference could bring it all down on the poor creatures below. Then again, how could I live with myself if I only rescued Nel and left the others to be feasted upon?"

Seanne lay silent, for what seemed like an eternity to Jun, then she lifted her head and whispered, "Then this is what must be done. Ask Brother Mina to set about digging a tunnel, through the side of the cavern that is always letting rocks fall. I believe it is the side closest to the outside and has become damp from all the water.

"At the same time ready the holes on the opposite side, which you and the others started long ago. When Brother Mina strikes the outside and the prevailing wind blows through the landslide, all the redness that devours will be extinguished. If the damage is severe enough, it may well force the King Rat to change his chambers. Either way, in all the chaos you should be able to rescue at least a few creatures from their menu.

"Then, they may well think they escaped of their own accord and seek them out in the usual places. I feel a few missing will not raise the King's suspicion. Such a tactic should lessen the chances of him sending his whole army after them." Seanne turned her muddied face to look at Jun with her good eye.

"Wise as always, oh Great Sulphur Crested Cockatoo. In the confusion, I shall use but a few warriors to aid in their rescue. Then if we are discovered, they may well think we have come through the hole Mina created."

"When will you try such action, Jun?"

Standing Jun moved so close he was nearly touching her beak. "There is no better time, than toward the end of this darkening. Sister Moon will hardly be throwing any light, thanks to the Grey Rain-bringers who circle once again."

Jun excused himself and left through the small opening, into the maze of tunnels weaving their way through the sanctuary. Deep in thought, he wandered along the damp passageways. He hardly noticed his fellow natives, sitting huddled against the walls. For the first time, in many lightenings, the damp musty smell had not bothered him.

Bowing his head, he entered his chamber.

Fena walked straight over to look up into his troubled brown eyes. "What is wrong, Jun?"

"Fena, Seanne and I have formulated a plan to rescue Nel. I wish Ji to accompany me, as he is small and agile. I am also on my way to take the invading mice to Seanne. She wishes to gain a translation from them of the exact layout of the cavern."

The female mouse shook her head and placed both front paws on Jun's shoulders. "Must you take Ji? Jun, he is only a young mouse."

Jun with a firm touch removed her paws. "Yes, but he is one who has been partially trained by my brother. It is

291

obvious by what he has demonstrated already, he knows more than most of these refugees about battle. Now come, I want you to be present," Jun said, ducked his head and left the alcove.

#   #   #

Trix stroked her daughter's brow lovingly as the memory of the poor young mouse's beating replayed in her mind. *These creatures are truly evil*, she thought.

Pulling Hatty closer, she whispered, "Hatty, my sweet mouse, what have they done to your beautiful fur? I love you with all my heart, my darling. Your father will come soon, we must endure until then."

Hatty, her damp fur stained with dried blood, was too weak to reply.

After finishing their work the King had ordered the two female mice restrained. There the brave mother and daughter sat with their hind legs tied to the walls.

Only mouse lengths away Nel lay asleep behind a large gate.

Trix and Hatty lifted their heads when King Yahn squealed and watched as his guards moved forward. Trix could feel Hatty's heart racing beneath her paw. Suddenly, with a loud sigh, the young mouse's body twisted and she began to convulse.

"Rega, escort the primitive females to the royal nursery and put them to work," King Yahn snarled and dropped his paw down next to his throne.

Lifting, Tongue the Bringer of Truth; he attempted to pull the sword free for the twentieth time. Furious, he flung the sword at his guard. "Feen, take this useless sword, which will not even leave its scabbard, and put it with my other treasures," the King commanded, returning to gnaw on a native's bone.

Hatty cringed as the guard grabbed her by the scruff of the neck, undid her restraints and dragged her away.

Trix waited until her legs were free, leapt to her feet and dashed to her daughter's side. Helping Hatty to stand, she barely winced as the rats whipped at her face with their tails.

#   #   #

Not far from the refuge Princess Squorth and her fellow spiders moved amongst the shadows.

From his position high in a tree, Bur could see a lot of activity in the surrounding area. "Princess Squorth, there are patrols of invading rats everywhere. They are forcing our natives to collect food."

"Yes, I have seen such things. Dri, of the Barn Owls, has just informed me of a refuge for natives. According to her directions it is above the vile creatures' nest. She left a few leaf falls ago to seek out the Refuge's Watchers. I have asked her to inform them of our arrival and seek advice. If Father Sky shines on us, they may help in our quest."

Bur scurried down the trunk of the tree. "A refuge above the rats' very nest who would dare such a thing? Now I realise why we have not seen any natives, other than those forced to serve the rats."

#   #   #

Prince Meric sat with his back against the damp wall staring at their guards. *The natives of this land puzzle me. Since our capture they have treated us with respect and fed us on a regular basis.*

Beyan wriggled his hind paw, in the mud, drawing pictures to amuse himself. "Meric, what do you think our fate will be?" he asked, moving his attention back to the vines which bound him.

Meric turned his head to look at his friend's muddied features. "I can not be sure but I do know this, if it had been our cousins, the rats, who had captured us, we would have been slain. Yet, after all our kind has done to these creatures they treat us kindly. They amaze me, when despite having little food themselves, they share it with us."

Just as Meric finished speaking, Jun and Fena entered the damp cell. The leader of the sanctuary bowed his head to the frill-neck lizard guards then stopped to speak to them. Bending down near the arch, Jun examined a stone and proceeded to the prisoners.

Beyan shivered as the native walked toward him, with a sharpened rock clenched in his paw. *He is going to slay me, here in these musty damp confines,* he thought. Resigning himself to his fate, he closed his eyes. *I shall never see the sunshine again.*

Expecting a jolt of death, Beyan was surprised when instead he felt his bindings cut. "He did not kill me! Meric, you are right these creatures are amazing."

The prince smiled as the native released him and bowed his head in gratitude. He had not thought for a moment they were capable of such an act; unlike the invading rats.

Moving to the stone arch, Jun signed with his paw to ask them to move ahead, in front of him. Meric and his companion complying moved out into the tunnel, flanked by Jun, Fena and the lizard guards.

Once again they walked back down the dark dank corridors of the refuge. The hackles on Meric and Beyan's necks stood on end as they felt legs kicking at them. The other natives lining the walls, who did not strike out, growled in their native tongues.

"I am glad this native mouse is in charge of us," Meric

whispered. "Even to one who can not understand their tongue, it is obvious the contempt we are held in." Yet, the Prince's heart felt pity for them, refugees in their own land.

Unsure of their destination, the two captive mice were relieved when they turned into Seanne's chamber. They knew from their previous interrogations, not another creature stayed with the strange old bird. Her work was far too important for her to have any distractions from sharing her quarters.

Signalling them to halt, Jun held his paw up and jumped forward alone to seek the wise bird's council. "Seanne, please ask these mice to show us the exact layout of the cavern below?"

Walking out of the shadows, the large bird lowered her head and turned her good eye to the captives. "As you are still with spirit this darkening, you must realise, we are not what you thought we were. We have treaties, laws and a common tongue that unites us. We are not primitives, to be harvested for work or to be eaten," Seanne said, bobbing up and down.

"I realise this fact now, old one. I am truly sorry for my part in all of this, as is Beyan. Tell me, why have we been summoned here, a trial or our execution perhaps?" Meric turned to look at the large blue tongue lizard blocking the entrance.

Seanne's yellow feathers on the crest of her head stood on end. "Must I explain again, we natives do not kill for killing sake. In fact, before your kind invaded our land, we were at peace. I admit in our history, there were a few times where natives fought others in battle. This is why we now observe our ancient rituals. For some lightenings now, all our kinds have lived in peace and celebrated sustenance together."

Meric scratched his ear with his paw. "Then why are we here?"

"I want you to show us the layout of the cavern below. We wish to rescue some of our kind from that depraved King Yahn. Your ruler will soon feast on them, if we do not." Seanne watched Meric's face for any hint of emotion and soon found what she was hoping for.

The captive's eyes widened as he threw a fist into the air. "He is not our King. He slaughtered my father and family," Meric protested. "Despite that, I shall not show you the caverns' layout."

Watching on from the side, Jun felt the mouse's anger and moved forward to restrain him.

Seanne shook her head at Jun and winked to signal everything was under control. "Then, there is little use in us wasting precious leaf falls conversing." In an attempt to manipulate her prisoner further she lifted her head and looked at the guard by the entrance.

"Since we first came here, my mice brothers and I have misunderstood this place. I am deeply sorry for our part in its ravaging and wish we had known how the creatures of this land coexisted. Perhaps we too may have had a treaty. Sadly, what has come to pass has. Nevertheless, I now ask for a chance to show there is some good in us. I beg you to allow Beyan and I to guide your kind to success below?"

Seanne's brow lifted. "Indeed, it would be advantageous to have such guides. I shall put it to Jun."

The old bird swung her head to the side, tilted it on an angle and translated. "The Prince wishes to guide you, Noble Jun."

Speechless, Jun stood staring into his enemy's eyes.

"Jun, you can not even entertain such a thought. They can not be trusted," Fena whispered.

Surprising even Seanne, Jun stepped forward and said, "Done." He then moved to stand right in front of them both. "Tell them, Seanne, if this is any kind of trick, to redeem themselves in the rat king's eyes. I shall kill them with my own paws. Now I must go and prepare. Please inform them of our plans." With that Jun hopped over to the archway, spoke to Ji, turned and signalled for Fena to follow.

Fena hopped up to Jun's side and tugged at his front leg. "They will betray you."

"I have no other choice," Jun confessed, in a distant tone as he headed toward the entrance.

"Hold, Jun," Bink, of the Bush Cockroaches called, from down the burrow. Finding the passage blocked by natives, Bink ran up the wall and along the roof of the tunnel.

Agitated, Jun looked up and snapped a reply, "What is it, Bink?"

"We have received news, from Dri of the Barn Owls. There is a Princess Squorth, of the Funnel-web Spiders, on her way with some bird-spiders."

Jun's mood changed in the wink of an eye. "By all that is sacred Princess Squorth, what grand news." Jun slapped Ji on the back with elation.

Allowing himself to fall to the floor Bink then stood on his hind legs. "That is not all, Noble Jun. Apparently, a Chieftain Mar and a Chief Antoni follow behind with many bull-ants. Jun, in the past lightenings they battled the rats on the far shore of Sister River."

The tall lean mouse crouched and laid both paws on Bink's shoulders. "Well tell me Bink, did they defeat them? For if they did not they may be leading them toward us."

Bink smiled, as best a bush cockroach can, "I am pleased beyond words to announce." Bink stopped for a water drip and then went on with a raised voice, "With the aid of all natives, winged ones and ground dwellers alike, the rats were defeated."

A cheer began to ring through the sanctuary as the news passed around. Jun realising the danger of such a thing, held up his paws and begged for silence. Within leaf falls, the refuge fell quiet.

"Praise Mother Earth," Fena sighed, wrapping her foreleg around Ji.

His eyes wide and sparkling, Jun said, "What else have you heard? What of the other communes, have they been liberated? Can we all finally return to our homes?"

"Perhaps I can better answer your questions," a voice Jun remembered from his childhood rumbled, "oh roller of rocks and plucker of hairs," Squorth said, but ten mouse lengths away.

"By my Father's fur it is you. Ento, Princess." Jun swept his front paw out in front of him and bowed.

As Squorth approached, all the creatures cleared a way for her and bowed in respect.

"Come, Jun, it is not like you to follow formalities. Where is the cheeky tongue and wit, I remember so well?" she said, placing a leg on each of Jun's shoulders.

"Fena, I did not think treaties were held with the funnel-webs," Ji whispered, watching in awe.

Fena moved closer to Ji's ear. "This is the spider I have heard tales of. She went against her own kind's wishes to save Chief Antoni, many lightenings ago."

Noticing the gigantic bird-spiders not far behind her, Ji's fur stood on end. Their bodies obviously forced into, what he once believed to be a larger part of the catacombs.

"Tell me, Jun, who are these that stand by your side so bravely?" Squorth asked, looking around with all her eyes.

"This is Fena and Ji; Pon's mate and Fila's son."

"Metcha, mice. Fila and Pon will be pleased to find you

two. Tell me, what of Nel, Nila, Hatty and Trix?"

Surprised, Jun's expression changed again. "Pon and Fila, they are with you?"

Sensing his happiness, Squorth smiled. "Yes, they joined me some lightenings ago. You see, our paths crossed while following the vile shadow creatures. Now, Jun, tell me of the others?"

"They are still alive. Well, Nel and Nila are, as for Trix and Hatty we can not say. Seanne said there were two native mice in the king's cavern but they were taken away. We are this leaf fall, making ready to free some prisoners."

"Some prisoners," Squorth said, looking Jun in the eyes. "You mean you are not, going to rescue all. Why Jun, where is the cunning that you once had? It is not like you to think small."

"Lightenings ago I might have rushed in but now I know better. For lightenings, I have watched and dealt with the evil savagery of these rats and mice. We have fought them physically, along with the diseases they carry. Those around you are all that are left, from those confrontations.

"I shall not risk them in an attempt to save others. Now if you wish to join our plan, then by all means do. However, if you do not, I beg you, Princess, stand aside," Jun declared, before he squeezed down alongside Squorth.

A rumble of laughter surfaced from Squorth's belly. "That is more like the defiant young mouse, I remember. But Jun listen, Mar and the others will join us before the darkness ends. Then by the River Stones, we shall rescue them all."

Spinning around he grabbed her hairy leg. "Are you sure of such happenings, Princess?"

Placing a leg on his head, she said, "I give my word, Jun."

"What of Father, has he travelled with them?"

"I am sorry I have to tell you this, Jun. Elder Briar's spirit was stolen, in treachery by one of the dark winged cockroaches."

"Father gone," Jun sighed. "I will take pride in disposing of a few of the ground creepers this darkening." Jun walked on ducking under the spider's legs, a fire burning in his heart.

#   #   #

Grey Rain-bringers drifted across the face of Sister Moon and for a leaf fall sent shadows across the land.

Bega leant back against a stringybark's trunk, closed his eyes and began to drift off to sleep. "Mopoke, Mo," he heard in the distance as he allowed himself to dream of better lightenings.

Si, the bat, swooped down and landed on a small branch beside him. "Ona, Elder Bega, I bring news from the Highest of Wedge-tails."

"What, what, what." Bega sat bolt upright searching for his staff. "Oh, Si, it is you. Please continue." Relieved, the bandicoot sighed and leant back against the tree once more.

"Sorry if I startled you, Elder. I was told that you were here on guard." Si draped his wings around his chest and smiled.

"Yes, you were told correctly!"

"But I was sure your eyes were shut," Si stated, in a cheeky tone.

Bega sat up as straight as he could. "Come now, Si, I hope you have not forgotten what I taught you, in the Circle of Knowledge and Defence. Remember, bat, good warriors never sleep but hone their senses at all times. Which is precisely what I was doing." Bega stared at the bat. "Now what of this news?"

"Just after mid lightening, Gre and other natives engaged the camp of mice, rats and cockroaches. A mighty battle was waged and, Elder, they were successful in defeating them."

"May the Baby Stars, in Father Sky, shine even brighter from this leaf fall on." Leaping up with surprising agility, Bega called, "Antoni, did you hear the news?"

Appearing from under a leaf, on a branch about five mouse lengths above Bega, Antoni scrambled back down the tree trunk head first. "Yes, Bega, I am pleased beyond words," he replied, leaping to his hind legs in front of them.

The tone in Si's voice changed. "Unfortunately, all the news is not good. So numerous were the invaders that many natives lost their spirits in battle."

"May Mother Earth, accept them," Antoni prayed, brought a front leg to his chest and solemnly lowered his head.

Letting go of the branch, Si, somersaulted to the ground and landed on his feet. "Sadly, many of the vile ones also escaped. Most fled further into the bush and are now being pursued by our natives. Unfortunately, some turned to the water and swam toward your position. I think they are heading back to their nest."

Bega slumped onto his staff. "This is indeed bad news. Tell me what of the others?"

"Those who are left have commenced crossing and should be gathered again by the lightening." Si crawled over to Bega, stood and touched him with his wing. "Elder, it saddens me to say that Highra was taken down in battle. He now lays severely injured on the other bank."

"Thank you, Si," Bega said, laying his paws on the tiny bat's head.

Some long grass parted and Mar appeared from the far side of the tree. Aided by Toe and Dodd, he stumbled over to his friends and groaned, "We must act swiftly."

Antoni was surprised, and pleased, to see his old friend conscious for the first time in many leaf falls. "Marcus!" he exclaimed.

The Chieftain of the Oak looked down at the bull-ant with a gleam in his eye. "Am I to understand I am under arrest, Antoni? Is that correct?"

Toe stood silently by his father's side, glaring at the bull-ant while signalling for his wasps to join them.

Holding the tips of his front legs out in front of him, Antoni said, "We have no time to debate politics. This area is full of rat patrols that force natives to gather their food."

Mar turned to look at his eldest son. "Dodd, has Adin come back yet?"

The large mouse shook his head with concern evident on his face. "Father, the strange one has not returned. Please stop talking in such a way; you can not possibly know it is Adin."

Turning and looking up at the steep slope ahead, Mar let go of Dodd and started to walk on. "Ah, dear son, that is where you are wrong. Upon this lightening, I found even more reason to bring our family home safely, for soon we will be whole. Now come."

With that, Toe and Dodd rushed forward to their father's side.

Antoni flung his four front legs into the air in frustration. "Stubborn, kangaroo mouse! Bega, have you seen his wound? It does not heal well. This past lightening, the healing herbs were flushed out by the force of Sister River's water. Have you identified the herbs and mosses the guardian used?"

"Yes, I did, but this bank seems to lack the moss." Bega lumbered over to Antoni and laid a claw on his head. "I am, however, ever watchful."

"I have no doubt, Elder. Now we go on." Antoni raised a front leg, drew fang and signalled.

The ground behind them burst to life with the movement of thousands of bull-ants, followed at the rear by Pon and Fila.

About halfway up the grassed incline Bri of the Barn Owls swooped down onto a rock above Mar's head. Without looking down, in case she was being observed, she spoke, "Chieftain, ahead lies a refuge of natives. It is there, Princess Squorth, Bur and his brothers, the bird-spiders, now await your arrival. Bink of the Bush Cockroaches is but a flap of wing away, under a log near a Sister Wattle, he will escort you." Then without even waiting for a reply, Bri was gone.

#   #   #

Further down the slope, Breath's and Bri's, kind swept in at the guards surrounding the native gatherers. For protection, the rats grabbed their captives and held them in front of them.

Not a creature noticed, as a scruffy native slipped in amongst the captives.

"Leave you fool, we now return to the rat's city," a young bandicoot pleaded.

Yet the stranger said nothing and went about gathering berries and grasses.

None of the guards, even thought twice about the extra mouse in their midst. After all, what native in its right mind would join the captives of its own free will.

#   #   #

Across the darkening's sky Breath's, of the Boobooks, shadow could be seen struggling to stay in flight. She sighed with frustration as her large cargo began to squirm. With a deep breath, she flapped her wings even harder.

"Owl, I am not accustomed to being carried like this," Slur hissed. "Ssince hearing my kind were needed; I have travelled for ssome leaf falls to reach this point. I have been carried by many a winged one. You are my worst carrier yet."

"Silence snake or I shall simply drop you. I will also order my sisters to do the same to those of your kind, they now carry," Breath said, annoyed by the snake's gall. "We are nearing the rat's most important nest."

"A large nest? Ah, this sshould be interesting. I will have ssome more rats to play with until I am ssatisfied justice has been given. I sseek compensation for the ssight of my eye."

"Remember snake, to tell Chieftain Mar and Jun my message. Inform them, my kind are taking as many rat guards as we can this darkening." With that, Breath released her cargo.

Without warning, Slur felt herself falling through the air. Landing with a thud she hissed, "Despicable creature."

"Queen Slur," a familiar voice whispered, "Follow me into the refuge please." Bega lowered his head and entered the partially concealed door.

The bull-ant guards stayed at their post as Slur slipped past. "Ah, Elder Bega, you must be gathering more information for your stories I ssuspect. This time, old one, ensure you tell the whole sstory," Slur said, sliding up behind him and poking her tongue out just enough to touch him.

Bega shuddered and walked on. "Um, um yes, Queen."

"Now take me and my kind to Chieftain Mar, this instant."

#   #   #

Pacing back and forth in the narrow tunnel, Jun waited impatiently for Mar to arrive. The memories of their childhood, spent wandering the forest and enjoying each other's company, replayed in his mind. Being his father's top student Mar became like an older brother to him. *In battle,* he thought, *I can not think of a better mouse to stand by my side.*

Bink, the bush cockroach, proudly led the Chieftain of the Oak through the labyrinth of dirt and rock tunnels, toward Seanne's chambers. Leading the legendary figure past the natives, huddled lining the walls, Bink enjoyed every water drip of his importance.

Despite his pain, Mar tried to acknowledge every creature who held out a paw to him in greeting.

The passage being too narrow for them to assist their father, Toe and Dodd closely followed his progress. They were both puzzled by, and in awe of, their father's popularity. While Bega had told many stories over the lightenings, Mar had never shared his personal story, regarding the treaty campaigns. Still, the two young mice reflected in their father's glory, reaching out and also shaking paws.

Turning to the rumbling of voices, emanating up the tunnel, Jun could just make out his friend in the distance. Relieved to finally see another warrior mouse, trained in the Circle of Knowledge and Defence, Jun rushed forward. Unceremoniously, he stood on his hind legs, flung his front legs around Mar and hugged him. "Marcus, by all that is sacred, I am glad to see you."

"Uh," Mar sighed, at the strength of Jun's embrace.

Feeling Mar's hind legs giving way, Jun tucked himself under his shoulder to give support. "What is this? You are wounded, my friend."

Ignoring the comment about his wound, Mar waved his sons forward. "Jun, these are my sons, Dodd and Toe."

"By Father Sky, they are like you. Metcha young mice," Jun said, offering his paw to Dodd.

With a gleam in his eye, Dodd returned the greeting by squeezing Jun's paw. When the leader of the sanctuary simply smiled and returned the favour, only harder, Dodd recognised the challenge. *This is my opportunity to prove my strength*, Dodd thought, gritting his teeth.

Leaf falls past as they stood there, eyes locked, testing each other's measure. Until this meeting, Jun had never met a mouse taller than himself, yet there Dodd stood before him a good head taller. *With your light grey fur, nearly blond in colour, you look so much like your father,* Jun thought.

The elder mouse's face showed no sign of strain, in fact he appeared to be enjoying the contest. Without relinquishing his grip, he continued speaking, "We must hurry and formulate our attack before lightening."

"Yes, Jun, we have had word of another great battle. Some of the vile creatures of the shadows, escaped and are heading this way" Mar moved over and parted Jun's and Dodd's vice like grips. "Careful, Jun, he is far stronger than I ever was. Since a young mouse, he has lifted log and rock in training." Mar moved closer to Jun and whispered, "It is as if he knew what lay ahead for us all."

"Wasps, wasps, keep away," the cry of many natives rang along the tunnels.

Jun stood on his toes to see past Dodd. "Wasps, what on Mother Earth?" he exclaimed.

Without a sign of fear, Toe moved forward and tugged on his Elder's arm. "They are my friends, Noble Jun. By order of the Guardian they travel with me for my protection," Toe announced, turned, hummed to his friends and did a jig; in response the wasps moved directly to the ceiling of the tunnel. "Fear not, they will stay to the roof of any cave, in which we travel. They have no wish to be trod upon or to accidentally sting a fellow native."

"Indeed, this darkening is full of surprises. Why, young mouse, I have never seen such a thing." Reaching down, Jun went to place his paw on Toe's head. However, when the wasps began to swarm he removed it. "A Guardian you say. Toe, you will have to tell me more later."

Toe held up his paw and told the wasps Jun was a friend. The strangest sound came out of the swarm, something like laughter. The wasps had known the mouse was a friend, but felt they had a menacing image to uphold in front of so many natives.

Jun shook his head in amazement. "Quickly, we must go to Seanne's chambers."

Bink bent down and spoke to a pigmy possum next to him, turning to Jun, he said, "Jun, a message has been passed along. There are other new arrivals, only lengths behind. Already in the tunnel, are a bandicoot and some no-legs."

"Mar, tell me, is it Elder Bega?"

Mar simply nodded as his friend helped him along the corridor.

"Why, I would have sworn that old teller of tales' spirit would have left him long ago. Especially, considering his condition," Jun said, with a smile.

"And what condition is that?" Mar enquired, knowing full well, if it was still the Jun he knew as a child, what the answer would be.

"Well, he is still fat is he not?" Jun said, with a laugh as they entered Seanne's chambers. The sanctuary's leader allowed Mar to sit on the only dry stone in the small cavern.

"That he is." Antoni's small deep voice answered from

behind.

"Antoni, I must be blessed. How be you, small one, ready for battle?" Jun asked, offering him his paws in friendship. "Boyor, great Chief Warrior Ant of Queen Zana."

"Metcha, Jun, one of mystery and disappearance," Antoni replied, scrambling to a rock above Squorth and Bur.

Unexpectedly, Bega's large frame appeared at the arch entrance to the chamber. "Mar, Queen Slur has arrived and wishes to speak to you immediately. She has entered this refuge under protest and will move no further. She is having a hissing fit, declaring the place too damp and cramped for her.

"The Queen is so frustrated she has suggested, she devour some natives to make room for her to travel the tunnels. I am afraid the refugees in that area heard the Queen make her suggestion and have scattered. To be truthful, Mar, even I had to enter on all fours and squeeze past the tunnel's occupants."

Standing with Dodd's assistance, Mar moaned, "I hope she was jesting." With a little effort he and his sons slid past Bega's large frame into the muddy corridor.

"You have not changed at all, round one." Bega turned to the voice coming from the shadows.

Raising his staff, the bandicoot grumbled, "Who dares address me, Elder Bega, in such a way?"

For a leaf fall Jun examined the old bandicoot's mud covered, greying features. Standing a good four times his height, even he still had to admit Bega would be an awesome foe. Without another word, he walked up closer to Bega and stood in his line of sight.

The bandicoot leant down and stared into the mouse's deep brown eyes. "Oh, it is you, maker of trouble. By the River Stones, I should have known you would be in the thick of it. Tell me, are you still using sap as a glue to secure large creatures' posteriors to their seats, little one?"

"Not for some time, but perhaps later, Elder. Maybe I could manage something after the battle, to your liking." He raised his paw to his forehead in salute and bowed.

Bega smiled when he saw Pon and Fila circle round the gathering natives, to come up behind their elder brother.

Tapping Jun on the shoulder, Pon poised himself as his brother turned. Once he had his full attention, Pon punched him in the jaw, followed by Fila heading him in the belly.

"Uh," Jun sighed, as the air escaped his lungs. "Why brothers, it is nice to see you too. Now what was that about?" he asked, regaining his stance and looking into his brothers' wild eyes.

"That was for all the lightenings, Brother, without word. We worried for you every leaf fall, you inconsiderate gum head." Fila stood ready for a retaliation.

"Sorry Brothers, I thought word may have reached you. Either way, with your mates and family, Fila, I did not think you would have worried about me," Jun said, turning to Ki the gecko and whispering. Ki fell on all fours and dashed out of the chamber. "Perhaps, what you are about to see will help compensate you in some way?"

Pon's heart leapt as Fena entered through a tiny arch. Rushing forward he embraced her and swung her around. Putting her down, he lay his paw on her stomach. "Why mate, you are with mouse."

Fena smiled and fell into her life mate's arms.

Fila, stood with a tear rolling down his cheek at the reunion. However, when he saw Ji move around from behind Fena, he began to cry, "My son, my precious mouse. Tell me of your Mother and Sister?"

"Father," Ji said, with his head over Fila's shoulder

looking at Pon and Fena, "they live but are in great danger."

When Mar returned and witnessed the scene, he suddenly found himself overwhelmed by the thought of having his family reunited. He and his sons then took up a position, to the left of Seanne, sitting with Jun.

"I am honoured, to have you all in my chambers," Seanne started. "This darkening we shall finally show these creatures, from other lands, we stand united. To save time, I shall explain our plan thus far." Seanne went on to explain everything, even down to Trix's and Hatty's positions.

Mar had sat entranced by the cockatoo's words, but when Seanne mentioned his wife and daughter, he felt a renewed strength pulse through his body. Placing one foreleg over each sons' shoulder, he looked to the ceiling and thought, thank Mother Earth and Father Sky. The other natives, concentrating on Seanne's words, did not notice as tears streamed from the Chieftain of the Oak's eyes.

#   #   #

Slee approached his king with great caution. Despite his and the other tunnelers' efforts, they were unable to unearth the rebel mice who had been causing havoc in the tunnels. Lenthric, Meric's second in command, and his followers had gone to ground in the mice section of the nest. The complexity of the small mouse diggings, were making it impossible to find them.

When Yahn noticed Slee making his way across the chamber, he placed a possum leg, he had been gnawing on, to the side of his throne. Reaching down, he picked up a bandicoot skull and placed it on his head. Then he donned a necklace, made from a collection of natives' teeth, and picked up a leg bone of a native rat to use as a sceptre.

"Come here, Slee."

The greying rat shook with fear as he approached the king.

"Did I not tell you, to report to me regularly about your search for those traitors?" The king's eyes narrowed to slits and his bloodied fangs protruded even further from his mouth as he spoke.

Bowing, Slee fell to the steps in front of Yahn's throne. "Forgive me, my King. Digging out the small mouse tunnels is proving harder than we first imagined. They twist and turn in every direction, throughout the nest, and all seem to be interconnected. Furthermore, we have found they conceal most exits with grass and mud doors. This makes it virtually impossible to tell where the mice may flee when we approach. I am sorry, Lord, but they may have already escaped to the outside."

Yahn swung his sceptre and connected with Slee's skull. "You had better pray you are wrong, digger; for if you are not, I shall personally take great pleasure in squeezing the life out of you." The fat disgusting rat threw the bone to the side and yelled, "First, Meric and Beyan escape the nest and now this. Oh, why can I not find capable commanders? Leave, Slee, and ensure you find those mice."

Blood pouring into his eyes Slee backed away bowing. Turning, he staggered back into the tunnel that had once been the King of Mice's entrance into the main chamber. "If I get a chance, I will collapse a tunnel on that beastly creature," Slee grumbled, slinking through the damp, dark crumbling corridor.

In the light from the flickering torches hung on the walls, the king's face took on an even more sinister appearance.

Placing his paw to his chin, he surveyed his chamber. The king's evil eyes surveyed the large rocky walls to the rounded ceiling. Then they wandered back toward the cages of captives which lined the far wall. Finally, saliva dribbled down his jowls as he examined the piles of native's bones scattered across the well worn floor. *How boring it looks*, Yahn thought.

While watching slaves enter with the food they had gathered from outside, he sat pondering his thoughts. *I know; I shall redecorate my cavern. Perhaps, some of the larger natives' skulls on the walls could brighten my nest up.*

The commander of the gatherers raced up to the throne. "King Yahn, our slaves have brought in an abundance of foods this night. Thanks to the rains so much more has grown in the last few days."

"Yes the rains, while an annoyance, were good to us in that respect. Tell me, Ine, have we feasted in thanks to the Rain Gods, yet?"

"No, King," Ine replied, lifting his head up to look at the king's face.

Yahn waved his paw with great arrogance. "Then we shall this coming morning, organise it immediately."

"Yes, my King." Overjoyed to be in his master's favour Ine decided to leave while he was in luck.

"Ine, make sure you save the plumpest and most delicate sacrifices for me." Yahn's teeth became wet with drool and he licked his lips.

"As always, King," Ine replied, stopping three rats' lengths away. "Shall I send for the Order of the Flame to join us?"

"Yes of course. Those loyal rats deserve the best at all times. Now make haste, the morn will soon be upon us." Yahn rubbed his belly with both paws. "There is nothing like a soft tender portion of native meat to start the day." His rat eyes went red with anticipation.

Hatty hopped over to her mother carrying a new-born

invading rat. "Mother that young rat, the one they all bow to, keeps looking at me strangely."

"I would say he is a prince, Hatty. Be ever watchful, my child, he has the eyes of his father, dark and evil." Trix took the baby off Hatty and laid it gently on some fresh grass.

The young mouse looked around the cavern in awe. Along the walls were small holes, dug in the soft dirt, to hold the newborns. Three torches hanging high on rock ledges sent a gentle light over the area. "So many baby rats; is it possible they are all direct offspring of the King?"

"As impossible as it seems they very likely are, dear Hatty. The King appears to do little more than feast and copulate. In fact, he is too fat to do anything else. It is a wonder he can even move to make children," Trix said, lying down fresh food of grasses and roots for the weaned offspring.

Another food gatherer brought forward offerings for the nursery and placed them at the entrance. Glancing at Trix from the corner of his eye, he moved closer. "Toemouse mother, you be. Yes, me know this. For many lightenings, me watch you look after little friend. Love him and miss him, you do, yes," he whispered.

Trix's eyes shot open and she went to turn to face him.

"No, not look, rats watch."

"Yes, Toe is my baby mouse," Trix quickly replied."

"Toemouse safe, with father. Me be here to help you find them..." Before Attic could finish, two guards moved forward and ushered him away.

Rushing over to Hatty, Trix straightened some straw as she spoke, "Hatty did you hear? Toe is safe with his father, praise Father Sky."

Sensing he would not be allowed to return, Attic turned and yelled in native mouse, "They be here. They be near. All be good, do not fear."

Having no idea, what the young male mouse had said, the rats lashed him with their tails anyway.

Grabbing Attic by one leg, one of the guards examined his ear. "This mouse is not one of the nursery gatherers. Look he has no markings to identify him."

"Mother, they have seized the young mouse," Hatty screamed, running forward. She soon found her progress blocked by the prince rat, his teeth glaring.

"Worry not," Attic yelled, "for I be me." Raising his front paw to his mouth, Attic placed two nails in. Within an instant a very loud high pitched whistle rang through the chamber.

Watching the prince turn to the sound, Hatty pulled out the sharpened stick from her pouch. Before Trix could yell at her to stop, Hatty had leapt forward and rammed it into the rat's throat. Blood gushing from the arterial wound the rat grasped his neck and fell to the floor.

Instantly, the other nursery guards scurried toward her.

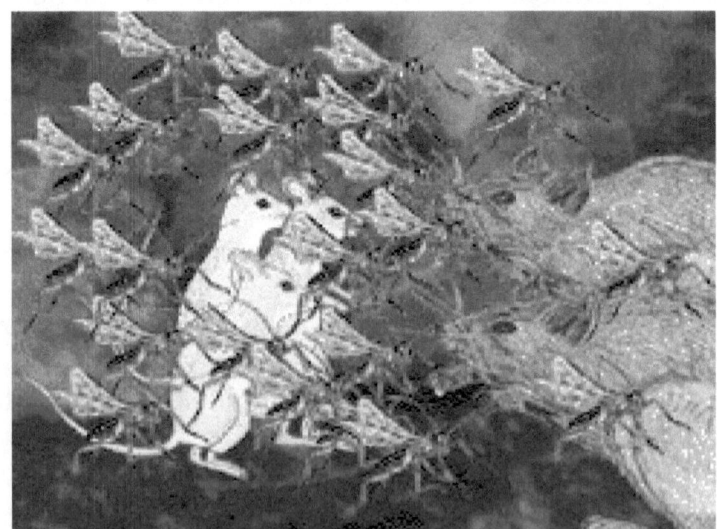

Attic, watching on, whistled again. Suddenly, the

guard holding him released his leg, when a native bee flew up his nose. Pulling out his stick, Attic blew again.

With a humming roar, the roof of the nursery disappeared behind a blanket of hornets and wasps. Arrow like swarms began to attack the guards with relentless determination.

Rushing into Hatty and Trix, Attic grabbed their paws. Kicking with one leg, he forced their way from the nursery. Then, after yet another whistle, a wall of hornets and wasps formed around Hatty and her mother. As soon as the protective shield was up, Attic leapt outside of its perimeter of safety to help his friends, the stingers.

#   #   #

Seanne finished outlining the plan of attack and solemnly lowered her head. "I ask that we now reflect on the plan in silence and pray for success."

Only the sound of water dripping down the walls broke the silence as a total hush fell over her chambers.

The gathering, in the sanctuary, had decided to open all the secret holes over the rats' nest. Princess Squorth and the other spiders would sail down on web with Bull-ant Warriors on their backs. All other natives would then enter through the holes the moles were to create.

A cry rang throughout the sanctuary, shattering the silence. After spiralling from floor, to wall, to ceiling, along the overcrowded corridor a muddied gecko entered Seanne's chambers.

Scurrying across the ceiling, Gef, the gecko rushed over those gathered to land on the ground near Jun. "From my observation point, above the rats' nursery, I have seen a great battle begin. A strange native mouse dared to talk in our tongue to Trix and they seized him. Hatty then slew one of the guards with a stick to the throat. With the aid of hornets, wasps and bees the young mouse has freed them. If we do not do something, they will be overrun and slaughtered." Gef's tongue flicked in and out with excitement.

Toe turned to look at his father and Dodd. *Attic,* he thought, *what have you done?* The young mouse started to fidget, his hind legs bouncing up and down in frustration.

Jun sprang to his feet. "We have no leaf falls left; we must attack! All natives to their positions."

Despite his seeping wound, Mar leapt to his hind legs with surprising agility. "Antoni, send word for the army to attack the wall facing away from Brother Sun. It will be there, the rats in the nest will try to escape from the battle. Bega, ask Queen Slur and her kind to enter through the main nest entrance. Bink, you go with Bega and show her the way. Father Sky and Mother Earth be with us." Adrenaline pumping through his veins, Mar moved swiftly out into the tunnel. Turning, he signalled for his astonished sons to follow him.

The sanctuary's tunnels sprang to life, as every native of the refuge moved to take their positions. Armouries, full of bows, arrows, staffs and sharpened sticks soon emptied. Driven by the thought of vengeance for the destruction of homes and the butchery of friends, their usually timid eyes glowed red.

#   #   #

The hum, emanating from the royal nursery grew to a roar as Ine hurried to his king's side. Visibly shaking the king's herald threw himself onto the limestone steps.

"What is that terrible noise, Ine?" the King demanded, waving a piece of bloodied meat around in the air.

"Winged insects are attacking the guards in the nursery sector. There are so many of them, guards report being unable to breathe. While some sting, other smaller black insects fly in and block their airways." Ine backed down two steps to ensure he was out of the king's reach. "King Yahn, it is with a deep heart I report, Prince Loak has been slain. Oh, Great One, what shall we do?" Ine's eyes shifted rapidly from side to side and his whiskers twitched.

Emotionless, Yahn took a bite of his mouse meat and thought for a moment. "Hah, I have other sons," he declared, throwing the scraps to the cockroaches inhabiting the shadows. "We shall dispose of the annoyances with flame. Send some of the Order of Flame forth, to help repel these insects. How dare they enter our nest and defy us?"

"While I have great respect for The Order of Flame, my King, they are insane in battle. Not only do they not hesitate to set themselves alight, but they also light any creature near them. Surely that will mean death to your children." From the corner of his eye, Ine could see more guards rushing toward the nursery.

Furious, Yahn picked up his sceptre and hurled it at Ine. "You dare to argue with your King? Do as I say, Ine. My children matter not to me, I can produce more. Send the Order, now! Ine, I want everything burnt or you will be sacrificed." The obese rat went red in the face as he tried to raise himself from the throne.

Bowing his head, Ine sneered at the King and left. Scurrying to a tunnel arch, Ine screamed, "Send the Carriers of the Flame to attack the nursery, set all alight."

Unnoticed, the herald slipped into a corridor and headed for the outside world. He did not intend to stay in such a hideous environment any longer. Shaking his head, Ine mumbled, "To declare war on primitive creatures is one thing, but to slay your guards and children is unforgivable."

The dark dank tunnels lit up as the flame carriers

poured out of their sector. Within moments the Ash Cathedral, usually full of worshippers, emptied to leave a solitary flame on the altar.

Not far away a muddied secret door swung open and with great stealth two invading mice rushed to the flame and extinguished it.

Within moments, all the passageways leading to the nursery began to fill with the Carriers of the Flame; in pairs, one carried the flame while the other fuelled it. Insane, they hurtled along setting bystanders alight as they went toward the battle. Their eyes red from the reflection of the fire, they screamed with delight at spreading the flame's word.

Chaos broke out as other nest inhabitants began panicking; fearing the flame all they wanted was to flee. As the corridors emptied, small trapdoors opened along the ceilings. Lenthric, Meric's lieutenant, signalled to wait until the rats were directly beneath them.

Keen to avenge the death of their king at Yahn's paws, the invading mice patiently waited. When the rats came past chanting, they flung the doors completely open. In one combined effort, hundreds of invading mice hurled wet mud at the flames to douse them.

The rats screeched with anger as the flames went out and soon lost any form of discipline.

Lenthric seized the opportunity. "For our King and families," he yelled, falling onto a muddied rat's back.

"For freedom or death!" thousands of muffled voices replied in unison. In an instant a myriad of other secret doors opened as fellow rebels joined with Lenthric.

Confined to the small corridor the rats' size worked against them during the attack. Using sticks, rocks and claws, the down trodden mice engaged the tail end of the flame column.

Trix and Hatty stood with their front paws over their

ears. The hum created by the shroud of stingers' wings was deafening. *What is going on?* Hatty thought. *Where is the strange mouse? What if he is dead?* Her heart full of dread she moved even closer to her mother.

They both jumped as the wall of wasps broke open and Attic leapt in grinning. "Me be here!" he declared leaning his wild scruffy face toward them. Seeing their expressions, his smile broadened.

The two female mice looked at each other in disbelief. They could not believe their eyes as he came even closer, held both paws to his mouth and asked, "Hatty and Toemouse mother miss me, yes? Me see by face, yes."

Hatty stared into his wild eyes. *He is quite mad,* she thought, pushing in to touch her mother.

"No worry, me have plan. We must go this way up path. Then you see where fat one keeps shiny things." The wild mouse moved round behind them and put a paw on each of their shoulders. "He be fatter than Elder Bega, yes?" Making a gesture toward his own belly Attic waited for a reply to his earnest question.

Witnessing their supposed saviour's behaviour, Trix became increasingly concerned. *He seems to be acting like it is all some game,* she thought, watching him step away from them.

Turning, Attic signalled with his paws and hummed. Immediately, the protective curtain of stingers changed direction. Hatty and Trix had little choice but to move along behind the wild mouse as the swarm followed Attic's orders.

While the natives in the centre could see no indication, the rats on the outside were still trying to penetrate the shield. With more wasps and hornets joining it with every leaf fall, the stingers curtain had become more than three rats in thickness.

Slowly, they climbed the slippery slope to the chamber

above the main cavern. "Quiet we be. Below the fat one sits. Near him many cockroaches, in the shadows they be," Attic whispered, holding a finger to his mouth. "Here we be." He held out his gangly front leg and pointed.

Toe's mother could not get over the wild mouse's innocence in the face of such adversity. Looking deep into his large brown eyes, she felt a twinge in her heart. *Why am I overwhelmed with the feeling I should be protecting you?*

Looking into the dark alcove Hatty saw Tongue, the Bringer of Truth, lying on top of a pile of ornaments. Leaping forward she grabbed it, even though she knew she could no longer draw it. Throwing it to Attic, she pleaded, "Draw it strange one! It could be our last form of defence."

Placing the scabbard between his knees, Attic, tugged and tugged at the sword to no avail. Lifting his front paws up to his shoulders, he shrugged. Returning his gaze to the jewelled weapon, he pondered their next move. "We be safe here away from rats, with friends help. Me think of plan to get outside now, yes."

#   #   #

King Yahn raised his huge rodent head and looked up at the swarm of hornets and wasps above his throne. Straining to see beyond the torchlight, his eyes narrowed and whiskers twitched. "My faithful creepers climb the walls and bring me the creatures the stingers are protecting."

From near his throne, thousands of black cockroaches crawled out of the fissure and commenced scurrying up the walls. Looking across the bones of the natives he had devoured, the king rat smiled. His eyes flashed red in the darkened cavern. *I shall torture them first,* he thought, *and then slowly eat them.*

To his pets' surprise, the stingers put up a strong resistance. The first waves of the attack found themselves covered in stings and were soon in retreat.

Taking to the air the black cockroaches began attacking in flight. The cavern hummed loudly with the sound of wings as a great aerial battle commenced. Within moments, black bodies began showering down in the king's chambers.

Yahn watched on as cockroach after cockroach fell before him dead, without gaining any advantage at all. *I could call for a retreat,* he thought. *No, if they can not defend me, what is the good in that? To die for their king, is the only honourable death.*

Yahn felt his throne vibrate, just before a loud rumble began to shake the cave. Unable to see the ceiling, through the battle raging above his head, he became unnerved. "To me, my royal guards," he called.

In an instant, hundreds of his most vicious protectors surrounded him.

#   #   #

Watching the guards leave their posts to race to the king's side, Nel realised help was coming. Leaning against the wooden bars, she watched the events unfolding before her eyes. A trickle of dust, showering her head, began to increase to a stream as the very ground she stood upon shook. *The ceiling is going to fall,* she thought, beginning to run.

"To the back of the pit," Nel called, racing past the other captives.

The pit filled with dust when a small stalactite crashed down and blocked the cell doors.

While the rats were unable to reach them, their tormentors, the black cockroaches poured over the stalactite in a dark wave.

"We can not escape through the entrance, but we can

fight." Nel screamed, picked up a stone with her front legs and smashed it down on a cockroach.

For the first time, the native captives began to fight back. Following Nel's example, they picked up stones to pound the black creepers to death. Lightenings of torture and watching friends' deaths drove their weary arms into a murderous frenzy.

When out of the dust, above them, a large bird-spider appeared sailing down its web Nel shuddered in disbelief. However, when at least three more landed, she became certain she had to be delusional. Weak beyond imagination she fell to her knees. *My head is spinning and my heart is bursting,* she thought, as her eyes closed.

Bur's deep voice growled, "Be not afraid, fellow natives, we of the bird-spiders have come to your rescue." His legs wriggled for a moment to find a solid footing, then he nodded.

The captives watched in amazement as Fila and many bull-ants leapt off the enormous spiders' backs. Leading the way, soldier bull-ants nipped at the cockroaches with their mandibles pushing them back from the trapped natives. Others seized the opportunity and led the prisoners to the spiders' backs.

When each spider was fully loaded, a bull-ant would signal to those above with a tug on the web. With this command, the creatures of the sanctuary began pulling the web back up. Upon reaching the rough entrances to the refuge the spiders waited for their passengers to disembark. Dropping into the foray once again, they span new webs then connected them to the old ones.

With desperation in his heart, Fila strained his eyes to search for his daughter. Placing his front paws to his mouth, he called, "Nel, Nel."

A young female pigmy possum, on its way toward the spiders' backs, broke ranks and hurried to Fila's side. "Metcha Mouse, she is at the back of the pit. Hurry, I fear she is injured, I shall guide you."

Touched by the small possum's bravery and concern, Fila lay his paw on the young native's head. "Go now, child, to safety. I will find Nel." With that he signalled to a bull-ant to guide her to the spiders.

A sharpened stick in each front paw, Fila jabbed and slashed his way to his daughter. "Nel," he called again.

"Father," a muffled voice replied, from under a pile of creepers.

Rushing forward Fila tore at the cockroaches, his body shaking with rage. He skewered creeper after creeper, splattering their guts all over his golden/grey fur. Deeper and deeper he dug into the dark soulless creatures until he could see Nel's, bloodied motionless body.

Throwing the sticks aside, he grabbed the last few cockroaches in his bare paws. One by one, he shoved their bodies' between his powerful hind legs and twisted their necks. Their necks' snapped, he threw their lifeless bodies to the side. *You deserve no better for serving the rats*.

Tears filling his eyes, he leant down and picked his daughter up into his front legs. "Please, my darling child, be with spirit." Lovingly, he drew her limp body close to his heart and prayed. Water clouding his vision, he became overwhelmed with grief and began to weep. His stream of tears dropped down on his daughter's dusty white chest, dampening her fur.

A gentle paw reached up to touch his cheek. "Do not cry, Father, for I am here."

Fila looked down into her beautiful eyes, shining with life. "By the River Stones," he cried, softly hugging her. With a nod of his head, he summoned some soldier bull-ants to his side. "Please create a defensive perimeter around us, so I can carry her to Bur."

In a fraction of a leaf fall, they had returned to Bur's side. Hugging Nel, he placed her to the front of the spider's body near his head. "Guard her well, great one."

"Have no fear of that," Bur replied, handing web to his bull-ant companion to tie her on.

Fila's soul felt lighter as he watched Bur climb back up the netting of webs. *For the first time in so many lightenings she is free,* he thought. Spinning around he returned to helping the remaining captives.

#   #   #

The wall of another cell crumbled away as a hole opened into the pit which held Fila's wife.

"Come, follow." Ena the mole beckoned, squinting his eyes.

With surprising speed the dark pit began to empty. As the last few natives left their prison a boulder crashed across its gate, ensuring the rats could not pursue.

Nila scurried along on all fours behind Ena.

Despite the natives' efforts the black cockroaches, were soon moving with great speed along the tunnel. In passing Ena squeaked to one of his kind hidden in a freshly dug side tunnel. A water drip later a roar hissed through all the escape tunnels as the moles and echidnas collapsed them on their pursuers.

#   #   #

Attic stood listening to the battle raging around them. No matter how hard he tried, he could not think of an escape plan. Just when he felt all hope might well be lost, Wi of the Wasps flew up next to his ear.

Hatty watched on as the wild mouse used hums and paw movements to talk to his friend. "He promised to help us escape, Mother, and yet here on this ledge we seem more trapped than ever. I can not stand being unable to see what is happening beyond the stingers."

"From the loud hum I hear, perhaps it is best we do not know." Trix turned to look her daughter in the eye. "I have faith in the strange mouse, Hatty, I can not explain why. Please, give him some more leaf falls to figure something out."

With fire in her eyes, Hatty replied, "As you wish. I warn you, Mother; I will not stay here much longer. The constant hum is driving me crazy. I have no wish to become a meal for cockroaches or rats. If I must lose my spirit, I would rather do it fighting."

#   #   #

A blood curdling screech echoed round the cavern as the first pair of flame carriers burst into the nursery. Their noses twitching with insanity, they screamed with delight as they began to set everything alight with flame.

In next to no time at least a dozen more pairs joined them. Driven by the excitement the flame brought they incinerated everything in their path; not a creature was safe. The stench of the smouldering corpses, they left behind, flooded out of the tunnels feeding their lunacy.

Swooping into attack, the brave wasps, hornets and bees did their best to contain the vilest of all the rats' kind. Their brave attempts were no match for the burning redness that sent them spinning to the dirt floor in flame. Relentlessly the mighty native stingers continued attacking, despite their massive casualties.

"Spread the word of the flame, let the flame cleanse the impure," The Order of the Flame chanted, their eyes reflecting the redness of the fires.

#   #   #

Attic's nostrils flared as he reached forward and signalled for the wasps to part. *Me friends stingers and bees losing spirits,* he thought, *and it be me fault.*

Before Trix and Hatty could stop him the wild mouse leapt out of the wasp barrier and back again.

Hatred in her eyes, Hatty leapt straight toward him, sharpened stick in her paw.

The guardian's eyes bulged as the young female went straight for his head.

With a jump and a roll she pierced a creeper through the heart, which followed Attic back in. Tears rolling from her eyes she stabbed the insect again and again. "I shall take your spirit, dark one, in payment for Elder Briar."

Trix moved forward and grabbed Hatty's front leg to stop her. Drawing her close to her breast she held her daughter, whispering, "My dear baby, what has this all done to you? Your eyes, once so full of life, seem so old. I promise we will soon be a family again and return to the Great Silky Oak."

The wild mouse watched on, longing to know such love. "Me must help friends. You stay here, yes. Wasp and hornet curtain protect you. Me friend Wi, of the Wasps, informed me many of our natives be rescued. Hairy legs carry up into holes above and seal entrances with web. You see no dark creepers can follow then. Hairy legs are very smart creatures, yes." Trying to lighten the moment, Attic laid a paw on each of his companions' heads and smiled.

Surprisingly Attic found both his front paws seized at the same time by the females. Trix looked up into his large brown pool like eyes and said, "We shall not be separated, take us with you."

"Much, much danger, this not be good idea. Me save you for little friend, Toemouse. He be broken hearted if me not return you safely. So no, me not take you." Attic tried his hardest to remove the grip on his paws, but could not.

"Take us with you, NOW!" Hatty stood, with gritted teeth, twisting his paw. Somehow she felt a familiarity in the larger mouse and asked, "Who are you?"

"I be me," he replied, only to find his front leg twisted even more. Having watched her, from the shadows in lightenings past, bring her brothers to their knees with a similar hold, he relented, "Ouch. Yes this be very good plan, Toemouse sister make." Turning he hummed and danced again. "We move back down ledge to where we came from, yes. First female with grip of bandicoot let paw go, please." Attic shook his paw, bent down, picked up the sword and moved in close to the wall.

Walking on to follow, Hatty kicked the cockroach, she had stabbed, off the ledge. The battle still raging between the dark creepers and the stingers slowed their progress. *I must get off the ledge*, she thought, *or I will scream.*

Leaf falls past as they hopped back down to the nursery. Upon reaching the bottom their protective curtain began to find itself overwhelmed for the first time. The relentless attack of the black creepers, combined with the redness, was too much for even the hornets and wasps to take.

Unexpectedly the wall of stingers parted to allow Wi to enter. "Hmm, hum hmm." Was all the females' ears could hear. Yet Attic stood there listening and nodding his head.

"Wi now say, soon all natives join us and attack. Should be exciting, yes? Me also send Wi to protect Toemouse, when little friend comes with father. Wi, you see, very clever wasp and has much respect from his kind."

"Is that all, your friend said?" Trix enquired, examining his concerned features.

Attic solemnly lowered his head and shook it, "Sad this be, many wasps, bees and hornets lay outside our shield without spirit. Invaders used redness to devour them."

Rushing up Hatty seized him by both his front shoulders. "And what of the smell of burning fur and meat? Tell me," she insisted, shaking Attic.

"The evil ones also set bodies of other invaders to redness and some rat babies." The wild mouse's face revealed remorse for the lost spirits.

Hatty stood examining his soft features for a water drip. Turning and walking back to her mother's side, she said, "I am sorry for the loss of your friends. As for the rats and their offspring let them perish and be done with it."

Hatty's body trembled as her mother shook her trying to bring her to her senses. "This is not like you, Hatty, my child." Releasing her, Trix ran past Attic and grabbed Tongue the Bringer of Truth. "They are only babies. If we allow them to lose their spirit then we are no better than the invaders." Screaming she jumped into the wall of wasps.

Defiantly, the wife of Chieftain Mar, Lady Trix of the Oak, stood in the archway to the nursery screaming, "They are infants who know nothing of evil. Adults have not yet been able to corrupt their minds with dark thoughts."

The cavern and tunnels hissed as Trix drew Tongue the Bringer of Truth. "No native or invader shall harm one of these babies." With a wild look in her eyes she stood firm, ready to fight against any creature who would dare try to kill the few surviving rat offspring.

Glaring past the dust and smoke, filled with the stench of death, the flame carriers stopped their advance. For a moment they stood mystified, amazed by the female kangaroo mouse standing in front of them waving a sword. As the very ground beneath them began to shake, they turned to look at each other in wonder. "What does this mean, Devor?" However, before he could receive an answer the walls of the cavern began to collapse, showering them with rocks.

#   #   #

With a great crash, a thunder rumbled through the king's cavern, then the wall closest to the rising of Brother Sun crumbled down. Rushing in Mar, Dodd, Toe, Jun and the others took the fight to the King's most savage guards. Pon and Fila leading the archers, not far behind, signalled for them to rain their arrows down on the rats.

Turning their attack away from the wasps, the cockroaches began to swarm on the archers instead. In the breath of a breeze, Pon and Fila found themselves under a black cloud of fluttering dark creepers. Their archers bravely continued to shoot arrow after arrow, downing as many as they could, until they disappeared into the darkness.

#   #   #

The rising dust clouds hiding how many attackers there were. King Yahn sat motionless, dazed by the battle raging around him; his fat rat brain unable to fathom how so many native creatures could fight together. "Flame carriers to me," he screamed, forced himself to stand and strained his eyes in hope of seeing the faithful come to his aid.

With blind obedience the flame carriers turned away from Trix and ran screeching into the battle.

The surviving Order of the Flame members soon

burned a pathway to their king and surrounded him.

King Yahn's soulless eyes narrowed and he laughed. "Foolish primitives you shall all perish by flame. Go forth and spread the word of the flame, my faithful."

The evil flame carriers rushed forward into the attack to set all alight.

However, as they did the Boobook owls' kind swooped into the cave and began to flap their wings. A chill ran across the battle scene as the wind ripped through the air, extinguishing the rats' flames. Having never had any training in paw to paw fighting, the flame carriers soon found themselves overrun.

#   #   #

When the wall of wasps parted Hatty seized the chance, leapt out and joined her mother. Determined to help, she nodded and stood by her side. "I have regained my senses, Mother." Turning her head from side to side, she asked, "Have you seen the strange mouse? He left through the other side of the curtain leaf falls ago."

Attic's nose twitched as he felt the wind blow across his face. After living in the wild all his lightenings, he knew exactly what the wind would do in the smaller tunnels. Humming and jumping about furiously, he pleaded with the stingers and bees to flee. His heart wept as he looked around at his friends' bodies scattered on the ground, like in the lightenings when the leaves fall.

"More redness comes," he yelled, hopping back to Hatty and Trix. At full speed he threw his body into the air and knocked both the females to the ground. "Stay in my protection. Soon you see why." Attic did his best to pull them in closer to cover them with his own body.

The wind from the owls' wings spun around the cavern and out into the smaller tunnels. Twirling up the passageways, reigniting all the smouldering bodies left in the wake of the flame carriers, it picked up more and more power. A rumble grew out from the entry tunnels to the nursery.

Holding the females even tighter, Attic said, "Tell Toemouse, he be best friend in all existence." Tears rolled down his eyes onto their dusty fur as the beast like fire's roar entered the small cavern. Feeling a tremendous heat building, Attic closed his eyes to the inevitable.

A water drip before the fire-ball hit, all the wasps and hornets in the area flew down. Selflessly, they created a protective shell over the trio, using their own bodies.

Hit by the realisation of what the scruffy mouse had done, Trix lifted a paw to his damp face. "Thank you, dear brave mouse," she said, closing her eyes as all the air around her and Hatty disappeared.

Like a giant wave, the redness washed across them burning everything in its path.

#   #   #

Fighting the much larger rats, the smaller creatures of the sanctuary found their casualties increasing dramatically. The cavern's stifling atmosphere reeked of smoke, dust and scorched bodies, making it difficult to breathe. Even with their nocturnal abilities, the natives could see but a few paw lengths in front of them.

Inspired by Mar's example the untrained natives continued to fight the rats, despite the massive loss of spirits. Mar led on, as lifeless bodies began to litter the bone covered floor of the king's cavern. The battle ground made even more horrific by the sight of dead stingers and cockroaches blanketing the bodies, like a shroud of death.

Where is my family? Spinning the staff above his head he tried his best to search through the smoke.

Pivoting on his powerful hind legs, the kangaroo mouse lunged forward to bring his weapon into contact with a rat's eye. Following through, he rammed the staff into its windpipe. Weary beyond his spirit the Chieftain of the Silky Oak fought on, hoping to gain a glimpse of his wife and daughter.

Not far from his father's side, Dodd thrust out into the murky smog with his pole and flicked his tail in the air like a whip. *This is not good enough, I am getting nowhere,* the large mouse thought. *Mother and Hatty could well need me; it is time for a change of strategy.*

Taking a gigantic risk, Dodd lowered his staff to the ground; unwrapping his roarer from his side. Coughing as he drew in a breath, he began to hurl it above his head, around and around in the darkness. The flat sharpened stone, attached to the spiders' webs, began to emanate a ghostly howl.

#   #   #

The long wailing cry of the roarer, cut through the air and into the tunnels. Soon its haunting lament began to grow, reverberating off every wall and ceiling. Once combined with the ominous stench of death, even the hardest of the rat guards began to shake in fear.

Moving its head quickly from side to side one of the king's guards felt an urge to break ranks. Nose twitching, it stood horrified by the frightful sound in the dank gloomy environment. Finally, unable to stand the sound any longer, it fled yelling, "Cats! Cats! Cats!"

Forcing himself to stand, King Yahn glared at the deserting rat. Raising his paw, he called to his guards, "Fools, it is but a trick. Stay by my side and protect me or I shall kill you myself." Drool oozed out of the rat's disgusting mouth as he continued, "I know of no cats in this land. Stand and fight to the death for your King."

The King of Rats strained his eyes, attempting to find an answer in the haze. *This sound is of pure evil,* he thought, as he racked his brain for an escape plan. *Even if it is some beast, my guards are expendable and I have other nests to go to. After all, I am the one my rats need to lead them.*

His eyes widened as a glimmer of fire light, from the nursery, broke through the murk for a moment. *A sign,* he smiled thinking to himself, *the gods are sending me to the gatherers' entrance near the nursery.*

Before the king could even give a command another guard broke down. "I tell you it is some beast from this land, come to devour us." Turning to look at the king's large fat body the guard yelled, "He is not worth losing our lives over. Follow me to freedom." In an instant the rat was scurrying across the dead bodies toward the hole made by the avalanche.

Heeding his cry many other guards turned, running toward the faint light filtering through the landslide. Panicking as they surfaced outside, they fled into the open and straight into the waiting talons of the hawks and owls.

Moving his grotesque body awkwardly down the stairs of his throne's podium, the king turned to his remaining guards. "Take me to the nursery, my faithful, and I shall reward you with riches beyond your dreams. We will escape through the gatherers' tunnel to my sons' nests. There we shall gather an army to bring down the wrath of the rats upon these barbaric creatures. We of the superior race are ordained to wipe these pathetic animals off the face of the earth."

Creating a defensive parameter around their king, the rats began their push toward the nursery.

#   #   #

Wi of the Wasps' heart fell into despair when upon his return he found the nursery entrance devoid of life. Everywhere he looked, bodies laid charred by the massive heat-blast from the fireball. Attic's friend of many lightenings flew to a large pile of the stingers kind. Seeing that it was nothing more than a scorched pile of bodies moulded together from intense heat, the little wasp became ill.

Swinging around to return to Toe, Wi caught the slightest hint of movement in his eye. Frantically digging into the pile of departed friends he dug deeper and deeper. His tiny heart skipped a beat as he came across the motionless body of his dearest of friends, Attic. Doing his best to find signs of breath, he was saddened to find none.

In pure desperation he landed behind Attic's ear and gently stung him with his stinger. The brave wasp then flew away a few paw lengths and prayed, to Father Sky, his plan would work.

Unexpectedly, Attic's paw twitched and then rose to his ear. Within a leaf fall, the wild guardian had forced his way out of the pile. "It was you who stung me, Wi. Me be sleeping and dreaming of other times and you brought me back." Attic reached out his paw and stroked the wasp's head. "Grateful me be, little friend."

Turning his attention back to Trix and Hatty he was pleased to see them both breathing. "Forgive me, stinger friends, for using bodies in such a way." Tears streaming from his eyes, he covered the female mice to hide them from the rats. "Hmm, hmm and thank you," he said doing a dance of gratitude. "Wi, return to Toemouse and protect him now, yes. Good friend, me owe you me spirit. Me promise, soon we play again."

Opening her eyes, Hatty could just make out Attic's figure moving up the ledge again. Where is he going?

Wriggling she tried to free herself from her mother's grip.

"Stay here with me, Hatty," Trix gasped. "We will do what, as I suspect, the wild mouse wants us to do. That is stay in safety and rest."

"Rest?" Hatty questioned. "How can I under a pile of scorched stingers' bodies?"

Rubbing her daughter's chest, Trix whispered, "These brave natives gave their spirits for us, child. If we were to leave here prematurely and have our spirits stolen, their sacrifice will have been for nothing."

"I understand, Mother." Hatty took in a large breath of the suffocating air and lay in wait.

#   #   #

Slithering up the slope to the main entrance of the rats' nest, Slur stopped. Flicking her tongue, she coiled around to face her guide. "I ssuspect the attack has already begun. If you have failed to get us here before any of the vial invaders escaped, Bink, I sshall personally sseek you out. You sshould make a nice ssnack before I celebrate ssustenance again."

"If that is the way you feel, Queen Slur, I suggest you hurry into the foray." Without another word Bink scurried away from the platoon of no-legs straight up a rocky outcrop.

Slur turned to her followers, "Blate, you and your brethren of the Black Snake, sstay concealed here outside. You sshould easily dispose of any that may evade our fangs and coils. The rest of us will head inside, this despicable place, and each take a passageway." Winding her way up to the arched entrance Slur turned to her kind and hissed, "Leave no invaders with sspirit."

Watching from above, Bink the Bush Cockroach sighed with relief. Spinning around and hurrying away he grumbled, "Good riddens, python, your kind has always given me the creeps. You should try being my size and running around in the grasses, I bet you soon would be lost, oh arrogant one. Oh arrogant one, that is good, I shall have to remember that. I will be able to recount to my offspring, how I stood up to the no-legs. Of course, I shall be their leader in my retelling." Bink chucked to himself as he hurried back to the sanctuary.

Upon entering the maze of tunnels, Slur waited as her followers moved with great stealth down each opening. Slowly but methodically she slipped with grace into the largest hole. "Come oh sspirit sstealers to Queen Sslur, there is no use hiding. We of the no-legs will ssniff you out wherever you be. Sso ssave us precious leaf falls and sseek me out."

Screams of terror hurtled out of the passageways as Slur and her kind began their attack. Disorganised and blind with shock the rats which were fleeing to the entrance turned back toward the main cavern. Taking no care, they charged away from the no-legs, pushing and shoving each other. Many of the rats catching alight as they squeezed past burning corpses.

"Take my ssight will you," Slur screamed, in a rage advancing through the tunnels. Clasping a rat in her powerful jaws she bit down and crushed it to death. Constricting yet another, she cried, "Please allow me to introduce myself as you run, I am Queen Sslur, of the no-legs. I have the honour of being a Sservicer of the Circle of the Great Oak commune. The very ssame commune you attacked unprovoked."

Slur blinked her eye and rotated her tongue. "Come to me rats sso you may die. Come to me sso your throats I can choke. There is no use hiding, I know you are there. I can feel on my back your evil glare. Ssstop hiding in the sshadows, for Mother Earth's ssake, come to me sso your bodies I can sshake.

"Please take off and run, it makes more of a challenge, indeed it is more fun. Be you rat, mouse or cockroach, please come cross my path. With one quick ssqueeze your sspirits will pass. Sso please come out and join me, do not hide instead. I promise little pain, for I will ssoon make you dead!"

\#   \#   \#

It had taken Bega, Antoni and the army far more leaf falls to reach their assigned position than had been calculated.

Approaching the newly made hole, leading into the king's cavern, Bega sighed with frustration. They had been surprised by the number of rats deserting the king's side, who turned and fought instead of surrendering. *I am too old for such battles,* he thought dodging an oncoming rat. The old bandicoot, his body weary beyond reason, rapped the fleeing rat across the neck with his staff.

The two friends fought side by side cutting a path through the wall of escaping rats. Finally, they stood atop a pile of rubble created by the avalanche. Straining their eyes, they could hardly see anything through the smoke, dust and swarming insects.

Bega watched on with envy as Antoni, and his army of bull-ants, scurried down the perilous slope with ease. He hated trying to climb on unsure ground at his age, let alone when he was constantly in jeopardy.

Watching as the bandicoot crawled down the slope, Chief Antoni sent his army into battle and waited at the bottom. *For once I do not admire your size, friend,* he thought.

His small ant face grimaced when yet more boulders and rocks slid from beneath Bega's large frame.

Realising, he was making the bandicoot even more nervous, the bull-ant walked away a few paces.

A smile of relief grew on Bega's face when his paws once again touched solid ground. Standing on his hind legs he dusted his greying fur and laughed, "That was not bad for an old bandicoot was it, Antoni."

The bull-ant ran to his side and looked up into the large brown eyes. "I am proud of you, my teacher. Even at your advanced lightenings you can still move with agility." Antoni's mandibles opened to reveal a smile. "Now I suggest you follow me, Elder, as it is much clearer closer to the cavern's floor. I can guide you through the smoke and dead bodies to Mar. I already have his scent."

"I am not so proud as to be foolish," Bega answered, touching Antoni's face with his clawed toe. "In all my lightenings, I have not fought in such terrible conditions. To be truthful, I am all but blind in this fog of death. The stench of the burning corpses in my nostrils makes me sick, to my oversized gut."

Bega's large ears pricked and he lifted his snout toward the ceiling. Before Antoni had a chance to ask him what was wrong rocks began to shower down on both of them. In a fraction of a water drip, a large chunk of the rocky roof came screaming toward them. Knowing there was not enough time to escape; Bega leapt forward, seized Antoni in his front legs and rolled onto his stomach.

Held tight in his friend's grip Antoni lay listening as the boulders pounded Bega's back. His heart broke as he felt bone after bone, snap in the old bandicoot's chest. "Why did you not simply roll away, dear Elder?" he said, as a tear left his eye.

Hit by the full force of a small stalactite, Bega's body spasmed, let out all the air in his chest and went limp.

Feeling his friend relinquish his grip, Antoni pried himself out from under his body and the rubble. Angry beyond words, the small bull-ant lifted a boulder ten times his own size off Bega's snout and threw it to the side. "No!" His small ant voice howled as he crouched down to feel for breath. "Please, Father Sky and Mother Earth, allow the bravest of all your servants to live."

Signalling for his warriors to dig Bega out, Antoni laid his face near the bandicoot's nostrils. When he felt a gush of air gently cross his face the ant whispered, "We shall dig you out, Elder, just hang on."

A groan came from Bega's mouth before he spoke, "Send your ants back into battle, dear Antoni. My body is broken beyond repair and I can feel my spirit leaving me. Ahhh... I have no wish to live another lightening, if I am to be a burden on my fellow natives. Ah, the pain has gone and Elder Briar has come for me. Farewell, brother Antoni, I am proud to have known you." Bega's body contorted. "Tell Chieftain Mar, I loved him as if he was my own son." With that, he was gone.

"NO!" Antoni shrieked, pushing a large rock out of his path. Returning to the battle, he no longer let the darkness impede his progress and found his way lit by pure unbridled rage. Leaping from rat to rat, he drove his spider's fang into the back of their necks, coldly, precisely, killing them in an instant.

#   #   #

Protected behind his wasp armour, Toe stayed loyally to the side of Mar's left paw. The young mouse's concern for his father's well-being had seen him send formation after formation of wasps to protect him. Despite his protectors' objections, Toe hummed and danced the order, "Leave me and protect my father." Just as he did, the rats overran and took Mar down.

Completely vulnerable Toe hopped over to a dead

native and tore two pointed sticks from its death grip. *I shall not let these demons steal my father's spirit,* he thought. Clenching his teeth, he held the two sticks in his front paws and flung himself at his father's attackers. In a water drip, he found his small frame flying through the air, knocked aside by one of the invaders. Standing, he shook his head and moved to re-enter the foray.

Wi was not pleased to see the events unfolding before his eyes. Flying down he blocked Toe's path and hummed loudly in protest, "Hmm, hmm, and hmm."

Even though Toe had not fully grasped the wasp language, he could tell his little friend was annoyed. He listened intently as Wi did his best to explain about his mother and sister.

"Mother and Hatty are with spirit, is that what you are trying to tell me?" He watched Wi nod and then fly away.

Flying in and out of the aerial battle, the small wasp flew with all his heart toward the nursery. Worried about Toe leaving himself so open to attack, he flew straight to Attic.

Toe, on top of the pile of rats attacking his father, struck over and over with his sticks.

A rat, turned, reached up with its front paw, pulled out the weapon and threw it to the side. Glaring at Toe, it turned its attack on him. Springing through the air, it landed pinning the young mouse to the ground. Drool oozed out of the rat's mouth as it drew back its upper lip to reveal its fangs.

Toe took in a breath of the foul air and prepared himself for his fate. "I shall not give you the satisfaction, Spirit Stealer, of seeing fear on my face." As the rat's head reared back, ready to strike, the brave young native closed his eyes.

Toe flinched, as he sensed the rat moving to drive its

teeth into his chest. His fur stood upright as the wind between their bodies escaped. *Now I shall see what is on the other side of existence,* he thought, *and where my spirit will go.* Praying he waited to cross over, but nothing happened. Opening his eyes, he saw his attacker's twisting body lifted off him by hundreds of bull-ants.

With fire in his eyes, Antoni hurled himself onto the rat's back and severed its jugular with his sword. Having dealt with that rat Antoni, his small body covered in a war paint of its blood, sprang onto another invader's back. Shrieking, he lifted the sword above his head with both front legs, driving it into the rat's spine.

Before he had a chance to move, Toe found himself shadowed by a spider descending on web. "Stay under my protection," grumbled Bur, of the Bird-spiders.

Standing, Toe was amazed by the fact his head did not even reach the giant spider's underbelly. From his position, he could see the spiders gliding down from the ceiling to join the wasps and ants. The natives tore at the pile of invaders, who had dared to attack their Chieftain, throwing them spiritless to the side.

"Father," Toe cried, watching Princess Squorth help to raise her friend. He was relieved beyond words when his beloved sire stumbled out from the pile of death. Running out from the spider's protection, he embraced Mar only to find the wounds worse than ever. "Mother and Hatty are alright. Wi told me they are safe at the invaders' nursery."

Not quite aware of his surroundings, Mar shook his head and thought for a leaf fall.

Bur's huge hairy legs moved over both of them. "Forgive me, Chieftain Mar, for interrupting. On descending from our webbed position in the ceiling, we saw the king and his guards moving in that direction."

"We must forge our way to my mate and daughter. I have come so far to find them; I can not lose them now. Antoni, Squorth and Bur, ask your armies to form a defensive circle and we shall pursue this devil creature ourselves." Mar threw his front leg over Toe's shoulder and allowed him to carry some of his weight.

Lost and bewildered by the carnage, Toe helped his father along under Bur's large frame. The soil of the cavern, damp with the blood of so many lost spirits, stuck to his hind feet. Feeling as if he trapped in a never-ending nightmare, Toe stared through the haze at the lifeless bodies. His eyes narrowing, he thought, *I have had my childhood stolen and can never go back.*

#   #   #

As Brother Sun's rays began to cut across the darkening, Prince Crier, of the Cicadas, turned to his leaders and chirped. In a leaf fall, thousands of his army poured down out of the gum trees chanting in chorus. Like a storm cloud, they began rushing in through the breach in the cavern's wall.

Dressed in full shell battle armour they engaged the cockroaches on all fronts. Hornet, wasp and cicada fought wing by wing, determined to drive the dark ones from their lands. Rising their chirping to an ear piercing screech, the Criers of the Forest seized the flying cockroaches and dropped to the ground. Freed from the aerial battle the hornets and wasps concentrated on diving down and stinging their enemy to death.

LIGHTENING OF THE WOODS FIFTEEN

Landing on the small gums, near the burrow into the rat's nest, the kookaburras warmed themselves in Brother Sun's rays. Turning their heads, the Jesters of the Bush waited for their leader's signal. King Kakka examined the ground before him, watching Brother Sun's rays as they approached the darkness of the chasm. The water drip the entrance lit up, he nodded his head and laughed. Within leaf falls hundreds of his kind joined him in greeting the dawn of the lightening, with a raucous call.

The kookaburras' salutation burst down into the nest to add to the chaotic noise already there. Reverberating off the walls, it joined with the cicadas' cry and the haunting roar of Dodd's flat stone.

Deserting the nest, terrified rats and cockroaches began pouring out of the hole created by the landslide. Blinded by the rays of light the escaping invaders ran straight into a trap. Sqweara the Highest of Wedge-tails, followed by her kind, dove in snatching a rat in each talon.

Still laughing, the kookaburras swooped in and pierced the cockroaches with their sharp beaks. At the same leaf fall, a platoon of goannas and echidnas swamped the chasm's opening to engage the rats also.

#   #   #

Hatty was the first to notice the king and his guard moving toward their position. "They are going to escape through the gatherers' tunnel. Mother, there are no natives fighting here any longer, what shall we do?" she wriggled nervously under the pile of dead wasps and hornets.

"Hold, child," her mother whispered, "and wait! Our only hope to stop the demon rat is to take him by surprise." Trix stroked her daughter's brow, with her free paw.

"You want us to attack the King and his guards?" Her mother's idea terrified the young female. Hatty began shaking with fear at the thought of the confrontation.

Spying out the small hole, they watched some of the guard pass. "Kick, Hatty, and jump to your hind legs." Holding Tongue, the Bringer of Truth, tight in her right paw Trix kicked with her powerful hind legs.

Hundreds of scorched stingers' bodies erupted into the air, only mouse lengths from the king rat. Yahn stood staring at the corpses showering down around him. He laughed when the air cleared and there before him, impeding his progress, were two female native mice.

"Ha, look at these primitives. Their lack of intelligence astounds me," he announced, waving his fat paw in front of him. "See how they stand defiantly in the arch, when they know we will kill them. What do they hope to gain? Kill them, and be quick about it."

Watching from above, Attic sent the remainder of his stinger friends to protect Toe's mother and sister. With a strange little war cry, the Guardian of the Bush hurled himself from the ledge, tumbling through the air.

Yahn took a step backward as the wild young mouse landed on his hind legs, two mouse lengths away.

"Fat one, not hurt friend's family," Attic said, leaning back on his tail to adopt a fighting position.

The King lumbered two paces forward to face Attic for the first time. The wild mouse spun around to check the stingers were keeping the guards away from Trix and Hatty. In a whisk of a breeze, Attic had completed a full circle and faced the king again.

Knowing full well the battle of the nest was lost, Yahn stood sneering at Attic. "You move fast, young mouse. It is a pity you do not have wisdom to match your speed. Look at you, small one, and look at my magnificence." The King Rat ran his front paws down his grotesque form, showing off his size. "What possible hope could you have of defeating me? Ignorant savage, you insult me with your challenge. Oh yes," Yahn taunted, "your small brain can not even understand language, can it? Perhaps on a better day I would have spared you for your bravery, but not this day. Guards, take him now!"

Watching the guards take the wild mouse Trix became enraged. Lifting her sword with both front paws, she rushed forward. The large sword swinging wildly from side to side, hummed as it cut through the air. "I shall take your spirit myself, vile one." Lunging forward, the Lady of the Oak severed an ear off the nearest rat.

As the other guards moved in to seize her, the king commented, "Look at her come. Watch and learn my elite, you may find this amusing." Yahn waved his claws at Trix calling her on. "Do not try to stop her, let her pass. THE FEMALE IS MINE." Yahn hobbled forward to meet her.

Laughing in Trix's face he said, "Why that last manoeuvre must have exhausted you, small one. Now young primitive female, I would bet you can not raise the sword again, let alone use it." Reaching out his front leg, he waved to the guards behind him. Eyes narrowing, the king laughed when one of his guards passed a young sugar glider for him to use as a shield.

Trix stopped and allowed the tip of the blade to touch the ground. *It is Glee,* she thought with a gasp. *I can not risk her spirit. She is such a friendly creature, the friendliest of all the nursery's gatherers. Where did they find her? I thought she had escaped.* She stood motionless trying to sum the problem.

Waving his paw in front of her the king signalled for her to disarm. With great reluctance Trix lowered the sword to the bloodied ground. Raising her tired body, she then took two hops backward away from the weapon.

The depraved king sneered, raised Glee to his mouth, and broke her neck. Flinging the body aside, he glared at Trix and snapped, "You know nothing of war. Never show any mercy! It is such a pity you can not understand, female, as on this day you may have learnt a lesson before you perish."

Before Trix had a chance to react, Hatty jumped past, a sharpened stick held in her left paw. "I can not bear your stench anymore, demon."

"Why this one is even more stupid than the other female. Leave her to me," he said, holding up a paw to his guards and waving it. "Is it not strange, how stupidity seems to run in the female side of any species?" Leaning forward he appeared to prepare for her attack.

Attic wriggled in his captors' arms as his stinger friends attacked their heads. He knew Hatty was not in the state of mind, she should be, to fight such a large creature. The more he fought, for his freedom, the harder he found himself restrained even with his friends help. "STOP, Toe's sister, the fat one will steal your spirit. Example, he wants to make of you, yes." Knowing, the sounds of the battle muffled his small voice, Attic lowered his head.

Springing forward, Trix grabbed the hilt of the sword again. Fatigued, beyond her lightenings, she took in a deep breath and raised it. Sweeping it around in front of her, she began to move forward.

Unexpectedly, the King dropped to the ground and rolled his giant frame, hitting Hatty like a boulder. With surprisingly agility, he stood again holding her in front of him as a hostage. "This has been amusing, but it must end now. I have other places to go and armies to build."

#   #   #

Walking slightly ahead of Jun and the others Meric and Beyan were pleased to see the rats suffering a great defeat.

"Prince Meric, how can we be sure that these creatures will not slay us after we have shown them through the tunnels?" Beyan turned his head and looked over his shoulder at the natives following them. "We foolishly thought them timid creatures and easily broken, yet they are defeating the rats. Rats may I add, who killed your father and your family. Indeed, we seriously underestimated their kind."

Prince Meric laid his paw on his friend's shoulder. "Ironic, is it not, the rats wiped our best royal mouse guards away in a breath and now are being destroyed by ones they thought, easily conquered. Unity, my friend, is the answer. I am sure if my father had known there were treaties amongst those of this land; he would have left here and joined them."

Rounding a corner, the prince smiled broadly as they ran head-on into Lenthric and the rebel mice. Unsure of the others reaction, Lenthric and Meric ran forward to meet each other. To Meric's surprise his former commander stood on his hind legs and then knelt before him. "It is good to see you, my Prince, please accept your sword of leadership from my humble paw." Lenthric held the sword straight out in front of him and bowed his head.

Stunned by what greeted his eyes, Pon turned and yelled back to Jun, "I told you, they could not be trusted! Now the Prince of the invaders is armed and has an army behind him. You made a mistake Jun. By the River Stones, the battle was almost won. Now we are seriously out numbered and will be their prisoners. I shall not allow it, by Father Sky and Mother Earth; I will lose my spirit first. Are you with me brothers?" Pon sprang forward his bow drawn, soon joined by Fila and Ji.

"I join you brother and so does Ji. I have no wish to be overrun again, like we were by the black creepers in the cavern. Here we have no wasps or ants to aid us, there is only us." Fila's eyes narrowed as he drew the web on his bow back and targeted his arrow at Meric.

Turning to face them, their postures alarmed Prince Meric. Dropping the sword, he raised both front paws above his head.

Jun jumped forward, realising the prince was signalling his willingness to continue as allies.

Unexpectedly, Meric's eyes lit up, he rolled forward, grabbed the sword and stood as Jun approached. Not another creature had seen the rat's eyes glowing red in the darkness of the tunnel's wall. The prince rushed forward as the rat from the shadows leapt at Jun.

Unable to see the rat's pending attack from his position, Fila let his arrow fly. Hissing through the air it cut into Meric's left shoulder, knocking him backward.

With amazing determination Meric tumbled, bringing his sword up into the rat's heart as it pounced. The rat fell to the dirt floor dead. Meric stood on his hind legs reached up and snapped the arrow off. He then offered a shocked Jun the same paw to help him stand.

A common cheer went out between foreign mice and native as they all turned to push the rats toward Slur and her kind.

Only leaf falls later, Slur, Jun and the rebels had successfully rousted the remaining invading rats out of the tunnels. Reaching the last passageway above the nursery, they all stopped and gazed in disbelief down into the small cavern. There below them, in the light of the smouldering corpses, they saw Hatty held captive by the King Rat.

Slur's tail stopped Ji when he went to climb down to help. "Sstop, young mouse, I ssuspect he wishes to use the child to escape. Ssuch a ssinister character will not hesitate to ssteal her sspirit. Sso listen to an old ssnake's wisdom and wait."

#   #   #

Aided by the wasps and hornets, the cicadas started overwhelming the cockroaches. Soon the black creepers began to desert the nest in their thousands, pouring out into Father Sky. With the native insects pursuing them, the cavern grew to a deathly silence.

The battle of the King's Chamber won, all the native forces followed Antoni, Mar, Toe and the bird-spiders. Slowly, they made their way through the haze of smoke, past hundreds of corpses, to the nursery entrance.

Moving out from under Bur's protection, Mar turned to the giant bird-spider. "Go to the ceiling, my friend, with your brethren and take Toe with you. With your kind once again in web, we may well gain an advantage."

"I agree, Chieftain Mar," Bur grumbled, crouching down. "Climb upon my shoulders, young Toe and we shall do as your father commands."

Defiant, Toe moved forward to protest. However, when he saw his father's expression, he reluctantly complied. In a water drip, he had mounted Bur and they were scurrying back up the webs and across the ceiling. Princess Squorth, of the Funnel-web, and Bur's brothers soon followed.

Crossing a pile of spiritless bodies Antoni stopped. From his position, he could now see beyond the king's guards to where Yahn held Hatty. Flinging Fang into the air, he signalled for his army to halt its advance. Standing there, he waited for Mar to catch up.

"The King Rat has Hatty, Mar," Antoni called, down as he past.

Moving forward, Mar tried his best to sneak around behind the cover of bodies to get closer.

"Hold, you primitives or she dies," Yahn screamed, opening his jaw to show his large teeth.

"He says he will kill her and have little doubt of it," Seanne screeched, through a hole above the canopy of webs. "We will comply," she told the king in his own tongue.

The water drip Dodd noticed Hatty in the king's arms, something snapped inside him. Rushing forward, using his flat stone as a machete, he began cutting his way through the guards. Nothing was going to keep him from saving his beloved sister. *I am tired of orders*, he thought slashing a rat across its neck.

Taking advantage of the distraction, Antoni signalled for his ants to go low. Mar continued to circle hoping to find a weakness in the guards' defence. Silently, above, Bur and his spiders span more webs and waited.

Yahn moved his fangs closer to Hatty's throat, howling, "Hold or she dies this instant."

"Cease or he will steal her spirit," Seanne shrieked, as loud as she could.

Seeing little choice, Antoni sprinted up to Dodd and tackled him. They both watched as the flat stone spiralled into the air to fall near the king's feet. Savagely, the king's guards grabbed them both to use as hostages.

When Mar saw his beloved mate held captive his heart near burst. *How I long to hold you, my love,* he thought.

As if reading his mind, Trix turned and their eyes met for the first time in lightenings.

Stunned, by her beauty, Mar allowed Yahn to see his staff.

Catching the movement in the dying light of the fires, Yahn ordered, "You mouse, hiding like a coward behind a body, come out and put down your staff. I see a resemblance between these here and you. Do as I say now."

Seanne interpreted the king's demands, "Stop, Chieftain Mar, he knows they are your family. He wants you to drop your staff."

The king's face took on a look of self-satisfaction as he watched Mar relinquish his weapon. "I do not know what creature you be that speaks our tongue and theirs but tell them this; I am leaving with this young mouse through the gatherers' entrance and nobody is to stop me."

Before Seanne could relay the message, Attic whistled a small, barely detectable, whistle. "I be me," he screamed, stamping on one captors' paw and biting the other.

Perplexed by Attic's actions, the king opened his mouth even wider to sink his fangs into Hatty. "Stupid savage, we have the other creatures as captives, so I can kill this one."

A wisp of air before he began to close his hideous jaws Wi, of the Wasps, flew in and stung him in the throat.

His neck swelling the king thrust his paws up, screaming in agony.

Released Hatty moved to hop away only to be confronted by a guard. Waiting for the precise water drip, she let her body go limp and fall to the ground. When the rat came up to kill her, she lunged into its belly, piercing her stick through its sternum.

Mar, picked up his staff, and with the aid of some bull-ants commenced attacking the guards. Seeing a gap Trix dashed forward, holding the sword. However, within a water drip she lay sprawled on the ground; the sword knocked from her grasp by the nearby fighting. Lying there watching the King gasping for air, she grimaced as he went to pick up the sword.

Unable to sit and watch any longer, Toe dove off Bur's back, seized a web and swung toward the battle. With a squeal, he rolled through the air, landing between the king and his mother. Grabbing the sword he turned to face the king, who struck him with his large paw. Flying across the ground into the guards, he flung the sword back to Trix.

Gasping for air the king lumbered a few paces and pounced on the Lady of the Oak.

Too tired to move, she summoned all her strength and held the sword blade up toward his chest. The king's giant frame met the blade with a hiss, driving the hilt into the sodden ground. Trix could do nothing but watch his grotesque form fall on her.

An unearthly cry echoed throughout the cavern as the King fell, to the damp earth, covering Trix completely.

Dodd, watching on, summoned all his strength and tossed the rat that held him over his back. Then as the rat stood, he used it as a spring board and bounced forward, leaping across the other guards' heads.

Antoni, still a hostage, gave the order for his bull-ants to bite as Dodd entered the main arena.

With all his might, Dodd pushed and tugged attempting to remove the King's body, knowing it would be suffocating his mother.

Hatty rushed to his side, followed by Toe and they lifted together. Finally, the body moved and they could see their mother motionless underneath.

"Use stick in Mother's throat," Attic yelled, kicking a guard between his hind legs. He watched as Toe stuck his hollow stick into his mother's mouth. "Now hold her nose and blow." Attic spun round on his paws and kicked two rats in the windpipe at once.

"Toe," Trix's gentle voice whispered.

Relieved, Dodd and Hatty helped their mother up; soon another large rat confronted them. Putting himself between his family and the rat, Dodd stood staring the rat down, "Take mother, Hatty."

At the same water drip, Jun, Ji, Pon, Meric and Beyan sprang out onto the webs and shimmied down. Bur and the other spiders launched themselves out of the webs, to land near the guards.

With a loud cry of war, Mar summoned all his strength and ran in to stand by his son's side.

Attempting to remove Tongue from the King's chest, Toe's body shook with fatigue. He never expected a paw, in the grips of death, to reach up and seize him. Thinking with amazing speed, Toe called, "Attic," flinging the sword to him.

On receipt of the weapon, Attic spun it above his head and returned it, point first, whizzing through the air. "Dive Toemouse."

Toe pushed to the side as the sword spun through the air severing the King's paw, ensuring his release.

Princess Squorth hurtled down from the ceiling and pierced her funnel-web fangs into the king rat. Her eyes lit with satisfaction as she allowed her venom to drain into his body.

Still staring at Dodd, the guard rat raised its paws above its head. "Surrender, my fellow guards, we are defeated and our king is dead."

The guard holding Antoni released him and thrust his front paws into the air.

Within a leaf fall, the rat guards had all conceded defeat; the natives quickly bound them in a group with webbing. Nobody expected the carrier of the flame to burst out of the gatherers' tunnel. Before any native could stop it, the rat leapt into the captive rats. "Die traitors!" Possessed by pure evil, it set itself and the guards to flame.

Aided by her children, Trix rose to her feet and made her way forward to embrace her mate. Flinging her front paws around his body, she felt how weak he was.

Watching on, Antoni turned away as they embraced. Glancing at the removal of Bega's body from the rubble, he noticed Attic bend down and gently touch Bega's paw.

"Farewell, large one, from you me learn many a thing," Attic said.

With the greatest respect, he stood quiet, for a leaf fall. After paying homage to his unwitting teacher, the Guardian made his way toward the opening, followed by the wasps and hornets. Turning, he could see Dodd, Hatty and Toe embrace their parents. With tears rolling down his cheek, he whistled. The remaining hornets lifted him and they flew toward the place where Brother Sun rests.

Not a creature noticed the dust move ever so slightly in front of Bega's mouth.

Mar, with his head tucked over Trix's shoulder, looked around for Attic. "Where is Adin?" he asked, in a distant voice pushing himself back from her embrace.

Trix, noticing the wound on his back, pulled him close once again, "My darling, Adin was lost to us many lightenings ago."

"You do not understand," Mar snapped. Turning he looked for his life long companion, "Antoni, where is

Adin?"

"If you mean the Guardian, Chieftain Mar, he left but a leaf fall ago. The wasps and hornets carried him away, after he paid respect to Bega's departed spirit."

"Bega is without spirit?" Mar gasped, collapsing. "And Adin gone!"

"Elder Bega was a noble bandicoot, my love, and we shall all miss him. However, please talk of Adin no more upon this lightening, for it taints the joy of our reunion."

"I tell you by Mother Earth's crust, it was our son," Mar mumbled, turning to look across the battle ground, to the bright lightening of the woods beyond. "No, I tell you it is him! We must return toward the setting of Brother Sun and find him!" Mar passed out, collapsing into his family's arms.

THE END

The story continues in the second book of the series:

"RESTLESS SPIRITS"

About the Author:

Kym Jade and family live on a small property in rural Australia. It is there, some of the native creatures used in the Spirit Stealers series can occasionally be seen running free in their natural environment.

Kym fights everyday to overcome the debilitating disease Myalgic Enchephalomyelitis and spinal problems to write and share with the world her books, stories and poetry.

In her action packed, fun, adventure, fantasy series Kym hopes to help increase awareness of the damage introduced species can do to native flora and fauna.

www.ingramcontent.com/pod-product-compliance
Lightning Source LLC
Chambersburg PA
CBHW020121070726
47497CB00020B/394